TO
THE VISCOUNT'S MANOR
CROSSROADS
THE BONESETTER'S HOUSE

ALSO BY MAGGIE O'FARRELL

FICTION

After You'd Gone

My Lover's Lover

The Distance Between Us

The Vanishing Act of Esme Lennox

The Hand That First Held Mine

Instructions for a Heatwave

This Must Be the Place

Hamnet

The Marriage Portrait

NONFICTION

I Am, I Am, I Am

LAND

LAND

A NOVEL

Maggie O'Farrell

ALFRED A. KNOPF
NEW YORK 2026

A BORZOI BOOK
FIRST HARDCOVER EDITION
PUBLISHED BY ALFRED A. KNOPF 2026

Published by Alfred A. Knopf, a division of Penguin Random House LLC,
1745 Broadway, New York, NY 10019.

Knopf, Borzoi Books, and the colophon are registered trademarks of
Penguin Random House LLC.

Library of Congress Cataloging-in-Publication Data
Names: O'Farrell, Maggie, [date] author
Title: Land : a novel / Maggie O'Farrell.
Description: First hardcover edition. | New York : Alfred A. Knopf, 2026.
Identifiers: LCCN 2025054367 (print) | LCCN 2025054368 (ebook) |
ISBN 9780593320648 (hardcover) | ISBN 9780593320655 (ebook)
Subjects: CYAC: Ireland—History—1837–1901—Fiction |
LCGFT: Historical fiction | Novels | Fiction
Classification: LCC PR6065.F36 L36 2026 (print) | LCC PR6065.F36 (ebook)
LC record available at https://lccn.loc.gov/2025054367
LC ebook record available at https://lccn.loc.gov/2025054368

Background art by me67kz / Adobe Stock

Map designed by Helen Cann

penguinrandomhouse.com | aaknopf.com

Printed in the United States of America
1st Printing

The authorized representative in the EU for product safety and compliance is Penguin Random House Ireland, Morrison Chambers, 32 Nassau Street, Dublin D02 YH68, Ireland, https://eu-contact.penguin.ie.

For my family—past, present, and future

seanchaí, m. (gs. ~, pl. aithe).

1. Lit.: custodian of tradition, historian.

2. Reciter of ancient lore; traditional story-teller.

Foclóir Gaeilge-Béarla/Irish-English Dictionary
NIALL Ó. DÓNAILL, 1977

PART ONE

A PENINSULA, STRETCHING OUT INTO THE ATLANTIC

HIS FATHER WAS EVER A MAN OF FEW WORDS. EVEN WHEN LIAM is on the other side of the world, with a new name and unfamiliar clothes, facing a committee of robed men who have come to sit in judgement of him, he will be able to recall the astonishing day that turned his father garrulous.

The morning had been a long one, Liam and his father out since dawn. A north-westerly breeze has been at them for hours, scrupulous in its self-appointed work of lifting the caps from their heads, in hurling a scree of water over them. Liam stands on what he would call a hillock and his father a drumlin or *tulach*, holding the end of the chain and the surveying pole in hands that are scarlet with cold. He is scrawny, in short trousers and a handed-down jacket that has been mended and re-mended by his mother. Her patches, with their fretted edges, have to Liam the fascinating appearance of postage stamps. He likes to rub at the stitches, those marks of maternal patience and devotion, with the side of his thumb. He imagines, at night, when he catches sight of the jacket hanging on a peg, that it might take off through the darkness on a journey across oceans and mountains, borne along by his mother's faceless, stateless stamps. Not that he would tell anyone this: at ten years old, he has lately attained the awareness that such flights of fancy should not be divulged.

The year is 1865, the place a narrow promontory of land lapped on either side by cold blue inlets: a peninsula, stretching out into the Atlantic, like an imploring hand, the westernmost scrap of Europe before it surrenders to icy cross-currents of a vast ocean. As Liam waits there, on his hillock, buffeted nearly off his feet by saline gusts, he brings up a hand to worry at the corner of his elbow patch—a minuscule snarl resides there, a place where his mother has been obliged to knot and retie her darning thread, something he knows she is loath to do.

He is startled by a sudden noise. His father, at the other end of the measuring chain, perhaps twenty or thirty yards away, reduced by distance to nothing more than a little peg man, like the ones his sisters make with fabric scraps, is yelling something at him—what Liam's schoolmaster would term an imperative—but the greedy breeze snatches away the words. Liam stands more upright, wishing to signal that he is paying attention. His father is gesturing, brandishing his arm. Could he be instructing him to straighten the chain or to move the pole? It is what he most often shouts at Liam.

The boy adjusts the stick with one hand, tugs at the heavy links with the other. His father is still yelling from his matching hilltop, still motioning, waving his tripod. Liam waits, anxiety trickling through his chest. He sees his father throw down his instruments and stride towards him. He licks the salt from his lips and tries not to shiver. His father doesn't like to see him affected by weather: a sign of weakness in a man, he calls it.

What does Tomás see as he walks from the pinnacle of one drumlin to the next (counting his strides, as is his habit)? The bedraggled figure of his only son, faithfully holding the surveying pole, a child dear to his heart, whom he will perhaps take back to their lodgings soon because this is no weather to stay out in, a person too young for the job he has been given.

If only it were so.

Tomás, as he feels the slope of the first drumlin level out under his boots and then the incline of the second start to lift him up, sees only this: a gradient of perhaps 1:3, topological landforms caused by glacial activity, a valley scraped and forced to submit to a U-shape by the slow force of ice, to his left the rearing structure of a high rocky outcrop of likely volcanic origin, a smoothness of moraine. And in the middle of this abundance of cartographic detail is an irregular greyish mark that does not belong there—a human, a small one, with bare knees, a cap, under which is some hair the colour of copper coins, and a surveying pole tilted at an inefficacious angle.

Without warning, his gaze, passing over the landscape, is arrested by a curious fissure in the southernmost slope. Filled with a dense copse, from which flows a reasonable-sized stream, it is a geographical feature not shown on the existing map sheet, making it Tomás's responsibility to measure and survey it for the necessary revision.

Tomás sighs. He removes his own cap and uses it to wipe the moisture from his forehead. He doesn't feel the cold, doesn't mind the rain. I am waterproof, he likes to say to the scarlet-jacketed soldiers who employ him for their great mapping project. The redcoats, who come from over the water, bare their teeth in a smile and roll up the charts and sketches he creates. Tomás is useful to them, he knows, not so much for his surveying and draughtsman skills—there are plenty to be found over the water who can do such things—but harder to find someone who has these abilities and can also speak to the locals in their own language. Tomás may be classified in their accounts and ledgers as a "labourer" but the soldier-men cannot do without him. He is the only one of their division who can measure and calculate, draw detailed draft maps in ink for the engravers to copy, and also converse with the people about where the boundaries lie, who owns which field, what this valley or that bluff is called and why, where might the ruins of this building be. He alone is able to parse a polysyllabic string comprehensible only to those who have lived here for generations: he makes *the-crossroads-under-the-bluff-where-once-a-hailstorm-killed-a-cockerel* read "Bluff's Cross" and renders *the-strand-where-the-yellow-periwinkles-gather-in-spring* into "Yellowcove." In a tent set up in a field or a town square, the redcoat sappers and surveyors will mill around behind Tomás, half listening, while he negotiates with a crowd of people a toponymic compromise over a mountain known by one name to those who live on its eastern slopes and quite another to those on its north. Or he untangles from several shouted accounts who the landowner was before this one, and the one before that. Then the redcoats step forward; they take these revisions away to their barracks and their camps; they collate them; they sign their names to Tomás's work; they print their maps and put them in a cabinet somewhere in their city.

So lost is he in his reverie that when he gains the higher ground and someone taps him on the elbow, he is startled to find a person of short stature, looking up at him, mouthing something.

"What?" Tomás yelps.

His son, Liam, quivering like a wet hound, speaks again but his words are whirled away into the fog. Tomás permits the child to cling to his damp jacket hem as he looks around them: a good vantage point, this. The land slopes away from the drumlin in all directions, as if he and his son are standing on a bolt of cloth tweaked aloft by immense and invisible fingertips. They are ninety feet or so above the unmapped copse to the south, a comparable distance to an old field boundary with a gatepost to the west, the volcanic outcrop behind them, the clutter of the village—or what remains of it—to be seen below. On an elevated piece of ground, a quarter of a mile away, stands the ruin of an isolated dwelling place, also absent from the map—roofless, walls bared to the sky, like crumbling teeth, a sapling sprouting from what would have been the chimney breast.

Anyone observing Tomás at this moment would see the muscles in his jaw tighten. It is a necessary but unenviable part of his current task to distil into inked symbols and ordered lines what has taken place here since the first maps were drawn. These new revisions must contain a cartographic record of the Great Hunger, the disaster that struck this land more than a decade ago now. Tomás must amend the hundreds of households in a barony to the handful that now remain; he must erase row after row of tenant cottages on landowner estates, which have been emptied and dismantled. The redcoats turn their eyes from this task; they prefer never to acknowledge the crisis that befell the country, the losses and deprivations it has suffered. They do not wish to make such marks upon their maps, which might lead to certain admittances. Tomás has determined, however, that his maps will bear an account of what happened, what was lost, if it kills him.

He twists away from the ruined cabin before it presses itself too firmly to his eye, inadvertently pulling his jacket from his son's grasp.

"What's that you're saying?" he snaps, aware that the boy persists in squeaking out some words.

"I said," his son falters, and it makes Tomás bristle because he can't abide timidity in his children, "will we be finished soon, Da? Because—"

"Finished?" Tomás thunders. "Finished? You want to know if we'll have finished this task soon? The revisions to the great map of the—"

"No, no, I meant only for today, Da, not—"

"—whole country? Will we have it finished today? Is it that you're asking me?"

Liam bites his lip. He worries away at the patch on his elbow. Tomás sees that the wet has spread over the boy's cap and jacket, turning the cloth dark. He sees that his bright hair is dulled by the rain to the dun of old envelopes. Water drips from the boy's eyelashes, his chin. A brief pang passes through Tomás but then he pushes back his shoulders: the soldiers are coming out to this place in a week; they will expect the new map sheet of this parish to be near completion. There is no opportunity for sentiment; no time must be lost.

"Away over there," he says, pointing, without looking at the boy, "to that copse."

The child lifts the surveying pole, which becomes tangled with his ankles, making him stumble, but he rights himself, and makes his halting way down the slope, towards the gathering of trees. Aspen, elder, Tomás is noting in his book, birch, oak—both ancient and new—and how odd it is that the place is absent from the last map.

"It's not on the map we have, so we'll need to locate the source of that stream before we do our surveying. Go on inside," he calls to his son's retreating back, "and tell me what you find."

Was it a mistake, he wonders, to bring the child along? But the boy must have a trade, must learn to work a job: Tomás will not have him cast out into the world without any prospects, so why not train him as his apprentice? The boy excels at mathematics and draughtsmanship, but Tomás senses resistance in the child, a part of him that yearns for something other. It is pure ingratitude, he has said to the boy's mother. He doesn't care for the work, doesn't put his back into it.

Ah, now, Tomás, she replied, he's young.

Ten isn't young, Tomás retorted, sure when I was ten—

Tomás had fallen silent, the words choked to a halt. He does not like to go down that vertiginous path, into those particular dark woods. It is Tomás's belief that it is always better to say too little than too much: many things are best left unsaid.

He slides his pencil back into his pocket. If his wife were here with him, on this drumlin (which is formed from eroded soil and loose shale gathered during the long journey of a once-mighty glacier, its power waning as it reached this exact spot, causing it to drop its gritty treasures, what a miracle, what a revelation), if she were standing here at his side, her shawl pulled over her hair to keep off the rain, he knows exactly what she would say. Be kinder to him, speak more gently, and he will listen to you. And she would be right, of course.

Tomás scuffs with a curled hand at his bristling chin. The problem is there is so much work to be done, so many field notes to take, so many mistakes to correct, so much history to preserve. He sees himself as that cursed man in the story—read to them once by a visitor—who was forced to push a boulder up a hill every day, only for it to roll back down each night. He can still recall the tale, the book with a red-leather binding, held in gloved fingers, as they all sat huddled together on their benches; he has been both intrigued and repelled by it ever since. He can imagine the grain of the boulder against his palms—it would be granite, he thinks, and he can feel the glistening flecks of mica pricking his palms as he struggles to find a shoulder-hold on the rock. He can imagine the exact tilt of the gradient, how much pressure he would have to exert against his back foot, pushing down with his calf muscles, straining, straining—

His thoughts are snipped short by the recollection that his son should have reached the copse by now. Tomás gives himself an almost visible shake: why has he allowed his thoughts to run along such fanciful pathways? He shades his eyes with his hand and peers into the mist.

9

Liam trudges the distance towards the cluster of trees tucked into a hollow between two hills. He glances back to find out if his father is watching him, but sees only a gaunt outline etched against a shifting, liquid sky. In an unaccustomed act of rebellion, Liam tosses the surveying pole to the ground. He's sick of carrying it, sick to his back teeth.

He moves towards the copse, talking in his mind to his sister, Enda, who is not quite a year older than him: Sick to my back teeth, he tells her. You should see the way he orders me about, like I'm a donkey or a dog, and you wouldn't believe the weather he has me out in.

Enda had been acutely disappointed that she hadn't been taken on this mapping expedition, but their father had said it was no work for a girl. Liam will tell her, when they get back, that she was the lucky one, getting to stay at home. He is exploring his own emerging back teeth, as he steps between the first tree trunks, feeling the hard, pearly nubs erupting from his tender pink gums.

Then he pauses. Later that night, he will wonder why. Was it that he stopped or did something stop him? Which way round was it?

The quality of light in the copse is immediately different, verdant and lustrous, glimmering with the trembling of the leaf canopy. The wind vanishes, as does the relentless rain. He is enclosed and enfolded, as if he has stepped inside the secret green house of a giant. Liam looks up: the tops of the trees separate and collide in the breeze, revealing and concealing the opaline sky. He sees the arrowhead leaves of an aspen entangling with the ripple-edge foliage of an oak, bending together like conspirators. Underfoot, the ground is spongy with damp. It oozes from the soil, the leaf-rot; it sucks and grips at his boot soles. He glances down and sees that there is thick, luxuriant moss, glistening and emerald-bright, blanketing everything: the humps of stones, the long cylinders of fallen branches, the ridged splay of roots, unidentifiable mounds that suggest loaves of bread or animal lairs. Or tiny graves.

Liam's mind reels, flailing desperately away from the thought.

Not graves, no, not here. Who would bury a child, or many children, here, in this desolate and soggy woodland? He knows, of course, about the terrible times in this country, when the Great Hunger struck, which happened not much more than his short lifetime ago, knows about the countless starved people buried in ditches all over the land, and the rest driven away in coffin ships. These mounds are too small, much too small, to be human children. And no one, surely, would inter their tiny, starved younglings in this lonely place. Would they?

He tries to marshal his brain, tries to form the kind of thoughts his father—who feels suddenly very far away on that ridge—would want him to have. Woodland, he forces himself to say aloud, although his mouth is now set so tight that he cannot push out the syllables. Mixed. Some trees easily hundreds of years old, perhaps several feet around. Oak and ash and—

Could they be graves? Liam shuffles forward a step into the copse, then another, taking great care where he treads. Only on ground, please, solid ground. He feels something clingy and sodden brush against his calf, like a pleading wet hand, and he cries out.

It's only the frond of a fern, curled into a little green fist, but the way his cry still rings in the trees does nothing to calm the fears that have beset him. All around, he now sees, ferns are beckoning to him, their spears piercing upwards through the moss, undeterred by its heavy, suffocating swags.

Trees, he tries to think. Oaks, ash, saplings and full-grown. He realises he can hear plashing and gurgling: water. What is the word his father uses? Irrigation. He will need to report this to his father in a moment, in half an hour, whenever he comes out of here: a number of streams, he will say, perhaps a spring or—

Behind him, without warning, there comes a sound so like human laughter that for a moment he is convinced his sister is there with him, that by some peculiar set of circumstances their mother has relented, sent Enda out after them, and she has managed to locate him here; she has crept up behind him, and she is mocking his fears, ridiculing his cowardice.

Liam whirls round. His sister will be there, she will.

She isn't, of course. He sees only branches meshed together, a confusion of trunks, the glitter of a stream winnowing through rock, the black shape of a bird opening its wings. Liam turns again, panicked, disoriented, and loses his footing. His boot is wedged between two rocks, and he falls, into the moss, into a little green mound, which collapses under him, soaking through his clothing instantaneously.

He screams, thrashing on the ground, trying to free his boot, yanking himself away from the mossy hump, picturing the skeleton of a dead and hungry child beneath him, its little bones now crushed to senseless white spillikins, its spirit rising up, angry at being disturbed, and wreathing itself around him.

His socked foot bursts out of the boot and, in a heartbeat, Liam is up and away, crashing blindly through the trees, branches and twigs lashing his face, leaves swiping at the tears on his cheeks, brambles snagging on his britches. He hears the gurgle of water, the ragged sound of breathing, the high-pitched keening of someone in distress, the *pip-pip-a-pip* of a bird's cry, and suddenly he is out. The copse has released him. The giant's unstable, lichenous house is no more. He is delivered back to the world. And it looks as he remembered it: soft parchment scrolls of mist, sloping hillocks, craggy rocks, the sea an indigo-grey line in the distance, and a forbidding figure striding towards him.

His father bears down on him and grips him by the shoulders. "Screaming, are you? Whatever is the matter?"

Liam cannot speak. His chest heaves up and down as he tries to draw in breath. A handkerchief is pushed roughly around his face.

"What happened? Where's the pole? And your boot, for God's sake?"

Liam points at the copse, unable to speak, resting his hands on his knees. His father, disgusted, lets go of him and tramps off to find the lost possessions without a word.

The day wears on, and Liam stands between copse and hillock, waiting for Tomás to return.

Towards the end of the morning, the rain slackens. Grey, piled clouds congregate above the far-off mountain and then, as if they have reached some mutual agreement, disperse over the lower slopes and the sea. A weak primrose tint casts itself over the hillocks, but the sun cannot quite break through.

Liam continues to stand. For a while, he keeps his shoeless foot off the ground, heron-like, but he becomes too exhausted and is forced to put his socked foot down on the damp earth.

A skein of marsh birds passes over his head, their cries a dissonant plucking on untuned instruments. Liam tilts his head, tracking their progress as they veer and bank over the green inclines and fields, towards the cragged cliffs that fall off into the pounding sea: a sole geometric shape moving among grand and yielding irregularities. How radiant, how lovely is the land—and yet how empty. It is as if he has passed through a rent into another realm where humans are unknown, where he is the only one, and will have to make the best of it.

A thin thread of relief stitches through him then, an hour or two later, when in the distance he spies a woman driving a brown heifer along a road invisible to him from where he stands, the switch in her hand flicking back and forth; a dog sprints ahead, waits for her, then sprints ahead again. From this distant signal of humanity, he draws small solace.

Still, Liam waits. His stomach begins to churn and knot with hunger. He knows that in his father's knapsack will be a slice of bread each for them, perhaps a waxy cube of cheese, but he dare not go in search of it. Liam's bladder has been uncomfortable for quite a time now, and he can stand it no longer. He turns his back and, wincing at the icy touch of his frozen hands on his most vulnerable parts, relieves himself into the grass.

The woman comes back along the road without the heifer, the dog gambolling ahead. A gentleman rides by in a gig, flicking his whip to the horses' backs.

Around mid-afternoon—Liam thinks, trying to discern from the blurred replica of the sun held fast by the clouds—he sees two fishermen returning home, their donkey laden with full creels on both flanks. Liam experiences a deep and sudden longing to be their child, to be a fisherman's boy, to be climbing up the hill back to a house where there will be a fire piled with fragrant sods and perhaps a dinner stewing above in a blackened pot. He wants passionately not to be the son of a map-maker, abandoned for hours now on a wet hillside.

When he begins to think that the light is fading, he summons enough courage to call, softly at first: "Da? Da?"

The bowl created by the stony mountain and the hillocks at its base tosses his voice back to him. Da, Da, the land repeats, mockingly.

"Da!" Liam's fear takes hold. "Where are you?"

Where are you, where are you, where are you? the hills demand.

Without noticing it, Liam has started to cry. His throat feels raw and flensed; he struggles to draw enough breath into his lungs. "Da, please," he sobs, quietly so that there won't be an echo. "Please."

He eyes the copse. Could he step inside it again? He thinks not. But has something happened to his father in there? Liam considers the little green mounds, the clutching branches, the rushy streams. His father would never be cowed by such things, would never be bothered by fanciful notions. He would stride through the ferns and the mounds, regardless, crushing all under his boots, his mind engaged only with the topography and the geology and the irrigation and the vegetation. He has a scientific word for everything he sees.

Could it be that Tomás, distracted by the work, completed his survey of the copse, exited the other side and, forgetting entirely about the presence of his son on the hillside, merely tramped back to their lodgings? Or even that he was so angered by Liam's failure to report back on the copse that he is punishing him by leaving him here, out in the open?

Liam feels either to be a distinct possibility and so, with one boot, soaked to the skin, too cold even to shiver, he begins a limping, dispirited descent down the hill.

~

At the end of the mostly derelict village is a lime-washed longhouse, still thatched, still with smoke coming from its single chimney. The widow living here has been the one to take in the map-maker and his son while they do their work: she has swept out the loft, putting down a pallet bed, with her second-best sheets and a woollen blanket each. During the day, while the man and the child are out, she will sometimes climb the ladder and peruse what they have left there. The man's belongings are a disappointment: no fancy clothing or any such thing as a pocket-watch to be seen. And the map-man has come all the way from the city, and is in the employ of the redcoats said to be making maps of the whole country, from top to bottom. A jumped-up, mind-boggling idea, if ever she heard one, and no good will come of it: it will mean only more taxes and tithes. So the widow-woman, all in all, has felt let down by her lodgers. Instead of expensive cloth and linens, the man has clothes that are darned and patched by needlework that the widow, after inspecting it by holding it up to the light; has grudgingly to admit has been done by a skilled hand. But the man has manners on him: he may not speak a word if it can be helped but he always wipes his feet at the door, and nods his thanks at table.

She is just setting about supper, scoring lines in a cross on the uncooked bread, riddling the fire to raise the heat, when the door creaks open and in steps a figure. For a moment her heart clenches, like a hand snatching for something out of reach, but it is only the map-maker's son. A delicate-looking child, with a flare of auburn hair and skin like mother-of-pearl. He sidles in sideways, wet to the bone. The widow presses a floury hand to her aproned chest, attempting to master her still-thudding heart.

"Child," she says, "what is the matter?"

There follows a garbled account of some misfortune up on the hill—the widow can make out something about trees, a hill, the rain, a surveying pole, whatever that is—but the child wants to know, is his father here?

"Here?" she repeats, puzzled.

"In this dwelling."

"But he was with you, up on the hill."

The child's head sinks and he sets up a terrible sniffling and sobbing.

The widow tuts and clucks, trying to quell the shudder that has passed through her. Hadn't she told the man to be careful up there, not to wander from the path, wasn't it said that people had vanished up on that mountainside, never to be found again, but he had looked away and told her not to fret.

She puts the bread into the crock and then the crock into the fire's ashes, and she sets about the boy, stripping him of his sodden clothes—and what kind of a man sends his child out in such weather? Children are a blessing, a fragile one, she would like to say to the man, have you no sense in that head of yours or is it only learning? She sits the boy before the fire and chafes him with a blanket to get the blood back into his bones. Never mind, she hears herself saying to him, don't you worry now. She sees her very own feet walk over to the cedar chest, which she has not opened for ten years or more, and then her hands removing the dried sea-kelp that keeps away the moths, and she sees her hands lifting out clothes: a shirt she had sewn so long ago it was almost hard to believe it had been her who'd laboured on that linen and not some other woman, that she had taken those buttons and stitched them there, and the grey trousers in warm wool. She had spun the raw fleece herself, then given it to the weaver, and hadn't the weaver said it was among the best he'd ever worked on? And from that cloth she had cut and made trousers, measuring the legs and the waist of her eldest, so that they would fit so perfectly, with enough length to allow for growth, for the winter to come, and then in turn to be passed down to the younger ones.

Here they are, the trousers that were never worn, not once, not by any at all, and here she is, touching them with her palms and fingertips again, when she thought she never would: she could not bear even to look at them but neither could she open up the chest and give them away. But here now are the trousers and the shirt, and one of the jerseys she knitted, and she is putting them onto the frozen, pale body of the map-maker's son.

By this time, the bread is ready, so the widow cuts some for the boy, and he devours it like a dog would a stolen cut of meat, and she has to turn away, for a hungry child is a sight past bearing. Gruffly, she says she will go up the road and find someone to look for the boy's father.

The peninsula men go out with lanterns and sticks and dogs; they know the land and the land knows them. They follow the field boundaries and the courses of the streams, and navigate their way by paths and trees, bushes and rocks. They search the hillside, they climb the mountain; they rove as far as the clifftops and the strand, calling the map-maker's name.

By midnight, they have returned. There is, they tell the widow, no sign of the man anywhere. They carry with them his curious instruments, found up on the mountainside—a straight stick with markings, a long and slippery length of chain, a metal tube of some sort with jointed legs—and these they lay, with care and reverence, on the widow's table. They stand there, all of them, for a moment, and they shake their heads.

The boy, put to bed in the loft, alone on the pallet, his belly full of her milk and bread, falls into an exhausted sleep. She watches over him, monitoring him through the long night, keeping off the men who want to rouse him and question him. She will let no one up the ladder and will pass the whole night there, in that chair, staying awake if she has to: she will protect this child because it is in her power to do so, and by God she will do it.

The map-maker had been with the widow for only a day or two when he had appeared next to her with books and papers under his arm. She had been spinning, her foot on the treadle, her fingers feeding in the carded fleece. He had fiddled with a string on one of his rolled charts for a while, clicked his tongue at the old mongrel by the hearth, cleared his throat and shifted from foot to foot, and she had wondered what it could be that he was building himself up to say.

With a final cough, he wished, he said, to ask her about the estate. Specifically, he said, scratching at his forehead, the changes that had occurred here since the last map had been made, over twenty years before.

She had raised her gaze from her work and she and the man had regarded each other for a long and complicated moment. She had allowed her foot to lift and the wheel to slow, its humming noise tailing off into silence.

Will we, she'd said, still holding his gaze, send your boy to fetch the eggs?

We will, the map-maker had agreed.

He had occupied himself in spreading out his papers on the table, and only when the boy, Liam, had left, closing the half-door behind him, had the widow gone to him and sat down at his side.

Looking down at his incomprehensible workings, she had told him what he had wanted to know. That before the Great Hunger, there had been over forty houses or cabins on the estate, each the home for a large and extended family, most of them down here by the shore, others up in the hills or spread over the peninsula. Now, she had said, plucking stray fibres of wool from her apron, there were only four dwellings left: herself, the fishermen, an elderly man living down by the cove, and two sisters at the end of the village. The viscount had given orders for the land to be given over to grazing, with sheep replacing tenants.

The map-maker had remained silent, scratching down some words in one of his books, scoring lines through numbers. Then he had tapped the table, drawing her attention to a large sheet of paper filled with lines and symbols, saying that here was the barony twenty years ago, and as she had looked, the scribbles and markings resolved before her eyes, into coves and hills and roads and paths and fields, all of which she knew, or rather had known.

It made her cry out in something like pleasure, to see the peninsula there upon the page, as it had been, to look down upon it, as if she were up in the air, a bird, or a heavenly angel, and it seemed to her a brand of sorcery, to be presented with this version of the place, as if the Great Hunger had never happened or it had been a terrible nightmare. Her amazement must have loosened her tongue, because she could point at the picture of a little box of one house, then another, and she could recall and relate. There, she heard herself say, lived a family of eleven, good people they were, they all died in the first wintering. And these people in the second, and these, and these, and them, and also them, and here and here and here.

They are all buried together, where this road meets the other. This cabin, they left after the rent was raised: nobody knows where they went. These people went to the workhouse and we never heard more. This family survived because the man was a good fisherman but the third wintering did for them. Then this field was taken over by these people, and she pointed at another house, and of course there was trouble over that, but most of them left for America and only the old ones remained behind, and they sickened, and in the end we'd to tumble the stones of the house around them, for there were none strong enough to take them to the graveyard, so they were buried where they lay. This cabin is gone, and this one, and this one, and this, and this, and this.

Her finger had paused over the viscount's manor, rendered on the map in strokes of ink. Although she hadn't been near it for years now, she could envisage the double-fronted mansion with columns and windows, the long curve of the driveway, the gatehouse, the stable block, the creamery, the glasshouses, the storehouses, the walled kitchen garden, the ladies' walk, the ha-ha, the boating lake. She found she could still picture its interior: the gun room that smelt of leather and oil, the Chinese silk curtains in the drawing room, the winding marble staircase that split in two under a stained-glass window that she herself used to clean once a week, the ladies in their sparkling jewels and gowns that trailed along the floors, their lapdogs nesting in baskets by the fires, the little boy-child, the heir, running through the hallways, a wooden horse on castors clattering after him. Her finger hovered over all these places, but it never landed; she did not touch the map here. All she said was, many of us used to be employed in the manor house, then, before.

She didn't say that every time she sees the tree at the crossroads, its branches shaped into plumes by the wind, she thinks of all the people who are buried in a pit beneath it. That every time she passes the iron gates of the viscount, she hawks and spits on the ground. That she will never work in that house again, never clean its windows or its parquet floors. When she goes to the town, she sees not the market stalls, full again, the people clothed and fed, but drifts of the evicted, gathering by the clock tower, their hands out, their clothing rent and patched. She doesn't say that a dream comes to her sometimes in which she will be moving through the peninsula as it was, in the before time, with all the cabins full, turf smoke unravelling from the roofs, the paths filled with youngers playing, the neighbours gathering and talking, and she walks among these people, whom she had thought were dead or driven away, and she is smiling to herself, to them, and always in the dream she feels an urgency to get home, to reach her longhouse, to be among her children, to be at the side of her husband, so she walks faster, past house after house, cabin after cabin, and she makes it to the final corner, and she sees her home, and she knows her man will be in the byre, his hand upon the cow because he always had a rare way with beasts, and she hears the sound of her children's voices coming from the open door, those three strong boys of hers and the baby girl, and she is hurrying forward, filled with eagerness to get to them, but always at that point she stumbles, she wakes, and the dream ends.

As they stood together in front of the out-of-date map, she said none of these things to the map-maker, but she thought perhaps he knew them anyway because he had rolled the thing into itself, he shuffled his papers, he shut his notebooks, and before he walked away, he reached out and patted her hand, only once, and roughly, which she didn't mind.

She had returned to her spinning, and he to his mapping, and nothing more was said.

Liam wakes to find himself in a dusty, low-ceilinged space, pinned down by heavy blankets. Above his head is the packed density of thatch; below him is an unyielding bed. His head aches and his skin has the tight, boiled feeling of too much warmth. He pushes at the blankets and sits up.

The widow-woman is asleep in the chair on the other side of the room, letting out light, snuffling snores. Liam gives a polite cough because he doesn't want to wake her. He is just wondering whether he could use the bucket without her noticing when his ears catch a noise outside.

As Liam will describe it to his sister, Enda, later: it is a flurry of words, a whooping, followed by a shout.

Liam frowns, turning his head first one way, then the other. Across the room, the widow slumbers on.

More shouts in a tone that sounds very close to gleeful. Then a cackle of wild laughter. Part of Liam wonders who would be making such a noise at this time of day, so early in the morning; another part of him feels a sinking sense of dread. The voice, the laughter had a familiar timbre to it, but it can't be his father. Tomás neither whoops nor cackles. Liam can't recall ever hearing his father laugh. It can't be him. Can it?

The door of the widow's cottage bursts open, squealing on its hinges. And then a huge voice fills the narrow space, pushing at its clay walls, its wooden beams.

"Where is my boy? Where is my Liam? I must see him— I—"

There is a flurry of scuffling and mumbling. Liam rises and tiptoes fearfully to the lip of the loft: two men are attempting to restrain a wild-haired man-creature, who is adorned with greenery. Ferns are stuffed into each of his pockets; he wears a rough-hewn crown of leaves around his head; there are rushes woven crudely about his wrists and ankles.

"*Mo mhac!*" the creature cries, upon seeing Liam. "*A bhuachaill!*"

It is hard for Liam to comprehend the scene below him, nor can he decide what is more shocking: his father's outlandish appearance, the fact that he is expressing affection, or that he is addressing him thus in front of other people. He always warns Liam and his sisters against speaking their native tongue anywhere outside their home because, he says, you never know when the redcoats might be listening and they would punish anyone, even a child, if they overheard.

"There you are," the person who bears a disquieting resemblance to his father yells, wresting himself loose. "I have so much to tell you, so much, you will never believe—"

Gaping down at his father, Liam feels something brush his sleeve: the widow has come to stand next to him. He looks up into her face to see if she understands the gravity of the situation, but her expression is one of resignation. She sighs, then turns to climb down the ladder.

"Mister," she says, as she steps down to the floor, "are you not ashamed to let your child see you in such a state? Where did you get the drink?"

She shakes a finger at each of the men holding Tomás back, and Liam recognises them as the two fishermen he'd seen the day before. "Which of you was it that gave it to him?"

The fishermen mumble, wasn't me, missus, not me.

"It was one of you," she insists. "I know it. I'll get it out of you if I—"

"My father doesn't take a drink," Liam says quietly, as he descends the ladder.

The older of the fishermen lets out a guffaw; the other mutters an amused aside in a low tone. Quick as a flash, the widow lands a sharp slap, first on the shoulder of the older man, then on the arm of the younger.

"He doesn't!" Liam protests. "Never."

The widow leans towards Tomás, who gives her a wide, blissful smile. She sniffs the air near his face and, for a wild moment, Liam thinks she is about to kiss him, to press her lips to his temple or his cheekbone, as his mother does sometimes when she thinks no one is watching. But the widow draws back. "He doesn't smell of the drink," she says.

"That's what I thought," the younger fisherman says, rubbing at his arm.

"And his eyes are clear enough."

"We found him up by . . . you know . . ." The older man drops his voice to a whisper, uttering some near-silent syllables. Liam's keen ears catch the words "well" and "waters" and "singing to himself."

The widow narrows her eyes. She reaches out, snatches the leaf-crown from Tomás's head and tosses it into the smouldering grate. Tomás lets out a roar of protest and, throwing off the restraining hands of the men, lunges forward to retrieve it, trying to restore it, ashes and all, to his head.

Liam, the widow and the men all watch this solemnly, warily: each of them is wondering what to do next.

The widow, of course, takes charge.

"Help me now," she says, beckoning to the men and to Liam. "We'll need to get him out of those clothes if he's not to catch his death."

Tomás, realising what is happening and reluctant to lose his new costume of rushes and ferns, begins to run about the room, yelping. He knocks over pots, he upturns buckets, he slides under and over the table, he bangs his head twice on the low rafters, all the while crying out incoherent words about layers of time and the illusion of ownership. Eventually, the fishermen, strong from lifetimes of labour, tackle him to the floor by the half-door, and hold him down while the widow strips him of his sodden jacket with grim and determined fingers.

"Shame on you," she scolds Tomás, as she might a child, "for being so bold. You lie there until I see to you."

She removes his boots and socks, his shirt, and Liam has to turn his gaze from the appalling sight of his father's bared limbs, the flash of dark hair at the centre of his chest. When the widow starts unbuttoning his trousers, the older man asks her if she would like him to take over the undressing.

The widow shakes her head. "It's nothing I haven't seen before."

For the second time, the widow goes to her chest and brings out a nightshirt in thick flannel, old and well-worn, and pulls it over Tomás's naked body. Liam sees the long, pale flanks, the muscled and hairy calves, the knobbed elbows all disappear inside the flannel. Then the three of them haul Tomás—more pliant and subdued now—to the chair before the fire, place a blanket about his knees, and then seem to consider their duty done. The men nod at the widow; one of them ruffles Liam's hair; they leave. The widow flings a piece of sacking around her shoulders and goes out to see to her livestock. And Liam is left alone with the man who looks like his father, but isn't.

He takes a step towards him, then another. His father is sitting in the chair, his head bowed. A strange, thin noise is coming off him, drifting into the air like smoke: a kind of humming or crooning, the pitch of which slides up and down, like a rosined bow upon taut strings.

"Da?" Liam says.

His father doesn't respond. Liam ventures closer. Tomás is intent on something in his lap. Liam peers over his father's hunched shoulder and sees that he is mending the leaf-crown, his ashy fingers threading the stalks into pierced holes, deftly and expertly. Where has his father learned to do such a thing? How does he know to make a hole like that and to weave the stalk just so and to turn the crown in his hands so that one leaf follows the next and then the next? Liam sees an oak leaf followed by an ash followed by an aspen.

He puts out a finger and touches his father lightly, ever so lightly, on the back, feeling the muscle through the unfamiliar nightgown. His father starts as if poked with a stick, and swings his head around. Upon seeing Liam, his face breaks into a delighted smile.

"*A mhic*," he says. "Come here to me." He reaches out and seizes him, and for a moment, Liam thinks he is about to be severely chastised, perhaps even beaten, which is not his father's way, but instead, to his horror, he is swept up into his father's embrace, onto his lap, the leaf-crown placed on his head, his father's arms around him, tight as ships' ropes.

"I have so much to tell you," his father breathes into his ear, "so much to say, I hardly know where to begin, but because you and I are for ever bound together in this, aren't we, and we must always work side by side, and there must be no secrets between us, so in that spirit—"

"Da," Liam whispers, hot with discomfort, with this flood of words, with the peculiarity of sitting on his father's lap, great boy of ten that he is, with the woven leaves that are slipping over his eyes, "where were you? We all thought—"

"Where wasn't I?" his father cries, delighted. "My boy, I have been everywhere and yet nowhere. I have scaled the heights, I have run to the depths, I have been abroad and yet have stayed within the reach and shadow of—"

"What are you talking about?" interrupts Liam, in desperation. "You . . . you seem . . . different."

"I am different. Everything is different. I have something for you, now, where is it?" His father leaps up, heedless, so that Liam tumbles to the floor, and begins to riffle through his pockets.

"Da, are you drunk?"

"I am not. Are you?"

"Me?" Liam is confused. "Of course not, but—"

"I found something, or something was revealed to me," his father is emptying his pockets, with hasty hands, turning out stones and twigs and leaves and Liam's lost boot, and discarding them to the floor, "and I took it as a sign that I was at last . . ." He becomes distracted by some ferns that fall out of one of the pockets and crouches to gather them carefully, as if they are nuggets of gold. Liam reaches for the boot and clutches it to his chest, finding a modicum of comfort in its familiar leather contours—his mother might have cried if he'd lost it, for it would have to do for Rose when he'd grown out of it.

His father straightens up, one hand filled with ferns and moss.

"My point," he says, with sudden urgency, "my point, Liam, child of my heart, is that everything we've thought until now—everything is . . ." He seems to lose focus, his fingers burrowing into the seams of his jacket.

"Everything is?" Liam prompts.

". . . is wrong."

"Wrong?"

His father beams at him, as if taking his repetition for agreement. "I knew you'd understand—I knew it. What we thought we knew—or perhaps I mean what I thought I knew, because I do not blame you, my son, for how is one so young to know?—is all wrong. About the land, about our history, and the intersection of both."

He seizes Liam's face in his hands, and Liam finds that palmfuls of damp moss and twigs are being crushed to his cheeks.

"I see it all now. I see that maps cannot be made with theodolites and poles and compasses alone. These are but playthings."

Liam gasps, dumbstruck at this heresy. He scans the features of his father's face, the red-calligraphed eyes, so close to his. Could this be a trap? Should Liam agree or disagree?

"They are?" he mutters.

"Necessary playthings," his father says, "but playthings all the same. How much more there is to the land! I have never before seen it thus. How layered, how nuanced is the geological form, especially when considered from the angle of human habitation and who . . ." Tomás holds aloft a finger for emphasis, and Liam takes the opportunity to discreetly wrest his head from his father's grasp ". . . who is laying claim to it. Or should I say whose claim is in the ascendant?"

Tomás paces to the door in his socks, whereupon he swirls around and paces to the fireplace, then back to the door. Agitated and pale of face, he runs his fingers through his hair, over and over again.

"My point is, my point is, my point is . . . that there needs to be a map of how this land really is, of how it has always been, of what lies beneath whatever order or disorder others might impose upon it. There must be a way to create such a document. And to do so would be an act of honour. Honour and resistance. The whole matter rests in our hands, do you see?"

Liam nods, then shakes his head because he has no idea what his father is talking about, but Tomás seems not to notice, reeling about the room, addressing his words to the air, to the rafters above them, still sifting through his pockets.

"I can begin the work, of course, but you—you—you must be the one who continues it, after I'm gone. What's important is that we begin right away so that when the soldiers come, we will be ready, won't we, and we will tell them, in no uncertain terms—" He pauses again, for he seems to have located whatever it was he had been searching for. He comes towards Liam on dancing feet, something gripped in his fingers.

"Look, now, what I have for you. This will explain everything. You will see as I do. Here. Open your hands."

Liam puts down the boot and obediently holds out his cupped palms. His father places into them, as reverent as a priest bestowing holy communion, a single pebble.

The boy looks down at it. It is about the circumference of a halfpenny, and smooth. Grey in colour, with a curious divot at one end. Four striations in white quartz run around its length. It feels cool in his palm, and curiously heavy for so small a stone.

He looks up at his father. Tomás is gazing down at him with suppressed delight and expectation.

"Now do you see?" his father whispers. "Do you understand?"

"So . . ." Liam looks from pebble to parent and back again, willing himself to comprehend what is happening, groping for an explanation.

"This is older than any of us, older than humans, older than the soil itself. It was here before us and it will be here after us. This hole here, do you see, you can place into it a desire or the name of your greatest enemy or that of the one you love best, and you will know, or can guess, without me telling you, where I found it."

"Where?"

"The well, of course."

"The well?"

"The spring. The *tobar*. In the copse. You saw it too, didn't you? I drank from it, deeply, and I believe you did too."

"I . . ."

"The well? You saw it—I know you did. The place where . . ." Tomás flaps his hands about his head, frenzied, his thoughts seemingly outrunning his words ". . . where everything meets. Where . . . where . . . You saw it, didn't you?"

"I saw a stream and—"

"Yes!" His father grips his shoulders in ecstasy. "Exactly! So, you understand. You don't have to say anything now. Just nod."

Liam hesitates. He curls his fingers around the pebble. Its underside, where it is in contact with his palm, has drawn into itself the heat of his body; its upper side is still cool. The tip of his index finger fits neatly into the divot. And because he is miles from home, from his mother and sisters, and because there is no one here to help him, and because the wild and deranged man before him seems to have replaced the only father he's ever known, and because he doesn't know what else to do, he nods.

Tomás lunges towards him, grasping him in an enormous hug, lifting him off his feet. "My boy, my boy," his father mutters, as he clasps a bewildered and terrified Liam to his chest. "We'll begin straight away."

"Begin?" Liam says, as he is put back on his feet.

His father rakes his fingers through his unruly hair, darting looks about him. "Yes! It was no coincidence that we happened upon that copse, that we were drawn inside. We were chosen for this task, you and I. So we won't delay. We'll start now, today."

"Start what?"

Tomás laughs, as if what Liam is saying makes no sense at all. "To redraw the maps, of course."

~

Liam, in his thirty-first year, in the humid room of his interrogation, rises from the bench and walks to the wall, where he presses his forehead into the cool distemper and runs a finger around the inside of his damp collar. The chamber is airless, with only one high window. In the restless Calcutta dusk, the strange, probing aerial roots of a banyan tree rattle against the pane.

Behind him, the men at the table murmur in surprise; one of them barks at Liam to sit down again at once. He ignores this injunction, keeping his interrogators out of sight. He grips with all ten of his fingertips the powdery surface of the wall.

From here, it is just possible to glimpse a section of the outside world through the single window. There is a parakeet feather resting in a fork of the banyan tree, its hooked filaments iridescent in the last rays of the sun, turning from blue to green to purple. He would like perhaps to stand on a stool, unlatch the window, to reach out and take the feather, to make it his, to put it carefully into the pocket of his garment, which is so drab and monochrome, after all. He would like to take it to his siblings, to give it to them, as if it might explain where he has been, what has happened to him or—

From the table comes a peremptory voice asking Liam if he can pinpoint the moment he went wrong or was led astray, and where God or his conscience might reside, where the Holy Father might have concealed himself, as if He is a lost handkerchief or wristwatch that Liam has carelessly misplaced.

"Did any of you ever see a *tobar*?" Liam interrupts.

The five other men look about in consternation and confusion. It is the first utterance Liam has made all day. He clears his throat and begins to speak to them of an ancient tradition in his country, where you make devotions to a well or spring, in the hope of a cure or the easing of a problem, dating from pre-Christian times, of course, but some were blessed by priests in an attempt to divert the people to the ways of God.

This is met with mutterings of disquiet, a single cry of outrage.

"My father set great store in—" Liam stops himself, again pulling at the tightness of his collar. "I made an offering myself once," he says instead, and turns his gaze back to the window, where the sky is just beginning to turn the deep indigo of early evening. "I didn't understand the power of it at the time—I was too young, you see—but now I wonder if it didn't in fact change everything, if it wasn't entirely instrumental in—"

"What has this to do with the matter at hand?"

"Hard to say," Liam murmurs, his eye still on the parakeet feather, its purplish sheen, its green depths. "Maybe everything."

Tomás doesn't sleep for three days and nights. Neither, much to Liam's relief, does he touch their charts, drafts or field books. Instead, he talks. On and on his voice goes, words and sentences pouring in torrents from his mouth. He talks about landforms, ancient and historic; he talks about rivers and their courses, from spring to estuary; he gives over an afternoon to discussing with himself the question of pagan wells and sacred springs. There is a whole evening during which he delivers a long disquisition on this world, parallel worlds, how to locate portals between them, and the ways and times each might be open to the other, until the widow yells at him to hush because there are some here who need to sleep. Liam slips in and out of slumber, and whenever he opens his eyes, his father is pacing about, muttering, or has taken himself off to wander about the peninsula. Tomás talks to the widow, he talks to Liam, he talks to the spinster sisters at the end of the lane, and to the old man who lives by the road; he follows the fishermen out to their currachs, and when they get tired of listening to him, he talks to their donkey.

Around dawn of the fourth day of his sleeplessness, he takes a breath in the middle of a soliloquy about soil to announce that they will be building a bonfire on the strand, as soon as there is enough light. He will require help, so Liam should get himself dressed at once and start collecting dry kindling. What is the bonfire for? Liam asks, from the safety of his bed, still half asleep.

Tomás lets out a huff of incredulous laughter, as if the answer is obvious, and says: To burn all the maps and the name books, of course.

Liam sits bolt upright. His hour has come. He must act. There is no one else. He snatches up his britches, yanks them on, he pulls his jersey over his head, and all the while he keeps up some chatter, to throw his father off the scent. Where will we find dry firewood, Da? he gabbles. Has he a place in mind for the fire? What about up near the dunes, or would that be too much of a danger to the widow's thatch?

Hands stiff with panic, Liam seizes the name books from beside his father's pallet and crams them haphazardly into the leather satchel. Down below, Tomás is talking about wind direction and how maps are acts of colonisation, enemy tools that must be destroyed, and Liam says, in a loud voice, Oh, right you are, Da.

All the while, he is grappling with the slippery drafts, the rolls of his father's sketches, slotting one inside another and tying them tight. So much work, so much labour: he would marvel at the extent and skill of it if he wasn't making sure to gather it up, petrified that he might have missed a single book or page. All those hours and days and weeks spent painstakingly at the widow's table, Liam at his father's elbow, ready to pass him ruler, ink, a new nib, a sharpened pencil, listening out for the curt test questions his father intermittently fires at him about elevations or the principle of triangulation.

When he at last has the satchel on his back and the maps under one arm, he hovers at the top of the ladder, heart hammering. Tomás, still below, seems to be engaged by a homily about patterns of precipitation. How will Liam get himself through the room and out of the door without Tomás seeing? He cannot let his father destroy these papers, hurl weeks and weeks of work into the fire, to erase all they have achieved out here on the peninsula to fit some new crazed design of his disordered mind. Liam will do whatever he has to in order to prevent it.

Tomás is over by the window, examining a spray of seaweed, holding it up to the light. It must be now. Liam bites his lip, looking down the length of the ladder, the stretch of floor to the door. He shuts his eyes briefly, summoning courage, picturing his mother, and Enda, and little Rose, because he knows that if his father is allowed to fling this work onto a bonfire, the redcoats will not pay him, and won't employ him again, and then where would they be? Turned out of their home to starve at the side of the road. Liam launches himself, rattlingly, down the rungs, trying not to weep with the worry of it all, through the room, and out of the door, into a mild dawn with everything in his arms.

As he bolts across the yard, pursued by his father's angry cries, it comes to him that he hadn't formed a plan of where to go or what to do next. He had only thought as far as getting all the papers down from the loft and out of the house. So he runs in zigzags, his head clanging with alarm, his arms piled high, feet skidding in the dirt, desperate to save the work but having no idea what he might do, where he could stash all this to keep it safe.

Luck is on his side because the widow, a quick-witted woman, spots him from her milking stool in the little byre attached to the house, and hisses at him to come to her. And together, the widow and Liam hastily hide it all in the rafters above the cow's stall, where Tomás will never think to look.

Moments later, Tomás comes roaring out of the cottage after his son and his work, still in his nightgown and his wilting crown of leaves. He finds only an empty yard and the widow innocently milking her cow.

"Where is he?" the maddened Tomás demands.

"Who?" the widow says, her hands working away.

"Mo mhac."

"I haven't seen hair nor hide of him all morning, mister. Now get inside and put on some clothes—you're making a terrible show of yourself."

Tomás grunts, stamps about the yard a few times, peers around the sides of the house, then goes back into the cottage. The widow, who is thinking that she hadn't accounted for this kind of trouble when she agreed to take in these lodgers, waits a moment, then says: "He's gone. You can come out."

Liam, concealed behind the cow, presses his forehead against its broad, silken side. He could stay here for ever, in this sweet-smelling place of straw and grass. Wedged between the lime-washed wall and the contented beast, he could live out his whole span of years here. Except, of course, for the matter of his mother and his sisters, far away in the Lanes. How he longs for them in this moment, with the cow and the straw and the *pfft-pfft* sound of the milk hitting the empty pail. For Rose's trusting hand in his, for Enda's boldness, for his mother's good sense. He recalls his mother, suddenly, bent over her work—she often takes in sewing for the people who live in fine houses in the big squares—and the slanting stitches she was using to fix a hole in a lace collar, stitches so tiny as to be invisible, as if done by the hand of a faery. She had murmured, to herself perhaps, or to him, that she didn't like the thought of Liam going so far away; she didn't like the family being parted down the middle like this. And she was right, as she always is: no good has come of it at all.

When Liam finally extricates himself from his hiding place and ventures back inside, he discovers his father at the table, busy with the drawing of his new map. He is also, inevitably, talking: "Now would you not agree . . ." Tomás is mumbling, either to himself or perhaps to the old dog curled up at his feet, as he dips his pen into the ink ". . . that myth is the close relative of fact? We're talking here about the earliest people of this country and . . ." he makes a long, sure stroke across the uppermost left-hand corner of his page ". . . the way they chose to go to ground. This in turn, of course, goes back to how land is history, and history is land, how everything you might see, rocks or trees or fields, is—"

"Da." Liam cuts across the flood of words—it is, he's discovered, the only way.

His father pauses in his speech but his hand keeps moving: Liam watches it add the miniature crosshatchings of rocks on one side of the line—which he now recognises to be the clifftop not far from here—and the sprouted marshland symbols on the other. Strange, he thinks, that his father seems to have entirely lost his mind but not his extraordinary cartographic skill. Tomás can draw geographical features freehand and with great rapidity, but can't answer a simple question.

"Did you eat your breakfast?" Liam asks.

Tomás looks at him quizzically, with eyes wide and dark as sea anemones. "It's so clear to me," he says to the dog, or perhaps his son, "that I don't know why I never saw it before. This is a country that has attracted wave upon wave of conquerors, those who seek to occupy and enslave, but now I alone see how we can resist. To map is to assume power. We can redraw the very land we walk upon, record it how it is, how it was, how it will be. We will not use their names, their estate lines, their plantation boundaries, their barracks: these shall be erased. The very essence of the land, the soil is exactly—"

"Da?"

"I must tell you, child," Tomás says urgently, placing his pen in his inkwell and taking up another, "that if any animal or bird crosses your path and asks for your aid, you must give it. Do you promise?"

"What about—"

"Promise!"

"I promise, but—"

"And if any bestows upon you such thing as a feather or a whisker or a part of its hide, you must keep it safe and return it, when asked, but only to its owner. You," he pokes Liam in the chest, before applying himself to the map, this time with a pen from his cerulean inkpot, "will sail the wide oceans. You will ascend the blustery summit. You shall be tested and found wanting but you shall break the bonds that hold you. You will live among strangers and learn foreign tongues. And if you find the rays of the sun too hot, or not to your liking, do you know what you must do?"

Liam stares at his father, at his glittering eyes, at the hand from which pour rivulets of blue—rivers, pools, loughs, an estuary—and he has to swallow a sob to say: "I don't."

His father, adding a sign to his map with a flourish, laughs. "Liam! It's obvious! You come back here!"

"Here?"

Tomás stabs the table with startling force. "Here."

Liam looks down. His father's middle finger, ink-stained, calloused on the first joint from the pressure of a pen, is pressed to his half-drawn map. Liam sees the contour lines, close together, of two inclines, a dwelling place just below, a minuscule mark in blue ink, from which flow seven streams, and in his father's crabbed calligraphy, the word: *tobar.*

"To . . . to the . . . well?"

His father grasps the cloth of Liam's jacket, a blissful grin cracking open his face. "Exactly so."

"Da." Liam passes his tongue over chapped lips, summoning his courage. He is telling himself he mustn't cry. "I don't know what you're talking about, I don't understand any of it. Please can you stop this? Can we go back to the way everything was, with you and me measuring the peninsula? I'll help you, I promise, I'll do everything you tell me. I'll hold the surveying pole straight every time—you won't have to remind me, I won't complain about the cold, I promise, Da. Please. Please don't be drawing this map. It'll only bring trouble for us. What happened to you . . . at the well that day? What was it that—"

But his father speaks over him, as he takes up the green-ink pen. "Now, as I was saying, myth is fact and fact is myth, and both are embodied in the land itself and . . ."

On the afternoon of the fifth day, the priest arrives.

Tomás would never admit as much to anyone, but even in his right mind, he cannot remember anything about his childhood, his parentage, or where it was he came from.

All that information, all those days and years and nights of living under a roof, up until the age of perhaps twelve, all those facts and names that might skewer and pin his identity: gone. All the conversations and meals, the work, the dressing and undressing, perhaps in the company of brothers and sisters, the animals they fed and cared for, the bedding, the cups and plates, the very soil they ploughed and sowed: gone from him. The people who reared him, gave birth to him, washed his clothes, tidied his hair for mass, fed him, plucked him off the ground when he fell: not a trace remained. The landscape of his home, its fields and pastures and trees and paths, the memory of his home's hearth or doorstep or rafters or bedding: vanished without trace.

All he has is the recollection of a long, frost-shirred road rolling out before him, and his name. The latter had been sewn, in a looping black script, into the breast pocket of a jacket he was wearing on the day he was brought to the workhouse. Embroidered there by the hand of his mother, he supposed, in the time before.

Of the frosty road, he knows this: that it cut through a V-shaped valley, with high peaks on either side, a deep and slate-grey lough filling its base, that he had been compelled to walk its length, very slowly, the dark shapes of the hillsides on either side of him biting into the sky, and that the weather had been bitter and chill, and dusk had been upon them, and the air was thick with the choking, sweetish scent of rot. It invaded his nose, filtered right down to the bottom of his lungs: ever after he would recognise the smell instantly, if he came across it. If he allows himself to delve into his mind, if he probes the memory at all, which he tries never to do, he senses that he had not been alone on that road. There were others with him, and they are hazy to him now, with indistinct voices. There was at least one taller than him, and some smaller, whose hands Tomás had held, and some of these figures had hair that shone bright copper in the flinty dawn light. Whenever Tomás finds himself ambushed by these thoughts, which isn't often, for he is assiduous in keeping them at bay, he recalls that he had no wish to walk this road, and very little strength for it, but that he had to, and that was that.

And then there exists a yawning gap in his recollections. His mind holds nothing more of the road, its geography, the cold dusk and the damp dawn, and the others who walked it with him, their little hands in his. The next he knows, unaccountably, is that he was found alone, on the outskirts of a village, begging for food, by two men with a cart. Tomás knew enough to fear these men, with their smiles and their soft voices and their strange clothes, buttoned black suits with white collars, their promises of help, the curious way they addressed each other as "Friend." He knew in the core of himself, he could not say why, that when they said "orphanage" they in fact meant "workhouse," which was a word that carried dread and shame; such a place would lock you away and you might never come out again, so he tried to run, tried to pull himself from the grasp of the men with starched collars, who had him by the wrist. He had been warned of the dangers of the workhouse, he knew, by someone who loved him. So he kicked out, wrested himself free, slipped through an alleyway between two dwellings, his bare feet skidding on rounded pebbles, but one of the men came after him and there was such a weakness in Tomás's limbs, and here now was the other man, waiting at the far end of the alleyway, and between them they caught him up, loaded him into their cart and took him with them.

Of the cart Tomás possesses a clearer sense. The sway and creak of the axle, the tittuping hoofs of the two donkeys pulling it, the filthy and stricken faces of the other children who were collected, as he had been, from villages and verges. The countryside reeling past, empty and denuded; patches of land mere churned mud pierced with drooping and blackened stalks, and the fenced and guarded fields of the landlords filled with waving, golden corn. A gulley outside a town with a curious humpy shape that he thought might be a haystack but when they got closer, it began to resemble a heap of human bodies, left there under the sky, and he tried to look away, because it had to be a trick his eyes were playing on him and he had no desire to see those entangled limbs, all bone and joint, the teeth stained green. A row of cabins with their thatch burned to cinders, doors split in two by the axes of the eviction gangs, furniture and crockery fanned out on the ground. The figures that rose from the roadside and hobbled towards the cart, so many of them, mile after mile of their brittle arms, their cries and entreaties. A bent-over creature standing at the end of a long path, half man, half dog, with the hair gone from its head and yellowish fur growing on its cheeks and neck, and how it stared to see them pass, and Tomás saw it was a young man, his face quite distorted by madness, and he was chewing, chewing on a mouthful of leaves. A tattered woman who ran with surprising strength alongside them, saying, Would you buy a cup, sir, would you buy a pair of spectacles, or a bawneen? and snatched with her bleeding fingernails at the arm of a child by the backboard of the cart, and Tomás had to prise apart her grip and slap her away, and he turned to see her crumple into a puddle of rags in the middle of the road.

When they arrived, after a day and a night of riding the back roads, they numbered eight in all. The workhouse was at the edge of an unfamiliar town with a river cutting through it; grey stone bridges arched over it, looking to Tomás like the lithe forms of sleeping sea monsters. It was a large, imposing stone building with high walls around it; he wondered what the place had been before these times, why it was here, and when he asked the men on the cart, they said it used to be a barracks for the redcoat soldiers, that the children would be looked after here and, no, they themselves would not be coming in with them—they would be leaving them here and returning to the roads to seek out more orphans.

Outside the workhouse iron gates were huddled groups of people, sheltering in the lee of the walls, and Tomás looked at them carefully, asking himself, did he recognise that woman with the dark plait, was there anything of note in that old man's scarred cheek? But the person opening the gate was brandishing a stick and slashing it towards these figures, shouting at them to get back, so the people melted away and Tomás was carried forward, through the gates, which clanged shut behind him.

He would ask himself later, when he had become a maker of maps, in an ever-simmering attempt to unpick the question of his origins, how long had he travelled on that cart? For how many miles, and in what direction? Had they taken a circuitous route through different villages or parishes? How far was the workhouse from his place of birth, from the road through the river-cut valley? But he had been only a child; he hadn't yet learned the ways of assessing distance or navigation, of recording and remembering names of villages and townlands. There was no chance he could ever retrace the cart's journey.

The workhouse was all he had now, was what he was: he was confined within its walls, its rules, its systems, its hierarchies. He rose at the sound of one bell; he ate at the toll of another; he set to work at the ringing of a third; he put away his tasks when told; he lay down to sleep at the final bell of the day. He was watchful, mostly silent. He kept to the edges of rooms, observing which boys to avoid, which he might safely bed down beside, which were most likely to steal food from his serving. He learned to keep a fist raised and ready to defend his plate, as others did, and to sleep in his clothes if he wanted to keep them; he learned that the best way to keep warm at night was to curl up with your knees pressed to your chest. For Tomás, it seemed, had decided he was going to live; he had discovered, to his faint surprise, that within him was an inexplicable but strong urge to survive. It gushed through his veins, lit up the branched tangles of his brain. It seized him by the scruff each morning and hauled him to his feet. He would not be going under, it told him, he would get out of here and live his life.

There were perhaps thirty children at the workhouse when Tomás arrived, housed in a long cabin at the back of the yard, girls in one dormitory and boys in the other. The wardens clothed these children in whatever was to hand, gave them a bed of straw and sacking, a slice of bread and one serving of thin meal porridge a day; they put them to work; they buried those who failed to wake in the mornings, with scant ceremony, in a pit just outside the walls. There was a school, of sorts, paid for by the same Christian society to which the men with the cart belonged; for a brief hour the young inmates might receive instruction from a visiting priest, or a listless schoolmaster would drill them in the basics of letters and numbers. It was soon discovered that when a slate was put in front of him, Tomás could write in a fluent script and perform sums; he could recite poetry in three languages. When the priest stood before them, Tomás found he could flawlessly produce the words of the catechism. The schoolmaster demanded to know who had put this learning into his head, but he could find no answer. Soon, the schoolmaster got Tomás to instruct the younger ones while he rested his feet on a windowsill and his head on a wall and fell into a doze. It was always Tomás the wardens displayed before the governors or visiting landowners who might be moved to donate to the cause of relief, as an example of their methods, and the fine people in their beautiful clothes nodded and smiled when Tomás spoke out his multiplication tables.

Otherwise, he worked, alongside fellow inmates, breaking up stones so that the redcoats could make roads with them, or cutting up hides in the shoe-mending workshop.

If stationed in the yard, Tomás spent a lot of time gazing through the railings at the town streets, at the twisting silver surface of the river, watching people come and people go, soldiers marching past in formation, scattering all before them, weapons gleaming, their sergeants yelling orders, the way the cobbles shone in the rain and yielded up billows of dust in the summer. The donkey cart continued to arrive, intermittently, through the locked gates, bringing more orphaned children to the door.

One day, Tomás was asked to go and take care of the cart's beasts. Strangely, he found that he knew just what to do: grip them by the harness, unhook the yoke from their soft necks, all the while speaking to them in low and reassuring tones, and rub a knuckle near their long-lashed brown eyes, then say, *Hup-hup*, and guide them to a bucket of water. He watched his hands and heard his tongue perform these tasks and knew, in an embedded, airless part of himself, that he had done it all before, and many times, in the unknowable life he'd once had. He found, too, that he knew to wedge the water bucket with a stone so that they didn't kick it over in their eagerness and thirst. As he stood near the beasts, inhaling their remote-familiar-upsetting-soothing scent, he noticed that a girl had climbed down from the cart, come up to the donkeys and, like him, was pressing her knuckle into their furred foreheads with a movement of such gentleness and care. It struck Tomás in that moment that these were qualities he had not observed in anyone for a long time, so he turned to examine her properly.

She was slight, of course, with something of the bird about her, a linnet perhaps or a thrush—that same brightness of eye, a quizzical tilt to the head. Most incredible to Tomás was the curling yellow hair falling to below her waist. He looked at the waterfall of it—it had been a while since he had seen hair like that—and decided not to tell her that the wardens would have it severed from her head in a matter of minutes. It was said they sold it to wig-makers. He looked at the tears spreading silently down her cheeks and knew that she, like him, had had another life and was now embarking on this one, and he was surprised by the urge in himself to speak to her, to ask her where she was from and who her people had been.

"What's your name?" he heard his voice say, which took him aback because he generally found speaking painful and unnecessary.

The girl paused in the crooning noises she was making to the donkeys and looked at him across their backs, as if wondering what kind of a person he might be. For a moment, he believed she wouldn't speak, that she would decide he was not to be trusted, that she would turn and walk away. But she cleared her throat.

"Seraphina," she answered. "But I'm always called Phina. And you?"

Reflexively, he touched a hand to the breast pocket of his jacket where his name was spelt out in black thread. Her eyes, unnaturally large in their sockets, followed this movement.

"Tomás," he got out, then fell silent, not because he had nothing more to say to her. He found, in fact, that he would have liked to ask her many more questions, such as had she scrabbled with her fingernails in the soil to see if any of the crop had escaped the blight, had she been reduced to living in a ditch with only branches to cover her head, had she been driven to eat grass or weeds that turned her mouth to a green cave and her bowels to water?

He was silenced because he didn't want to say to her that the wardens would shortly be taking not only her hair from her but her name too. "Seraphina" would, he knew, be deemed too ornate for a starveling. So he said nothing but stood with her as they petted the beasts. And when some of the others ran up to her, saw the fine woollen shawl she had about her shoulders and tried to snatch it, Tomás stepped towards them and thumped two of them in the side of the head—he found that he knew how to do this, too—and told them to let her alone. The shawl, patterned, with a long fringe of tassels, he had seen was much too big for her, it was of a size meant for a grown woman, but she clutched it as if her life depended on it.

Her name Tomás was right about—and the hair. It was cropped to her scalp that very night, and she was informed by the wardens that she would henceforth be "Frances." They also took the shawl, saying it was far too smart a piece altogether for a girl like her.

With a sure and righteous hand, Father Joseph pushes open the upper section of the widow's half-door and surveys the scene before him. A single long room, cast in a dim pall, despite the patchy sunshine outside; a waning fire cracks and grumbles in the grating; three fish recline, open-eyed, in a bowl of salt on the windowsill; a couple of smoking rush-lights rest on the wooden board that serves as a table.

At the table stands a man. Father Joseph is particularly interested in this man—reports have been reaching him in his wind-blasted chapel, an hour's walk away, of the map-maker and how his mind has been turned, his wits lost. There has been a certain amount of disorderly speculation about a spring up near the mountain, and the effects of its supposed magical waters, but Father Joseph has always been firm about such heathenish nonsense. He'll have none of it, he has told his flock. There will be no blessing of wells in his dominion, no praying to false pagan deities, no reliance on witch-doctoring or curers. So he has come all this way, his soutane flapping in the breeze, his head wrapped in a scarf to keep off the cold, to peruse this person for himself, and to put paid to these rumours of hydromancy and visions, to show the whole parish who has the upper hand here. That hand being his own. And God's, of course.

What does he see, from the threshold of the cottage?

The man is younger than Father Joseph had been led to expect, perhaps close to his own age. The priest takes in the wild hair standing up off the brow, the crown of wilting leaves, the several days' worth of beard-growth. He sees the intent and focus of the man as he makes marks on the ledger and page before him with blunt and inky fingers. He hears the mumble and hum and sudden laughs that erupt forth from the poor soul's mouth. He observes the bared legs below the tattered hem of the nightshirt, and the way the shinbones curve away from each other, the lumpen ankles, and he knows enough about the effects of malnutrition to recognise that before him stands a man who lived as a child through the terrible times and there are not many of his age to be seen, unless—

"Come in if you're coming, Father," the man says, without looking up.

Father Joseph feels himself turning scarlet, for some reason. Then he fumbles for the latch, and steps inside.

"Shut the door," the man commands, still without raising his head, "if you please. Draughts are the very devil to my papers, and I must keep them in a particular sequence, you see, otherwise . . ." He trails away, searching for something under his ledger, behind an inkpot.

"What is it you seek?"

"My . . ." the man mutters distractedly, getting down on his hands and knees to search under the table ". . . the . . ."

"Your name is Tomás, is that correct?"

From under the table: "It is."

"I am Father Joseph."

A noncommittal hmm.

"You are named for one of Christ's apostles," Father Joseph presses on—he always feels it best to make some connection between a challenging situation and the scriptures. "He who was the first to recognise and acknowledge His divinity, His grace, and—"

"And the one who doubted the veracity of the Resurrection."

Father Joseph pauses, trying not to betray his surprise. He has heard the map-maker was a learned man, but he did not expect to encounter the word "veracity" in this cottage.

"You know your scripture," he says, after a moment's pause.

Tomás straightens up. "That I do." He places, on the table before him, four stones, one at each corner of a piece of unrolled parchment. "I was schooled, in part, by men of the cloth."

"Oh? And where were your people from?"

Tomás's eyes narrow. "My people?"

"Your . . ." Father Joseph flounders. Like a man stepping unknowingly onto the wet terrain of a bog, he is alert, instantly, to his error. "I meant, before . . . before the . . ."

The man shifts his lips against his teeth, as if his mouth is dry. His eyes glitter with madness or rage, hard to tell which.

"What about you, Father? Where are you from? If I'm not mistaken I detect perhaps an accent from across the water."

Father Joseph clears his throat, finding himself wrong-footed once more: how febrile and agile is this man's brand of madness.

"Ah . . . you are . . . What a fine ear you have, Tomás, I commend you. I . . . I was born near a place called Cliffony, which is in—"

"Sligo," Tomás finishes, then stares at him, unwavering, his chin lifted. "But?" he prompts.

"But . . ." the priest gives a weak laugh, hating the sound of it ". . . you are quite correct . . . My father . . . he borrowed money for a passage to Liverpool before . . . just as all the trouble was starting . . . and so . . ." Will this sentence ever end, will he ever finish what he is saying, and why is he saying this? ". . . I lived over in England—"

"I thought as much."

"—but I made sure to return as soon as I was ordained. I requested to come back here to do what I could for my country, in its hour of—"

Tomás holds up a hand. "The hour of need, Father, has passed. A long time ago."

"Well, I feel that need still present. How could it be otherwise? We all of us still live in the shadow of the—"

"Please, Father." Tomás closes his eyes. "I do not wish to speak of this." He heaves in a huge breath, then lets it out. "Now, as much as I have enjoyed our conversation, I must ask you to let me return to my work."

Father Joseph, gathering himself, shaking off the discomfort of their discourse, steps forward. "Your work?"

"Yes." Tomás bends over the table.

"And this would be the maps for . . . ?"

"Your redcoat friends."

The priest ignores the jibe and bends over the uppermost page. He sees incomprehensible marks, brown lines that fit inside each other like the whorls of a fingerprint, squiggles of turquoise worming through green, odd words written upside-down and right-way-up and at veering angles. And then, like holy tongues descending, it all hits him in a rush: there is the crossroads under the bluff, the meandering river he crossed not so long ago, at that very footstickbridge he sees before him as a tiny pair of parentheses, the inclines of the valley with the contour lines rushing towards each other, the soft undulations of the land as it bows down to the sea.

"Ah," he says. "Oh. What a beautiful sight, a sheer—"

He stops. Something is wrong with this map, its leaf-hued inks and azure expanses of sea, its neatly fitted ochre lines and flea-sized houses. Beside him, he hears the mouth of the mad map-maker lift in a smile. It suddenly strikes him.

"But this map is in . . . the wrong language. Don't the soldiers—"

"Wrong?" Tomás murmurs.

"Surely they would require the mapping to be in—"

"They do," he replies, with an emphasis on the first word, "but the error of this way has come to me of late, so I have abandoned it. I will do their bidding no more. I am making my own map. I will never again cede to their version of geography, of history, of linguistics and toponomy. Instead of the map sheet they ordered, I will deliver them this one. And then they will see the truth."

In consternation, the priest looks again over the map. Where he might expect to find settlement names and townland boundaries and north arrows, he sees: **Hill Fort**. He sees: **dolmen**, **stone cist**, **tumulus**, **evicted village**, **pre-colonial kingdom** and **navel**.

His finger lands, scandalised, on the final marking, a minuscule knot of blue, from which flow the lines of several streams. "What is this?" he asks.

Tomás reaches out and pushes away his hand from the map. "You wouldn't understand, Father."

"I might."

"You wouldn't, I assure you."

Tomás gestures to the markings, to the—Father Joseph doesn't like to admit the word access to his mind—*navel*.

"It never ceases to amaze me how assured you priests are of your place in the scheme of things. What you refuse to see is how recent is your hold here, that the land was inhabited long before you and your kind ever arrived, with your crosses and your prayers. You will never understand how the land remembers, how deep the roots grow, how fast the stream . . ."

The man talks on and on. How he talks! Father Joseph arranges his face into his listening expression, allowing the torrent of words to flow past him. The rumours, Father Joseph sees, are quite true. The man has been robbed of his senses. But he, Father Joseph, sees it is more than that: far more.

What is before him, in this low-thatched room, is a clear case of possession. The man has been invaded, led astray, by a dark and malign force. Father Joseph knows this foe—he has been warned about him in school, in sermons, at the seminary, in the Good Book itself; he has studied him and his wiles; he is trained in how to vanquish him. With an internal tremor of something resembling excitement, he sees that the Devil comes clothed to him today not in his customary guise, in scales, with hoofs and a tail, but in the form of a misguided man. Father Joseph sees through it all, and he quails not, hesitates not.

With measured yet purposeful footsteps, Father Joseph goes to the bag he left by the door. He sends up a quick prayer of gratitude: he thanks the Lord most humbly for setting him this task and assures Him that he will do His bidding here on earth. His hands shake as he undoes the bag's fastenings but he tells himself that he is composed, he is ready.

He takes in a breath of the room's salty, smoky air, lets it out. He fishes from the bag his Bible, his candlestick, his tinderbox, and he recites the necessary words, and what grandiloquent, irresistible words they are, a direct appeal to one of his favourite saints: "St. Michael the Archangel, defend us in battle. Be our protection against the wickedness and snares of the Devil . . ."

He has always wanted to perform an exorcism.

Liam, who has been sent to gather seaweed on the shore with a basket on his back, is climbing up the dune with his cargo of bladderwrack, great swags of it, the blistered slithery ribbons trying to escape the creel. He is startled by the sight of the widow hurrying down from the cottage towards him.

"We're not to go in," she is saying, her face lit up. "The men are with him now, and the priest is come so—"

"The priest?"

"Yes, he will see to your father, don't you worry. He's going to drive out the devils. All will be well again."

Liam does not like the sound of this. He puts down the creel, unhooking his arms from the straps, and runs towards the cottage. Not for the first time, he wishes Enda were here, or his mother, because he cannot manage this on his own. As he rounds the byre, the fishermen are leaving, their caps in their hands, saying, Yes, Father, of course, Father, it was no trouble at all, Father, just call us if you need us to subdue him again now. Liam weaves through them, hurling himself towards the door of the cottage, where he sees, just for an instant, the awful sight of his father, that strong and imposing man, tethered to the table like a beast about to be butchered, bindings around his head and chest, his wrists and feet, a strip of linen cutting into his face as a gag.

"What have you done to him?" Liam cries. "Let him go!"

Before he can reach him, he is caught around the middle by someone stepping quickly out of the shadows. Liam twists around to find a stranger, a priest, in a smooth black soutane, with a halo of brown curls around his head. He holds Liam fast by the ribcage, ushering him back outside, uttering soothing words, how he will help his father, he will have him right as rain again, just wait and see, but how Liam must not come into the house until given permission, whatever sounds or cries or thumps or noises he hears.

Outside the door, the priest puts a hand to Liam's head, and Liam feels the press of all five fingers, like a circlet or a woven crown, feels himself kneel before this man.

"All this must be very frightening for you," the priest says softly.

Liam raises his eyes, sudden tears pricking at the lids. At last, someone who understands, someone who sees the truth of this situation. Liam is afraid. Liam is terrified. He knew it but couldn't find the words: this man, this priest, sees it all.

Under the all-knowing hand, Liam nods.

"You will be frightened no more. Your father will be quite well again soon. I promise you that. Do you hear me?"

"Yes, Father."

"Can you give me your word that you'll stay out of the house until my work is done?"

Dumbstruck, Liam nods. He would have agreed to anything this man asked of him.

"Now, I'm told the soldiers will be back in two days to collect the maps. You have kept them safe, have you not? The, ah, original ones that you and your father made?"

"I have."

"Aren't you the clever one? Do you think you can finish them yourself? If I give you the pens and inks from your father's chest? And all the necessary papers?"

Overwhelmed, Liam shakes his head, then nods, then shakes it again.

"I know you can do it," the priest whispers. "I'm told you've a good head on your shoulders. We'll work together, you and I. I will restore your father to himself. And you can finish the maps. The soldiers need never be aware of this."

"I don't know."

"If they come and the maps aren't ready, you know what will happen, don't you? Your father will be in trouble. You have a sister, I hear."

"I've two."

"Then do it for them. And your mammy. The soldiers will go away, pleased, and they will pay your da and things will go back to the way they were."

"The way they were," Liam repeats wonderingly, and how is it that this man, this priest, has divined that this is exactly what Liam desires, for things to be the way they were?

"Good man," the priest urges. "We can fix this between us. You and me."

The hand on Liam's head tightens to an iron band. The priest begins to murmur in Latin, and the words to Liam are like rainfall after drought. They fall upon him with a gentleness that is both merciful and absolving. He wants it to go on and on. He opens his mouth to breathe in the blessing so it might live in him for ever.

The widow comes panting around the corner, lugging the abandoned creel. She sees the priest standing before the boy, reciting a blessing, and she quickly puts down her load, kneels and folds her hands.

The fishermen, away up the path, pulling at the bridle of their donkey, turn and see three figures outside the yellow longhouse: the boy, the widow, the priest. They pull the donkey to a halt and lower their heads.

Up on the path, the viscount is riding by, out hunting with his son, a young man lately back from his studies abroad. They glance down, reflexively, at the cottage below them, at the figures standing outside it, but they see nothing of any note, just some tenants and a padre, indulging in one of their strange superstitions. They ride on, in silence. A brace of pheasants swings from the gibbets of their saddles.

As the priest finishes his recitation and removes his hand from Liam's head and turns to go back into the cottage, to what awaits him there on the table, to the work ahead, Liam stares in rapture at the man before him. He sees an absolving smile, a pair of wise brown eyes. He sees a representative of reason and sense, the very opposite of a ranting fool dressed in ferns. He sees the end of uncertainty and fear. He sees the face of God.

How does a child committed to a workhouse ever make his way out of it?

Tomás thought his way around this conundrum when he lay awake at night in the dormitory. He turned it over and over in his sleepless mind. He considered it from every angle as he lay on the straw pallet he shared with three or four other boys.

Most days he rose before the morning bell was rung, easing himself out from under the coarse blanket. He would find an empty stretch of floor, perhaps over by the window, put a hand into his pocket and draw out what was stowed there—one or two pale slivers of raw chalk—and circle them in his palm.

It was possible to find them while you crossed the yard if you kept your eyes on the ground. Easy to bend at the knee, snatch one up and hide it in your pocket. The chalkstones were purest white, soft and crumbling in texture, and if pushed against a wall or a floorboard, they left a trail of themselves, in whichever direction you might choose.

It was a ritual he would enact until the very end of his life, when he was an ancient, bearded enigma, living half wild, given to wandering roads and byways: to rise before anyone else and, taking whatever was to hand, begin to draw. The rasp of chalk against floorboard, its dissolution into a powdery line that could be coaxed into a shape, which became a thing, real and recognisable. While the other boys slept on, Tomás drew as if he were a bird flying up near the clouds, looking down on the land below. He drew the workhouse, seen from above, as if the roof had been peeled away by a gale, its confining walls, the road curving away from it. He drew rivers, real and imagined, with bridges arching over them. He drew woodlands and lakes, houses and fields. And sometimes he drew a long road cutting through a deep valley, which ended with a village clustered around a cross. Every dawn, via the chalk in his fingers, he found his way back to what he thought of as the source of his life, the fuse through which he might one day solve his troubles. The habit helped him to think, soothed his mind: as his hands moved and his eyes followed, he was able to form plans and conjectures.

By the time he had filled all the available floor space, the morning bell would ring, and Tomás would be sent with other boys either to the yard, where they broke apart rocks, or to a low-ceilinged basement, where they were put to work operating looms or mending shoes with stitching and glue. Good trades to have, the wardens said. So he learned how to prise off a sole worn through at the middle and how to measure and cut a new one from toughened hide, how to tap tiny nails in around its edges so that they wouldn't work themselves loose into the wearer's foot, how to patch leather, and how to repair a broken heel with a metal rim. He was instructed in the operating of a loom, learning the warp and the weft and how the two must be kept at a certain tension, one against the other, the shuttle passing back and back. The work he loathed most was oakum-picking, where he had to tease apart the fibres of old ships' ropes, his fingernails splitting as the day wore on, his palms raw.

The girls, he knew, were in a room next door, where they were set to the laundry or the cooking, or taught needlework. He kept an eye out for Phina, the girl he'd met by the donkeys, among the others, as they were made to file from one building to another, her golden hair shorn. She would always nod at him imperceptibly, and if they happened to be close, she would ask, in a whisper, How are you? and Tomás was able to say that he was getting along. He never said he was exhausted or hungry or had had his feet scarred from the cold or that his head pained him after a day of breathing in the smell of glue. He never said how glad it made his heart whenever she nodded at him or asked after him, or how often she rose to his mind when he was working with his chalk pieces in the dim light. Or how the expressive arches of her pale eyebrows and the dip at the centre of her upper lip had somehow become, in his mind, intermingled with his remembered valley and the frosty road.

He couldn't stop himself gazing at her across the clamour of the refectory or at the far end of the yard, and he discovered within himself the desire to give her something, to put into her hands an object that might bring her happiness, and to have the pleasure of watching a smile rise to her wan face.

A chance came to him on an icy winter's day when he was sent to the head warden's office with a message from the corpulent man in charge of the loom-work; Tomás dashed through the sleet, towards the office, where he knocked, handed the folded slip of paper to the warden's lackey, then waited to see if there was any reply. Through the crack in the door, he caught sight of a blazing fire, the heat of which was weaving out towards him, making his head swim, bringing bright spots to the edges of his vision. The warden was standing with his back to the grate, his coattails pulled apart, the better to warm his behind; Tomás saw him take the message and read its contents. In a chair beside him sat a woman Tomás recognised as the warden's wife, and he saw to his shock that she was wearing the shawl that had been taken from Phina when she arrived. Tomás pressed his eye to the crack. He was certain of it: it had that fine wool weave of purples and greens, the cross-layering of grey, a pattern of triangles, a fringe of sky-blue silken tassels.

The door was abruptly yanked open, and a lackey ordered him to wait. Tomás tore his attention from the shawl, the wife with her complacently folded hands, and he nodded.

Then Fate, for once, went his way. As the warden strode to his desk to scribble a reply, the wife began to take her leave; she pushed herself up from her chair, gathering the shawl about her shoulders, then moved towards the door, which the lackey jumped to open for her. She stepped past Tomás, head averted, as if he were invisible, and turned to bid goodbye to her husband. The conscious thought of what Tomás was about to do failed to pass through his brain because he saw his hand reach for the narrow, blunt blade he wore slung about his neck on days when he was at the loom, a tool intended for the nicking and severing of strands that had become tangled in the machinery, and quick as a diving swallow, the same hand darted forward and sliced a single tassel from the shawl. He had it stowed in his pocket before the wife or the warden or his lackey could see.

Back at his place in front of the clacking, shunting loom, he was appalled at his daring, appalled and exhilarated. He wished he had snatched the whole shawl away from that woman, had yanked it from her ample form and run off with it under his arm—how little she deserved it. But what if he had been seen? What if someone had caught him taking a weaver's knife to the warden's wife? How close he'd come to a shocking beating, or worse. He had to force himself to take gulps of the dusty, dank air to slow his galloping heart.

The scrap of shawl-fringe remained in his pocket for a week, then two. He liked to twirl its silken weave about his fingers. Almost a month later, he was caught day-dreaming while he was meant to be mending boots, and he was lashed on both hands and told to collect the night-buckets from all the dormitories. He made sure to walk tall, not to show how the lashes stung and sang with pain, or how excruciating it was to lift the handles of the reeking buckets. He took two to the midden, then another, and then he went to the door of the girls' dormitory to fetch the last. As he bent to lift it, his shirt-tail wrapped over his palm, Phina was suddenly there beside him, her sleeve brushing his. She spoke in a whisper, barely making any sound at all. I heard about your beating, she said, and I'm sorry for you. Tomás stared at her, aware that he must cut a pathetic figure, filthy and bleeding, stinking of foul midden air. He glanced over his shoulder, then back, and eased his fingers into his pocket, and the brush of cloth against his injuries was agony, but then he held out the blue tassel and watched her face change from puzzlement to recognition to disbelief to overwhelming joy. She didn't smile, as he had hoped, but instead whispered, Tomás, Tomás, with tears in her eyes, snatching the tassel to her chest, and his name in her mouth was like water to a thirsty throat, how did you ever—

At the sound of footsteps behind them, they stepped apart, silenced, the girl hiding herself behind the door, and Tomás seizing hold of the bucket. As the footsteps crossed the yard, then died away down a flight of stairs, he heard himself murmur, We have to get out of here.

The words were out of his mouth before he had time to think, and he was horrified to realise he had used the word "we." The awful presumption of it, implying that he wanted or assumed she would be coming with him. What a fool he was, he chided himself, bending to heft his noxious pails, to think that a girl like this would ever—

We must, she said.

Tomás raised his eyes to look at her, aghast. She had said "we" back to him. He'd heard it, very clearly. Which meant—

How, though? she asked. Her hand reached out and she hooked one of her fingers into the frayed buttonhole of his jacket.

At the sound of boots on gravel, they turned. Someone else was coming and, by the sound of it, a warden. Phina snatched her hand away, shrank back into the shadows, but her eyes were still on him, waiting for his answer. Tomás had to go, now, if he was to avoid another whipping.

I'll think of something, he whispered, and darted away.

To find a route out of the workhouse became an obsession for him. How to get himself—and her—out and away? He observed movements around him, assessing what exits might be available to them. A group of boys not much older than Tomás was dispatched over to England to work in factories; some of the girls were sent to be servants; other children were hired out as workers on farms over the summer months. He watched these departures from the cobblers' bench or at the loom, his fingers holding the cold hammers and needles. For a while, he longed for this, to be digging and gathering on the land: perhaps he would be taken in by the people, perhaps he would be met with kindness and welcome. But then he saw the children returned to the workhouse after the harvests were in, beaten, ill-used and fewer in number, with stories of hard work and no food, of being made to sleep on the earth, like animals. Whenever the wardens began looking for farm-workers the next year, Tomás hung back, hoping not to be chosen.

A year in the workhouse became two. The Great Hunger was coming to an end, it was rumoured, and the bad times might soon be over. Yet what was Tomás to do to get them both out of the place?

His voice was deeper now, his shoulders broader. He knew that it wouldn't be long before he was sent away to a factory or a farm as an indentured labourer, for ever to be a cog in a machine. How would he ever get away? How would he find her again if he was sent over the water? As he stood by the window at night or chalked the thousandth iteration of his road, Tomás gritted his teeth and swore to himself that he would find a way.

Like everything else in life, it didn't happen as he might have expected. It was the road, in the end, that saved him.

Liam is meant to be in the byre, finishing his father's work on the redcoats' maps. He has been given a plank to balance the pages on his knee. It is mid-afternoon; the day is blustery, with brief flashes of pelting rain. The widow has taken her cow up to pasture and he ought to be hard at it, but the task of completing the map sheet and the name books feels enormous and insurmountable in scale, like trying to climb a mountain, the summit of which keeps on disappearing into the clouded distance.

Instead, Liam has put it all aside and crept out of the byre. Checking to see if any are watching, he treads on anxious feet around the perimeter of the longhouse.

His father has been in there now for nearly three days. The priest has bolted the door and covered the single window with cloth. The widow passes food at regular intervals through the top of the half-door. What can be happening?

Liam presses the whorl of his ear to the door and hears—what? Footsteps, snatches of Latin, under which it is possible to make out the hoarse panting of what sounds like an animal. Liam tries to cling to his image of the priest's kindly face, the light of God he saw in his eyes, but he is filled with the horrifying knowledge that it is his father making these terrible noises, that the priest could be doing awful things to his da, that he needs his help—he must get to him.

Liam cannot stop himself: he grips the latch on the door and rattles it to and fro, wailing, Let me in, let me in. I tell you, if my ma hears of this, she'll skelp the—

A hand comes down on his shoulder. The widow has materialised beside him and is steering him back towards the windowless byre that smells of dung, saying, There now, there, come along with me.

"I won't," Liam says, "I won't come," but his feet are walking ahead of her. "My da . . ."

The widow seats him on the milking stool. "Your da," she says, "is a lucky man. Getting the priest out here and him a stranger in these parts."

"But . . ." Liam tries to clear his mind, tries to get a grip on the situation, which seems to get worse by the minute. "But he has him tied to a table, and his mouth stopped with—"

"Shh, shh," the widow says soothingly. She dips a ladle into a bucket, and hands him a bowl. "Drink this."

"I don't want . . ." But Liam accepts it and stares at the opaque surface of the milk. He swallows it down, feeling its frothing warmth flood through him, hoping it might nudge him towards a place of calm. But his heart still feels too heavy for his chest, and he longs, suddenly and acutely, for Enda and her unquenchable bravery. She would batter down that door and give that priest a piece of her mind.

"He has him tied to a table," he says again, aware of the weakness of his voice, wiping his mouth on his sleeve.

"It's for his own good," the widow says. "Back to your work now."

Liam sets down the empty bowl and moves slowly towards the papers. His body feels unwieldy, his joints stiff from his thin bed of straw. He seats himself on an upturned barrel and picks up his father's pen.

He would like to say to someone, anyone: I can't do this. I'm ten years of age. Please don't ask me to do this. He would like, more than anything, never to have come here, never to have set foot on this ragged tongue of land. He has to resist the urge to drop his head to his arms, bury his face and give in to the desire to cry.

Come on, he tells himself. There's no other way. They cannot return to the Lanes with empty pockets. There would be nothing to eat, nothing to pay the rent-man. His mother would weep with despair. She would have to take in more sewing; Enda would have to leave school and find work, perhaps in the factory, and then who would mind Rose? He has no choice.

He has the name books; he has the notes; he has his father's draft maps and sketches. He tries to breathe evenly. He tries to tell himself how incredible it is that something so undulating and varied, so ever-changing as land, can be set down, with a handful of symbols and coloured inks, as something so flat and orderly as a map. Truly, Liam forces himself to think, as he dips the pen nib into the inkpot, it is a kind of alchemy.

All he has to do is look up the new redcoat terms in the name book and inscribe them on the draft maps; he must cross-check with the lists and the field notes, and he mustn't make a single mistake with either spelling or translation or location. One tiny slip-up, his father told him, before he went mad, can cause a cascade of error and inaccuracy.

With his tongue pressed against his bottom teeth, and anxiety scrabbling in his throat, like rats in a chimney, Liam double- and triple-checks the name book, his bitten-down fingernail under the entry, then carefully, carefully, so as not to cause an ink blot, he inscribes the words, Bannan Cliffs, at a point where two roads meet. He cannot use the cursive he has been taught at school: he must use cartographer's script, with letters blunt and clear, so that they match the rest of the map.

He finishes the final *s* then leans back, fearfully surveying his work. Will it pass? Has he managed to imitate his father's flawless penmanship?

He compares *Bannan Cliffs* in his penmanship to *Yellow Cove* and *Bluff's Cross* in his father's, written there last week, before the disastrous trip up the hillside, when his father cared only about—what was the phrase?—setting down a faithful representation of the land's history and geography. A good surveyor, he has told Liam, over and over again, must be the *seanchaí* of the land. The *B* of Liam's *Bannan* is a little uncertain, the *s* in *Cliffs* too squashed. Terror seizes Liam by the scruff of his neck. Has he set down a faithful representation of the land's story? Will the redcoats notice? Will they pay them? He has heard his mother and father talking at night, when they think the children are all asleep, and it is always with a fraught tone. He has heard his mother express a fear that the landlord might turn them all out onto the street, and he does not like the sound of that at all, the turning out, and where would he keep his school books, his lunch pail? Where would he do the exercises set him by the masters? Where would his mother cook their tea?

Liam takes a deep breath to steady himself. He doesn't have time for panic. He scans the columns of the name books, the headings of "List of Names to be Corrected," "Recommended Orthography," "Description Remarks and General Observations," all filled with his father's slanting black hand. He notices, in the margins, small but exquisite sketches Tomás has made: a dolmen, an architrave, a clock tower, a corrie, a remark about "a flock of sea swallows filling a marsh." Behind him, the widow is singing under her breath; she is clattering her ladle against the side of the churn, skimming off the cream. He dips his nib, wiping it carefully against his britches, and runs his finger down the list in the name book for the next words. He finds the entry: *stormy-inlet-where-herring-shoals-gather* has been recommended to be renamed Shoal Sound.

The pen nib meets the map's paper and Liam guides it through the swerves of the initial *S*.

And Tómas? What is he thinking as, through the wall, Liam inks the translated names of the fields and hills and villages and forests and valleys?

Tómas is scarcely thinking at all. He has pulled himself back from the contours and boundaries of his body; he has folded himself into a small space, a wintering plant hiding in the merciful dark earth. There is himself, Tomás, and he is tied to a table, and there is the being near him, a dark and breathing shape that looms over him, murmuring and muttering. Tomás has no trouble keeping this person at bay. He has strong defences; nothing can breach his moat or scale his ramparts.

"Accept God's grace," this black-clad form tells him, "cast out the canker. Ask for His divine forgiveness."

Burning candles are held over him and they weep scalding tears onto his skin and clothes, and Tomás does not flinch. Incense, acrid and choking, is burned beside him, and he coughs but will not speak. The sign of the cross is inscribed in the air, and Tomás merely shuts his eyes. Prayers, long and circular, are incanted, fervently, near his ear. Do what you will, Tomás would say to the man, if the gag wasn't stopping his mouth, nothing you do can touch me. "Repent," the priest urges him, with increasing agitation, spittle spraying from his lips. "Repent."

Tomás will not repent. He has nothing to repent for: he is as certain of this as he is of his own name, as he is of the orientation of magnetic north. So when this priest comes near him, with candle or book or bell or beads or incense or cross, all the tools of his trade, Tomás gives an insolent grin, his lips curving up above the gag.

"What did you see?" the priest demands of him, over and over again. "You went up the hill, didn't you? You went to the well. What did you see there? Tell me, my child. Confess."

Tomás swivels his eyes towards the man so that they are gazing at each other, inches apart.

"Did the Devil appear to you? Did he? Tell me all. I can help you. Did he clothe himself in human form or did he come to you as an animal? Did you call to him, did you summon him? Did you? Did he sing, did he speak to you, did he offer you something, did you make a bargain? Did you perhaps make him some kind of promise?"

Tomás lets out a muffled guffaw. He shakes his head, and an answering anger, smothered but there all the same, flares in the face of the priest.

"That well," he hisses, through clenched teeth, "is a heathen place, pagan and godless. If you struck any manner of bargain there, I must tell you that your soul is in danger, grave danger, and if you fail to confess, you are condemned to burn for ever in the fires of—"

Tomás closes his mind to the man's ranting: he slams the door, he throws the bolts. The well, he thinks, the well. Not the term he would use for it. "Spring," perhaps. "Pool." "Source." Cartography doesn't contain a term for what it is, which strikes Tomás at this particular moment as a mark in the well's favour. The place eludes definition, something this priest will never comprehend. Beside his ear, the man is still gabbing about hellfire and damnation, and Tomás wishes he would hold his tongue so that he can think, find his way back in his mind to the copse, the streams, the wellspring or source or font, or whatever it might be.

Why had he gone in there? Tomás ponders this. Why had he left the drumlin and gone down the slope?

And then across his mind comes the flash of a small, damp figure, trailing a surveying pole, disappearing into the mist.

Of course! It had been to find Liam, for hadn't he heard the boy cry out? That was it. Tomás had been standing at the base of the escarpment, noting the striated nature of the rockface, indicating a slow but dramatic battle of ice versus igneous rock, when that peculiar noise razored the air. A sharp scream, like that of a seabird, had driven away all thoughts of glacial battles and made him swivel around. A second cry. Tomás had frowned and peered into the mist.

Whatever was up with the boy now? Sighing, Tomás had placed the instruments on the ground, covering them fastidiously with his knapsack, and made his way down the slope to the child, who was carrying on about a lost boot or some such nonsense.

Tomás had left him there and had gone to retrieve the boot. He had entered the copse from a west-north-westerly direction, pushing his way through the trees, slashing at the branches and undergrowth with his stick, and around him he registered nothing but an interplay of terrain and irrigation, the subterranean spring having carved, over millennia, its own place in the rock, in the hillside. He saw only water moving through a landscape, and untended woodland; he was thinking of how he would map it, in blues and greens, on a page, decorated with the minute insignia to denote both deciduous and evergreen trees. Then he had reached the *tobar* or the spring or the source. Even then, when he was still in the mindset of civilian assistant, it struck him as a peculiar, arresting sight.

The rock smooth, the branches curving over and around, the waters deep and clear, with a mineral-green tinge to them, the rushing streams. So arresting was it that he had paused, his boots on the pool's lip. He was still thinking along his habitual tracks: how surprising it was to find a pool like this, so circular, of such a depth, and so hidden. How deep was it? It must be several yards down, perhaps even—

A different notion had entered him then. So concealed was this place that it didn't exist on the map, had failed to be recorded. Tomás could picture the sappers who had surveyed the area for the initial map sheets, slapdash creatures, who had not bothered to walk up any further than the boreen, completely failing to record this pocket of woodland, hidden in the cleft of two hills.

The copse was old, even he could see that, the trunk of that oak so wide it couldn't be spanned by the arms of two or three men, the boughs of those ashes gnarled and twisted together to form one many-limbed giant.

No one, he might venture, had been in this place for a very long time: the moss underfoot was lush and springy, the stones and fallen trees covered with its thick, bright blanket. Ancient stumps cradled the supple growth of saplings, their decaying matter feeding the newer life, the next generation of their particular species. All around him was the sense of growth and renewal and the teeming circularity of life; he fancied he could almost hear the roots drawing up moisture and nutrients from the soil, the dissolved leaf-fall, the decaying fallen trunks, the many streams. Absently, as he leaned over to retrieve a small leather boot wedged between two stones, he was wondering to himself, with a certain element of glee, whether even the viscount of the manor knew about this place. Wouldn't he have ordered these trees to be felled, the wood to be cleared, the timber to be sold or utilised? Because that is what landowners do: they squeeze every last shilling to be made out of the land; they drive away anyone who might—

Tomás had busied himself wiping Liam's boot against a mossy trunk to remove the mud, turning to take a last look at the pool.

He would have to come back, he decided, as he bent over the water to cup and lift a mouthful to his lips. The taste was startling, in its way, with a sharp, peaty coolness. He swallowed it down, then wiped his chin. He would return tomorrow, with his instruments, for the whole place must be surveyed from scratch, in better light than this, if he was to include it on the new map sheets.

What if he didn't, though, what if he let it be?

The notion was shocking to him. As Tomás stood in the copse, his fingers still wet from the pool, his mouth and teeth cold from its water, he was overcome by a powerful dilemma. Accuracy was his skill and his vocation: he was paid to rigorously record and set down every feature of the land, yet he found himself suddenly seized by an urge to break the rules, just for once.

Tomás knew that if he were to survey this copse, to record it upon the map, within weeks, perhaps even days, the viscount would send up a party of men to fell all these trees for timber, to divert the water for use in the manor house, and that would be that. This woodland, which had been here since the beginning of time, would be gone, claimed, erased.

It could exist on the map, or it could exist on the land. Tomás felt the insolubility of this predicament behind his eyes, in his temples, like a headache. The trees around him seemed to seethe and shake, pressing their branches closer; the silver streams ran towards him and away from him; the air was at once abundant and scant. The choice, he saw, was his. His life's work was to map but he did not want to be the one to condemn this place.

Tomás crammed Liam's boot into his pocket, anguished. He was a man of habit and principle. Impossible for him not to record this copse for the map, surely.

He would do the surveying, of course he would.

He put out a hand and his palm met the wet, rippled trunk of a blackthorn tree, his fingertips finding clefts in the bark. The very words were enough to sicken him; he thought he might retch, as if he'd ingested something rotten. With a searing clarity, he saw himself as the lapdog of the redcoats, taking their money, helping them to tighten their hold on the land, touching his cap at them, yes, sir, no, sir, whatever you say, sir, here's the name book, here's the map, will I carry that for you, sir, will I do the readings, here are my calculations and my sketches and, oh, I see you're signing your name to them there, thank you, sir, you're very kind.

He was a betrayer, a traitor of the worst sort. The redcoats had plucked him from poverty and early death, yes, but they had made him work like a beast for almost no pay. Well, he would do their bidding no more, as from this moment. This copse, it seemed blindingly clear to him, could be the one scrap of this whole country that hadn't been taken by the redcoats or the landowners for their own purposes. It might be the one place they had never set foot. It could be the only remaining slice of the country still free of them. He, Tomás, would not be the one to hand it to them on a platter. He would never work for them again.

Tomás groped his way forwards, filled with a loathing—for himself, for the soldier-men—so sharp and bitter that his mouth was stinging. He was crawling on his hands and knees over the damp, leafy ground, and when he came to the smooth edge of the pool, he drank from it again and again, desperately, deeply, to ease the pain in his gullet, to slake a thirst he hadn't known he had. In its shadowed depths, he saw the flick of a fish but it was the face in the surface of the water that caught his attention, a haggard visage that resembled his own yet wasn't. It belonged to someone he had known long ago, someone who had since been obscured to him, someone who had loved him, had cared for him, right until the very end, and a great flare of shock and joy rose in Tomás, for the face was looking gravely at him and seemed to be on the verge of speaking, of asking him a question—

That accursed priest is at him again, tugging on his ear, pouring what feels like hot oil into it, and onto his hands, his throat. Tomás hisses at him, like a cat, thrashes his head about, desperate to keep a hold on the reflection in the pool, the vision, whatever it was, the look of dismay on his father's face. Will this priest just leave him be so he can work out what it is he must do, what his father was trying to say to him?

It comes to Tomás, now that he has been dragged back to the room, that it has been a long time since he ate. The sun has set twice since he was tied here, which means he hasn't taken a bite for over thirty-six hours. The notion takes up residence inside him. He breathes around it, feels it swell and fill his body with dread. Far worse than the tethers and the gag, the priest's endless prayers, is the sudden awareness of a certain sour, aching hollow at his core, just under his ribs.

As the morning wears on, Tomás becomes distracted. The copse, the waters, the face he saw all begin to slip from him because the emptiness in his belly is deepening. It is stirring, it is stretching wide its fanged jaws. Tomás knows this atrocious creature and he wants nothing more than to grab it by the neck and throttle it with his bare hands if it dares come any nearer.

It is, of course, hunger. Tómas is hungry.

The dark-robed figure who keeps him here, away from his boy and his work, receives whatever sustenance he needs. Tomás watches as, at midday, the priest opens the top hatch of the door, just a little, just enough to allow a platter or a bowl to be passed through. And then the man fills his mouth, daintily, a forkful at a time; he chews methodically, swallows the food, and licks his lips, while Tomás's stomach groans with nothingness, feeding off itself.

Tomás shuts his eyes. He will not give in, he will not hand this person the satisfaction of knowing how the clean scent of milk, the tang of a mealcake drives nails through his innards. Perhaps worse than that is the sense of something shifting, gathering itself, like a dark storm cloud out at sea, and Tomás fears it, fears what rains and storms it may drop when it reaches land.

At suppertime, on what is perhaps the third dusk of his confinement—he has lost his bearings in time by now—the plate that is handed through the half-door is something else. When the priest bears it through the room towards him, Tomás turns his head away but it's too late. The first drops of rain from that ominous cloud have begun to fall, to wet his head, for he has caught the waft of it, the drifts of steam from it have entered his nostrils, have infiltrated his gullet, and he recognises it as the smell of colcannon.

Colcannon: made in a scalding pan, the fat at a sizzle, slices of onion softened to translucence, with kale and cabbage thrown on by the handful, a pinch or two of salt to make it good, and then the potatoes, and Tomás cannot think in this way, he cannot, he must not: he has to clamp down on thoughts such as these, must not permit them entry.

The storm cloud within him, though, is roiling and rumbling with thunder and he is at once here, in this cabin, inexplicably tied to a table, but just for a moment he is also standing at the side of a taller person. There is a fire before them, its logs and turf throwing out a ferocious heat, and in the glowing crevices there are caverns and castles to be found, and the younger Tomás is seeking them with his eyes and dwells in them, and in the pan there is, of course, colcannon, which the person beside Tomás, who must be his mother, works at with a spoon, and as he lies there on the table he finds, with a kind of blunted incredulity, that he knows it was his father who carved the spoon for her, with his whittling knife, from a branch of birch. Despite himself Tomás tries to seize this mote of memory; he snatches at it, to hold on to it. He wants nothing more than to tell his wife about it: the colcannon, the woman beside him, the whittling knife. He would like to say to her: Listen to this. And: I will make you a spoon from birch myself, so I will, in the evenings when we sit together at the hearth, and you may use it to make colcannon for our children. There is nothing—nothing—he wants more in this moment than to be sitting at a table, with his three children and his wife, about to eat such a meal.

The priest is shovelling the colcannon into his gob and Tomás is forced to listen, and his own stomach is howling, and the sudden recollection dissolves. Hunger is all very well in itself: if you leave it be, it can be borne, but if you wake it, with a smell, with even a scrap of food, it comes back at you with double the strength.

Tomás grimaces, squeezes his eyes shut; he doesn't want the storm to continue, for it to drop its entire load of rain, as clouds always will when they blow in off the sea and meet the immovable rockface of a mountain. He gropes back along the rope thrown to him by his mind, tries to find his way back into that room, to that fireside, but instead of his mother and the pan and the spoon, he finds at the end of the rope those things he never wants to see or revisit, such things as would drive a person out of their mind.

He is in the eye of the storm now; he can hear the screaming of the gale, feel the dart of each icy raindrop. He is forced to recall things he has expended much effort on trying to forget: for example, the sucking of stones, to slake the craving within, and the way the grit lodges in the pits of teeth, under the tongue. For example: the crying, the endless crying, of the youngers who lie together on a sack filled with bracken. And being sent out to stand at the gate to wait for someone, anyone, to rise up from the road so as to be able to hold out a hand to ask for a farthing, please, a morsel, all the while hearing the squealing noise of the earl's pigs over the hill, which are hungry too, because it is your father's job to feed and care for them but he is too weak or ill to do this task. Also, for example: clothes that are worn to flitters so that the wind can find its way to your skin, and the scrabbling with freezing fingers in the mud to see if any of the lumpers survived, even one, maybe two, and then the awfulness of another kind of digging, the very worst kind, when the arms are so tired and the ground is so heavy and sodden. How he and perhaps his sister have to fill in the hole, over three of the youngers, over their father, and they heft stones on top of it, as well as they are able. They have to take them from the top of the walls their father built, a beautiful patchwork of stones in all sizes that surrounded their cabin, for their father had been an expert wall-builder, in his time, and they do it in the full knowledge that soon the eviction men will come and turn them out onto the road, for their father is dead and cannot work for the earl now so they cannot pay their rent, and the next day or the one after that they will have to walk to the next town in the hope of relief.

On the table, Tomás whimpers and thrashes his head from side to side, because there comes something unthinkable, the worst of all, and he needs to fend it off, shield himself from it. He has spent all the days since keeping it out of his mind, away from his thoughts, but this priest has forced it there, he has summoned it, and Tomás fights against it, he rails at the storm, he tries to hold it off. He is a strong man, he can do it, so he can, but it comes anyway: a noise reaching through the darkness of perhaps their last night under the cabin's roof, a strange scuffling and snorting, a tussle just outside the window. He had raised himself up to look out—and how he wishes he never had, how he wishes he had lain there, like the others—and there in the moonlight were the earl's pigs, broken out of their pen and through the walls of the family's yard. Hefty, bristling creatures they were, digging insistently at the soil with fleshy snouts, displacing the stones with their filthy grubbing, and they had in their mouths, their slavering and horrible jaws—they had—they had—and Tomás was unable to look away—his mother and his sister saying, Whatever is it? from the floor by the hearth, stirring as if they too would stand and come to the window, so Tomás had said—he had said—Nothing, nothing at all, go back to sleep.

Peculiar gasping noises are coming from his throat, and he seems to have no control over them, no way of stopping them, and a slick of sweat is breaking out of his brow, down his back, and he doesn't know how there is moisture enough in him for that, but the body is a curious thing, what it can survive, how it continues to breathe and exist despite everything. He lunges against his bindings, letting out a shout from behind his gag. He wants this priest to know he cannot be broken, that he will never give in. He survived the eviction; he survived, unlike his brothers and sisters and mother, the terrible trudge along the road in search of relief that wasn't given; he survived the workhouse when many others did not; he survived his apprenticeship; he survived—that. Look at him now. A wife, children, a job where he is not at the mercy of landlords or crops and their failures or the vicious whips of the gombeen men. He would say to this person beside him, if he could, Look at me, man, I survived the worst thing you might possibly imagine, and I will not be felled by the likes of you.

The half-door opens and a hand reaches in again with a bowl, and even from the table, Tomás can catch the scent of baked apple, fragrant and hot, filtering into his nasal cavity: sweet and blistered peel, the floral scorch of honey. He turns his head away quickly but perhaps not quickly enough for, against his will, he finds a string of words coming from behind the gag: *Please, please, mister, can you spare a morsel?* Somehow these words strike against him like a flint. They shame him, and he knows his mouth and tongue have spoken them before, and this thought forces a deep gouge through him; it seeks out the weaknesses in him and blasts them apart. He sees again the reflection of his father's face in the surface of the pool; he sees the beautiful wall he had to dismantle, stone by stone; he hears the unholy slabbering of pigs fighting over something. He sees, unbelievably, over by the hearth, that his father is standing there, in the room with them, dressed in his smock and britches, looking straight at him, and his face is bruised and rueful, and Tomás thinks he has come to ask him why he didn't do better at the job of covering his grave, why he didn't drag more stones over it or stamp down the earth. I'm sorry, he gasps, I'm so sorry. Smithereens, is what Tomás thinks. I am smithereens.

The black-garbed one leans close, the plate in his hand. Tomás can see the steam curling up off it.

"Do you repent, my child?" he says, still chewing.

"Can you spare a morsel?" The words force their way out of Tomás's throat. He shuts his eyes, tight, in case his father is still there at the fireplace, watching him plead like a beggar.

The priest smiles. He is all forgiveness, all heart. He holds the plate above Tomás. The apples, two of them, filled in their empty cores with hazelnuts and honey, crowned with a spoonful of the widow's cream and a scattering of—

"Repent, my child. Repent and then we may cast out the darkness, the—"

Something in Tomás snaps. He almost hears it go, like the breaking of a cart's axle or the snapping of a bootlace. He rears up, straining against his bindings—he possesses great physical strength, he can bear two children on his shoulders, he can pick up a sack of grain and carry it a mile, he can lift his wife off her feet and across the room, even after all their years together, so surely, surely, he can break these bonds—and from somewhere near his belly, he roars: "I am not your child! You are not my father! Give me some food, man, for the love of God!"

Next door in the byre, his finger moving from word to word in the name book, Liam hears the roar, but not the words, and his head swivels around on his neck, fear rising up in him like floodwater.

Father Joseph stands, arms aloft, face lifted to the heavens, sacred words flowing from his mouth. The moment is close, he senses, when he will triumph over the Devil, when he will cast him out of this poor unwitting sinner, for the man is speaking now, in hoarse and unintelligible noises, and in them he hears the unmistakable note of regret.

His first exorcism! Father Joseph feels invincible, bathed in glory, filled with light. He is a vessel for God, his representative on earth. Running through him like fibres of gold in cloth is the Holy Spirit, the glorious work of the Lord. He is brimming with love and forgiveness. He will triumph, he will win, and this sinner will be saved.

As soon as possible, he will write to the bishop; he will pen a moving yet modest report of what has occurred here, in this rude dwelling, in which he will appear as the humble country priest doing battle with Beelzebub. The bishop will surely be impressed, perhaps might even consider a visit to the site of this miracle and reward him with— But, no, he mustn't get ahead of himself, all in good time.

With a tremulous breath, he opens his eyes and is a little dismayed to see not heavenly ladders descending from the sky or visions of the Holy Virgin, but smoke-blackened rafters, the sleeves of his robe, smattered with food stains, the dirt of this place and his bitten-down fingernails.

No matter.

Father Joseph allows his gaze to fall on the object of his prayers and impassioned pleas, the focus of his and divine love. *A simple working-man,* is how he will describe him in his letter to the bishop, *educated but unspiritual.*

"Do you," he says, in the sonorous voice he learned at the seminary, "repent?"

Words—or at least the approximation of them—emerge from behind the spittle-dark gag, rattling like stones in a bucket. Father Joseph smiles down at the poor sinner before him: the moment of conquest is nigh, he is certain. *Far from easy was the task*, he will say, *but I persevered in the face of evil.* He will drive out the devils within this poor man—he will hook them out, as a farmer pulls worms from the hoofs of cattle. There surges within him a thrum of excitement at what form the Devil has chosen to take this time. *Beelzebub appeared to me there as a*—Father Joseph's mind teems with possibilities—*a scaled and fanged serpent, a hideous half-man and half-goat, a legged eel, a raven, a large and furless cat.*

"Do you repent?" he asks again, with a tinge of impatience.

As he looks down upon the man on the table, held there by bonds of love and forgiveness, it happens. He, Father Joseph, witnesses good prevailing over evil, sees proof of God's goodness and righteousness.

The man begins to cry.

Tears pool in his eyes. He attempts to blink them away, tries to deny their existence, even to himself, but Father Joseph sees them slide out of the corners of the man's eyes, cutting clean paths through the sweat and grime coating his skin. And then, just as Father Joseph had hoped, the full release takes hold. *The sinner broke down*, he will say, *and sobbed like a child.* The map-maker's fists are curled, great gouts of repentance wrenched out from deep within. The noise of his weeping spirals up towards the thatch, and Father Joseph, all the while, is darting looks this way and that, hoping to see the devils, for he has heard that it is possible to see them leave the body at this moment.

Disappointingly, his gaze is met by a row of iron spoons on a shelf, a cup hanging from a hook, a faded wooden chest by the window, a nimbus of blow-back smoke sliding about the room, seeking exit.

He rallies himself: he has succeeded; he has triumphed; he has cast out the evil. He is able to lay consoling hands on the man and he has every hope that this man will confide in him now, will tell him exactly how the Devil appeared to him, what he offered as a bargain for his soul, and he, Father Joseph, can write it down, word for word, in his letter. His heart swells and lifts with what he knows is the will of God, the force of Him, not pride, never that, and he holds out his arms again, this time in victory.

~

Liam has tried his best with the maps. He has completed the draft sheets, as well as he can. Any remaining pencilled notations he has copied over with ink. He has done what he can with the mathematical calculations. He hopes, fervently, that the redcoats won't notice anything amiss.

He is sitting on an upturned bucket in the byre, rolling one of the drafts into itself and attempting to tie a length of cloth around it to keep it scrolled, but his fingers can't seem to make the knot. Again he feels the lack of Enda, she with the clever hands that can do anything, bind up Rose's straggling hair, twirl a spoon through all five fingers and back again. She would snatch this map from him and have it trussed up in seconds, handing it back before he even realised what was happening.

He is trying for the third time to tie the fastening when he sees something at the corner of his eye and looks up through the open doorway of the byre.

The priest is stepping out of the cottage, leading a stooped figure by the arm. For a moment, Liam thinks it is an old, infirm man, his shoulders bent, his face bearded, some elderly villager he's never met before. The widow is fussing around, bringing out a stool; the man is being lowered onto it. Then he sees exposed feet that are familiar to him, the hem of a striped nightgown. The hand that tremblingly grips the priest's has fine dark hairs on it, and its nails are rimed with ink.

Liam flinches as if slapped. He flings aside the map and runs towards them. "Da," he cries. "Da!"

He squirms himself between the bodies of the widow and the priest: he won't let them keep him from his father, not this time. He gets a handful of Tomás's sleeve and hauls himself towards him.

"Da," Liam says, placing a hand on his father's face, much as his mother does when she's checking if any of them are sick, "are you all right, are you—?"

"He is restored," the priest says, in a voice of modest triumph, and Liam can tell without turning round that the man is smiling, "to the Lord, and to us, and to—"

"Is it back you are, Da?" Liam says, touching a finger to the skin rubbed raw on his father's wrists.

The widow is shunting him aside, saying not to fuss, not to worry, let his father take a bite now. She is placing a thick slice of bread, slathered with butter, into his hand, and a cup of milk.

Liam watches as his father, who hasn't yet met anyone's eye, stares down at the bread. He tilts it one way, then the other, his fingers trembling. He lifts it close to his face, then lowers it. His lips move soundlessly. Liam leans closer.

"What was that, Da?"

". . . not too much," his father is muttering, and his voice is thistledown, the sound of it smothered by the chatter of the widow and the priest behind him, "little by little."

His father wants the bread, Liam can see, but is unable to eat it. This strikes the boy as peculiarly upsetting. "You can eat it, Da," he says. "It's for you."

"Is it?" his father whispers. "Is it for me?"

"It is."

"All of it?"

His father raises the slice, but as it approaches his mouth, Liam is appalled to see tears spring from Tomás's eyes and course down his cheeks. He makes no effort to wipe them away; instead, they sink into his new, scraggly beard. Tomás, with a shaking hand, presses his teeth into the crust and takes the tiniest nibble Liam has ever seen, but his father chews as if he has a whole mouthful.

Mutely, Liam takes the milk from his father's hand and replaces it with his own fingers. Next to him, the widow is saying how the priest has worked a miracle, right here, in her very own house, and the priest is chuckling bashfully, saying, No, not at all, a miracle you say? Liam holds the cup to his father's lips, watching him take a minuscule sip, and he wants to say: Do you call this restored? The man is like a ghost: this is not my father, this cannot be him.

The next day, the redcoats come. Two of them, mounted on glossy-flanked horses, buttons gleaming in the sun, their mouths hidden by moustaches. The widow has shaved Tomás, who is still not speaking or meeting anyone's eye, and dressed him in his best shirt and trousers, rubbing the mud off his boots. He stands next to Liam by the cottage door, holding his hand, or is it the other way round? Is Liam holding his father's, wedging his shoulder into Tomás's side so as to remind him to remain upright, to show the right balance of deference and confidence?

Ah ha, quite so, the redcoats say, in their odd, hee-hawing way of talking, far back in the throat, hardly opening their lips. Yes, yes. Rather. Seems to me. They unroll the new map drafts, they flick through the pages of the name books, then stow them all in their saddlebags, and remount their horses. Just as they are about to leave, one leans down from the saddle and holds out a drawstring purse. For you, Tommy.

Tomás's eyes remain fixed on the ground. So it is Liam who steps forward and takes the purse, who weighs the slippery coins in his palm, who nods his thanks and watches as the pair ride away, their horses breaking into a canter, tails swishing.

Liam grips the purse to his chest, letting out a breath. He can hardly believe they got away with it. It feels as though the top of his head is missing, that the sea air is circulating around his brain, his eye sockets, so sharp is his relief.

The widow shades her eyes, following the two red dots as they progress down the track, towards the crossroads, as if to be sure they are really leaving. Then she puts a hand on his shoulder. "Now," she says, "we need to think about getting you home."

What happened to Tomás was simple, in its way. First, a harassed British-army corporal rapped at the workhouse door, requesting to see whoever was in charge, and then, shortly afterwards, the warden was seen to rush about, rounding up some boys.

The corporal was the commanding officer of a surveying division, which only that morning had lost its chainboy. The unfortunate youth had been ordered to wade into a fast-flowing river while carrying the heavy, forty-yard length of chain. The boy had neglected to mention his inability to swim, and the water proving deeper than anyone could have expected, the worst had come to pass. Most unfortunate. Nobody's fault. The corporal would write to the boy's family, of course, but the incident left him under enormous pressure. These map revisions had to be done and they had to be done quickly—the initial maps were such an unqualified disaster that the government was keen to set the situation right. Truth be told, the corporal wanted nothing more than to finish the amendments and get the hell out of this godforsaken country. His division was now a man down and he had to find a replacement chainboy—and fast—if he was to keep to the schedule. Riding past the gates of the workhouse that morning, he had hit upon the idea of recruiting a youth from within its walls: it was a scheme both inspired and economic. So here he was.

Tomás would only later discover the fate of the dead chainboy. All he knew at the time was that the warden burst distractedly into the basement where they were oakum-picking, beckoned to five or six of the boys and, as an afterthought, seized Tomás by the collar.

Tomás was dragged into the daylight, coughing from the oakum dust, half listening to one of the others asking the warden where they were going. The warden was replying that some redcoats had appeared, wanting a chainboy, and the lot of them better be on their best behaviour, no messing, did they hear him? What is a chainboy? one of the boys asked, and the warden muttered something about land and measurements and the fecking British army and cess tax and the drawing of maps and—

Maps? Tomás repeated, as he was shoved into line beside the others.

He looked at the army officer, who was standing at a slight distance, wearing some kind of fancy waterproof coat that came down to his ankles, and the other, younger, soldier, who was being ordered to examine the workhouse boys. He stepped forward to peer into ears and mouths, saying some short words over his shoulder to the officer.

Tomás couldn't make sense of this scene or these people. He didn't know what a chainboy was or what maps had to do with taxes or the army, but what he did know was this: here was a chance, his chance.

He straightened his spine, trying to appear tall, lifting his head, as he had seen soldiers do. As the young redcoat sapper came down the line of boys, Tomás shuffled his feet ever so slightly forwards. The man had to take notice of him, he had to.

The sapper pulled out the boy next to Tomás, then another further along. Tomás could see a rash of pimples on the sapper's neck; there was a powerful stench of drink off him. Tomás cleared his throat, raised his chin even higher, almost on tiptoe now. The sapper paused, looked at him briefly with bleary eyes, then walked past.

Gripped by devastation, Tomás watched as the sapper poked the chosen boys in the stomachs, rolled up their sleeves to examine the muscles in their arms. Tomás had only seconds to stake his claim. He pushed one hand then the other into his pockets, found a piece of chalk, and stepped out of line, towards the yard wall into which, he knew, was built a particular stone, beautifully smooth and gratifyingly large.

Ignoring the hissed command of the warden to get back in his place, Tomás began to draw. From under the tip of the chalk, he brought forth lines, straight and curved, intersections, crosshatchings. Behind him, he sensed people gathering around him, felt their gaze and their interest, felt it gradually dawn on them that what was emerging on the wall was the workhouse in which they were currently standing, seen from above. The driveway, the dormitories, the workshops, the gravepit, the river that coursed past. Never mind the people begging outside, the starving inmates within: none of them existed in this stark, factual version. He made paths, doorways; he slanted buildings one way, then the other, making the whole workhouse focus on one point at its centre, the yard.

Without looking around, on the neighbouring stone, he began a quick sketch of a deep lough, pooled in the V of a valley, with high mountains on either side, through which was winding a long, wretched road.

"Remarkable," he heard someone say, and he turned.

They were all standing in a semicircle around him. It was, he divined, the officer who had spoken.

"Doesn't look very strong, however," the officer murmured. "We do need them to be hale and hearty."

"Oh, he is, I can tell you that," the warden cut in. "He's used to hard work, all my boys are, and this one has his numbers and his letters and—"

"Name?"

"Tomás," the warden supplied.

As the sapper peered at Tomás's teeth, and examined his hair for lice, the officer put his head on one side.

"Thomas," he said, renaming him with a casual and proprietorial sweep of his palm. "Does he speak the Queen's English?"

"I do," Tomás piped up.

"As well as the local lingo?"

Tomás nodded. Only when he was being led to the warden's office did he realise that he had succeeded: the job was his. He couldn't comprehend what this all meant, what would happen now: there were white spark-holes in his vision and his fingers were tingling as if deprived of circulation. The warden was up ahead, saying to the officer in the long coat that he was losing a worker, a fine worker, and happy though he was to be of service to them, could they see their way, etc.

Tomás had begun the day oakum-picking in a workhouse and ended it as a chainboy for the redcoats. He was allowed to bed down in the barracks' stables, up in the loft space, and he could arrange the bales of sweet-smelling straw into whatever shape was most comfortable for him. A soldier told him to get some sleep because they would be up at dawn and would be marching twenty miles by noon. They found him a pair of boots, and a cap, and gave him scraps from the mess kitchen: a half-cooled plate of stew, a hunk of bread. It was the finest meal he could ever remember eating. As he lay in the straw, he eyed the length of chain, a jointed serpent made of metal links, which had been laid beside him. His job would be to carry it and take care of it, to lay it out nice and straight for the surveyor chaps, to push its metal teeth into the ground to hold it fast, he had been told.

Folded into his hand were several chips of chalk from the workhouse. He had looked for Phina, in the sewing room, before he left, but couldn't find her. He had seized the arm of another girl and pleaded with her to tell Phina he'd gone, taken away by the surveyors. Tell her, he urged, his face scarlet, that I'm sorry but I had to go. Tell her I'll be back. I'll be back for her.

~

As they cross the river, Liam allows himself to feel the first tinge of relief. They are nearly home, five streets more, perhaps six.

He and his father take the winding passageway up from the dockside, Tomás's laboured pace making Liam want to urge him on, like a horse. They turn left, then left again.

The vista of the Lanes, where Liam has lived all his life, opens out before them, and he could cry out with relief: the wide cobbled street, criss-crossed every three or four tenements with narrower lanes, where more brick buildings are crammed in, like teeth. Railings run along the fronts; most of the street doors stand open; women in aprons with babies on their hips talk across the stairwells to each other; and the expanse of cobbles is filled with children running back and forth, skipping, fighting, playing hopscotch, swinging on a rope that has been knotted to a gas lamp.

Liam would like to throw his arms around these railings, these gas lamps, these children, all of it. The familiarity of it all makes his eyes prickle. Surely if anything can restore Tomás to his former self, it will be this.

For the entire journey back to Dublin, through the low-lying central counties, Tomás has barely raised his eyes from the mesmerising turn of the cart's wheels. Liam might have suspected that his father was angry with him but for the way he clutched at his hand, even while they walked, almost as if Tomás were the son and Liam the father. Tomás is still gripping it now, and Liam wishes he wouldn't. He wants to extract his hand, retrieve his arm before any of the lads see it and rag him for it—a boy of his age, holding hands with his da. As they round the final corner into the Lanes, Liam tries to ease his fingers away, but his father's grip convulses and tightens, as if he is a man afraid of getting lost. Liam feels shame then: what does it matter if the other boys see, when this is his da and he needs him?

"We're home," Liam says, his voice creaky with disuse, for it is dispiriting to keep up a one-sided conversation, and he'd given up trying many miles back. "Da, look—we're here."

To Liam's dismay, Tomás shows no sign of having heard him or of even noticing where they are. Liam comes to a stop. All the way home, during all those miles and miles of trudging across wet ground and rocky places, he had kept the hope alive that this would be the moment his father would come back to himself: here, at the mouth of the Lanes.

"Da?" he says again.

He remembers his father telling him once that the Lanes had been built for wealthy people, that once upon a time each of these houses would have been home to just one family. Liam had laughed, not believing him, because nowadays there was a family, sometimes more, crammed into each room. But his father had insisted, said it was true that cities, like everything else, were subject to the forces of change. As he had spoken, his hand had been drawing on a scrap of paper a rough sketch of the place, the wide main street, the narrow lanes across it, like rungs on a ladder.

"Da, will you look? We're—"

Liam's query is cut short because a person—short, swift, barefoot—is barrelling towards them, hair flying, mouth open in a joyous yell. Rose hurls herself towards her brother and her father, arms pinioning their knees, hands gripping sleeves and hems as she proceeds to scale the edifice of her father, a cat up a tree, climbing until she is aloft, one leg over his shoulder, shouting at the top of her lungs for Enda and their mother, yelling to all around that her da and Liam are back.

Liam, finally released, turns to their father, curious to see how he will take this. Tomás drops their bundles in surprise, and for a moment, he doesn't move. Then his hands tremble their way to Rose's back, to the wild spring of her hair, as if he needs to check that this child is real, not just some apparition. Rose is gabbling, in a rush of words—something about a dog, or perhaps a doll, and cabbages and a baby.

"A baby?" Liam says.

". . . and Mammy told us it wouldn't come out unti—"

"Rose, Rose," Liam cuts across the torrent, "are you saying that Mammy's to have a baby? A new baby?"

Rose looks down at her brother and nods, delighted with her task of imparting the news. "It'll be my baby brother or sister. We don't know which yet. And it won't be borned for a while, Mammy says."

Liam glances at his father. Tomás's face is wearing a strange expression, like that of a man hearing a distant strain of music.

"Da?" Liam says. "Did you hear that?"

Tomás frowns, clears his throat, as if he might speak, Rose perched on his right shoulder, her arms held out, like an acrobat's. This, Liam thinks, might be the very thing to coax his father out of his shell: another baby in the family.

His father eases Rose to the ground, gives her head a cursory pat. Rose is still talking, about a loaf of bread Mammy has made, tugging Tomás by the hand towards their tenement, and Liam has suddenly had enough of it all. Leave his father to Rose, to their mother, to the news of the new baby, he has had it with trying to take care of him.

He edges sideways, away from his father, first one step, then another, and it is the furthest he has been from him for days now, and what easement he feels as the distance increases. All the while, his eyes are scanning the street, the groups of children, for the tall, gangly figure of Enda.

She must be here somewhere—she has to be. Nothing can keep her in the house in the hours between school and supper: not their mother's appeals for help, not even the exercises from the schoolmaster, which Enda likes to do later, with awe-inspiring speed and concentration, before bed. Liam wanders up the street, one hand trailing rhythmically along the railings, the other shoved into his pocket. Wherever can she be?

This street and its alleyways are Enda's domain. His sister rules it as a fierce but fair monarch. No child will stand alone here, waiting to be asked to join a game. No one is hit or cuffed. No one is made fun of for having no shoes or for wearing torn clothing.

He is just about to give up and go into the tenement to seek her there when he hears the timbre of a particular voice—clear and melodic, rising conspicuously above the singing of others, accompanied by the inevitable slap of a wet coir rope on cobbles. "*Stands the lady on the mountain, who she is we do not know, all she wants is gold and silver, and a man to—*"

Enda's favourite skipping song. Liam's head snaps around, and there she is, at the other end of the street, his sister, inside the blurred orbit of the rope, the shape of which contains her like a house or the innards of a whale, and she a leaping Jonah, feet flying, pigtails jouncing on her shoulders. Above her is a great mass of piled cloud, stately as a galleon, passing over the tiled roofs.

Despite himself, despite everything, Liam smiles, flooded with the feeling he has had all his life: that whenever Enda is near, everything will turn out well. He cannot help himself. He sets off at a run, calling her name, and the sound of it makes her falter in her leaping, makes the song stutter then cease, the wet rope come to a smacking stop against Enda's leg.

She stands there, among the other murmuring girls, regarding him, her chest heaving, her hands on her hips, skinny elbows pointing outwards, as if considering how she feels about his return.

Liam swallows. Is Enda angry with him? Should he not have yelled her name and ruined her game?

To his immense relief, he sees Enda's face break into a smile, and she murmurs, almost to herself: "Li."

She hops over the rope, lying on the cobbles now like an inscribed letter, and tilting her head sideways, in such a way that means he should follow, she sets off at a sprint towards the end of the street, and Liam falls in beside her, and they run together, towards a brick wall that separates the Lanes from a small patch of scrubland.

Enda does not let a thing like a wall get in her way: she makes a leap and hauls herself onto it. Liam has no choice but to follow. It takes him three attempts to find a foothold, but he manages it eventually. Enda balances her way along the top of the wall, but Liam cannot pull this off; she waits with patient forbearance at the end while he shunts his way along on all fours.

She drops down to the other side, into a thicket of bushes. By the time Liam joins her, among the waxy-skinned laurel stalks, she is cross-legged, examining a scab on her shin.

"So," she says, with studied nonchalance, as if the answer is nothing to her, and he is reminded of how jealous she was that he went on the trip, not her, "how was it?"

Liam, still panting from the exertion of the climb, shrugs. "It was . . ."

His speech suddenly collapses in on itself like rotten floorboards. He gulps for air, for steadiness, gripping a branch.

Enda looks up, piercing him with her gaze. Her eyes are said to be blue but Liam thinks that, like their owner, they are more complex than that. They remind him of nothing so much as the sea: shifting, indistinct myriad shades, green in some lights and azure in others. Inside the half-light of their secret den, they are the dark turquoise of deep, dangerous waters. She watches closely now as, on an overwhelming impulse, he delves about in his pocket, extracts the pebble his father gave him, the one with a hole, which came from the well, and he flings it from him, into the bushes, just to be rid of it, to put the whole episode, and that dreadful place, behind him.

Enda frowns, watching to see where the pebble falls. "What?" she whispers, as if she knows already that his reply will contain secrets. "What is it?"

She reaches out a hand—grimy, with a tidemark of what looks like mud crossing her palm—but she doesn't take his or give a comforting caress, which is not her way. She flicks him on the bare knee with a finger. "Tell," she says.

Liam scratches his nose, which is prickling as if he might cry, and wonders how to begin: the redcoats, the priest, the widow's house, the two hillocks, the odd little graves, their father in his garrulousness or bound to a table or reduced to a silent husk of a man. At what point does this story start? Where are its edges, its boundaries?

"There was a copse," he blurts, "and—"

"A corpse?" Enda straightens up, thrilled.

"Copse," he repeats, and sees that Enda isn't familiar with the word, but she will never admit to it, so amends it to "a little group of trees."

“Oh,” Enda says, with palpable disappointment. “And?”

“Well, Da went in there and when he came out,” Liam says, already aware that his account sounds hollow, will fail to impress his listener, but how is he to communicate what happened back there, how can he explain? “He was . . . he was . . .”

“He was what?”

“Different.”

There follows for these three children a confusing time.

Liam gives to his mother the money he has carried back from the peninsula and watches as she tips it into her hand, looks carefully over the coins, then counts it out into two piles: the larger one to clear what they owe, the lesser one to put by in case of lean times, as she likes to say. These coins are put into a stitched pouch and hidden behind the flour bin. That done, she collects up the first pile of coins, ties her shawl in a firm knot and goes out, first to the rent-man and then to pay off their accounts at the grocers.

When she returns, with promising parcels under her arms, she smiles at them all, but Enda and Liam observe that she has not returned with rashers, jam, sugar and eggs, as they had hoped, just some milk and butter. They glance at each other, then away, both gleaning that the money from the redcoats hasn’t been quite enough to ease their mother’s anxiety about how they will manage.

More worryingly, their father lies in bed, a felled oak, under all the blankets they own. Curled into himself, face to the wall, he is silent all the day long. At night, however, he wakes them, over and over again, with wild thrashing about, his muttering and yelling—about swine and ghosts, stones, and something about a wooden spoon—making Rose cry, the neighbours hammer furiously on the wall, and Enda get up to pace about the room.

He is ill, their mother tells them, he can’t help it, God love him, and they repeat these sentences to people who enquire, to anyone who knocks on their door. When the other inhabitants of the tenements ask the children what ails their father, what is the name of his sickness, they do not know what to say.

A fever, their mother tells them one morning. She quickly amends this, that same afternoon, to "a distemper."

Rose says the new word to herself as she arranges her doll and its bedding on the pavement, tasting its syllables, trying out different emphases: dis-*tem*-per, *dis*-temper, distem-*per*, *distemper*. She cannot penetrate its meaning. Temper, she thinks, as she tucks sacking over her doll's cloth limbs, is a bad thing, something that might bring punishment on your head, especially at school. It is something that comes in "fits" and "outbursts"; a child must learn to control it; it makes a person feel hot and suffocated, as if their chest is filled with smoking coals. But last night, when Rose had tiptoed to the bed where their father lay, he didn't seem to be suffering from anything like that. How could this be the same gibbering terror who tore about and yelled in the night? He was utterly still, a person carved from stone. A new scraggly beard covered his lower face; his eyes flickered back and forth under their lids; as Rose had watched, she saw a line of water seeping from the side of them. It was not so much tears as a slow leak, as if tiny streams were flowing out of her father, down his temples and into his hair, and Rose had lifted the hem of her pinafore and wiped them away.

As she sits on the edge of the pavement with her slumbering doll, her feet in the gutter, she takes the hem of her pinafore and holds it up to the light. She can see that the water from her father's eyes has left a stain, near the seam, shaped like a small island.

Rose lets her hem drop. She looks up the street, she looks down. A grey and chill day it is. No sign of Enda or Liam, only a couple of boys across the way, hurling around a ball made of rags knotted around a stone. As she watches the arc of the ball, hears the shouts and exhortations of the boys, the knowledge that something unusual, something unaccountable is happening in her house spreads through her, like damp through a wall, leaving a trail of blackened spores in its wake.

In the ensuing days, however, Rose is the only one of the children who will go near Tomás. Enda comes back from school and goes straight out again. Liam, by contrast, tries to avoid going anywhere. He finds he needs to stay close to the house, to Rose, to his father, to his mother. What if something were to befall them all while he was gone? Who would defend a sick man, a pregnant woman, a small child, if not him?

He tells his mother he can't go to school because he has a stomach ache or a sore leg. His mother lets him stay at home for a day, then two, but on the third day, she shakes her head and says, in a gentle voice, "Back to school with you today, Liam."

"But, Mammy—"

"You'll fall behind on your lessons, so you will."

"—I have this awful pain."

"Where?"

"In my . . ." he glances at his father, lying on the bed ". . . my head?"

His mother, standing at the table, where she is spreading butter on the end of a loaf before cutting off the slice—one for him, one for Enda, one for Rose—follows his gaze. Her eyes light upon her husband for a moment, then she waves the buttery knife at her son. "You're to go to school, and there's an end to it."

Liam slowly takes the bread and stows it in his pocket. He submits to a swift wet comb through his hair. He ties the laces on his boots. He follows the familiar route, but on the threshold, his classmates barging past him into the schoolhouse, something tugs at him, insistently, inexorably, reeling him back.

He spins around, he dashes sideways down the street, back, all the way back to the Lanes. He pushes at their door, he climbs the stairs, to the very top, where they have a room, at the rear. In the doorway, he pauses, arrested by the tableau of two figures, lit from the side by a shaft of sunlight filtering in through the window. A woman—Liam has to blink before he realises it is his mother—is sitting on a chair drawn up to the side of the bed. His father is propped against a rolled-up blanket, and his mother is lathering his face with white soap.

It is an act of such care and attention, her hands moving carefully, expertly, rubbing and coaxing the foam about his chin and cheeks, and all the while she talks to him, in a quiet undertone, wiping the soap from his mouth, putting down the bowl of water and picking up a razor. She lays a towel around him and applies the razor to his face with gentle, deft fingers. *Chhhruss*, says the blade against the stubble, *chhrrrruuus*, as it carves its way through the soap, and then she wipes it on the towel, and turning him to face the other way, she shaves the other side, talking, talking all the while. Liam cannot move, so struck is he by this sight—his parents, alone, without them, carrying on their lives, with no children by, apart from the one in his mother's belly—and the way his mother cares for his father, her hands enacting this simple task.

It will be a moment that will return to him again and again, when he is a grown man and far away from them all, seeing his mother caring for his father like this, and the understanding that she is mending him, in much the same way as she turns a collar or darns the heels of socks. His father will be made well again, his rents and holes stitched up by her.

"There now," she is murmuring, and Liam can just about hear her, "just turn this way for me, like that, yes, my love, we'll soon have you right, I know we will, and all this will pass, like everything else, and we'll be set again, just you see if we won't, but for now you stay there, right where you are, you're not to worry about anything, we'll manage, so we will. I can always take in sewing again, and the girls can help me, so you must do nothing but rest and get better, do you hear me, get your strength back, but first give me your hand, yes, like this, here, not much to feel yet but this baby will be a fine one, I know it, a strong one, another boy, I believe, it knows you're there, it can hear its daddy, and we can't wait to meet it, can we?"

The baby, who is the size of a pear, senses its parents' movements as a concertina of space and a flickering alteration of its light. It considers the saline taste on its tongue, and the shape of the handprint before it: the slices of light between the fingers, the breadth of the palm, its alternating intervals of light and shade. The baby wriggles with a flicking motion, a fish in a stream, taking in a sip of fluid. Here I am, it says, I am here.

"That's it now," Liam's mother says. "You can lie back down, sleep some more, rest now, my love, rest."

Liam, unseen and silent, turns away. His mother is taking care of things, as she always does; his father looks more like himself, with all that beard growth gone. Liam goes back down the stairs, one boot after the other. At school, he will be whipped for his lateness, but no matter.

His mother, hearing her son depart once again, smiles, but doesn't turn her head. She leans forward, over the bulge of the baby, and presses her lips to Tomás's brow.

As a chainboy to the mapping team, Tomás's job was to move the measuring chain in a series of straight lines so that the soldiers could get accurate measurements from their trig points. He was also expected to heft heavy instruments along paths and tracks, up mountains, along shores.

The most crucial part of his job, however, was translating for the surveyors and the sappers whenever they had to ask farmers or villagers where this boundary lay or who owned that field or what was the name of the river. Tomás stood behind a seated soldier as the local people queued up, one by one, to answer questions, and Tomás spoke with them, then told the redcoat what the responses were. More and more, he was handed the pen and told to write it all down himself because the redcoats had no sense of the spelling involved, of the many regional variants of *cloch* and *droichead* and *gaoth* and *sliabh*. Whenever he sat at the table, the map sheets before him, he always surreptitiously pressed his hands to their inked marks, almost as if he would make a print of them across his palms, because it was clear to him that, with a map, a person could never get lost. With a map, a person could always know where they were.

He learned quickly and eagerly, always seeking an opportunity to ask a question or a chance to perform a new task. By standing beside a redcoat surveyor and adopting an attitude of helpful deference, he was able to observe and memorise how the mysterious theodolite operated. It must, he saw, be steadied and levelled on its tripod, with tiny water bubbles to position inside three different markers; it must then be centred, bringing the vertical axis to match a gravitational marker. Angles were read and recorded, spoken aloud, and then the next bluff or outcrop could be recorded, as long as the instrument didn't move an inch.

When instructed to take down the instrument and pack it away, Tomás always first sneaked a look through the lens, holding his breath so as not to steam up the glass. Inside the theodolite was a world untroubled and hermetic, where mountains and trees, buildings and roads hung upside-down, where the sky was a pellucid sea that collected in the bottom of the lens, and the sun shone its beams upwards, like stalks of barley.

Tomás did not shy away from what he saw around him, never shirked in committing to the record what had occurred in these places in recent years. He set it all down: the ghost towns, the weed-lush fields, the mass graves, the workhouses, the Famine roads that led nowhere. He corrected the earlier surveyors' inept manglings of the language, their cavalier erasure of history. Maps can be read for many things—geography both natural and man-made—and Tomás made sure that the Great Hunger was inscribed on his drafts and in his name books, that it was recorded, in symbols and writing, that its effects and scars would be seen, its evidence and testimony unmissable, for all time.

He followed his division wherever they were ordered, from coast to coast, over river and bog and valley and mountain, and this journeying fed his restlessness. He learned that there were days when the rain came down more heavily than usual, and the surveyors kept to their tents, wary of what they called "a wetting," the sappers to their bottles of stout, so he was able to slip away, to wander at will. The weather was of no consequence to him; he moved through the drizzle like a fox. He learned that he must never contradict a soldier or a redcoat surveyor, even if he knew their calculations were erroneous, that seaweed should be consumed if a man wants to keep his teeth, that the cerulean ink intended for the sea may be mixed with gorse flowers to achieve the emerald hue needed for fields, that the land, his land, contained such astonishing variety—river valleys and coves and shallow waters and pounding waves and lime-cut wastelands and cragged peaks and lowland and towns and cities and streets and woods—and that he had never imagined such bounty. He learned that everything he saw—quarry, hospital, weir, castle—had a minuscule corresponding symbol. The blisters on his heels hardened into calluses; he rubbed pig fat into the seams of his boots each night. He was tireless, his division said, sometimes ruefully, always ready to press on, to urge them all another mile or two down the road; he never rested, never allowed a mistake to filter into the books or the charts, and he was rigorous at winkling out every detail, every twist in a road or a stream.

After two years of this, he was no longer an apprentice chainboy, the commanding officer told him; he was still classified as a labourer but he had been promoted within that category to what was called a civilian assistant and would receive a salary.

The thought of this—the shillings and pennies that would be coming into his pocket each week—kept him awake that night. Coins that would be his very own, to spend, to save, to purchase life's needs. Some men, he saw, from looking around himself, sent money to families back wherever it was they came from; others squandered it in shebeens or county fairs. What would he do?

Tomás cut and sewed a little bag out of canvas—such tasks came easily to him, from his time in the boot-mending workshop—and wove a long drawstring of leather through its top, and into this he put every coin he was paid. The drawstring he then tied around his waist: he slept with it under his shirt, to the amusement of the sappers around him.

What are you saving for, Tommy? they cried. Drinks for all of us? A tumble with a woman? New boots for you to wax? A fine suit of clothes to go a-courting? Come on, Tommy, don't be shy, you can tell us.

He ignored the taunts but privately he wondered: what would he do with this money? The revisions project was coming to a close and his division was being disbanded. There would be more work for him, he had been told, and he should present himself soon at the offices in Dublin. But what should he do for now, and where should he go? This question was pressing on his mind as they came, like the closing of a compass's circle, to where he had begun, the town where the workhouse was located, at base camp for the mappers.

That night, he slipped out of his hayloft, climbing down the ladder, easing open the door, and tiptoeing through the barracks—he needn't have worried, as everyone else had disappeared into the town, in search of drink and more. The dark was thick and absolute, clouds standing resolute between him and the moon, but Tomás could have found his way about a place he didn't know with a blindfold over his eyes. He kept to back-streets and lanes, to the shadows, hoping he wouldn't meet any of his division, because he didn't want to be asked where he was going, or why. It wasn't something he could have explained to himself.

The walls of the workhouse were visible from the main street as Tomás crossed it, moving from one alley to another. Further down, towards the river, was the sound of carousing and shouting, the light of an inn spilling like shattered glass onto the cobbles. He barely glanced towards it but kept going.

When he came to the gates, locked of course, he paused for a moment, then moved left, skirting the walls. No lights here, no candles illuminating the windows. He saw the hulk of the main building, with the children's dormitory behind it, and the shoe-workshop; he saw the yard, where he used to find the chalk stones; he saw the warden's office, with a line of light under the door.

His sharp eyes noticed two figures flitting across the yard from the kitchens towards the dormitory: he recognised, somewhere in himself, the bandy-legged gait of a barefoot workhouse child, the risk such a being might take to grub around like an animal at the back door of the kitchens to find even a morsel of extra food, and he let out a low whistle.

One child froze, causing the other to barrel into him. Tomás whistled again, and the first child took a step towards the railings, then another.

"Who's there?" the child whispered.

"Tomás. You might remember me—I used to be here myself. Come on over here, will you?"

"We will not," the second child said, in an urgent tone. "We've to go."

"I won't hurt you. Come," he beckoned to them, "just for a minute."

The children approached the railings, warily. Tomás saw that one was clutching a handful of peelings, the other a strand of cabbage.

"Have you anything to eat, mister?"

Tomás felt in his pockets. "I don't," he admitted, anguished. "I'm sorry."

"Ah, sure, I remember you," the first child said, leaning up against the railings, unfazed, as if it weren't at all extraordinary to disappear from this place for almost two years, then reappear in the middle of the night. "You're the lad who got taken away by the redcoats, isn't that right?"

"It is," Tomás said. "I was."

"And how did they treat you?" the child said conversationally. "Aren't they a terrible fierce lot and—"

"Let's go," the second boy hissed, tugging at the sleeve of his friend. "What do you want with us, anyway?"

"I . . ." Tomás felt his words desert him, as if they had been written in chalk and sudden rain had washed them away. What did he want? Why had he come? "Would you know . . . a girl . . . ?"

The child grinned. "There are lots of girls here. Would there be one in particular you were thinking of?"

"She's called Seraphina."

The boys, listening, considering, shook their heads.

"Or Phina?"

Again, they shook their heads: no.

"The wardens call her Frances."

The taller boy, the more gregarious of the two, pushed a carrot peeling into his mouth and chewed energetically. "Isn't that the one whose daddy came back from Merikay for her?" he mused, addressing his friend. "She has the yellow hair, and the curls, a—"

Tomás gripped the railings with both hands. "Her father came for her, did he, all the way from America?"

"He did." The boy chewed again, then swallowed. "But he was asking at the office with her other name, Seraphina was it, and the warden was a new one and he only knew her as Frances, so he told the man there was no one by that name here, no daughter of his."

"And he left?"

"He did."

"Without her?"

"Without her."

The three of them contemplated this story in appalled silence. Tomás was very aware of the painful thud of his heart, a compression in his throat.

"And then," the boy continued, and even his jauntiness was dimmed, "she heard about it later, but it was too late, your man her father had gone, and she went wild, didn't she?"

"She did," the second boy said. "They'd to lock her in the shed."

Tomás leaned his forehead into the cold iron of the railings; the images assailing him were disjointed and senseless. The father sailing all the way back from the New World, in search of surviving family, him tracing her to the workhouse, and then to be turned away. The girl realising her daddy had been so close, and no way to reach him, and then her restrained and shut in the shed. He didn't know how to piece these strands together, how to stitch them into a narrative.

"Did she . . ." He had no idea of what he needed to ask, he didn't know how to proceed.

"But now she's to go to the other side of the world in a big boat."

"A boat?"

"Yes, her and all the older girls. The wardens said that there's a penal colony, far away, on the other side of the world, stuffed to the gills it is with just men, and no women, so they've been told to send workhouse girls out there because—"

"A penal colony?" Tomás demanded. "Was it Australia? Phina's being sent to Australia?"

The boy nodded. "That was the place. The dormitory for the older girls is empty now—they all went yesterday. They're to be wives or servants for the—"

Tomás reached through the railing and gripped the boy's arm. "Where were they sailing from? Do you remember?"

The child struggled against his grip. "Hey, leave off, I don't know, it was a big boat, they said, but—"

At that moment, a cloud slid back and away from the moon and a silvery light splashed down on the place, the yard, the three of them, and the second child seemed to be struck by a thought: he opened his mouth and uttered a word.

It was an approximation of a placename, with one or two extra syllables to it, but recognisable as a port not twenty miles from there. Tomás swung his gaze towards the boy. He spoke the name of the town, and the boy thought about it, then nodded, yes, that was the place.

In his bed, in his home, years and years later, Tomás opens his eyes. He sees: sunlight lying stretched out in a strip along the floor that rises up and over the table and a chair, down to the floor, over the rag-rug, and up again to lay itself over the bed, across his feet. He sees: a jug held aloft over a bowl, and a twisting rope of milk reaching up towards it. He sees: a pair of boots, his, by the door, one leaning its open mouth into the other. He sees: a woman standing by the bowl, her hand attached to the handle of the jug, her face wearing an expression of abstraction.

Tomás parts his lips. He is fearful of looking around too closely, at the corners of the room or the black mouth of the hearth, in case his father might be lurking somewhere, looking at him reproachfully, perhaps missing a limb or part of his face. He doesn't know how long he's been asleep, weeks or even months, but he is aware that he is now awake and feeling several things: the inexorable swish-swish of blood along his veins, a strange stiffness in the joints of his hips, a healing itch in the skin of his wrists.

He finds also, to his surprise, as if it has been gathering itself together while he slept, like a mist, that in his head is a plan. A clear and attainable plan. He blinks, awed by the glow of it. He regards it from all sides, like a man who has come across a great heap of gold coins by the wayside, and cannot believe they are there for the taking.

Tomás moves his tongue inside his dry mouth. He blinks his eyes, open and shut. He clears his throat.

"May I," he begins, and his voice is hoarse, "may I have some milk? I've a terrible thirst on me."

The woman turns her head, puts down the jug, her face opening to him like a flower. He extracts his hand from the bedclothes and holds it out to her.

~

Tomás ran through the dark streets, his breath ragged. At the barracks, he rolled up a blanket, strapped it to his back, and woke one of the sappers, a young lad not much older than himself who occasionally shared his tobacco with him. I'm going off for a day or two, Tomás hissed into his half-awake ear.

Wha'? the lad muttered, turning over in his camp bed.

Reconnaissance, Tomás said, giving his nightshirt a shake, tell them for me, will you? The sapper nodded, blearily, and dropped back into sleep.

Tomás slipped into the night, blanket roll on his back, his cloth-purse of money hidden beneath his clothes, a thick coat buttoned up to the neck. He looked at the Pole Star, consulted his compass and set off, summoning to his mind the maps of the area he had perused and, in the case of one slice of the county, drawn up.

Near dawn, a farmer with a cart of cabbages stopped for him and took him a good portion of the way; near the county border, he exchanged a penny for the hind end of a loaf; he lay on the turf to drink from a stream. By the time he reached the port, it was mid-morning. The air around him was still, hung with grey vines of damp, and this fact spurred him on: wouldn't a big boat, as the workhouse boys described it, need a good wind to fill its sails? Surely weather such as this would keep a craft in harbour. Even so, he quickened his steps, hastening to the quayside. To miss this boat, to arrive too late: it would be the end of him.

The dock, in an estuarial inlet, was busier than he had anticipated, with fishing boats and ships large and small lined up along the harbour wall, tethered by great ropes and chains, gangways stretching from deck to quay. Sailors shouted and yelped to one another in languages Tomás couldn't comprehend; crates were hoisted above him to land with a crash on wooden decks. A cow was being led on a rope towards a ramp, and the beast was not pleased at the idea of being taken onboard, lowing and tossing its head. It occurred to

Tomás, with dismay, that there was a distinct and frisky breeze here, down at the docks. The flags on the ships' masts were snapping and tugging, the rigging rattling, the furled sails straining against their ties, as if they, too, were keen to be out at sea.

Which is the boat bound for Australia? he asked a sailor with barely a tooth in his head, who was standing by a wooden craft. The man glanced at him, up and down, then shrugged, casually catching a thick rope tossed to him from the deck. Ask further down, was his response. Tomás hastened along the harbour, weaving in and out of heaped nets, lobster creels, woven baskets, piles of discarded fishbones. The smell was overwhelming: salt mixed with fish mixed with unwashed crowds mixed with damp wood. It was a place of departure, of the fear and trepidation of those leaving, and the grief of those left behind. Tomás saw an old woman in a bonnet clinging wordlessly to the hand of a young man; he saw a woman with a baby at her breast, and two more children tied by their waists to her wrist, her face set in a mutinous scowl of panic as she looked down into the heaving green waters of the harbour; he saw a fisherman and his wife sitting imperturbably on a box, scraping their catches with the side of their knives, the scales cascading around them in a blizzard of silver. He saw these things but he also didn't see them, for what was filling his heart and his mind was the thought of a girl wrapped in a fine shawl, standing near a pair of donkeys, her blue eyes looking into his.

The ship for Australia, he said, to anyone who would listen. Where is the ship bound for Australia? People shrugged or shook their heads or pushed his clasping hands off their sleeves. A uniformed harbour official with a ledger under his arm gestured down the quay; a sailor with bare browned arms uttered something in a foreign tongue and pointed, with a blackened fingernail, to a large ship right at the end of the curved harbour wall.

Tomás broke into a run. The ship had high sides, punctured here and there with meagre square windows that looked like a host of disapproving eyes. Its sails were at half-mast, filling and emptying with air; figures were at work in the rigging, climbing up and along; a crate of something was being dragged across the harbour next to it; a man in a bicorn hat stood at the wheel, conferring with a person beside him, and together they were consulting some kind of document. Perhaps a map, Tomás thought irrelevantly, as he stopped by the man dragging the crate.

"Is this the ship bound for Australia?"

"Eh?" The man didn't stop his hauling.

"The penal colony. Are you heading there?"

"We are, but we're to put in first at Tangiers and then—"

"I need to speak to one of your passengers."

He grimaced, panting, and Tomás, realising that the crate was too heavy for one, saw his chance. Bracing his hands to its side, he threw his weight behind the crate and it began to shift over the cobbles.

"I'll help you," Tomás said.

Eyeing him, the sailor grunted, but accepted his assistance. The gold hoop in his ear glittered in the weak sunlight: Tomás had heard that they wore them so as to pay for a burial, if they were lost at sea. He wanted to put out a hand and touch it, for luck, for himself and for the sailor. Together they hauled the crate—filled with what looked like sacks of oats—towards the gangway.

"It's one of the workhouse girls," Tomás said, in a low voice. "Have you seen them?"

The sailor glanced towards the officers at the wheel, then back at Tomás. "I have. They are already below, far down in the hold. There's a man from the workhouse with them."

"Take me down there, will you?"

They were reaching the deck, the crate between them. The sailor narrowed his eyes at Tomás as he struggled backwards, the muscles in his arms standing out like cords.

"Give me your coat," he said.

Without hesitating, Tomás unbuttoned the army greatcoat he was wearing and handed it to the man.

"And that blanket."

Tomás unstrapped the roll from his back and pushed it towards the sailor, who paused for a moment, glancing again at the uniformed men, then gestured towards a hatch.

Tomás followed him across the deck and down through the hole, finding a foothold on a narrow, slippery ladder. The space below was half lit and close, filled with jostling bodies and people calling to each other, pushing this way and that. There were packages and luggage stacked in passageways, bottles lashed together, doors opening and closing, sailors rushing, passengers arguing and shoving. Tomás heard the noise of a pig from somewhere and the cluck and flap of chickens; there was a strong odour of quicklime and something else, perhaps overcooked meat. He had to be quick to keep up with his guide, who stepped surefooted through the chaos, not looking round once to check that Tomás was still with him. Tomás had to barge his way through clusters of people, past passengers coming in and out of their cabins—he was so frightened by the thought of losing his sailor, and also by the awareness that the ship might cast off and leave, without warning, and he would be trapped here, on his way to the other side of the world, where he would have to begin all over again, and never see this land once more. It was a horrifying thought but he spurred himself on with the idea that Phina was on this ship, that she was almost within reach.

The sailor monkeyed his way down another ladder, along a narrow corridor, and then down a third. The air here was foetid and sour; water and a kind of green rot oozed down the panels, and there was very little light.

Tomás was just about to ask how much further they were going—he was gripped suddenly by the idea that this sailor was tricking him or leading him into some awful trap, perhaps to murder him and steal his money—when the man stopped, so abruptly that Tomás rammed into him.

"Here," the sailor said, pointing at a narrow door with a high step.

Tomás knocked with his knuckles, seeing, from the corner of his eye, his sailor leaving, climbing up the ladder and away. He knocked again. And then he looked down and saw that the door was barred from the outside. He lifted the iron bar, let it clatter to the floor, and he pushed the door open, stepping inside.

The space was dim, strung with lines of greyish linens. The floorboards were strewn with thin drifts of sawdust; boxes and cases were scattered about. In one corner, a group of figures could be seen, crouching low, clinging to each other, their frightened faces visible to him, like pale petals pasted on the darkness. He saw them shift, shrinking away from him, tightening their hold on each other.

"Who are you?" one of them called, in a shaking voice. "What do you want with us?"

"I'll do you no harm," Tomás said. "I promise. I'm looking for Phina—Seraphina. Is she among you?"

There was a susurration of whispering, heads turning, hands gripping other hands, and Tomás wondered, grimly, what had happened to these girls to make them so afraid.

"What would you be wanting with her? If she was here?" It was the same voice again. "Which she isn't."

"I've come for her. For Phina. You might know her as Frances. I mean her no harm," he said again, because it seemed important to keep stating this to them. "I'm wanting . . ." He stopped. It hadn't occurred to him, throughout this whole escapade, what his plan was. He hadn't formulated what he wanted with her, hadn't articulated it to himself. He had been focusing on getting here, and preventing her from being packed off like this. Beyond that, he hadn't thought.

"What?" the bold girl demanded. "What do you want with her?"

"I want . . . I want . . . I need to speak with her . . . I was sent away, you see, with the redcoats, to make maps and . . ."

There was a murmur and then a distinct titter. Tomás faltered to a stop, his face suddenly scarlet. It was possible he had made a dreadful mistake in coming here, it now occurred to him. She might well not remember him, might feel nothing for him. This was a grave error. He should go.

"S-sorry," he stammered, "I'll—go . . . I—"

"Tomás?"

A figure was standing up, separating itself from the huddle.

"Yes," he said.

A silhouette moved towards him, its outline blurred, but he could see a mass of curls about its head, and feet that were stepping precisely over the boards. Then a slight, cold hand was taking his, claiming him. Tomás pressed the hand in his, pulled it close to his side. Then they were stepping out of the door together and he could see more of her: the dust-coloured dress she was wearing, that she was thinner and taller, of course, but her eyes were still the same frank blue, and the way she held his hand was full of such trust, such certainty, and his heart seemed to quiver within his chest because he had never felt these things before, or had no memory of feeling them, and he had no idea what he had done to deserve her faith, but he pulled her through the bowels of the ship, through the hordes of people, moving quickly.

At one point, near the second ladder, they were accosted by the workhouse warden, who squawked at them, at Tomás, saying to let go of the girl, what did he think he was doing, he was a blackguard and a gurrier, but Tomás put his elbow into the man's chest and shoved him hard up against the wall of the ship—it was the only time he let go of Phina—and he was forced to punch the man in the jaw, which was a sad thing because the man was old and not nearly as big as Tomás, and there was blood, but it had to be done, he would not let this man take Phina from him and send her to a penal colony to be a servant or worse, and Tomás wiped his knuckles on his trousers, took Phina's hand again, and then they were up on the deck, and he made straight for the gangway, and then they were down it and onto the dockside, and Tomás said, Run, can you run, we need to get away from here. So she ran beside him, and he could see she was weakened, but she was brave, this he knew, and she did the best she could, and before much time, they had left the docks behind them and were mingling with the people on the streets, losing themselves, but still Tomás was uneasy, so he struck a bargain with a family who were heading away from the marketplace with their children on a cart, and he asked them could they put Phina up there with them for a spell, and he would walk alongside, and they said yes, and an hour or so after they had escaped from the ship, Tomás and Phina were taking the road away from the town. Their hands were still joined, it didn't seem safe to let go, not yet, and Phina turned to him and said, I knew you'd come for me, I knew it.

Impossible, Phina thinks (as she crouches over a tub by the pump at the top of the Lanes, scrubbing at an inexplicable stain on a smock of Enda's), the situation is impossible. She doesn't know what to do: her husband, returned but unrecognisable, scarcely enough money in his pocket. She doesn't raise her eyes to meet those of her neighbours today; she hasn't the appetite for talk, doesn't know what to tell people who ask after Tomás. He is sitting up in bed, he is taking a little food and drink, but he still stares off into space, he whispers to himself, he starts and jumps at nothing, he still wakes screaming in the night, he barely speaks. It is as if his very soul has been stolen away.

Perhaps, she thinks (as she pegs out the damp laundry, clothes-pegs gripped between her teeth), it is best to do nothing, to wait.

On the other hand (as she takes a comb to Rose's hair, trying to untangle the knots and snarls, blocking her ears to the shrieks of protest), maybe she should be trying to find out what has caused this change, to get him to speak. What would be the best thing? What would a good wife do? She feels, yet again (as she leans uncomfortably over the hearth, blowing on the wood, trying to coax the embers into life), the lack of a mother in her life, someone with experience of marriage, someone to advise her, to say, yes, husbands do this, they take to their beds in silence and look like the living dead, just wait it out, or, no, this is not usual, and this is what you must do. But no use, of course, to dwell on these things. She has him, she has her children, and that is more than some.

All the same, she thinks (as she stirs strips of hot cabbage into broken-up bread crusts over the sulking fire), for all Tomás's strangeness and taciturnity, this is not like him. All the same, the other men on the street go to and from their jobs, if they have them. Tomás has always been a good worker, never squandered his money or time in bars, never taken to his bed like this.

The problem, as she sees it (she is dipping a ladle into the bucket of water to make the tea), is that there is no one for her to ask. She could try one of the other women or even the priest, but what would she say? He went away out west and then came back like a ghost? We've no money coming in and what savings I have won't stretch for long and I don't know what to do and I've another on the way? She's tried asking Liam what happened but the child just looks fearful and mutters about the maps and the redcoats and how the widow they lodged with helped him.

Her husband has gone from her, is what she thinks in dark moments (turning over in bed, trying to find a comfortable position, listening for the individual rhythms of her children's breathing, and that of her man beside her), and will perhaps never come back, might never work again. She will birth this child, God willing, and then what will become of them? Even if she could find more sewing work—and there's always a desire for new frocks in the big houses—whatever will she do when this baby comes? She'll have her hands too full for fine needlework and won't be able to afford the embroidery silks, the narrow pins. Tomás needs to get well, and fast, if they are to keep a roof over their heads, and have coal in the grate. She doesn't like to dip into the money she keeps in a pouch behind the flour barrel, but it will soon come to that. Some mornings she finds it hard not to yank the blankets off him and say: Stir yourself, for the love of God, and go out to work.

On a day when the rain has been coming down since dawn, Rose is fractious, unable to play out. Phina has had to devise tasks for her to keep her occupied until her brother and sister come back from school—holding a hank of wool while Phina winds it into a ball, shaping a bit of bread dough into animals. Instead of staring blankly out of the window, Tomás watches them with an unsettling intensity from the bed, his face unmoving; he doesn't respond when Rose pats his arm or asks him, will she fetch him a cup of water? So Phina is astounded when he suddenly pulls back the covers and rises to his feet.

He seems unaccountably tall as he stands there. Rose is as surprised as Phina is, staring up at her father with an open mouth, the scrap of dough clutched in one hand.

"Are you . . . ?" Phina says, her throat fluttering with equal parts relief and panic. "Do you feel . . . ?" not knowing how her sentences will end.

"I have decided," he says, "what we must do. I have made a plan for us."

Phina, unnerved, blinks. "And what is that?"

He seems not to hear or acknowledge her question.

"We are rootless," he says, apparently to the ceiling, "we are landless. And worse than that, we are at the beck and call of the enemy. My father," he mutters, "is ashamed of me."

Phina gropes blindly for Rose's hand and grips it in her own. "Tomás," she begins, in a voice that sounds calmer and more amenable than she feels, "let's not be hasty in whatever it is you've—"

"Do not concern yourself, woman," he cuts across her. "Because I know what to do. How to save us."

Tomás moves quickly about the room. He picks up his trousers, which have lain over the back of a chair for the weeks he's been in bed. He pulls them on, tightens the belt; he reaches for the jacket, which is hanging behind the door. All the time, Phina follows him, anxiety mounting as she asks, where is he going, what will he do, and whatever did he mean about his father? But he has lapsed back into silence and there is a peculiar glint in his eye, that of a man with a task on his mind, that of someone who has reached a decision. He fits his hat to his head, nods at his wife and daughter, then leaves, the door swinging closed behind him.

"Da's gone out," Rose remarks, reaching for the button tin in her mother's workbox.

"He has."

Rose is regarding her, trying to glean what all this means. Phina is careful to keep her face expressionless; she turns to scrape at the base of a pot, trying to quell the urge to hurry out the door after him, to see where he goes. Rose lifts the lid of the tin and all the buttons, shiny and smooth, spill out onto the table. Their paired holes stare up at Phina like so many tiny eyes.

Enda and Liam are seated at the table, giving exemplary performances of children concentrating on their exercises, Enda with the end of a pencil in her mouth, Liam with his chin resting in his hand. Their mother is across the room, darning a rent in Enda's jersey, Rose cross-legged at her feet. Every few minutes, Enda cannot help but raise her eyes to regard her mother, and Liam also looks up; their gazes will lock for an almost unbearable moment and then they will look down at their schoolwork once more.

Liam is labouring over a Latin text, his finger moving along the line from word to word, and sometimes back the way it came. Enda has ten long-division sums to solve for the next day. She sighs, plucking the pencil from her mouth, and leans over her work. If the two of them don't finish these exercises by tomorrow, and correctly, they might get the strap, but Enda is finding it hard to bend her mind around it all. How is she supposed to think about twelve times nine when she can see that her mother's eyes are swollen from crying, when her parents seem not to be speaking to each other beyond, Will you take a cup of tea? I will, or Is that you heading out again? It is, when Enda, checking behind the flour barrel, has seen that the pouch of her mother's savings has disappeared?

It is impossible. Enda sighs again and Liam peers at her from under his cowlick of hair; she tips her head in the direction of the flour barrel and widens her eyes, hoping Liam will cotton on to the fact that the money has gone, perhaps stolen, but he gazes instead at the kettle, puzzled.

Like sudden rain, the solution to one of her sums falls upon Enda. She snatches up the pencil and writes a series of figures in a fierce cascade, ending with an emphatic and underlined *= 327*, then flings down the pencil, triumphant. Of all her lessons, Enda likes mathematics the least—there is nothing for the mind to snag on and wonder about, just the rightness and wrongness of it. She would never admit to anyone that it comes easily to her: numbers that stack up in one column, fitting into each other's vacancies like stones in a wall. It makes a kind of dull, prosaic sense to her but she finds no pleasure in it.

The savings behind the flour can't have been stolen, she thinks, because how would anyone have found them? And a theft wouldn't explain the tension between her parents, the heavy, crackling atmosphere in their room, like the air in the street gets before a thunderstorm. Their father is out somewhere, this Enda knows, but she has no idea where. None of it makes any sense: he came back from the mapping, spent weeks lying in bed, then suddenly rose up, and has been absent for days now, only returning at night-time when Enda and her siblings are in bed. Her mother, if asked about this behaviour, draws in her mouth and just says, He has matters to attend to, but will not say what these matters might be. Enda has begun to suspect that her mother doesn't know any more than she does.

Enda wishes to know what the matters are; she wishes to know very much. She also wishes to know what is going on in her household and where the money has gone and where her father is and why her mother doesn't ask him and why the two of them refuse to exchange a word with each other.

She sighs, then glances up to find that Rose is now standing at the table, staring at her, eyes wide, as if to drink in as much information as possible. She has that doll of hers clutched to her chest; one of her hands rests upon its back.

"What?" Enda snaps, half her mind still engaged with *three into thirty-seven, carry one*.

Rose says nothing but keeps looking at her, unblinking. It is enough to tip Enda's precarious equilibrium over a cliff.

"Mammy," she cries. "Rosie won't stop staring at me."

Their mother across the room lifts her darning to her mouth, bites off the thread, and, without turning round, says, "That doesn't sound like a terrible crime."

"She's putting me off," Enda says, kicking her heels against the legs of the table, which joggles the inkpot, which in turn sprays a fine mist of ink onto Liam's page.

"Enda!" Liam shrieks. "Look what you did."

"I didn't do it," Enda shouts back. "Rose did it."

"I did not," Rose says, indignant. "I never touched it."

"You did."

"I did not."

"Did."

Liam starts to cry, scrubbing at the page with his cuff; Rose joins in, saying that Enda is a horror. Her mother is saying, "That will do from all of you, I'll thank you to remember that—" when the door opens and their father steps inside.

A gust of the stairwell enters with him, air that is chill and moist:

it eddies its way around the cramped room. Enda feels it coil about her calves, then move on towards the windows. Her father's hair is pushed off his brow. He is grinning. His eyes meet theirs. He looks, Enda is able to think, even in the face of the howling and shouting going on around her, like himself again, like someone restored.

"What the devil is going on in here?" he asks, with good humour. "Fighting like cats, are you?"

Enda darts a look at her mother, at Liam, at Rose. They are all silenced, wary; Liam's cheeks are wet with tears but he gazes at Tomás, mouth trembling, as if unable to believe what he sees. Their mother's brows are pulled together; she has one hand pressed to her middle.

Tomás bends to hoist the snivelling Rose onto his shoulder. "What do you cry for, *a leanbh*? Why such a sad look on your face?"

He bends his knees, bouncing her up and down, her head dangerously close to the rafters, her hair tossing back and forth. Rose's sobs turn rapidly to giggles and she clutches at her father's collar, dislodging his cap. Enda can recall sitting up there herself—she can almost feel the sensation of being that high and that close to her father. For a moment, she can feel that she is Rose or that Rose is her, one of the two, that time has collapsed and she is tiny again.

Enda feels no relief at the change in Tomás. Something is amiss, she knows, and she both does and doesn't want to find out what it might be. She is filled, all of a sudden, with a desire to go back in time, to when she was younger, Rose's age perhaps, to when life was simple, to reverse, like Liam's fingertip on the Latin verse, to the start of the sentence, to make sense of it all. She certainly doesn't want to be eleven, sitting at the table, doing her mathematics, about to hear whatever it is her father is going to say.

So when her father puts Rose down—she clings to his leg, of course, just as Enda used to, begging for more—and pulls out of his jacket a folded square of paper, saying that he has had a letter, that he has some news for them all, Enda is not surprised. What her father is saying is at once shocking and not shocking at all. It makes no sense and perfect sense. Of course, she wants to say, I felt this coming. But also, What are you talking about, how can you say that?

Her mother is aghast, her hand to her mouth, and she is saying,

Tomás, Tomás, what do you mean you took the savings, the money I'd put by. How could you do such a thing? Why could we not have talked it over? Liam is open-mouthed, aghast, and he is looking at Enda as if she has the power to stop this.

"It's so simple," their father says, looking from Phina to Liam, his palm resting on Rose's hair. "I have in my hand a letter from the land steward of the viscount's estate, confirming everything. I used the money to lease a cottage and some land out where Liam and I were mapping. We will leave the Lanes. We must. We're barely getting by here, and you, Phina, you're worn to a thread with worry. We will go out to the peninsula and live there. It is," he urges them all to see, "the answer."

"The answer to what?" Enda demands.

Her father looks at her, for the first time, and he smiles. "To everything," he replies.

PART TWO

THE EXACT PLACE WHERE, MILLENNIA LATER, LIAM WILL STAND WAITING FOR HIS FATHER TO REAPPEAR

SOMEWHERE IN TIME, A CHILD IS CLIMBING UP A HOLLOW CARVED out between two hills. Her hand grips the unruly fur of an enormous grey dog, which stands as high as she does. The animal pads beside her, companion and protector, its golden eyes scanning the landscape around them for predators or potential dangers, as it has been trained to do. Lengths of sealskin have been tied over the soles of the child's feet and she wears a string of pierced cowrie shells around her neck; the dog has been given a matching adornment, and it tolerates this indignity with benign resignation. The child's head is lowered and she is allowing her hair to sway from side to side with the motion of her walk. The sound of the name given to her at birth, by her father, might be written as "Brith."

Several steps behind—Brith can hear the swish of footfalls through grass—is her mother, who carries a smaller child on her back, and in her hand a basket, filled with lichen and a leaf-cup of hazelnuts. When they left the gates of the fort earlier, her mother had said they were going to gather mushrooms, but with the peculiar insight of youth, Brith knew that wasn't true. Ever since her father left the fort almost a whole season ago, walking off into the darkening blue hills with both his hounds, never to return, her mother has taken to these long and aimless searches, sometimes with Brith and sometimes without. The other women of the fort say she is sore-grieving her man, she is still seeking him, that they must let her do as she will, but wasn't he always an odd one, and that's what comes of taking one of his kind as a mate, a stranger, a meanderer.

Brith's course this morning—and it is hers because her mother seems to have no particular destination in mind, and is letting Brith choose their way—takes them to the exact place where, millennia later, Liam will stand waiting for his father to reappear from the copse.

The land, however, in the time of the child with the sealskin shoes, is very different from Tomás's day. The mother with the basket, the wolfhound and the children move through thick woodland: trees, trees and more trees cover the slopes, through which fall scattered coins of sunlight. Their feet press down into the thick, blackened leaf-fall. Around them, the golden air is stitched with pollen and the inexplicable flight paths of bees, and teems with the sounds of a forest: birdsong, the creak of branches, the insistent tapping of a woodpecker, the drip of moisture from foliage, the secretive rustle of unseen creatures moving about the undergrowth.

Brith, who is ahead and in charge, is taking as her guide the stream, which sparks in the sunlight, cutting a narrow channel through the hillside, weaving itself around rocks and tree trunks, appearing and disappearing, diving underground then springing up in unexpected places. Brith likes its eddies and gurgles, the way it flounces over the ground, smoothing the pebbles in its path; she likes the way it cools the earth under her feet and the sprightly waving of long weeds in its current. She sings as she goes, a breathy, near-silent song, for herself and herself alone: *Ai-yee, ai-yo, ai-yee, ly-ah, ly-ah.*

The dog, which is in fact the one leading the procession, decides it is time to pause. It bows its noble, heavy head to the stream and commences a noisy lapping. Brith watches it for a moment, then unhooks a shallow wooden cup from her belt and dips it through the surface, watching as a matching cup rises up out of the water to meet it. The stream is icy, despite the warmth of the day, as if it has sprung from deep within the land, and it tastes of rock, of the colour green, of peat, and something else she can't identify. The taste dances on her tongue; she swallows and feels it cutting a cool, confronting path through her middle.

Mother, she says, and she knows without turning that her mother is stepping past her—Brith is still at an age when proximity to a parent is a necessity, a means of survival. *Taste this.*

She holds out the cup, still half full. She cannot explain why but she wants to give this to her mother. She wants her not to be sore-grieving any more, and she has an obscure sense that the stream-water might help and soothe, might offer answers to questions they cannot articulate. And so into her field of vision bends her mother: sleek brown hair bound into long plaits, a smooth brow, a strong and freckled arm, dark lashes casting shadows on pronounced cheekbones. It will be a few years before Brith realises that her mother is an uncommon beauty, sought out as a bride by a passing stranger from an ancient wandering tribe, and the reason her father joined their hill fort, curtailing his journey to elsewhere, giving up his ways and taking to living in a hut, inside a fort, to putting his shoulder to a plough and his hand to a spade. For now, however, on this bright morning, she is just her mother, as constant a presence as the daylight or the sky, a person who gives her food, the one who lies beside her at night, the one who lights the fire each morning, the one who untangles Brith's hair, who laces up her tunic.

Her mother's lips touch the skin of the water. She drinks and swallows. Brith waits, anxiety building. Will her mother see? Will she understand how special this stream is? Will she, too, sense that it offers them answers to unknown conundrums? Her mother wipes her mouth with the back of her hand and smiles.

The dog watches them with its implacable amber eyes.

Laying a hand briefly on Brith's head, she moves away, up the path, and as she does so, something in the stream catches Brith's eye: there! A flash of gold. Seen and then concealed by a twist of water, then seen again. There it is now, caught in a cleft between two stones.

Brith steps into the stream, eagerly, first one foot, then the other. Instantly, her feet are encased in what feels like ice. She bends and slips her fingers into the water, her mind filled with the idea of an enchanted pebble or a nugget of amber. She will give it to her mother, no, her father, when he comes back, or she'll keep it for the baby, when he's older. She feels the silky glide of the water, stones that are slippery with brownish river-fur. Her thumb locates something hard yet delicate, and there is a slight clinking noise. Her fingers close over it and she lifts it out, and there, in her palm, as she stands in the appearing-disappearing stream that runs through this wood, between two hills, is a ring. Impossible to believe, and astonishing to see: wrought of beaten gold, with a swirling design of interlocking circles, and two scaled beasts, each swallowing the legs of the other. Brith feels the weight of it in her hand, its cool circumference, and she cannot draw breath.

She knows this ring. She has held the hand that wears it almost every day of her life. She has traced its woven paths, its smooth curves.

Brith closes her fingers over it, quickly, as if that raven circling the sky overhead might dive and snatch it from her with its blackened beak. She grips the ring fiercely. She brings her fist to her mouth to stave off the dread that is invading her; she squeezes shut her eyes. She will never tell. It will be a secret she'll keep. The thought swings through her, like a burning stick through night air. She will tell, she will call to her mother and show her what she's found and her mother will be able to explain it, will offer a reason as to why her father's ring is here, at the bottom of this stream.

The ring presses a circle of pain into the clammy skin of her palm. She won't tell. She will. She won't.

Brith lifts her head. The ends of her hair are wet from when she leaned over to pick up the ring. They stick like water-weeds to her tunic. Beside her, the dog shakes itself, droplets flying from it, then fixes her with an appraising gaze.

Her mother is a short way off and has seated herself on a flattish rock in the shade of an oak tree. She has undone the neck of her tunic, lifted the baby from her back and begun to feed him.

Brith waits for a moment, watching her mother, who is leaning against the oak's rippled trunk, face turned up to the sun. She will be there for a while, Brith knows. Her younger brother is a hungry one: she has heard her mother telling her father this, and her father gave his laugh that showed all his teeth, lifting the baby from where he lay near the hearth, saying that it's only right, for he is to grow up strong, and become a warrior and a hunter, like himself.

She thinks again of the word the other women had used for her father: meanderer. Brith had folded it into her mind as soon as she heard it and, unbeknown to her mother, had taken it to the fort's teller. He lived in a hut at the edge of their fort, all by himself (although Brith had heard people say, often with a sidelong look, that he was far from lonely), and it was said that he held in his head all the verses and histories of their people. Brith liked the teller's long beard, which was woven with beads and shells, the curved knife he carried tucked into his belt; most of all she liked his hut, which was decorated with feathers and whittled animals and switches of hazel and figures fashioned from the heads of corn. Her father had been a particular friend of the teller's, and the two of them had spent much time working alongside each other in the fields or walking out together, to the woods and the shore, their heads bent in conversation. The teller had once told Brith that her father had taught him tales he had never heard, from the times before, when the land was new-made and the streams had just begun their flow.

So when Brith asked the teller about the word, "meanderer," the teller had regarded her thoughtfully, his head on one side. He had been squatting in front of a dying fire in the long-hut of the elders, casting for them, to see what the future might hold, scattering seed-pods into its bright embers, watching them explode in the heat. Your father, he had replied, after a long silence, did someone say this about him? Brith had nodded.

It means, he had said, one who wanders, one who settles not in a single place.

But he settled here, she had cried, stabbing the ground with a finger, he did.

I know, the teller said, and he put a hand to her shoulder. I know he did. What this person meant was that your father was—and here he corrected his utterance, not unnoticed by Brith—your father is special, marked out. He belongs to a tribe who were here long ago, before us, before any of this. The teller's arm swept around the long-hut, the circular walls of the fortress that enclosed them in its embrace. As you know, our people came to this land from far away, over seas and over mountains; we came and built forts and ploughed fields and grew crops and kept animals. But we were not the first: your father's people were already here. They did not farm the land but instead walked among its valleys and hills, its shores and lakes, always moving, never settling.

Meanderers? Brith asked.

The teller nodded and gave her a smile. He reached out and stirred the embers in the firepit. In the shadows of the long-hut, the elders muttered among themselves—of portents and crops and weather and the storage of grain. Brith paid them no attention.

Nobody, the teller continued, knows where they all went, what happened to them. All we know is that they are not here now. Some say they left or sailed elsewhere in boats or died out; others believe that your father's people disappeared into the ground, by some mysterious magic. That their roaming became harder, with so many of their places suddenly farmed and fenced, so they merged themselves with the very land itself, passing into the trees and the rivers and the stones and the bushes and the briars, never to be seen again.

Never? Brith had swallowed, forcing down something hard in her throat. Never to be seen again?

Perhaps never. The teller had taken her hand and filled it from his pouch with dry seedpods, closing her fingers over them. I believe, he said, that your father may be the last of his kind. He indicated that Brith should do a casting, should throw the pods onto the collapsing structure of the fire, and she did so, sending sparks up into the air. Unless, of course, we consider you, he had said, and your brother. For you might have his ways in you. You are half him, are you not?

Brith had shut her eyes, finding that the sparks were still living on the inside of the lids, vivid in their dangerous dark. I am, she'd whispered. I am.

To distract herself from this recollection—and where is her father, where did he go that night, he would never leave them, as some insinuate, but did perhaps something bad happen to him, did he meet an enemy or a person from his old tribe, someone he had wronged or deserted to be with them, for he cannot have magically dissolved into the land, as the teller suggested, he would never leave them—Brith buries her hand in the dog's pelt, gripping the leather collar adorned with shells, and begins to push her legs against the swift-running current. Wavelets crest over her shins.

III

She swishes forward, along the bed of the stream, up the hillside, her sealskin shoes—made by her father, who slew the beast and carried it home on one shoulder, throwing it down at their doorway and kissing her mother, and saying, Now, shoes for all of us, and gloves for the cold season—slipping easily over the stones. She wades upstream, keeping one eye on her mother, still reclined against the tree, head resting on its bark, the baby at her breast, and the dog of course moves with her. The stream widens, narrows, turns a sharp corner. From branches above her is released a sudden shower of ash keys, which flutter downwards, whirring in circles, until their wild flight is put to a stop by meeting the water's surface, where they are apprehended and whisked away downstream. She is surrounded by dense greenery now, and the ground is covered with small, mossy humps, and she is just about to turn around and go back to her mother, who will worry if she finishes feeding and can't see Brith, when she sees something so surprising it stops her in her tracks.

A deep and startling pool, contained and protected on all sides by smooth and pale rock, its blue-green waters so utterly still that they hold a replica of the branches above. Brith stares, dazed, nonplussed. She has never seen anything like it, on all her wanderings around the place, either with her mother or her father. The land here is lush, marshy, wooded, running with rivers and streams, every hollow filled by a lake, covered with thick swags of greenery, fringed by wide beaches with fretted waves, but never has she come across the like of this. There is, she now notices, one area of the pool that purls and quivers, as if something live lurks just below, sending out concentric ripples, which trap the sunlight in shards that hurt Brith's eyes. As young as she is, Brith knows that this is the place the stream begins: a spring, her father taught her, or the source. A willow bends over it, protectively, its outstretched tips disappearing into it. A single oak leaf wanders and skitters on its surface.

Brith gazes at it, mesmerised. She is assailed by contradictory impulses: to turn and slosh back downstream, to run, to return to her mother's side, to stay, to keep looking, and also to move forward, to investigate, to perhaps immerse herself in those depths.

She does what she will at all moments of uncertainty and indecision: she strokes the fur of the wolfhound and inserts a thumb into her mouth, sucking it meditatively, the pad notched into the arch of her palate. It takes her a moment to realise that it carries the taste of the stream water—that tang, that purity—and she quickly pulls it out again.

Go or stay? Retreat or investigate the pool? She looks down at the dog, which raises its head to meet her gaze. She knows the right thing to do would be to go back to her mother, perhaps to tell her about it, and then they might look at it together. But part of her knows that her mother might well sigh and say the baby is tired, they should get back to the fort, they can come another day. Can Brith risk that her mother might say they should leave, that she might never get to return here?

She cannot: she takes a step forward, then another, her legs heavy now because the stream is getting deeper, the nearer she gets. The dog comes too.

Only when she reaches the lip of the rock does it become clear just how deep the pool is. Crossed spears of sunlight fall into it but only so far, and beneath their yellow illuminations Brith can see depths and more depths of water, darkening to obscurity. She peers downwards, her eyes straining for signs of the bottom, a rock, a shelf, anything, but there is nothing. It appears to be a watery shaft that falls from her feet, down, down, into the earth. The pool is endless. And she is pervaded by the strange sense that her father is near, that he is here, that she might turn her head and see him standing beside her, spear in his hand, hair held back from his eyes with a strip of leather. She turns her head, of course she does, but he isn't there, and somehow the feeling shifts to the suspicion that her father is here but is somehow unable to make himself visible or audible to her, that he is held apart from her, shouting, calling her name, but try as she might she cannot see him, cannot hear him.

She is about to call to him, to say, I am here, where are you, when she sees, with a jolt, something in the depths of the pool.

Carving slow half-turns in the blue is a lithe and indistinct shape, with fins and a sinuous flicking tail: a lone fish is stirring the pool's secret depths. Staring at it, she has the peculiar sensation that she is tipping forward, falling, drawn down by some strong and irrepressible force; she has to tighten her hold on the familiar, rough-haired neck of the dog, not to be lured into its watery snare.

Hello, she murmurs, without knowing why. *Hello, fish.*

The fish turns, almost as if it has heard her, its tail and head forming a near-circle, turns again, then rises up through the water, its scaled length flexing around the ripples, its colour brightening and brightening as it comes towards the light.

Brith, filled with a sudden dread, stands very still, watching it, and the dog, sensing something, emits a low growl.

The fin on the fish's back breaks the water first, then the delicate splay of its tail. It swirls round twice before its mouth edges itself out of the pool: a wetted, lipless opening with a greyish tongue.

Give me the ring, a voice says, or seems to say.

Brith staggers, half falling into the water, soaking herself up to her waist. She flails, making a grab for the smooth rock but is sure to keep hold of the ring.

Who said that? she hisses, shivering. The voice was faint and rasping, like the sound of pebbles raked by a wave. She must have imagined it. She cannot really have heard it. People always say to her that she spends too much time dreaming, that she never keeps to a task.

The dog is crouching low, its belly in the water, and it gives a volley of warning barks, and the voice comes again, unmistakably, and she knows she is not dreaming it, or imagining it, that it is not the sound of a breeze through the branches, or the gluggle of the stream.

Give me the ring. It's mine.

She snatches her hand close to her chest and glares at the fish, whose gleaming beads of eyes hover just below the surface, its lips moving.

It's my father's ring, she says, her words shaking with rage and something like fear.

Give it. I need it.

The fish, whose silvery length is speckled with peculiar spots, each ringed with a paler circle, giving it the appearance of having numerous eyes all over itself, is of a type she hasn't seen before. She has watched her father put brown trout into a trance with his hand, then snatch them dripping from rivers, seen her mother net pink-bellied salmon in the shallows of loughs, then roast them on sharp sticks over hot flames, and how delicious is the skin when its edges are blackened by fire?

But this fish looks nothing like them. It executes a circle of the pool, its tail giving angry flicks, its downturned mouth still above water, trailing a V of ripples after it.

You shan't have it, Brith whispers. *You shan't.*

Give it to me, quick, the fish orders, and Brith finds its voice so terrible and somehow so familiar that, without thinking, she puts not her thumb but the ring into her mouth—again that cold, clear taste—and holds it on her tongue.

The spotted fish thrashes angrily, disturbing the waters so that the pool's edge laps against the rock. Brith tells herself she isn't afraid, she is the daughter of a warrior who came from over the hills, accompanied by two huge dogs, a man who wore a yellow-bright ornament about his neck and a ring on his finger, and loved her mother, and her, and the baby. He loved her so much that he gave her a precious pup from one of his dogs, to protect her. He would never have left them, never, unless—

I will not, Brith starts to say, *I—*

And with the second "I," her throat contracts and she gulps, without meaning to, and suddenly the ring is gone from her tongue and she feels it sinking down inside her. Down, down it goes, down her throat, which aches and protests, down her middle, into her stomach. Brith has swallowed her father's ring.

She turns, sealskin shoes slipping on the wet stones, and runs, the dog crashing through the stream beside her, away from the pool, from the hateful fish, from its depthless watery spell-working, from the copse of drooping willows and the floating oak leaf, and when she finds her mother, she clings to her back like a sodden mer-child, sobbing about a fish that talked and a pool with no bottom and how she never wants to walk here again, and can they please, please, go home?

Her mother embraces her tightly, with the spare arm that isn't holding the baby. She rocks her to and fro, she croons to her, she sings her a song, and she fears a little, too, for this daughter of hers, who is so passionate and so singular, and who takes life not at all easily, but seizes it with both hands, and how this child does remind her, how like him she is, and what pain it gives her to see this. Pain and joy, an equal balancing, a vying bright anguish of the two.

The dog paces to and fro, hackles bristling, snapping at the empty air, its head turning one way, then the other, as if aware of invisible foes in the valley around them.

As it turns out, Brith's mother is right to fear for her. In the years that come, her father never does return. The mother, being so fair and so good, has many offers but she accepts none because she will keep herself for her man, the father of her children, who may come back, he may, and these refusals, of course, make a few enemies. What does come to the fort is a bloating sickness that takes many of their young people, Brith's brother included. They bury him at dusk, in a mound, with his little axe and his horn cup, so that he will never go thirsty or hungry in the next world.

Then the crops fail, first one year and then a second, and the bloating sickness comes again, and many of the huts inside the fort lie empty, and the elders decide that there must be a sacrifice to appease the gods, and it should be a young maiden, and at a meeting of the men it is decided that the best would be the girl Brith, for she is beautiful, like her mother, and the gods may be pleased by her. What is not said, but thought by all, is that Brith is an odd girl, unlikely to be chosen by any man, the progeny of the meandering stranger who came by that time, with wild hair and gleaming weapons and a pair of hunting hounds, who took a liking to one of their own, and then disappeared, who knows where? There are rumours that, soon after he settled among them, the man had a cache of golden treasure and buried it beneath the ground; many have tried to find it, digging deep in likely places, and even more have tried to get the girl and the mother to tell them where, but they claim not to know anything about it, and this refusal to yield up the location of the treasure angers the elders, angers the warriors, and infuriates the other women. The girl has a tendency to stare into space instead of putting a hand to her work, and tells stories of talking animals and spirits of the forests. And she is always accompanied by the enormous grey dog, given to her by her father, and trained by him to protect the girl, almost as if the man knew he wouldn't be around to do it himself.

The only one who will speak against sacrificing Brith is the teller. She has the gift, he points out to the elders, and she has already memorised several important tales. She should be his apprentice, and should take over from him when he passes into the next world. But because Brith has no father or brother to argue for her, to offer her protection, because she is yet to be sought by a man, and because her mother has refused all advances, both honourable and otherwise, the teller's pleadings are ignored and she is chosen.

The elders are not fools: they take the precaution of snaring the dog with meat and tethering it to a rock—its teeth would be enough to tear off the limb of a man—but they had not reckoned on the will of the mother. When the men come for the girl, in the middle of the night, her mother realises at once what is happening. She implores and screams; she shuts Brith and herself into their hut, barring the door with a staff of blackthorn that had once belonged to Brith's father—he had soaked it in brine and strengthened it with the blood of magpies. But it is not enough to keep out the men: they batter down the door, splintering the blackthorn staff in two. A sudden wildcat, Brith's mother seizes up the broken pieces and lunges at the men, injuring one of the elders on the arm, so that they are obliged to ask the young warriors to come and lash her hands together. She pleads, then, she falls to the ground and her hair covers the feet of the men. *I beg you*, she says, *please, not her, she is all I have*. She says she can help them find treasure, she thinks she knows where her man might have buried the gold. *Let me show you*, she says, but they say it is too late for that. She offers herself in Brith's stead: *Take me*, she says, *I will go, I won't fight you*. And when the elders shake their heads, she kicks at them with her strong feet and whispers to Brith: *Run, my girl, run*.

Brith does run. She flees through the hut's broken-down door, whistling for her dog, she darts through the gaps in the huts, and it is near night-time, so she can find her way via the orange glow of the firelight coming out of the doorways. She whistles and whistles, desperate, her lips stiff with fear, and the dog appears beside her, a gnawed-through rope flying from its neck. She and the animal sprint out through the open gate of the hill fort, because the people standing there are not expecting a girl to come hurtling towards them out of the darkness, then past them, her feet pounding the soil; they make it over the bridge and the moat. Brith runs, as her mother bade her do, she runs and runs, down the hillside, then veers into the forest, and she doesn't know where she's going, or how she will survive, for she has no axe, no knife with her, nothing to keep her warm, just the tunic she is wearing and the leathers on her feet. But she has the dog, old now, but still as sharp and courageous as when her father trained it. They run together, she and the hound, and it is as if there is a guiding wind behind them, powering them, assisting them, because she slips through trees and over rocks like a deer, and she doesn't know where she is heading, except perhaps she does because she thinks she recognises those two hills: they look like the ones that cradle the pool she saw that time, and she thinks of her father's ring, perhaps still lodged somewhere in her body, because she looked for it, she poked and sifted through her own stinking waste, but never found it, and she feels its pressure, its heat, as she runs, a glowing circle of gold at her very centre. She has the strange idea that if she can just find that spring again, the pool, her father will be there to save her, to show her how to disappear, as he did, how to dissolve herself into the earth or the trees, so that they may never find her. She runs.

They come upon her at dawn. She and the dog are curled around each other at the base of a tree, nose to tail, head to chest. The hound, of course, hears them and leaps up with a terrible gargling growl, but they have anticipated this and so they shoot it through the heart with a single arrow. Brith is too stricken, then, to run, so she remains lying on the ground where they found her, her arms thrown around the animal. They haul her up, they bind her hands behind her back, they offer her the bowl of food they have brought for her—milk-soaked grain—but she refuses. She weeps silently and looks only at the still-warm animal, her tears falling into its silver-grey coat. They put a plaited noose of leather around her neck and lead her to their altar, a raised and flat piece of ground, around which fork two of the streams flowing from the sacred spring, where the first rays of sun will fall upon the face of the standing stone. They pray. They chant. They beat their animal-hide drums. They imbibe fermented liquid made of barley. They raise their hands to the skies, to the rising light. They anoint themselves and their sacrificial maiden with water from the spring. The teller recites a tale of their ancestors; he leads them in a song. He looks away as they tie a length of cloth around her eyes so that she won't see the dull gleam of the knife, she won't know it's coming, and when they cut her smooth white throat from ear to ear, the teller tries to whisper to her that it will be quick, her agony will not last long, because he wishes her to have a friendly voice beside her at the moment of her passing, but he doesn't know if she hears him, either before she falls to the ground or after, and he watches, then, as the streams turn red, as the earth pulls her lifeblood into itself, drinks it down.

The young warriors are called upon to dig a pit, further off, away from the sacred stone, in the lower sodden ground. She is tumbled into it, her hands still bound; the teller is the one to say that the dog should be beside her, that a creature of such loyalty should be with her in the next life. The elders shrug, no longer interested in the girl, her empty corpse: they have made their sacrifice, they have fulfilled their task and done it well. The teller himself walks back up to the woods to fetch the dog's carcass, stiffening now in the cool of the dawn; he extracts the arrow and hurls it away into the undergrowth, and he hefts the dog back down to the altar—no, he will not accept help. He takes out his own knife from his belt and cuts the bindings on Brith's hands, arranging the animal next to her, taking time to place them both in a pose of dignity, her arms around her beloved hound, and before he steps away, he puts a brief hand to her hair. He cannot say why, which is odd because words are his skill, he has no other, but he feels in the very hollow of his bones that the fort's elders have made a grave mistake, that this sacrifice can bring only ill upon them all. Brith was a marked one, a special one, she was their link to the first people, the last of their kind, she should have lived; she and her hound should still be among them; she could have saved them, had she lived; she could have led them into the coming age. With a sense of portentous dread, he knows he has failed her. But he says nothing. The elders motion to the young men to cover the bodies, and Brith and her hound are sealed up together, the wet earth falling onto them like heavy rain, and there they stay, two creatures curled around each other in the dark, lips sealed by densely packed soil.

Harsh winter follows wet spring follows baking-dry summer follows harsh winter. A sickening fever sweeps through the fort on the high, rocky mountain. A low yield at harvest. Those who are able leave, strapping food and hides to their backs, leading away their animals on ropes. The teller moves to a willow cabin he builds for himself, down by the shore, where he lives out his remaining days, alone and in silence, his tales kept to himself. The elders, one by one, expire. A neighbouring tribe comes one day, from across the lough, and steals the remaining cattle and grain, and before they depart, they burn the fort to the ground. For several years, the remains of the hill fort are still visible: sometimes others will come and carry off a beam or a hearthstone but eventually nature reclaims it: grass and moss and trees engulf the fields and the foundations of the huts. Ivy climbs over the rock where the elders tethered the dog. Discarded pottery and tools are subsumed by brambles and moss. Soon, there is only a double ridge around the hill, and faded circular marks in the ground, and few remember that there was ever a fort there at all. All that remains of Brith's people, and of her father's people, is a particular breed of dog, found only in these parts, with silver-grey fur and a heart that loves too well, and nobody knows why or where it came from.

(Unseen, in the marshy bog, however, like a tuber folded into the soil, Brith's body survives, against all odds, by some alchemical process of peat acting on water acting on gas, and they are the same colour now, Brith and her hound, fur and skin and teeth and bone and eyelid and plaits leached to a golden-brown, almost indistinguishable from each other; they might be one eight-limbed being.)

Some time later, perhaps a few years, perhaps hundreds—it's hard to pinpoint in the colossal lifespan of a landscape—a woman from down by the shore climbs up the slope between the two hillocks at the base of the mountain. She moves rapidly, some might say agitatedly, losing her footing on the slippery grass, ferns clutching at her garments as she scrambles. Behind her comes a man, her man: he moves slowly, some might say resignedly, an ash stick in his hand, his head bowed, as if embarrassed. They are not young, they have perhaps lived twenty-five summers, but their bodies are strong, from work and toil. The climb is nothing to them. A large dog trots alongside them.

Unbeknownst to them, and indeed any of the people on the peninsula, at exactly the same moment a Roman general, on a reluctant posting in a windswept and rainy northern extremity of the empire, is bending over a table, looking at a country on a map (a rudimentary version, compared to Tomás's later ones, but surprisingly accurate for its time) and considering its value. A land girdled by sea, shaped like a dog, at the furthermost reaches of their scope. To invade or not to invade? The general thumbs his lower lip, speculating. He makes calculations of the battalions that would be needed, the ships, weaponry, food, uniforms. He glances at the map again, assessing possible gains: crops, land, tin, gold? Perhaps even slaves, although he has heard the inhabitants of this island are barbarous and savage. The map is turned one way, then another. The general sighs. He shivers. He pulls his furs more closely around himself, gazing out into the rain. He decides, no, they will not venture forth to this other country across a howling and restless sea. They will leave it be.

The woman on the peninsula, who is in fact a distant descendant of the teller, turns, unaware of what her country has just avoided, looks up into the sky and, seeing the position of the sun, nearly at its apex, calls to the man, gesturing upwards. The language she speaks is nothing like the one Brith and her mother used all that time ago, nothing like the one spoken by the general with the rudimentary map, but what she says could have only one possible meaning: *Hurry up*.

He regards his woman as she continues up the hill, her narrow back, her long switch of hair, and he sighs. He doesn't hold with what they are doing, doesn't believe it will bring her what she wants, but he has agreed to put aside his work, not to go out into the shallows of the sea in search of shellfish, and instead come with her on this mission. Why? Because he loves her, because what she wants, he wants, although he will not admit it. He does, he thinks, as he watches his feet searching for footholds in the damp, grassy ground, desire what she pines for. He would like a child, as she would; he would like a baby to lie between them in their hut; he would like to return in the evening to a woman and a child (he will not allow himself to think, *children*, no, that would be asking too much, just one would be enough, please).

In their lifetimes, which by modern standards are short and troubled, but by theirs are long and fortunate, they have seen great change upon the peninsula. Holy men with shaven pates have come over land from the east and built themselves a large stone dwelling place down by the marsh, where they keep bees and gather the moist green marsh plants and sing together, and sometimes the sound of their song floats out over the roofs of the huts, and the man, and his woman, and their people listen and wonder. And other men have come from the sea, and these men are not shaven-headed or holy, far from it, they have huge straggling beards, and possess great height, like giants they are, and they have broken down the doors of the monastery, and carried off some of the treasures and, yes, killed some of the holy men, staving in their skulls with cudgels. When these giants come, the people in the huts run—they seize up their tools and their children (if they have them) and what food they can carry and they sprint deftly away, melting unseen into the woods and the clefts in the hills, and there they stay, watching and waiting, until the giant men have got back into their boats and sailed away. The huts are sometimes burned by the giants, sometimes only pillaged, and then they set to, repairing the roofs, straightening the chaos, instructing the older children to keep watch by the shore for the giants' boats, with their many oars and their carved heads of terror.

Perhaps they will come again, perhaps not. Nobody knows. After the last time, which was the worst, the man, his woman, and their people went to the broken door of the holy stone place and offered help: there had been seven holy men and now there were only two, and scared they were, and injured, and not enough to make good their house. So they helped them, and his woman had tended the holy men's wounds, for she has the skill and the knowledge for this, and afterwards they placed their hands on her forehead, making a cross upon her brow, and spoke in words that were strange, and later that night, after he and his woman had lain together in their hut, she said: Perhaps that will help. What? he'd said, although he had known and it gave him a heavy feeling in his heart's core. The holy men's words, she said. The man had turned over and spat into their fire, which fizzled and protested. Better you'd visit the old wellspring up on the hill, he'd muttered, without thinking about it, because hadn't his mother and his grandfather said there was a place of water at the base of the mountain that was sacred and inhabited by spirits, and would give whatever was asked of it or whatever it was you were in need of, one of the two, if you paid it respect and then you drank deeply from it? He'd been taken there as a child, when he fell from a tree and injured his shoulder: a strange and eerie place it was, encircled by trees, its rocky banks strewn with a clutter of objects. Seashells, he had seen, as his grandfather dipped him into the icy waters, immersing his aching and mangled shoulder, making him cry out with shock, clay pots, a brooch, several bone hairpins, cups, plates. When he asked his grandfather what all these things were for, why were they left there, his grandfather, long dead now, of course, told him that people left them as offerings or gifts for the pool and the wise and ancient spirit said to reside within.

His woman, of course, could think of nothing else. So here they are, climbing the slope, an amber amulet gripped in her hand which she will drop into the spring as an offering, and it is all his fault, or is it the fault of the holy men, with their strange double-tongue speak, or perhaps even the marauding giants in their curving ships? Where can he lay the blame?

He watches as his woman disappears into the woods, picking her way carefully through the trees, and he leans on his stick, waiting. He will not go in with her: they have agreed this. Better she goes alone. He sees the hill rise away from him in one direction and in front of him the roughened face of the mountain. He sees that the earth here is grooved with tiny streamlets, many of them, all coming out of the woods, and a flattened network of otter-runs. He sees, further off, a flat piece of land, slightly raised, around which the streams curve: a large and upright old prayer stone stands there, alone and dignified. He moves towards it.

Wild irises grow in a knot at one end of the flat ground, their knife-like leaves spearing up from the grass, their complex yellow petals opening to the sun. The man walks to the stone, places his hand upon its rough face, the dog at his heels. He taps the earth with his stick, turns one way, then the other: mountain behind, hill to one side, hill to the other. Bathed in sunlight, sheltered from wind. He lifts his face and sniffs the air: peat, grass, moisture, clover.

The dog, meanwhile, is having a very different experience. First, the woman has gone off on her own into the trees and this feels extremely wrong and the dog doesn't understand why the man isn't more concerned about this. And then there are cross-currents of confusing smells in this place: a hint of smoke, then a whiff of humans the dog doesn't know, followed by the thinnest scent of dug earth, and something else, which alarms and excites it—bones. It turns, first one way, then the other, so fast that it can see the confounding, vanishing whip of its own tail. It growls, then yaps, a deep and throaty noise, and snaps its teeth at the air near the stone.

Hush, the man says absently, and the dog is incensed by its owner's inability to see that this place, this patch of ground, is an unquiet one, that they are not alone here. It barks again, more insistently, staring intently at the man, trying to communicate its unease.

But the man frowns. *Lie down,* he orders.

The dog paces one way, then the other, anguished. It wants to obey, it really does, but how can it? There is to be no lying down here, no resting, not on this soil, which seethes with disquieting scents, and not in this air, which roils with something the dog cannot name. Bad things have happened in this place, the dog knows, and worse is to come.

A short whistle from between the man's teeth, and the dog drops to its belly. It fidgets and frets, turning to scratch its flank, then gnaw at the fur on its paws. From out of the woods it sees or seems to see, just for a moment, not the woman but the smirred form of a stranger, carrying the dead body of a dog that looks distressingly like itself.

This place, the man is thinking, will get the first rays of the morning sun. It is entirely hidden from the rest of the valley, from the holy house, from the cliffs, from the shore, from the huts. It cannot be seen. They might be safe here, he and his woman, and perhaps their—

He turns. Why is the dog yelping and carrying on? The animal is writhing on its stomach, making a high-pitched noise of upset.

What ails you? the man says crossly, but he waves his hand. *Away you go, then.*

The dog, released, springs up, an arrow from a bow, and sprints away, settling further down the slope, away from the flat ground. Ears flat, hackles up, watching over its people closely from a distance.

And then the woman emerges from the trees, and she is smiling, her face and tunic are wet, and her hands are empty, and she smells of herself and also clean water, and the man goes towards her and they embrace briefly, and the dog is mollified. It shifts sideways on its great paws, filled inexplicably with the feeling that all is well in its world once more.

Despite the dog's misgivings, the man, with the help of others, builds a new hut, sheltered by the standing stone, on the flat patch of high land. He moves his belongings and tools; the woman, pregnant now, brings the hides and pots and utensils. They live there, near the sacred spring, for many years, bringing up their son, and when they die, the son finds a wife to join him there and they bring up their children.

Their dogs, all of whom come from Brith's father's hunting hounds, drink deeply of the spring waters and will never enter the hut, for some reason, but choose to sleep further off, near the edge of the wood, their heads resting watchfully on their paws.

Season follows season; year follows year. The descendants of the man with the ash stick abandon the flat ground at the base of the mountain—why live so far from the shore, so distant from the monastery and from others?—and settle where the widow's house will eventually be built. The giants in their boat come again, and again, and then they are never more seen on the shores. The holy men increase in number, more arriving over land and by sea, and the monastery gets bigger, sprawling now all along the marshy shore, with huts clustered around it. The monks exchange honey and candles and healing herbs; they employ a number of men to tend their goats; some of the women from the huts will spin their fleeces into yarn. One of the monks, a thickset man with an iron cross around his neck, gets into an altercation with one of the people's high druids: a fight ensues, and the thickset monk kills the druid with a single blow of his meaty fist. The people from the huts disappear into the hills, then, like in the bad times, leaving the goats and the spinning wheels to themselves. The thickset monk is seen to ascend the slope, to the very copse of trees where that druid would invoke the spirit of the water; other monks come behind him, hands hidden up their sleeves. The murderous monk goes into the trees and the people hear him saying his prayerful words, crying out, his fellow monks responding in a murmur. *I bless this holy well*, he calls out in words they understand. *It is now a place of God.* The people murmur to each other; some of them laugh. How can the murderous monk make their sacred spring his own? How could it ever belong to his invisible God? What a preposterous notion. They ruffle the fur on their dogs' backs and settle further into the concealing vegetation, content to wait out this strange visit, waiting to see what the holy men might do next.

A king whom none of the peninsula people has ever seen sends out armies and these soldiers knock down the walls of the monastery with battering rams made of oak trunks. They sever the heads of all the monks from their shoulders, they steal the honey from the hives, they roast the goats, and the scent of charred flesh quivers in the mist. When the soldiers march off, the women pick over the remains, collecting the goat bones to make soup, saving any pots or beakers or tools they can salvage. They leave the iron crosses, out of respect or perhaps fear: they don't wish to invoke the wrath of the holy men's invisible God. They make visits, on their own or sometimes in groups, to the sacred spring, to make offerings and imprecations, always careful with what they say and how they conduct themselves, for the spring is said to bestow what is needed, not necessarily what is wanted, which is not always the same thing. What they want now, more than anything, is for this peninsula and for the whole country to be left in peace, that they be allowed to live as they please and how they please, without the incursion of others.

History, however, has other plans. The country is encircled by sea: its western coast is abraded into inlets and loughs, the land giving way slowly to water, and faces a vast ocean. The sea is ice-cold, threaded with great shoals of herring that flitter by on huge currents. Seaweed accumulates on the jagged rocks and on the white-coral sands of the bays, and seabirds stalk the estuaries, their slender legs dipping into grasses. The opposite eastern coast lies close to another country; on clear days, across the narrow sleeve of sea between them, the neighbouring land may be seen from higher ground, a bluish shape on the horizon, like something glimpsed in a dream.

The other country, however, is very much real. Larger and more populous, with organised and extensive armies, it crouches on the far side of the cold grey channel of water, and it eyes the smaller country speculatively. Its rulers take advice about the dog-shaped land's strategic significance, its discomforting proximity, its fertile plains, its tribes, its chieftains, that long and complex westernmost shore lying open to all comers from afar. This coastline is of great interest and concern to the larger country: might it not at any moment be invaded by anyone? Could it not be used as a stepping-stone or a back door for an invasion of their own shores?

It is decided that the larger country should claim its dog-shaped neighbour, just in case, to tame it, to subjugate it, before anyone else does.

The patch of flat land around which the streams flow, where the ancient elders had their altar and invoked their gods, not far from Brith and her dog's place of burial, is indifferent to the bloody and fearsome shifts going on around it: all land is. One tribe gives way to another; high kings attack chieftains; chieftains invoke the aid of a foreign army; another tribe slaughters and drives out a third; the people from one side of a river snatch the territory of those from the far side. And while battles still rage throughout, the monarch from the larger country across the water arrives, ostensibly to implement the orders of the Church and restore order, but instead he has his own agenda. He smiles at the high kings with his mouth while his hands take the citadel from them. He promises the tribes and the chieftains that he will help them but banishes the indigenous people, driving them back into woodlands and wild places. Then he leaves, satisfied, sailing back across the narrow sleeve of water to his country, leaving behind a garrison filled with his soldiers. The monarch is pleased, all in all, with the outcome. His country now possesses a colony: the first of many.

The old altar at the foot of the mountain experiences these shifts and brutalities in ways that are imperceptible to the humans who walk upon it. All the land knows is that its trees are felled and cut—for houses, for fire, for weapons, for the walls of fortresses—and this leads, first, to an increase in water in the soil, and then a mysterious dryness as some of the streams vanish, their beds hardening in the summer sun. There are fewer birds, of course, because if trees vanish so do their inhabitants, and so after a while fewer meadow flowers grow, as no seeds are dropped. Insect life increases, which means that more crops are devoured by their swarms. Some winters, therefore, are long and the people grow lean. The wild irises spread, gathering in the still-wet places, the fissures in the earth where the surviving streamlets run, their blade-like leaves a sign to anyone passing that water can be had. Lichen blooms on the sides of the remaining trees; the branches rattle back and forth in the wind, unprotected by the once-dense forest.

What lies between the mountain and the shore now looks very different. The country has been conquered, ruthlessly and systematically, by an army commander from the colonising country. He has confiscated the lands and given them to his most loyal officers; they have established their plantations and estates, and the peninsula people—whom the landlords call "wild ones"—are forced back to live in the scant and rocky places, to work in the landlords' fields, and pay heavy tithes.

Hard times, then, here on the peninsula, and many are compelled to climb up the hillside, to visit the ancient wellspring, to ask for relief or assistance, or merely seek a chance to speak their woes, to tell them to the water. And a woman carrying a baby on her back, in much the same way as Brith's mother did more than a thousand or so years ago—they might even be mistaken for each other, at a distance—notices the flat piece of ground, and points it out to her mother, who walks alongside her, who in turn points it out to her man. He glances at it, grunts, doesn't make a reply. They enter the copse, they make their devotions at the well, and return to the plantation below. Later the next day, however, the man returns with two of his sons. They walk one way across the raised piece of ground; they walk the other. One son notes, as others have before him, the way this piece of land is sheltered, by the two hills and the mountain behind; the other gestures to the streams, the upright rock. The father stands upon the earth there, looking down on the field boundaries of the foreign landlord, and sees how distant they would be, how hidden, how nobody could find them, unless they knew exactly how to get here. The sons face the father, awaiting his verdict. The father turns, looks up the mountain and the copse, whistles for his dogs, which have disappeared into the trees. Then he nods, and the son shrugs the pick from his shoulder and strikes it into the ground, in celebration, in defiance, breaking into the sod.

(Below, far below and off to the side, in the marshy bog, Brith's body feels this strike, the slender jigsaw of her finger bones clicking together, the leather noose loosening around her neck, the delicate beaded spine of her dog shunted minutely towards her, their entwined forms nestling ever closer.)

The man and his sons dig foundations into the flat ground, in a shape as circular as the ring that resides in the sealed purse of Brith's stomach. They hew stones from the mountainside and carry them down, one by one, and place them carefully, incorporating the strong standing stone into their structure (Brith and her hound feel each thud, the packed peat around them shifting, the slow currents of soil moving them sideways). The walls rise around the men, and then they bring the marram thatch and lay it in a dense covering that will keep away the rain and the wind, and there they set themselves up, the chimney blowing smoke into the sky, the men working the landlord's fields and tilling their own meagre crops and paying the tithe each month, the women birthing the babies and knotting the nets and gutting the fish and keeping the children from the well and fetching the water, and so it goes for many generations, and battles are fought across the country, again and again, and crops are burned and people go hungry. Some rise up against their oppressors, and the invaders try to banish their language, and men are killed and babies slaughtered and women hung from trees by their hair and others thrown into the sea with their hands tied, but the peninsula is quiet, mostly, as long as the people pay their landlord and do his work.

Five generations of the people who dug the foundations live between the hillsides at the base of the mountain, each one adding new walls or beams to the house. The last is a family with nine children. The Great Hunger comes and their crops disintegrate before they can lift them from the soil. They survive the first winter, by relying on shellfish and nettles. When the blight takes the second year's crop, the father goes to the viscount, their landlord, for help, but none is forthcoming and the viscount instead raises the rent. Two children die, then three, then the grandmother succumbs; with each passing, the woman of the house makes a mark in the rafter above the fire. Taking his four remaining children with him, the father goes again to the door of the viscount but his land steward tells the man he is behind with the rent, and if he wants relief he must leave, give up his house and his plot of land, and go into the county workhouse. We will not do that, the father says, through gritted teeth, we will not leave, it is our land, we've lived on it for hundreds of years, but can you not help us, man, my children are starving to death?

The end comes, for all of them. By the time the next year of the Great Hunger comes around, the house on the hillside is empty, the windows boarded up, the thatch burned. The following winter, gales remove the roof altogether, and the chimney stack tumbles down in the frost. The streams continue to flow, the irises bloom in the spring, the lichen softens the grey of the stones, birds flit in and out of the broken door of the house. And one morning, in moist and misty weather, a man holding a knapsack and a compass climbs the mountain, his child trailing behind him, a surveying pole and chain in his cold-reddened hands. First the child, then the man, goes into the little copse, which is all that remains of Brith's dense and expansive forest. Not long after that, the same man returns with his wife, and all of his children, one of whom still resides in his wife's belly. They climb the hillside, the smallest daughter aloft on the man's shoulders, the wife leaning heavily on his arm, and he shows them the tumbledown cottage with an air of hesitant pride; he gestures at the mountain, the stream and the copse, like a magician revealing a particularly spectacular trick.

Phina stands, canted forward, one hand on the windowsill of the ruined cottage, the other pressed to her lower back, catching her breath. Her knuckles graze the rough grey stone, and she takes great gulps of the cool, fast-moving breeze, which carries the scent of both sea and earth, salt and vegetation. She imagines, fleetingly, that the child podded up inside her is experiencing the same thing: a heaving of its little lungs, a racing of its tiny seed-heart.

She starts to take in what is before her, what her husband has squandered their money on, what he has pulled them from home and carted them across the country for. They are standing, her family and herself, at a breach between two hills, with a large, steep, rocky mountain behind it. All is green: the grassy turf, the moss, the cluster of trees some distance away, the tall stems of flowers edging a little stream. They are on a level piece of ground, elevated above the wet bog, stretching from where she is standing to the lip of the hill, a surprising place, like a platform or perhaps a stage, dug into which is the shell of a house. Grey stone walls, Phina tells herself—and the child, for she believes the unborn share not only the blood and food of the mother but also her every thought, so she tries to confine herself to good and pure conjectures alone—with two blank-eyed windows, the remains of a chimney stack, no roof. She repeats this to herself, to the child: this place has no roof. The doorway has rusted hinges, to which cling the splintered shards of a door. Inside, Phina can see through the frameless window if she bends her knees, is a hearth, from which is growing an abundance of wet-petalled harebells and a bare-branched sapling, and the crumbling walls of what were once two separate rooms. The furthest wall is partly made up of an enormous, incongruous rock, the slope of which juts into the back room.

This place, she remarks to herself (and the child, don't forget), in an unruffled voice, would need digging out. A week or so for that task. All the fallen stones within require placing without, which would take her husband the best part of another week. The walls and chimney would have to be repaired: a job for two perhaps three men. The windows. The fireplace should be cleared. They would need thatch. Fencing about the place, a byre, a henhouse, a place for the drying of turf, perhaps a loft. To make it liveable, in its most basic sense, will take months. And there is no money, as far as she knows, to do any of these things, no money at all: what little they had saved, Tomás has used to pay the viscount for the lease and the first month's rent.

Breathing more evenly now, she straightens up, still keeping one knuckle on the house, as if trying to ascertain its character, or perhaps locate her feelings about it. She looks one way, down the valley, towards the lough and the village where they have left the cart to which all their worldly possessions are lashed. She turns back, and sees that Enda is climbing up the chimney breast, chattering about nests, about the journey, her fingers and her feet searching for footholds in the stone facing as she talks; Liam, further off, is hunched into himself, a bird beset by rain, looking down at his feet.

Phina turns, at last, to her husband. He is stepping in and out of the doorway, putting out a hand to tap the stonework, bending to peer up the flue, moving from one end of the tumbled cottage to the other, showing Enda some swirled markings on the rock in the wall. Where is Rose? Phina shoots glances, one way, then the other. She whirls around, looking down the path, then up towards the steep mountain, seeking a flash of gleaming dark hair, the red jersey the child is wearing. Just as panic is seizing her by the throat, she feels her hand brush up against something soft, and she looks down. Rose is right beside her, almost under her skirts; her face is tilted up, searchingly, her green-brown eyes—the colour of acorns, Phina always thinks—fixed on her mother.

She looks again at Tomás. He is smiling, for perhaps the first time in months, his cap pushed back on his head, leaning on the hearthstone, the harebells brushing against his trousers. Phina is filled, instantly, with rage, head to foot, like a pitcher receiving milk. She would do anything for Tomás: she will bear his children, she will cook his food, she will patch his worn-out clothing, she will rise when he does, she will sleep next to him, she will nurse him if he is sick, she will not mind his bouts of silence and withdrawal or even madness, she will soothe him if he is out of sorts, she will put her arm around him at night if he is besieged by monstrous dreams. There are things he has done for her that can never be repaid: they are bound together for eternity, and they both know this.

Even so, Phina lifts her chin and clutches Rose's hand closer to her side. She says: "We will not be staying here."

Tomás turns. He examines the set of her face, the line of her mouth. Liam, outside the house, shifts uneasily at her peremptory tone. Enda, sitting on top of the cottage wall now, looks down at her parents. Rose steps even closer to her mother's skirts and slides her thumb into her mouth.

"We will not," Phina states.

Tomás crushes his cap in his hands, he shifts from one foot to the other.

"Ah, now," he says, "a little fixing is all that's needed, I'll get the—"

Phina turns away. She makes a beckoning gesture that brings Liam and Enda to her side with uncharacteristic swiftness, for they can see when their mother means business, and with her children gathered about her, she descends the hill. She has no idea where she is going, what she will do now, because she cannot go back to their tenement in the Lanes: the upstairs back room is no longer theirs. She has no home and nowhere to go, but she will walk away, her head held high, grasping the hands of her children, her dignity intact.

Tomás, standing in the cottage he has leased, must watch as the figures of the four people dearest to him recede into the distance, until the mist swallows them whole.

The widow is outside her house when the woman and her children reach the cart. She has on her headscarf, knotted firmly under the chin, and her apron; the milking pail rests at her feet. She makes no pretence that she's not been waiting for them to come back.

She looks at the map-maker's wife, five months gone if she's a day, her face sallow with exhaustion and something else as well. She takes in the woman's shawl, knitted in an intriguing slanted pattern, her mud-encrusted boots, the way she puts a hand to the boxes and bundles on the cart, as if to steady herself. The man must have stayed up on the hill again, and how the widow would like to say to this woman, his wife: It's no use, they will never be told, that one least of all, and we will always be pulled along in their wake, buffeted this way and that.

There is the boy, Liam, for whom she feels a particular dart of fondness, a little girl-child with dark hair straggling over her eyes, quite unusually pretty but this, of course, must never be mentioned, and another girl, nearly as tall as her mother, all knobbed elbows and knees, a scowling set to her mouth, the same copper hair as her brother.

"Well, now," the widow addresses them.

She regards the wife, the wife regards her, the cart between them, and she sees that the woman could burst into tears with one ill-placed word or one wrong gesture, and who can blame her?

"You'd better come in so."

The widow observes that the wife, without being asked, makes sure the children remove their boots before they step over her threshold; she bends, despite her advanced state, to untie her own. From the corner of her eye, as the widow fusses with kettle and water, she watches the wife making sure the children's hands are clean, wiping them with her damp apron, the way she gets them all sitting down in a row on the bench.

The widow swings the kettle over the fire. The wife takes cups from the shelf. The widow places half a loaf on the table. The wife takes up a knife and cuts thin and even slices. She gets the children to say grace; she ensures they say please and thank you. When the boy reaches out his hand for a fourth slice, he is stopped in his tracks by an imperceptible shake of her head.

The widow and the wife sit on opposite sides of the table, each eyeing the other with what they believe are secret, assessing glances, steam curling up from their cups.

"A peculiar notion," the widow ventures, "of your husband's. To be taking you from the city and bringing you all out here."

The wife considers this with a sigh, then gives a short nod.

"When most," the widow continues, "are going in the opposite direction."

"True."

"You," the widow says, "will stay here."

"We won't."

"You will."

"We couldn't put you out."

"You must."

"But there are so many of us and—"

"I have room for you all and plenty more."

"It's good of you but we couldn't, really. The children and I will . . ." the wife casts around, despairingly, for what they might do ". . . we will . . ."

"You will stay here, with me, until himself has fixed up that house. That place has been a ruin for years. I don't know what that husband of yours was thinking, or the viscount for that matter, but then, of course, he and his kind are a law unto themselves. It's the work of weeks to get that cabin to a state where you can keep the rain off. And you can't be delivering that child up there in a roofless cottage."

The wife casts her eyes down, and the widow sees that she has her. "You'll stay here with me and there's an end to it."

~

When Tomás returns down to the shore, he finds his children at play: Enda has Rose on her back, with Rose's hands over her eyes, and Liam leading them around and around the widow's house. Inside, Phina and the widow are standing over a steaming laundry pot, laughing at something, their four hands employed in scrubbing. There is a general air of mutual approval, of female complicity. He glances at the long table, then away, feeling oddly wrong-footed, for he had expected to find Phina sitting forlornly by the cart in the mizzle, surrounded by miserable children, grateful that he'd returned, in a perhaps more pliant frame of mind. He had not counted on this situation: Phina finding a place at the widow's side.

"I thought," Tomás began, "that if we fixed up a sheet from the gable wall, then—"

The two women look up with identical scornful gazes.

"I'll not go back," Phina says.

"They're stopping here," the widow says.

"What?" Tomás says, astonished. "But we agreed—"

"We did not agree," Phina says, wringing out a cloth, twisting it into a rope between her hands. "Far from it. You took the money. Without telling me. You said there was a house for us. That," she dips her chin in the direction of the hill, "is not a house. I will not live in an eviction ruin. How could you ask me to do such a thing? I'll not have this baby on a hillside. I will not—"

"All right, all right," he cuts across her testily. "If I mend it? If I put on a roof?"

Phina seems to consider this. She slaps the wet, steaming garment back into the water. Tomás is sure he sees the widow mutter something to her, from the corner of her mouth. Phina gives her an answering flex of her eyebrow.

"There must be a roof," she says, pointing at him in a way he has never seen before, one hand on her hip. "Windows. A door. A proper floor. A clean chimney that draws the smoke. And," she says, delivering her trump card, "you're to go back to making maps for the redcoats."

Tomás is aghast. "Never," he says heatedly, shifting from foot to foot. "I will never do that again. I told you—I'll not take their money, I'll not be in their pay, in their—"

"Then I will not live in that place."

"Phina—"

"And neither will the children."

Tomás grips at his jacket cuffs with tense hands. He glances from one woman to the other and sees that they have cooked up these terms between them. Why did he ever let her come down here on her own? Why hadn't he followed her when she walked off?

"Come away outside," he says gruffly, "just the two of us, and we'll talk all this over."

"Oh," she murmurs, "now you want to talk."

The widow bows her head, as if to hide a smile, and Tomás cannot believe that this alliance has been formed so swiftly, so completely, in the time he was up the hill. How do women do that?

Phina lifts her chin, wiping her wet hands on her apron, and advances upon him.

"Listen to me, Tomás," she says, in a soft and—to him—menacing voice. "I know you want this life, with your own land, your own little house, beholden to no one. But that is not really how things are, is it? We will still be beholden, will we not? To the viscount, because we'll owe him rent, every single month. And we'll be at the mercy of the land, all its ups and downs. We," she circles a hand to include him, herself, the widow, "know only too well how that can end. I will not let my children go hungry. I will not be turfed out of my home. You may fix the cottage, you may sow your crops, you may keep a cow, and I will milk it for you, and I will put your dinner on the table, every day, but I will only live here on this peninsula if you continue to bring in those wages. If you won't do that, I will not stay."

Tomás stares at his wife, so diminutive and determined, her belly pushed out with their unborn child. He opens his mouth to speak, then closes it again. He removes the scarf from around his neck and, for want of anything better to do, throws it down on the table. Phina gives her husband a final nod.

"A roof, mind," she says. "A hearth. A chimney. And you working on the maps. Then," she finishes, turning back to the laundry, "we'll see."

The house on the hillside, ruined and empty, has waited a long time. Rain and sun and wind have acted upon it in the last few years, winter storms finishing what the eviction men started, sweeping away the remaining thatch and the mud sealing the holes between the stones. Once a roof is gone, a house is vulnerable to all manner of abuse. It can simply disappear, dissolving into the soil, to be covered by greenery.

Not this house, however. Ravaged but standing, it still possesses, lurking in its structure, signs of its provenance: a strut cut from the copse in the time of the monasteries, a siltstone threshold taken from the rath, compacted earth containing the lifeblood of Brith, and bundled rags above a window, stuffed there in wintertime by the eldest child of the last family to call it home. This house is a thing both ancient and disjointed, an entity of addition and subtraction, a palimpsest of stone and wood and caulk and mud. Its existence here, on the peninsula, is proof that everything was once something else: nothing goes away.

At the corner of its gable wall is the standing stone, partially occluded by the rocks packed in around it, and the mix of caulk and lime that holds the structure together; the outermost plane of it, decorated with interlocking swirls, faces the breeze coming off the inlet; its solid curve forms part of the chimney breast. No one who has lived in the house, the first being the man with the ash stick, has known that this stone was conveyed here from northern regions in the last ice age, and deposited on this mountainside, where it rested for thousands of years, later to be canted upright and made into a sacred menhir on the instructions of druids, who perhaps recognised that the stone was unusual, different from those around it, but had no idea why.

On a blustery morning, Tomás appears, stepping through the doorway, and to the house's astonishment stoops and sets to, clearing its innards of rubble and stray vegetation. He lifts each tumbled stone from the earth floor and carries it outside the walls, stacking them in the sunlight. He spends a while examining them, then selecting them, one by one, to rebuild and repair the walls.

Each stone is fitted, snug, in and around the planes of the menhir, which holds up the gable. The older fisherman, who comes ostensibly to help, but mostly to talk, conjectures as to how this great beast of a rock got here at all, upright like this, handy or what when you're putting together a cabin. Tomás runs his hand over the carved markings, the stippled and glittering granite surface, looks to the north, but says nothing.

With the use of long sticks, the chimney flue is poked free of leaf-fall and nests, and the hearth can once more exhale. Then the wait for the thatcher begins. He comes when he comes, the house hears the fisherman say to Tomás. It'll be any day now.

A month goes by. Winter gives way to a bright, warm spring. Tomás watches the patches of damp—maps of the house's history—vanish from the walls. The children continue to sleep in the widow's loft; the widow by the fire; Phina in the back room, where Tomás joins her, late at night, letting himself in through the door, sliding into the blankets beside his wife, bringing the scent of the hillside, of the house with him, lime-wash, fern, soil, tree sap.

The thatcher appears one morning in April, leaning his ladder to the wall, instructing Tomás to hand him up rods of willow and hazel, bundles of sedge and heather. The man works his way from one end of the house to the other, talking of the yield from his fields, a lad from over the way who fell foul of the law and ended up in gaol but escaped by shimmying through a drain.

"So you want to mind how you go," the thatcher says, whipping a hazel switch back and forth in the air, testing its pliability, "or you'll end up crawling your way through a drain." He ties a rod into place, fingers quick and deft, and reaches for another. "A man of few words," he remarks to the rod, or perhaps the house itself.

Tomás, his face set, hands him up another armful of sedge. The part of him which turned garrulous that day, the vision he had of his father's face in the surface of the pool, feels distant, unreachable, like mountains seen through mist. He doesn't think about it. It didn't happen. Or if it did, perhaps he just dreamed it. The ordeal with the priest he has buried so deep within himself that the only signs—observed by sharp-eyed Phina—are a flinching at the sound of the angelus bell, and a curious new aversion to bacon. He will go to mass, once a week, in the company of his wife and children, because it isn't possible to live in a place like this and not attend; he will even kneel and take the host upon his tongue, but he will not shake the hand of Father Joseph at the end; he waits, instead, at the churchyard gate until Phina is ready to leave.

He turns away from the thatcher abruptly, without a word, and takes up a spade, carrying it on his shoulder to a patch of bog. There, he nicks and portions and lifts the peat into neat sods. These he arranges into the shape of a hive, for the wind to dry them. He is a man, he is a husband, he can provide warmth and shelter for his wife and children, for the baby to come. Let the thatcher do his work, and Tomás will do his.

By the end of the following day, the cottage has acquired a thick lid of thatch, the straw-ends trimmed and shaped to a massed curve, the gables snugly covered. The rain slicks off it and the wind skims over it, as if the elements are surprised by this development and wish to test its properties. Inside, the space is unrecognisable: it is dim, contained, suddenly warm and, above all, Tomás feels, as he stands there, looking up at the new wooden rafters, safe.

The house is lime-washed, the floor is smoothed, the bed is brought up the hill and put together in the back room, straw pallets for the children are laid down in the loft, the lean-to is stacked with kindling, legs are hammered to a board to make a table, pegs fitted to dovetail joints for a bench, a drying line tied from sapling to hook, a patch of soil turned over, weeded and sown, an enclosure constructed for the beasts, which Tomás is determined will soon arrive. He will pay for them, he has decided, out of his next wages from the redcoats because, yes, he has agreed to go back to survey for them; he will calculate and draw up their map sheets; he will accept their money; and if this decision was hard to make, he tells himself he is doing it for Phina, it is all for her, because without her he would be nothing; he would crumble into dry leaves, to be carried away by a breeze.

The house waits for them, the interlapped birch planks of the door expanding and settling into themselves in the sun, the joists of the roof creaking with the unaccustomed weight of the thatch, its twin windows eyes that watch the boreen for the arrival of these new inhabitants. The stones of the walls absorb the lick of lime, taste the sluice of stream water that is scrubbed over them by the bucketful. They listen to the whistle of the thatcher, the chat and chaffing of the fishermen, the laboured breath of the map-maker as he hefts wood or mud or sticks of furniture or kindling. They hear the crackle and hiss of a fire in the hearth, and they feel its warmth gradually spread itself over their innermost sides.

(Brith, in her hidey-hole, is not unaffected by the change: the footfalls ease her and her dog slightly closer to the surface, to the air, and the sound of voices calling back and forth to each other reaches the tawny shell-whorls of her water-filled ear.)

The family come, eventually, on a windless day, when the sun is at its apex, flooding through the trees, illuminating the dew held in the fold of each blade of grass. They carry bundles and pots and spoons and buckets, the older girl sprinting ahead and her course takes her right over the heads of Brith and her dog, but all she feels is the pleasant oozing suck of the bog between her bare toes. The boy-child seems wary, looking one way, then the other, shifting the bundle strapped to his back. The smaller girl has a hen tucked under each arm: haughty creatures with feathered pantaloons and onyx-bead eyes that they keep imperiously trained on their captor, who murmurs to them as they walk, Not far now, soon be there, wait until you see where you're to live.

The father unlatches the door, holds it open, and one by one they shuffle inside.

The house holds its breath; the people hold their breath. House and people assess each other.

Liam smells dried rushes and the sharp resinous pinch of newly cut wood. Rose feels the orbit of heat from the fire and she puts down her hens, with care, one after the other, and watches them start to peck and scratch at the dirt floor. Enda spies eight curious notches cut into the beam above her head and wonders who made them and what they might signify. Phina sees the table, the bed, the hearth, the thick and sheltering roof.

Enda spies the ladder to the loft and, within seconds, she has shed her various loads to the floor and has darted up it, calling to the others to come. Rose leaves her hens to follow her; Liam begins to unstrap the pack on his back.

The house observes how each of them settles themselves into their new home. Tomás walks around the outside of the walls, three times, then leans on the haggard wall and contemplates the hillside, the clouds, the stack of turf; his heart is inflating until it feels as light as a balloon. He has them all here, safe; he has pulled it off; he has found them a home, some land they can call their own. He fixes his eyes on the wavering shape of the copse, its trees jostling in the breeze, and he feels an uncharacteristic urge to give it a nod, to say to it, Here I am, here we all are, we will take care of you.

Later, when darkness has wrapped itself around the peninsula like a cat settling into sleep, when they have eaten the soup Phina has made, when they have all taken themselves to bed, there is a thick, febrile silence throughout the house. The rinsed-out bowls lie inverted on a cloth; the fire has collapsed into a soft mountain of cinders; the door creaks against its new bolt; Phina lies on her side, breath washing softly in and out of her parted lips; Tomás sleeps hunched into himself, his hand clenched around a fistful of his wife's hair; Rose is curled up as near to Enda as her sister will permit, Liam on the other side of the loft.

Everyone is asleep, apart from the baby. It inhabits its briny, warm world with its eyes open, thumb inserted into its mouth, listening to the silence, to the peristaltic pops and gurgles of its mother's body, its soothing cardiac tempo, the creaks of the rafters, the susurrations of its father's breathing.

Not impossible, of course, that there are remnants of others here in this place, stray elements or traces of the people who walked this land before, come to inspect the new arrivals. Who is to say that such overlaps never occur, that the woman who wished for a child, the man with the ash stick, the meaty-fisted holy man, Brith herself, the little starvelings haven't tiptoed in or slid under the door or eased themselves through the caulking or filtered in through the thatch to look down on these people in their beds? Why wouldn't they, if they could, peer at Rose as nightmarish images of pursuit and threat flit through her mind, as Liam wrestles nocturnally with caverns and streams? What would stop them leaning over the living to feel the warmth of their sleeping breath, the longed-for tick-tick of blood along their veins, to observe the enviable flush of life in the redness of their lips, in the tint of their cheeks?

Perhaps this is why the unborn child is awake, because it senses the presence of these ghosts; perhaps it is the only one attuned to their hesitant shuffling, their phantasmic sighing, their wistful longing, their grief at their inexplicable and eternal incorporeality.

The baby sucks on its thumb, meditatively, musingly, eyes flicking back and forth in the darkness, ruminating, cogitating. It pedals one foot, reflexively, then the other, ankles knocking together, as if readying itself for motion. It is in no hurry, however, to leave its aqueous seclusion. It is biding its time.

~

As summer takes hold of the peninsula, drawing delicate white flowers from the wet bog and miniature blue arrows of swifts from the eaves, it becomes apparent to Phina that her family are taking the move here in very different ways.

Tomás is invigorated, full of fire and plans, unrecognisable from the man who lay in bed for weeks. If Phina looks out of the window, she might see him digging the little field, or instructing Liam in the correct way to harness the donkey, or constructing a henhouse, or pulling weeds, or spreading kelp on the drills. It hangs in the air between Tomás and Phina, like an invisible skein of spider silk, that this is a life familiar to them both, from back then, from before, that its rituals and routines are inscribed in their bodies and minds, that they know how to do it, what comes next in their list of tasks. It is their original map: the rising at dawn, the baking of bread, the milking of beasts, the tilling of soil, the gathering of eggs, one eye on the weather at all times, the other on the land or the youngers or the fire.

As for the children, Enda is besieged by restlessness, an inability to remain in a chair for long or settle to any task: she must explore, she must find out everything, right now, this very moment. She is out after breakfast, often until dinnertime, when she returns filthy and barefoot, her boots tied around her neck, her pockets filled with purple berries or pine cones or shells from the strand. Liam, Phina has been surprised to observe, does not share his sister's curiosity about the place; he doesn't, for the first time in his life, want to fall in with whatever Enda proposes, preferring to sit inside, reading a book the priest has lent him, his face lily-pale. Enda asks him to come with her, she entreats him, she stamps her foot and says, What's wrong with you?, but he will not oblige her with his company.

And Rose? Rose will not leave Phina's side. If Phina is placing the washed pots on the mantel, there Rose will be. If she is riddling the grate, Rose will be crouched next to her. When she is using the small axe to cut firewood, Rose is at her side, her first two fingers inserted into her mouth, her doll clamped into her armpit. Trying to sweep the cobwebs from the walls with a broom, Phina sees there is nothing else for it, and she makes Rose her own miniature broom from a stick tied with birch twigs, so that the child can do it too. Phina has to learn not to step sideways too quickly, or backwards without looking, because Rose is always there, beside her, behind her, half a pace away, eyes fixed on her, as if wanting to read her mother's thoughts, as if needing to study how to be, how to navigate this new life.

On a day when the weather is still, the sun a pale eye behind a veil of cloud, she raises her head from a mixing bowl to see that Rose has something in her hand, which she whisks back and forth as she narrates some story to herself, something that flashes blue and purple in the light stretching in through the door.

"What have you there, Rosie?" Phina asks absently, half a mind on her baking, the other half on where Enda might be.

The child is sitting cross-legged on the floor, at her feet, talking to whatever it is.

"A feather, is it?" Phina says, wondering will Enda be home for her tea or will Tomás have to go out searching and calling for her again.

Rose is murmuring, in her high and fluting voice; Phina catches something about a faery on a mountain, a lady with enchanting hair, and she is smiling to herself when she sees, pincered between Rose's fingers, the tassel, the one from her mother's shawl, the one that Tomás produced from his pocket in the workhouse. Rose has it upturned on her hand, its silken trails forming long blue hair around one of her fingers.

Phina turns and bends in one swift movement, her knees cracking, and catches Rose's wrist.

"Where did you get that?"

Rose, shocked from the orbit of her game by the sharp tone of her usually sweet-tempered mother, stares up at her, open-mouthed, her eyes starting to swim with tears.

Phina is filled, instantly, from head to foot, with scorching shame.

“Ah, don’t cry, *a leanbh*,” she says, and she clasps Rose to her chest with floury hands. “It’s only that . . . I . . . I . . . Wherever did you find it?”

“Sorry, Mammy, sorry. It was in a—” Rose begins but the rest of the sentence is swallowed by her sobs.

“Where?” Phina says, rocking her child but at the same time prising the tassel from her grip.

“In a box under the bed. I’m sorry, I’m sorry.”

Phina lifts her and settles herself in a chair, with Rose on her lap. She tells her over and over that it’s all right, she’s not vexed, it’s just that the tassel means a great deal to her.

“Why?” Rose asks, turning to regard her with large, wet eyes.

Phina looks back at her. She feels the astounding wholeness of her daughter’s body, its small spine, the wing-stubs of shoulder-blades, all folded inside her arms; she feels the shrugging twist of the unborn one between them. Over in the corner, Liam raises his head, alert to some change in the room. Phina feels a choking swarm of words in her throat. Unlike her husband, she has perfect recall of the time before, the life she had, her people. The strange thing, she would like to say to her daughter and her son, about this new house, their new life on the peninsula, is that she finds it returning to her here with such startling clarity, in vivid flashes, and how she greets them with a desperate grasp, gathering them to her. She remembers: crouching with her sisters to crack nuts on a flagged floor in slanting sunlight. She remembers: a yellow-washed wall, and her brothers when they returned from the fields, coming in through the door, shrugging themselves out of their jackets, pulling off their boots, and how they would shove each other, like bullocks in a pen, fighting to be first to wash themselves at the bowl of hot water their mother set on the table. There were two neighbours, an elderly woman and her brother, living down the lane, who used to let them ride on their pony, she and her sisters clinging to the stiff little mane. She recalls all the talk that surrounded her father leaving for America, whether they would all go or just him or if he might take one of the boys, the decision that he would go alone, initially, then send for them all, and there was the rush of preparation, the packing of a bag, the discussions about papers and tickets. She can picture him with them, the way her mother would rub his scalp with her fingertips, how he would balance Phina on one of his shoulders—just as Tomás does with Rose, she could have said—and the trembling, eloquent sound of his pipe when the neighbours would come after dark and sit by the fire, and someone might sing, and another might accompany her father on a fiddle or a drum. And she has a sense of her mother talking about her father, who was away across the sea, and how one day he sent a shawl, the like of which they had never seen before, and how happy it had made her mother; she kept it folded in linen, and only brought it out on Sundays. Soon, her mother would tell them, whenever she tucked it about herself, its silk tassels shimmering and swaying, very soon, their father would send them enough money for their passage, sure it wouldn't be long until they were all together again.

Phina recalls all this, the cracking of nuts and the brothers and the pipes and the shawl and the talk of papers, and she also recalls what came after, the fearful things, and these reside in a different chamber of her heart, and she is careful to tend to them, these moments and the people held in them, for it is the first thing she does upon awakening, every day, to recite a silent prayer for them all: *Eternal rest grant unto them, O Lord, and let perpetual light shine upon them.* When any thoughts of the awfulness intrude, snagging Phina's mind, like a sleeve catching on a door, she invokes the remainder of the prayer, and she recites it with fervent rapidity, over and over again—*May-their-souls-through-the-mercy-of-God-rest-in-peace*—and it is partly for them all and also for the child she had been. Because when they all passed, one by one, when the yellow house sank into silence, it was as if the opaque shades of blindness fell upon Phina. She had turned the key in the door, she had sat by the empty fireplace, and kicked her heel against the hearthstone, because she didn't want to be the last one left, and she was too frightened to go into the other room, so she would sit by the burned-out grate, with the shawl wrapped around herself.

When the pounding came at the door, for a wild moment Phina thought it might be her father, returned from across the sea to fetch her away, and she would say she was sorry, she tried to save them but she hadn't known how. It wasn't him, of course, it was just the old neighbour who had once had the pony, and he had a man with him, and the two of them were telling her she couldn't stay here and, dear God, what was that fearful stench, come away out now, child, and up onto this cart, we'll take you to a place you'll be looked after. Phina had struggled, she had clung to the chair, and said, I'm to wait for my daddo, he'll send for me or he'll come back on a big ship, I was told I was to wait. The neighbour said he would tell her daddo where she was, if he came, he promised, but she was to be a good girl, to go along now. God love you, the old neighbour said, placing a trembling hand to her hair, and together he and the man lifted her up. She had wanted to ask, where was the pony, could she not ride it one more time, but she was afraid of the answer, so she said nothing, just watched as the old neighbour got smaller and smaller, as the track between her and her home unribboned behind her, stretching out until the yellow-walled house was so little she could have pierced through its centre with a pin.

Phina sits on the edge of her chair, her arms around Rose, her fingers clutching the tassel. She sees that Enda is now standing on the threshold, her outline aflame with glaring daylight, a dishevelled fiery vision.

"It belonged to . . ." she begins, then abandons the sentence. How to tell this story, where to begin, how to pick out the words?

"It was cut from a shawl that . . ." But these are words she cannot utter.

Her children wait, their eyes upon her.

"It was sent all the way from America," she begins. "But . . ."

"But what?" Enda demands.

"Your father . . ." she tries cautiously, and this feels feasible, so she continues hesitantly, like a person uncertain of welcome might step into a house ". . . your father saved it . . . he cut this scrap off it and gave it to me."

Phina stands, gently easing Rose off her lap, her words suddenly drying up like a streambed in the heat. She stows the tassel with great care in her skirt pocket. Her children watch her do this. Then she swallows, several times, before turning away, back to her mixing bowl.

With mutinous deliberation, Enda scuffs her clogs against the verge so that they become clotted with thick, claggy mud. This is forbidden, of course, and she'll have to clean them later, with a stick. A tiny act of resistance but solace must be found in small doses, wherever it resides.

They are walking to the lough to collect the eggs, a task that must be performed twice a day. Rose and her mother have gone on ahead, hand in hand. The basket bangs against Enda's leg, its sharp weave snagging on her stockings, so that she has to pause and kick it, every now and again, her toe connecting with its creaking wicker. Tears, angry and salted, sting her eyelids and she tries to allay them with a knuckle but somehow they elude her, trickling down her face.

Fiercely, she sticks out a tongue to catch them. She never cries. She's not a baby. She prides herself on not crying, not even when she fell down a flight of tenement stairs back where they used to live.

At the thought of the Lanes, Enda catches her breath. That they have gone from there, might never return, never see it again, is beyond comprehension. She feels its loss like a wound, a pulsing rent in the skin of her side. There, she had known who she was: the stretch of cobbles between the rows of tenements had been her world. If she suggested a game, all the children in earshot would run to join in; if she wore her hair in two plaits, every other girl followed suit. The nuns at school had told Enda that if she worked hard she could be a teacher one day, and Enda had liked to think of herself standing in front of a classroom, opening a book to read aloud to rows of pupils.

Here on the peninsula, though, she can see that the only things lying before her are the baking of bread and the sweeping of floors and the milking of cows, and the interminable time these tasks take, and the way they must be done every day, over and over again. It's intolerable. Gone is her world of the cobbles, her eager acolytes who would play whatever she came up with, the nuns who loved her for her neat handwriting, her future as a teacher. All gone.

Over the bluff are her mother and Rose, and they are entering the part of the boreen where the hedgerows on either side have grown up to almost touch, forming a manner of tunnel, with the twisted fibres of tree roots and ferns curving up on either side of her, and the branches and leaves linking into a roof overhead, and Enda imagines she could slip through the roots and trunks, leaving behind all that—

Her thoughts are interrupted by a call: "Enda! Hurry now. Bring the basket."

Enda sighs again and, when her mother turns away, gives the basket another kick. Her mother had the idea of setting up the hen-house on the islet in the middle of the loughan that fills the hollow below their house. No fox will get them there, she'd said. They'll be safe and sound.

Which is well for them, Enda thinks, as they emerge from the tunnel of the boreen onto the lough's shore, but who's the one who has to tuck up her skirts and wade through the water, basket over her arm? Enda, that's who. And she must then deliver the eggs to the widow, who has made an arrangement with Phina to sell them in town on market day, who knows the best place to set up the stall, and the light-fingered people to keep an eye out for, and she'd be going anyway to sell her cheese and her dulse. She has said that, come winter-time, she'll be glad to take Enda with her for company on the road, and that way Enda can learn the trade.

Enda stops, slams down the basket and, without looking at her mother or her sister, sits down on a flat stone to pull off her clogs. There is nothing she wants less than to learn the trade. The very idea of being a market-seller appals her.

If her wide-ranging discontent, her grief and irritability could be traced, like the delta of a river, to its source, it would be this: Liam and his long absences from the house. He leaves at dawn, a slice of bread in his pocket, and isn't back until near bedtime.

It's not so much his absence, Enda thinks, as she steps into the water, which is the colour of strong-brewed tea, her feet finding the smooth pebbles beneath the weeds and water-murk, but the unfairness of it. The priest had come up the lane from down below; they had seen him from a long way off, his black robes swirling about him, his hand holding a hat firm to his head. Her mother had gone quickly inside to build up the fire, put a kettle on to boil. Enda had pulled at Liam's jersey and said, Come on, let's go, we don't want to sit and listen to him. But Liam, to her astonishment, had said, Actually I do. Enda, still gripping his sleeve, had been unable to believe it. I'm not coming, her brother said, without looking at her, without taking his eyes off the approaching figure—and how had the priest known where to find them, how had he known the way because the path was winding and confusing?—and Enda said, What?, and Liam said, I'm staying.

Worse was to come. The priest stepped into their house and their mother offered fresh milk and griddle cakes spread with butter, and the priest said he couldn't, and then he said, he might, and then he ate several, placing them hot in his mouth, as if his tongue had no feeling. Their father, upon seeing the priest, had made himself scarce, disappearing beyond the haggard wall, muttering something about how he needed to turn the soil. The priest had ignored his exit and summoned Liam to sit at his side. Rose leaned on her mother's knee, sucking her thumb; Enda stood in the doorway but she was near enough to hear that the priest had decided to establish a school, not much to speak of, a hedge school, you understand, for the handful of children in the area, taught by himself, the priest placing a modest hand to his chest, with a laugh, and the boy would be most welcome. He touched Liam on the shoulder and said that he was aware of the young man's considerable gifts, and Liam grinned up at him like a gom.

Disgusted, Enda had pushed herself away from the door jamb. She was opening her mouth to say, What about me, would I not be welcome too? The priest had turned his head towards her, but with his eyes flickering shut, as if the wind had blown grit into them, so that he was looking at her yet not seeing her. He had said, his hand resting on Liam's shoulder: we will only be taking girls of a certain age, so this one—here he waved his other hand towards Enda—would be too old for schooling, I think.

Enda had stamped her foot. She'd said, That's not fair, I want to, please, can I, I want to go. The priest had looked off to the side, a tight and paltry smile on his face, as if to say, Now this is why we don't take the older girls, see what we'd be getting ourselves into. Liam had said nothing, had spoken not a word, hadn't thought to stick up for her at all.

Perhaps, Enda thinks, as she arrives on the islet, hauling herself out of the water, causing the hens to tilt their heads and gabble to each other, she shouldn't have stamped. Perhaps she should have reasoned. Enda kneels, slides a hand under a hen's soft undercarriage and feels two eggs, which she draws out and places in the basket. She looks up, almost involuntarily, at the mountain, its outline stark against the sky, the mysterious ridges in the earth around one of its lower edges, as if someone at some time in history had dug circles around it. The widow says it is a faery fortress, and has told them never to walk into it. Enda stares at the circular ripples, thinking that she should have said, I have gifts too. I'm better than Liam at arithmetic, at recitation, at grammar, at geometry, at handwriting. Everything, in fact. He can't keep a column of figures straight in his head or write a sentence without smudging ink all over his sleeve, but I can. Let me show you. Let me try.

It wouldn't have made any difference, Enda knows, as she steps back into the water, basket over her arm. That priest is someone whose ideas are very fixed, as if nailed to a door. Whatever she had said, whether or not she'd stamped her foot, wouldn't have persuaded him. And so Liam goes off, each morning, to the hedge school, and now he leads a life that is closed to Enda, away from her. He won't even share with her what he's studying because, he says, the priest has told him to keep it to himself, that learning can be dangerous to those who do not understand. This smarts like a lash, that Liam does what the priest asks, that he chooses the priest over her. She must stay here, beneath the mountain, all day and all night, and she cannot see any way out of it, any gap in the tunnel she can slip through.

On the shore, skirts blowing sideways in the breeze, wait her mother and her sister, their faces turned towards one another. As she wades through the waters, her mother lifts a hand and waves to her, as if Enda is a boat and Phina is guiding her into harbour.

It is only a week later, perhaps two, of the same monotonous tasks, animals fed, animals milked, meals cooked and eaten, then cleared away, so that there is very little to distinguish one day from the next, when Phina comes to find Enda. She is wading knee-deep in the stream, creating miniature dams to re-divert the flow, her dress hitched up, and Phina tells her to come out of there and take a loaf down to the widow. Enda says she won't. Phina says she will. Enda says she can't. Phina says she can.

Then, her mother does something intriguing and unexpected. She lays the loaf, wrapped in a cloth, on a flat stone and says that it's a shame Enda won't go because the widow has something for her.

Enda, flummoxed, watches her mother walk away. Why should she get out of the stream? Why should she take the bread down? And what can the widow possibly have for her that she'll like? It's probably something dull, Enda tells herself, as she stands there, the icy stream water flowing around her numb legs. Something like knitting needles or a bolt of cloth that Enda will have to pretend she's delighted with, and then she'll be expected to spend every evening stitching or purling, being grateful. Enda pulls a face and kicks at the water so hard that the spray reaches the bank, and in the droplets, just for a moment, appears the startling arc of a rainbow.

She spends a while kicking again and again, summoning the miniature rainbow, gratified every time it appears. Then, eyeing the wrapped loaf, she steps out of the water, shivering, contemplating the path down the hill.

The widow's table, when she arrives, is set with two cups and two plates, as if it's all been pre-arranged. Enda sits, simmering with suspicion: whatever plan her mother and the widow have cooked up she is sure she won't like. She reaches out for a slice of bread from the plate in front of her and sighs; the widow is outside, fetching some of the cheese for Enda to take home with her.

Enda chews on the crust. Beneath the table, she feels the twitch and pull of her leg muscles. She has grown so much recently, her skirt hem seeming steadily to creep up her calves; sometimes, when she rises in the morning, she could almost fancy she is closer to the thatch than the previous day. She will be twelve next month, which seems extraordinary to her, a number on a cusp, a hinge between childhood and adulthood. She feels at once too young and too old for everything—too old to engage in all the pursuits she has loved up to now, exploring and climbing, but too young for the pastimes of a woman, all that tedious cooking and minding. She wants to be twelve but also dreads it: childhood already feels to be at an arm's length and moving here, to the peninsula, seems to Enda like closing a door upon it.

Without warning, she feels again the salt-sting of tears under her lids. What is the matter with her? Fiercely, she bites her lip, presses her thumbnail into the opposite palm. When she feels a wet trail down her cheek, she dashes it away with her sleeve.

"Here."

The widow has materialised behind her, putting a cup of milk on the table. Enda nods her thanks, not trusting her voice to speak, and takes the cup. She doesn't say that milk turns her stomach, especially when still warm from the udder, as this surely is. She takes the tiniest sip of the frothy white liquid and attempts a smile.

"Drink it all down," the widow says. "It's for those growing bones of yours you need it."

Enda nods again, watches from under her lowered lashes as the widow moves across the room and opens the doors of a little cupboard built into the rafters. A wooden box is placed on the table at her elbow, the lid lifted, and the widow is saying that this belonged to her husband, God rest his soul, and she thinks it is time for someone else to have it.

The interior is wadded with fabric, fashioned to curve, lovingly and exactly, around the frame of a fiddle. Enda stares at it, her eyes still wet with unshed tears, and the instrument sits there, in its box, presenting itself for view. The four strings, held proud of the burnished wood, arching over a carved bridge, the bow with its parallel bones of wood and horsehair strapped into the lid, the scrolled holes that conceal a dark interior, and Enda wonders what it might hold, what notes and melodies might be trapped in there, waiting for release.

The widow is lifting out the fiddle and putting it, with care, to Enda's collarbone, taking one of her hands and fitting her thumb to the notch, curling the fingers around the instrument's narrow neck, placing the other hand on the strings, and telling her to pluck. Pluck, she says, pluck away there, keep going. The widow listens, head cocked, eyes half closed, then tightens some of the black pegs at the top, loosens others. Enda keeps plucking and they both keep listening. This string should be five notes higher than this one, the widow says, and this one, and so on. Enda feels a shift, almost as if the fiddle is coming alive, or waking up from a long sleep, the strings falling into alignment or agreement, finding their correct pitches, That's it, the widow says, with a rare smile, that's it. Do you hear it now?

She presses one of Enda's fingertips to a string, then another, and the narrow cord pushes back up into the skin of it, but Enda doesn't mind because it is an interesting discomfort, a necessary one. The widow gives her five notes of a song about a river: she hums it, then asks Enda to play it back to her, again and again. The tune must become part of your head and your bones, she says, and you will take the fiddle away with you. When you've mastered this tune, I'll give you another.

Enda has the bow in her other hand now, and she is keeping it at a cross to the strings, and the widow is moving it with her hand over hers, over the strings, still humming the song, and the same notes are coming out of the fiddle, haltingly but definitely there. She, Enda, is bringing it forth. She is making something happen.

Mesmerised, she looks down along the strings, which look to her like a shining road, leading off into the distance. Her shoulder lifts and stretches, an up stroke, a down stroke, her fingers moving on and off the strings, and she listens to the differences, the alterations in tone, the language in which it speaks to her.

What might alert the child inside Phina to the change in the family's circumstances? It could be the quality of the peninsula light, which is not funnelled down between rows of terraces but is a lustrous grey glow from all sides. Or the richness of the fresh milk that spores into its minuscule bloodstream, or perhaps the startling oxygen-rich blasts of bog air when its mother takes the midday meal to its father, who is out footing turf. It might be the constant auditory presence of its next-in-line sibling, whose voice is higher in register and whose mouth is on a level with its head—the ebb and flow of questions, expostulations, reaches the unborn child as a muffled, watery song. Or the sound of Enda's fiddle as she practises, hour after hour, the first halting steps of a ballad or a tune.

It hangs upside-down, like a circus acrobat, in its briny cave, thumb in its mouth, waiting, absorbing everything this new landscape will offer it.

Rose doesn't like the whine of wind down the chimney. She doesn't like the bulky thatch above their heads, or the chittering birds that land upon it. She doesn't like the louring manor house, with its numerous chimneys and its iron gates. She doesn't like the fields and bogs that, at night, are filled with all manner of animals—badgers and foxes, owls and hares—that shriek and battle, scuttle and devour each other.

What she does like, however, is the donkey. A mournful yet intelligent beast it is, with long-lashed brown eyes that are full of sympathy for her fears and worries. If she whistles, it will come, plodding over the field towards her, to rest its head on the stone wall, and she will rub the soft fuzz behind its ears and whisper softly to it.

It is here, sharing secrets over a wall with a donkey, Liam off at school and their father gone to see the viscount's land steward, that Enda finds her.

"Come with me," her sister commands, from behind her. Three words to strike dread into Rose's heart.

Without turning round, Rose recognises this mood of her sister's—bored, restless, belligerent—and she knows the best thing to do is to steer clear of her until it passes. Enda has been practising her fiddle all morning, until Phina begged her to stop, just for a moment, so she could hear herself think.

"I won't," Rose says. Then, curiosity getting the better of her, she asks: "Where?"

"Away," Enda says, with a sweeping gesture. "We'll explore."

Rose takes a step to the side, aiming to dart past her, but Enda is too quick: she steps into Rose's path and grabs her round the arm.

"Come on," she says, half pleading, half ordering.

Rose twists uselessly in her grasp. "Let me go. I just want to be in the house. Please, Enda."

"Frightened, are you," Enda jeers, "of being outside?"

Rose thinks of the black and impassive waters of the lough, the way you can see the weather coming at you from a long way off, slow and inexorable as an army, the jagged bulk of the mountain behind them, and says: "Yes."

Enda is taken aback by this honesty, flummoxed. She casts a nervous glance around her, as if whatever Rose is afraid of might be coming for them. Then she squares her shoulders and changes tack.

"Rosie," she wheedles, "we . . . we haven't played out together for ages. Not since . . . well . . . ah, come on. Don't you always have a good time with me?"

Rose's tender heart is softening, of course, at the sight of her queenly sister brought so low as to be begging for company. Enda takes her by the hand, and off they go, waving farewell to the donkey, pulling long grasses from the verge, and Enda is showing Rose how to wedge them between your thumbs and blow on them to produce a hilarious squawking noise, tripping together along the boreen, pushing sideways through the walls of the green tunnel and out the other side, until they are in a place Rose has never been, a damp and marshy stretch, which pulls and gobbles at their feet. White and lilac flowers grow low to the ground and tall irises hold up their folded blooms to the sky; water pools in the low places, in their footprints. Rose would like to crouch to examine the peaty puddles, to see what might live within them, perhaps pick some of the flowers for their mother, but she can tell that Enda won't stop. Enda's mood is high, her cheeks flushed, her hand hot over Rose's; she jumps with a flourish over the small streams that cut through the bog, reaching back to help Rose, and Rose can feel the calluses the fiddle strings have left on her sister's fingertips.

Before Rose realises what is happening, they are walking between two gentle hillocks, towards a dense cluster of trees. She comes to a halt, pulling Enda's hand.

"Da said we weren't to go in there."

Enda's gaze darts longingly towards the thicket, then back to Rose. "He didn't."

"He did. He said: Never go into the copse."

Enda treads back and forth, biting her lip, a flighty horse held by a bridle. "He meant a different copse. Not this one."

Rose shakes her head, folds her arms. "I'll not go," she says. "And I won't tell on you but if Mammy asks—"

Enda lets out an explosive, thwarted sigh. "Fine," she snaps. "We won't do it, then. But instead . . ." Enda thinks, furiously, standing on one leg, tapping a foot against her calf. "I know," she says, seizing Rose's hand, and pulling her back towards the boreen.

"What?" says Rose, anxious, for she has visions of Enda riding off on the donkey's back, or her setting it free or—

"The faery fort," Enda breathes, imbuing the words with drama and deliciousness.

Relief rises up in Rose, like a wave upon a shore, then pulls back, revealing dread and unwillingness. "I thought . . ." she begins, as she and Enda dive through the bushes and into the green lane, brambles and twigs clutching at their clothing, their feet swallowed by bog and sedge.

"You thought what?" Enda says distractedly, set as she is now on her course.

"Didn't the widow say no one should walk into it because—"

"There has to be somewhere we can go!" Enda screams, gripping her hair with her free hand, dragging Rose along until she is forced to break into a run. "Liam told me that Father Joseph said it has nothing to do with the faeries, that it was made by people who lived here in ancient times, that they built walls in circles, to keep out their enemies, and it's called a 'rath' not a 'faery fort' and—" Enda breaks off, catching sight of her destination, and she lets go of Rose's hand to sprint ahead.

Rose clambers wearily after her. "Enda," she cries, "Ennnnn-daaaa! Wait for me, waaaaaaaiiiiiit," but she knows her words, bleated and fluting, are useless. Enda never waits for anyone.

Rose toils up the slope towards the rath, her legs aching, her breath coming in ragged pants. She can see, up ahead, the ringed mounds of the fort, softened by time but still discernible, the high and craggy mountain behind, a bird revolving through the clouds above with wide wings that end in finger-feathers, the tall form of her sister scaling the first grassy mound and disappearing from view.

"Enda!" Rose shrieks. "Where are you? I can't see you!"

She breaks into a run, her feet slipping on the turf, envisaging her sister kidnapped by faeries or the *púca* or the ghosts of long-dead people or whoever it was used to live here. She will have to do battle for Enda's soul; she will have to challenge the ancients to a duel, using her wits and strength; and she must be sure to keep one eye closed at all times so that—

Her sister's bright hair rises out of the grassy rings as she ascends another mound and sinks out of sight again. Not captured, then, not carried off into the earth.

Rose reaches the outer ring, entirely out of breath. She will not go into the fort, she will not. Let Enda face the faeries, the ill luck; she will remain here, just outside, close enough to watch Enda as she explores, but still at a safe distance from whatever it is that lives here. She lets herself collapse to the ground, then crawls forward until she can see down into the fort. There are three rings of earth, fitted one inside another, all covered with grass and moss. The fort is shaped like a bowl, gently sloping to the centre. In one place, just to Rose's left, is a gap or an inlet in the perimeter, and it looks to her like a gate or a doorway, and she is picturing a procession of little men and women, coming in and out, when Enda suddenly shouts: "Rosie, watch out!"

There is an unaccustomed chime of panic in her sister's voice. Rose scrambles to her feet, snapping around her head to see whatever Enda is pointing at.

A monstrous, shaggy beast is streaking over the hillside, bounding towards them. It has appeared from the direction of the copse or the bog, and has masses of grey fur, enormous long legs, and a rag of tongue lolling from its mouth. A dog, but larger than any she has ever seen before: it is a hound from Hell, and is coming for them at a sickening speed, its fearsome stride gobbling up the distance between them, fangs gleaming white in the sun. A scream unfurls from Rose's mouth, like a flag in a breeze. She blunders blindly towards her sister, for she represents the only safety around, up one ridge, down another, up the second, then she hurls herself down the slope of the fort and Enda catches her, wrapping her arms around her, and still the hound comes, nearing the fort, leaping the first ring and then the second, and Rose is screaming and Enda is screaming, and Rose will always remember this, even when they are grown women and living apart, that Enda thrusts Rose behind her, she places herself between Rose and the Hellhound, she surrenders herself to the beast's jaws. Rose clutches Enda from behind, crying and sobbing, her eyes squeezed tight, waiting for death.

A taut and ominous pause. Rose tightens her grip around her sister's waist. Is the animal crouching, readying itself to pounce? Will it tear them limb from limb? Will it rip out their throats, first Enda's, then hers? She hears Enda's heaving breaths, the hammering of her heart.

Suddenly, incongruously, her sister lets out a laugh.

"Look," she says.

Rose opens her eyes a crack. She sees: the grass surrounding her dusty feet, a triangle of Enda's brown skirt, and a set of four grey paws.

"I think he might be friendly after all."

Rose peers out from behind her sister. The dog is before them, ears flat, tail whipping questioningly back and forth, head tilted to one side. His face, Rose sees, is extremely expressive, with tufts for eyebrows, anxious furrows on his forehead.

Rose steps out from behind Enda, all fear evaporated. She moves towards the dog. He knows and she knows they won't harm each other: there is an unspoken tether of trust weaving itself between them. She stretches out her hand, her eyes locked on the dog's, and clicks her tongue. "Here," she says to him, "here, boy. Where did you come from? We won't hurt you."

The dog flicks up his ears as if listening out for some distant signal. He takes a wary step forward and sniffs Rose's fingers. After a long moment of assessment, he anoints her wrist with a lick.

Rose turns towards her sister, face alight, hand buried in the dog's fur, her mind already leaping ahead to the animal never leaving her side, even at night, where he will sleep alongside her, protecting her from robbers and thieves and nightmares; she will make him a blanket all of his own, she will feed him and brush him and he will never be hungry and she need never be alone again, and says, "We can keep him, can't we?"

Two miles north-by-north-east, Liam sits in a draughty schoolhouse, his feet tucked beneath his seat; on the desk before him are some lines in Latin.

He reads them to himself, syllable by syllable, hoping they will yield up their meaning, as an apple gives out its juice: *Nascuntur et alio modo terrae ac repente in alio mari emergunt velut paria secum faciente natura quaeque hauserit hiatus alio loco reddente.*

Father Joseph has told him that he looked out this passage specially for him. It will be difficult, he said, laying a hand to Liam's shoulder, but it might well lie within your reach. Now let's see if you'll disappoint me or surprise me.

Liam presses his left hand to the page. The thought of disappointing the priest makes his stomach clench around its breakfast. He has to do this, he must. *Nascuntur,* he reads, *et alio.*

Around him, he hears the sighs and chalk-scratches of his classmates but he will not lift his head to see how they are faring: they have not been given a special passage in Latin and are working on their arithmetic. Liam keeps his gaze on the lines. *Nascuntur,* he knows, is a word that means "arise" or "to be born," and *alio modo* is "in another way." But what kind of a sentence begins with "arise and in another way"?

Liam feels the prickle of sweat beneath his collar. It makes no sense. He is going to be a disappointment to Father Joseph, who will not be angry, but Liam can picture the dismay that will fill the eyes of the priest when he admits that he can't prise the meaning out of the passage.

Arise and in another way—what? He reads the words again, and takes in an unsteady breath. It's no good: the sentence has slammed its door in his face. Liam feels panic swarming like ants over his skin. The priest has singled him out for praise; he says, often, that he has high hopes for Liam, that he envisages marvellous things ahead. Liam wants whatever it is that Father Joseph sees for him—he wants it desperately. He wants, more than anything, to be able to live up to what plans the priest might be making for his future. By coincidence, his father, ten miles or so away, is also staring down in dismay at a page of written words. Tomás is standing in a field station of the redcoat surveyors, just over the county border. He is holding a sheet of paper upon which are written the details of his next commission: the map of a remote island off the west coast.

They leave next month, the paper informs him, and Tomás cannot believe this has come so soon, so hard on the heels of his last commission. He wants nothing more than to stay in his cottage, on his land, with his wife and his children and his animals. Every fibre of his being revolts at the thought of setting out with these soldiers, to live alongside them in tents, to eat their food and have to endure their jokes and banter. The journey, Tomás can see, will be long and the task arduous.

Tomás raises his head, struck by a cheering thought: he will take Liam with him. It will be good for the boy to set himself to some work, to get back to his apprenticeship. The child is always at his books and, Tomás thinks, with a dart of unease, is far too much in the thrall of that priest. This trip will be a good opportunity for Tomás to have his son to himself again, working alongside each other, like before.

The division will set out before winter closes in, the sergeant tells him, and they'll be lucky to be back by spring. Tomás nods, folding the piece of paper and sliding it into his pocket.

His daughters, Enda and Rose, are walking slowly along a ridge, up and over the drumlin where Tomás stood a few months ago, the wolfhound in step beside them. They are discussing the best way to ask their parents about the dog and how they must—no, need to—keep him, and they are putting off the moment, just in case the answer is no, because neither of them could bear that: the dog chose them, it found them, it belongs with them.

In his schoolroom, Liam struggles on, hope waning. He has found no crack, no entry into the Latin lines: they elude him. He has raised his head to seek Father Joseph's aid but the priest stands looking out of the window, his back to them, and Liam is unable to call out to him, for he can't trust his voice. His palms are slick and cold, and then suddenly, from nowhere, he recalls something Enda said to him, when he had been labouring over a different translation, back when they were living in the Lanes. Find the verb, she'd said to him, across the kitchen table, always start with the verb because it is the key that unlocks the whole sense. What do you mean? Liam had said to her, and without looking up from her own page, Enda had replied: The verb gives the sentence its purpose, its motion, so if you work out what it's doing, how it interacts with all the other words, everything will fall into place.

Liam passes his tongue over his dry lips. Verb, he tells himself, where is the verb? And then he sees it is the very first word: *nascuntur*, from the infinitive *nascor*, which means "to be born" or "to spring forth." Something is being born. But what? His eyes slide backwards, forwards, backwards again and pause on *terrae*. Which means "land." It is, he sees, a sentence about land, about the earth. Land is being born or formed.

Joy invades him and he has to prevent himself from leaping to his feet. "Lands are also formed . . . in another way," he tries, then returns to find the next verb, and the next, and they appear before him, like stepping-stones leading to a far bank: *emergunt*, *faciente*, *hauserit*, *reddente*. He grips his pen, thinking, thinking. What would Enda do here? How would she navigate her way through this? And at the thought of his sister, the lines start to break over his head, like a wave.

In a kind of ecstasy, he dips his nib into the inkwell, flattens the page—for Father Joseph has given him the privilege of a pen, no slate and chalk for him, and Liam feels his work must always live up to this—and writes: "Lands are also formed in another way, suddenly emerging in a different sea, as if nature were compensating the earth for its losses, restoring in one place what it has swallowed up in another."

Father Joseph, who has been watching Liam's struggle all this time in the reflection of the window, turns around, a slight but perceptible smile on his face. The child is gifted, certainly, and several cuts above any of the others, but Father Joseph has noticed of late that there is something more within Liam, something exulted. Something that he himself might mould and steer. Staggering to think that this boy came from that troublemaking heretic of a father, and how dare the man shun and ignore him, an ordained priest, in front of his congregation, week after week at mass, refusing to shake his hand or meet his eye? It beggars belief, after everything he did for him. Not a hint of gratitude, not a semblance of repentance or respect will the man show him, almost as if he has forgotten the triumph and glory of that exorcism, and how can it be that the bishop never replied to his letter, that he, Father Joseph, has never received a shred of recognition for his efforts, for all his inspired labour on behalf of the Lord? But God works His mystery in many ways, and He perhaps always intended for Father Joseph to tread the path of humility, to take on the role of this exceptional child's saviour and spiritual father. And what more perfect way to demonstrate to Tomás the error of his ways, to teach that most arrogant of men a lesson? There's an irresistible symmetry to it all. In plucking away the son—no, guiding the son—Father Joseph will show Tomás that a disrespect for the Church will never go unchallenged.

Father Joseph intends to do the Lord's work, always. He will save this boy. He will lift him out of that rude and elementary cabin on the hillside; he will divert him from a future of toil and set him instead on a path of righteousness and glory. And his eejit of a father won't be able to do a thing to stop it.

Father Joseph walks triumphantly to the blackboard, and surveys his modest flock. He smiles at them, holds out his arms.

"Boys," he says, "let us pray."

Rose and Enda are ready when they re-enter the cottage. They have it all arranged, the case for keeping the dog, how he doesn't seem to belong to anyone, they don't know where he came from; they have promised each other that they will remain calm, they won't cry or shout. They will talk like grown-ups to the grown-ups, and Liam will be on their side, they are sure. As they reach the haggard, the dog hangs back, he paces the perimeter of the cottage; he will not come inside. Rose slips her hand into Enda's. They are ready.

When they go through the half-door, however, all this talk flies from their heads; it takes wing and flaps out of the open window. For, inside, everything has changed. The fire has been built up so that its flames roar alarmingly up the chimney; the room smells, to Rose, of strangeness, like a mixture of salt and old railings. There is a bucket stuffed with stained sheets and cloths, a lid placed precariously over it. A pair of scissors lies discarded, blades open, upon the floor.

Phina is sitting by the fire, feet apart, several blankets wrapped around her. Her hair is curiously disarrayed, with strands falling to her shoulders, her face gaunt and clammy-looking, but she is smiling at them, beckoning, as if she has something she wants to show them.

And indeed she does. Come and meet your new brother, she is saying, his name is Eugene. The baby who has been inside their mother for so long is now outside her. It is in her arms, tucked into her side. Rose cannot understand how this came about. Her mother looks as she always did—there is no rent or tear in her to let the baby through—but out it has come, for here it is. Or here he is, rather, for the baby is a boy, like the dog outside, which no one has yet mentioned, and Rose feels that she, too, must not say anything about him yet (although she means to take him some of the crusts she has spied on the table just as soon as she is able). Instead, she will peer over the edge of the shawled bundle her mother is holding, and here now comes the source of a memory that will be vivid and present in her mind for ever: the first sight of her brother's face, night-dark eyes gazing beyond them all at something only he can see, tiny star hands grasping for stray explanations for what has happened to him, how he came to arrive in this bright, jarring place. Rose places a finger into his palm and instantly his fingers close over it, gripping it fast, taking possession of it, the second creature of the day to claim her, to say: You belong to me and I belong to you, and we must stick together, you and I.

Eugene, named for Phina's father, is the first baby born on the peninsula for a long time, and is therefore lucky, the widow tells them, a sign of better times ahead. She comes each morning, making the long hike up the hillside, to mind the house and instruct Enda on how best to be a help to her mother, to bake the bread or to hold the infant so that Phina can attend to these tasks. Neighbours start to arrive, as news of the birth spreads. It seems to Enda that every day, someone comes walking up to view this child: the fishermen, the pair of sisters from the end of the village, the elderly man who lives down by the cove, a silent woman and her two grown-up sons. They shuffle into the cottage, removing their hats and shawls; some bring buttermilk for Phina to drink, to build up her strength, others a basket filled with shelled hazelnuts or a handful of newly gathered mountain sage. One man brings a beautiful cradle carved from bog-seasoned oak and says he wants the child to have it, as there is no one in his house who will use it now. The widow takes over the fire and boils the sage into a green paste, which she insists on spooning into Phina's mouth, to bring in the milk, she says. Intriguingly, the pair of sisters produce from somewhere inside their capacious skirts a glass bottle, stoppered with straw: they tilt it over their arthritic hands and sprinkle drops of it onto Eugene, who opens his eyes very wide. The sisters are murmuring about how they made a special devotion at the well, at dawn, to collect it, and how the remainder in the bottle should be poured carefully away, into wet earth, never dry, and not used for household tasks because water from the well is powerful and—

What well? Enda cuts across them to ask, and the sisters glance at each other and say, The sacred well, girleen, the *tobar* in—

It does not escape Enda's notice that, at this point, Liam leaps up, clearing his throat and upsetting a cup so that the sage liquid spills over the table top, pungent fumes rising from it, and then the widow is scolding and the sisters are fussing with cloths and mopping and the conversation is forgotten. Liam slips out and Enda watches him, eyes narrowed. Liam is for ever leaving the house these days; he cannot easily stay within its walls; he is holding some secret within himself, Enda suddenly sees, and she wants to know what it is. She looks at her brother as he steps through the lit rectangle of the doorway, and she looks back at Eugene, her other brother, and his tiny face sparkles with glimmering drops of the mysterious water, his rosebud mouth opening and closing on them, as if he has things he would tell them, if only he could.

He will have a long life here, the widow says as she peruses his face, hungrily, avidly, taking Eugene in her arms and walking with him to the light of the window. Babies, Enda has noticed, cause people to behave differently, to gather together, to gaze, to utter ridiculous sounds, to allow flickering expressions of hope and sadness and longing to transform their otherwise stolid faces. Even her father, Enda thinks, isn't exempt: she has spied him, at night, working on his map preparations, with Eugene in the crook of his arm, looking down at the baby, as if he can find in his face all the answers to everything he ever wanted to know.

She doesn't understand what it is they all see there, or hope to see. Eugene is a baby: he sleeps, he eats, he cries, he pees. That's all.

Enda rises from the bench at the table, ignoring Phina's requests for her to fetch the eggs, deaf to Rose's voice saying, Where are you going, can I come too? She steps out of the door and, shading her eyes against the summer sun, she looks one way, then the other. An inkling of what is bothering Liam has suddenly occurred to her.

She calls his name, twice, hurling the sound like a ball into the air. She wants to find him, wherever it is he has gone, to fall into step beside him. She would like to ask him what he's brooding about and say to him, It's this island, isn't it? You're not wanting to go with Da, are you, you don't want to be his apprentice? Now why is that? Would it be that priest-teacher of yours filling your head with notions, for who wouldn't want to strike out like that and see such a place? A great column of rock in the sea, Da says. What a sight that will be.

She would like to see it herself, is the truth of it. She would like to travel towards it on the boat, off the edge of the charted world, to feel the swell of the sea currents beneath her, to go to a place that doesn't yet appear on any map.

Enda runs, hitching up her skirts. She cannot help it, she must move her limbs, make her heart hammer in her chest, for she cannot abide the sitting that women must do: by the fire, at the table, at the pot, by the cow, by the tub. She runs to the field, to the boreen, to the haggard, to the stream, but there is no sign of Liam anywhere. There is only the dog, standing a short distance away, staring into the trees, ears pricked, as if waiting for a signal.

The new baby is a source of quiet and straightforward pleasure to Tomás. It's not always easy to get at the child, so surrounded as he is by visitors and women, so often is he either asleep or at suck or having his lower areas cleaned, but Tomás totes him outside sometimes, when he comes in from the field. He likes to position the crib near his chair of an evening, while he makes plans for the mapping ahead, so that he can glance down on the infant's face as he slumbers; the flicker of dreams animates his tiny eyebrows, his pout of a mouth. All your cares seem to fall away when regarding this countenance. Four children is a good number, it seems to Tomás, a solid and dependable one. A table has four legs, as does a chair or a bed, and now his family has the same evenness and stability.

The child is watchful, quiet, rarely cries, and if left near a source of light—the window, the glimmer of the fire—will stare at it for hours. He has black hair, like Rose, and blue eyes, like Liam and Phina, and Enda's determined brow, and when he sleeps he clenches his fists, almost as if, it seems to Tomás, he holds a spear or a sword in them, as if he is ready for battle. Eugene looks like all of them, yet none of them: he is entirely and singularly himself. The rare noises he makes are questioning, quizzical, as if he is requesting an explanation of the world he has entered: Ah-blee? he says, from his crib. Ai-ah? Bubbles of noise rise from him, float through the air of the cottage and out of the half-door, to hover around the flat platform of land.

Ga-nang, Eugene demands of the dust motes, the bowls on the shelf, the birch trees, the birds of the sky, the tiny yellow marsh-flowers. Yee-ur?

How much there is to do! Phina must feed the infant and cook and milk the cow and collect the eggs. He, Tomás, must ready himself for when he leaves on his commission. He must scythe the grass and feed the beasts and dig the drills; he must chop the wood and fix the loose window; he must mulch the fields early, ready for the next planting. He must prepare all that he and Liam need for this trip to the island, get Phina to check over their clothing and boots. So much to think about, so much to take care of. His head, it seems to him, is split in two: this house and his family occupy one half, while the other is filled with thoughts of the island, said to be a remote and barren place where the people speak their own dialect. He doesn't wish to go, and yet he does. He would like to stay here, to see the winter in this cottage, yet the scale of the commission gives him darts of excitement: to map those cliffs and draw the corresponding sketch, his son at his side. He cannot help but anticipate the pleasure of the work.

The thought, however, that he will be working once again for the redcoats crouches like a toad at the back of his mind. He made a promise to Phina, or she dragged one out of him, and he sees that she is right: they cannot live here without the money he will make from the work; he cannot pay the rent and feed the children without those wages. So he goes to call on the viscount's land steward, pays him four months' rent in advance, and checks, several times, that the man understands Tomás will be back, that the family are not to be turned out of the cottage, that he will be returning with money in his pocket to pay whatever arrears might be outstanding. Then Tomás walks out, a few evenings in a row, to knock on the doors of the neighbours, to ask them to keep an eye on his wife and children while he is away.

Tomás is in the byre with Liam, forking hay and thinking about the islanders, the steep and craggy columns of rock they call home, which are possibly basalt or even granite, when he happens to glance out of the doorway and sees, to his amazement, an enormous dog.

There, in the yard, lying alongside Rose, stretched out on the ground, a patch of sunlight printed across its belly, looking for all the world as if it belongs here.

Tomás flings down the fork and comes out into the open air.

"Whatever is that?" he demands, his finger extended towards it.

"The dog, Da," his daughter says, without looking up.

"I can see that," he blusters, "but what is it doing here?"

Rose laughs. She rolls over, her legs in the air, then back, fitting herself ever closer to the beast. "He lives here!"

"Does he, by God? Since when?"

"Since ages."

"Rose and Enda found him," murmurs Liam, who has come up behind them, "the day Eugene was born. Have you really not noticed him before?"

Tomás strides to the haggard; the morning is warm, bees cross-stitching the late-summer air. Phina sits at the cow's side, her hands working beneath, baby tied with a shawl to her back, saying something to Enda about putting down that fiddle and taking some eggs over to the elderly sisters, and Enda is saying she shan't, she won't, send Liam instead—

"Phina," Tomás calls, "did you know there's a dog here?"

"Mind what I say, Enda. Liam has studying to do," Phina is saying, and she dips a finger in the froth of the milk and inscribes a hasty cross on the beast's side. "You mean Bran?"

"He has a name?"

"Da," Rose says, from her place on the grass, "he's called Bran. You know that."

"Since when," he calls to Phina again, "do we have a dog?"

"Go now," she murmurs to Enda, "and take the basket." She turns to Tomás. "Since ages," she says.

Tomás walks over to the dog, to get a look at it, or rather at the dog-and-girl combination, for the two lie entwined together on the ground, like one being, Liam standing above them. As Tomás gets close, the dog jerks its head up, alert, awake in an instant at the sound of footsteps, giving a warning rumble from its throat.

"Growl at me, would you?" Tomás exclaims, but he stops in his tracks because a dog like that could break a man's arm if it was minded to do so. "A good guard dog, is he?"

"Of course," Rose says dreamily, pressing her nose into the fur of the animal's neck. "He won't let anyone come near when we go out walking."

Tomás considers this. "And does he snarl at you like that? Does he bite you ever? Does he show his teeth?"

"Not to me. Only to anyone he thinks might harm me."

He wants to object, because opposition is his first instinct, because no one asked him if a dog could come and live with them, because the animal is so huge and ferocious-looking, but his imminent departure presses upon his mind.

"He'll take care of you, then, while Liam and I are gone?"

"He will. He always does." Rose bends over the animal and whispers in his ear: "You don't need to worry about Da. He won't hurt you."

It seems to Tomás, however, that there is something strange about the animal. It seems to him that the dog's gaze rests on him more often than not. When Tomás is sitting at the table for his meal or putting on his boots by the door, he feels the press of the animal's gaze, as if it knows too much, as if it sees everything.

He says this to Phina, late one night, as they sit by the fire together. She is nursing the baby before they take to their bed, the bundled form held against her; he is also peculiarly aware of the hovering presence of his father in the room, perhaps near the doorway or over by the ladder, his face full of disappointment in him, for failing to give him a peaceful resting place. Tomás will not look, however, will not seek him out. Sure enough, the dog, which had been asleep by the fire, keeps raising its head with a low growl, the fur on its neck bristling, its eyes glowing like coals.

Phina looks at him, warily, searchingly, and Tomás thinks again, as he often does, of seeing her for the first time, beside the cart, her mother's shawl around her.

"You're saying," she whispers carefully, "that you think the dog knows things about you?"

Tomás nods, his stubble rasping against his collar. Over by the window, to the left of Phina, the form of his father presses on the darkness, making himself briefly visible, his arm missing from the shoulder, taken of course by the swine; Bran leaps to his feet and lets out a bark. Phina shushes him, orders him to lie down. Tomás blinks, hard, and then the apparition is gone.

Phina's expression is careful. "What kind of things?"

He cannot look up, he won't, and he cannot voice his shame for his wife. "Bad things," is all he can say, willing Phina to understand the worst about him, his failure as a son, but how could she? The thing is unimaginable, after all.

Phina clicks her tongue, puts a hand to his cheek. "Sure, what bad things are there to know?"

Tomás springs up, shaking off her touch, scattering and shedding his thoughts: he will not dwell on such things, he will not. He starts rattling the fire-irons, tamping down the turf.

"Tomás?" she says.

Quick, he thinks, talk about something else—anything. He paces from one side of the fire to the other, keeping close to its light, avoiding the room's dark corners.

"Do you ever wonder that Liam perhaps doesn't want to be a mapper?" he blurts out, surprising himself. "Sometimes he seems—he seems— Well, as if he . . . I don't know what that priest has been filling his head with but if I find out—"

He hurls the poker away from him and sits down, his head in his hands, his eyes shut tight. He waits, now, for Phina to say something reassuring. That he is imagining things. That Liam is looking forward to the trip out to the island.

But she doesn't.

"My love," Phina smooths the hair on the back of his neck, "are you . . ." even with his eyes closed Tomás can sense her selecting her words, trying to erase the concern in her voice ". . . quite well? You don't . . . think that your . . . your melancholy from last year might be returning?"

Tomás opens his eyes in astonishment. He looks at the floor, at his socked feet. "Not at all," he snaps, "why would you say that? Aren't you the one insisting I take this work?"

Phina rises, lifting the baby to her shoulder and rubbing his spine. She walks to the door and back in the slow way women have when they are carrying an infant. "Have you talked to Liam?"

"Talked?" Tomás repeats, shocked. "Whatever do you mean?"

"About the island. About being your apprentice. About missing school."

Tomás fidgets with the cushion on his chair, crushing it between his hands. "What is there to say?"

"It may be . . ." Phina says, and Tomás feels she is once again selecting her words ". . . that he needs to be persuaded, that he may not wish to come or—"

"Not wish to come?" Tomás stands up so abruptly he knocks a plate to the floor. "What have the boy's wishes to do with anything? He has no notion of how lucky he is, to be given a chance like this."

The next day, however, he leaves off halfway through his scything. He finds Liam sitting at the table, bare feet resting on the dog, a book propped up against a bowl; the boy is copying something, his tongue pressed into his inner cheek, his fingertips blackened by ink.

"There you are now," Tomás says.

His son looks up from his copybook and his eyes are like two birds' eggs, implacable and still.

"We'll be off next week," Tomás begins gruffly, "you and I."

Liam blinks slowly, as if having trouble understanding the meaning of this sentence, or as if his thoughts are still with his lesson. Tomás glances down at the page beneath his son's hand, expecting to see mathematics or algebra, but he sees instead that it is some kind of psalm or prayer that Liam is writing out. Why would you be copying that, he is about to ask him, but, fleetingly, he has a peculiar and uncomfortable sensation of a crevasse zigzagging through the ground between the two of them, as if they are in the grip of a seismic event and the floor of the cottage is splitting open. He has to shake his head to rid himself of it.

"Off where?" Liam asks.

"To the island, of course." Tomás shuffles his feet, puzzled. Again, the sensation that the ground is shifting and that he is standing on one side of a huge fissure, with Liam on the other. He tries to remember what Phina says to him about Liam: try to talk to him with kindness, don't be too brusque.

"We'll have ourselves a grand time, won't we," he raps the table in what he hopes is a jocular fashion, "out there in the ocean? You and me together, like before. We'll be rowed out there on a boat, I'm told, like . . . like seafarers or . . . or explorers."

Liam glances down at his hands then back up at his father. "But I'm not wanting to miss school," he says, in a distant, almost formal voice.

"Ah, now," Tomás blusters, "what boy wouldn't like a few months away from the desk? Sure, your friends will be eaten up with jealousy. There'll be Norse ruins . . . seabirds . . . some interesting rock formations . . . We'll be the first surveyors on the island, did you know that?"

"Father Joseph says I need to be preparing for my examination in—"

"I wrote him a note," Tomás cries. "I gave it to him, after mass, it must have been a month ago now, so the man knows full well that—"

"He says I shouldn't be going if I want to pass—"

"You're *my* son!" The words, emphatic and furious, appear from nowhere. "And I say you're going."

Liam is silent, staring down at his psalm or whatever it is. Tomás presses a fist to his mouth, trying to bring his fury to heel. Why does the boy look so shifty, so reluctant? What is it that has come between them?

He tries again: "The redcoats have some fancy new tools, I hear. I'll be needing all the help I can get. It'll be just the two of us. With a couple of *dundarlán* sappers in tow, of course, but it will be a real adventure, won't it?"

Liam still says nothing.

Tomás stares at him, floored. He is filled with an urge to grab him by the shoulders, to give him a shake, to say, Whatever is it, whatever is wrong, why won't you look me in the eye, I'm your father. This island will be the making of us, as a mapping team, can't you see that? Then we will always work together, you and I, like a pair of hands.

He shoves his own hands into his pockets, then takes them out.

"We'll make a deal, will we?" Tomás says, trying again for a jovial tone. "You help me out there, and when we get back, I'll help you study for the examination. Every night, if need be. How about that?"

Liam lays down the pen he is holding and turns a page in his book.

"So," Tomás says, after a moment, "that's it, then. We're all set. We'll leave in a week."

Days later, in the early dawn, Liam hurries away from the house, pushing his arms into the sleeves of his jacket. It is that time of day when the clouds are a darker blue than the sky behind them. He has timed it perfectly, he thinks, before anyone else is awake, even the baby: no one will wonder at his absence for a good while. The dog is still asleep by the hearth, so Liam needn't worry about being followed or given away by barking. His father, who is a devilishly light sleeper, is away with the redcoats already, finalising the arrangements at their base camp.

Liam passes through the yard, past the pump, through the field, the donkey's soft nose rising into the air to sniff at his scent. Liam puts out a hand and strokes the damp nap of its face.

He moves quickly onto untended ground, his boots finding footholds between the gulleys and streams. He is trying not to think too much, not to dwell, is keeping his thoughts practical.

The rim of metal presses into the skin of his palm: whatever happens, if he falls, if he stumbles, he mustn't drop it.

It has to be his most precious possession, an item that means everything to him. Liam has spent sleepless hours pondering this; he has thought about it as he made the long hike down the hillside in the mornings, as he walked the long road to school, as he returned in the evening. He has considered all his treasures, one by one: a penny he found on the road, a piece of coral from the beach, the whitened jawbone of a fox, complete with teeth, a hawk's feather. And then, in bed one night, his mind offered up to him the saint's medallion, given to him by Father Joseph the first time Liam had performed his duties as altar boy at mass. He slid his hand beneath his pillow and felt it there, its smooth edges, the raised effigy of the saint, the tiny stars adorning the halo, the loop of metal at its top, and he had been filled with a bright, sharp pain because of course this was his thing-most-precious, his treasure, because it would hurt him to give it away, but wasn't that what Father Joseph would call the essence of sacrifice?

Liam casts a look over his shoulder. The cottage is further away now: a long box with a covering of thatch, a cursive slant of smoke rising from one end. Inside it is his family, minus his father: his mother, his sisters, his baby brother. None of them know what he's up to; none of them know what is in his head.

The copse reveals itself suddenly, from behind an incline, just as it did that first day; it is almost possible to miss, if you don't know what you're looking for. Liam stops again, his heart punching at his ribs, from either the climb or fear.

He doesn't want to do it but he must. He doesn't want to do it but he can't not.

He shifts from one foot to the other; he puts the medallion into his left hand, then back to his right; without intending to, he lets out a whimper of distress and the sound scares him, so he clamps his lips shut.

He looks up and around. The two hillocks, the high mountain ahead. The darkness has faded even more, draining from the sky. It won't be long until daylight and then his mother will wake up and they might come looking for him. It must be now. Now or never.

He incants these words to himself as he moves forward, towards the copse, and steps inside. *Now or never, now or never, now—*

It is the same yet different. There are the tussocks, and he is careful to tread between them, and there the twisting stream, but the sense of a green house is gone. The oppressive and frightening atmosphere is absent. It was, of course, spring when he was here before and now the leaves are almost off the trees and the ground is thick with rust and yellow and brown, with layer upon layer of discarded wet foliage. It's possible to see out through the trees now, to catch a glimpse of the mountain and the valley below.

Liam hears his laboured breathing and the thudding of his heart as he picks his way along the stream, moving upwards, and he hums to himself, just for the comfort of the sound, just so his thoughts won't run along the tracks he fears—the little graves, the laughter he heard here, his father's madness, the loss of his boot—and he realises it's a song Enda has been playing, over and over again, but he doesn't care because anything that distracts his mind is welcome.

The well appears much more swiftly than he'd anticipated. He'd imagined a long trek through the wet trees, or having to search for it among the trunks, but he sees that he's been tracing its path all this time and here it is: the holy well, the sacred spring, the very thing that altered the course of all their lives. Without it, he knows, they would still be living in the Lanes, his father would never have become garrulous and then silent, and he would still be sitting at the back of the classroom, watching as Enda put up her hand to answer every question the master asked.

Liam pauses, stock still, in a stance of polite obedience, feet together, fingers laced, before recognising it as the pose he adopts when serving at mass, and he drops his hands to his sides.

What he feels is a faint sense of disappointment. He'd expected it to be much larger, with statues, perhaps, or offerings tied to the trees, signs of pleas and heathen devotions: Father Joseph had described such practices at school. He had told them, as he stood at the front of the class, that in ancient times people had worshipped things they could see, the seasons and the land; they believed in hydromancy—and wasn't that a beautiful word, boys, derived, of course, from the Greek?—and they made offerings of their most precious possessions in return for wishes fulfilled or curses made.

But instead of a watery dell of druidical promises, this is just a pool, roughly circular, deeper than he might have guessed, and somewhat unremarkable, with a great deal of greenery growing around it, ferns and lichen, a blanket of moss, complex webs of ivy. He shuffles forward, wanting and yet not wanting to look down into the waters.

The surface is dark and implacable. He can see in it only fragments of the inky sky above, striated by black branches, a hovering image of his own chalky face. There is a faint stirring from the far side and he can picture his father rumbling something about subterranean water tables, then tries to banish the thought, because he doesn't want to think about Tomás and this well, about what happened or might have happened, he doesn't want to drink the waters or get them on his skin or his clothes, not at all—he doesn't want to catch the madness or the distemper or whatever it was—he wants to make his plea and get away. So he squeezes his eyes shut, he grips his medallion and he says the words he rehearsed last night, as he lay awake under the thatch: "Please let me not go to the island tomorrow with my da. I don't want to go. I want to stay here. I . . ." He swallows, passes his tongue across suddenly dry lips, wondering what, if anything, to say next, and then he hears the following words, in what sounds like his own voice, "I don't want to be a mapper, I want to be a priest."

Liam's eyes spring open. He is all astonishment. He hadn't meant to say that last part: it seemed to spill out of him without his will. He hasn't even thought it or articulated it, but now he has heard it, in his own voice, he knows it to be true. He wants to be a priest; he wants to wear long black robes, to take mass, to hear people's confessions; he wants to lay his hands on the crowns of heads and say, Bless you, my child; he wants to be a man of God, to have a face as serene and unlined as Father Joseph, a life of regularity and rules and duties all laid out for him. He wants the soothing chime of the bell to punctuate his days, to be wrapped in trails of incense smoke; he wants to stand before a row of kneeling people, saying the stirring words, Behold the Lamb of God. Liam can hardly breathe for excitement. It is as if his whole life, the years ahead, have been unrolled before him, like a beautiful woven carpet.

He gazes at the dark waters, confounded, amazed. He watches as an arm—which must be his because there is his jersey sleeve, his shirt cuff—extends over the pool, as the fingers uncurl. The medallion drops, turning and turning, flashing gold in the remaining light, the face of the saint with the halo of stars appearing and disappearing. There is a discreet, gulping sound as the well receives it, and Liam watches it tumble into obscurity, swallowed by the dark depths, never to be seen again.

Immediately, from just behind him, comes a noise: a horrible, hair-raising, tortured squeal that razors the air, that shrinks the skin on his body. Liam jack-knifes into himself, simultaneously cringing and spinning round, a shriek of fear leaving his mouth.

"Who's that?" he cries, stumbling to the side, splashing clumsily into the lip of the pool, his boots soaked, water instantly invading his socks. The sound comes again and he flails blindly in a circle, as if to ward off an enemy, arms windmilling, but there is nothing behind him, to the side, in front of him except trees, trees, trees and leaves, leaves, leaves, the gurgling of the spring, which he mustn't fall into for he feels very strongly that he might never get out. Then he's off, sloshing, lurching, desperate to get away from this place, crashing through branches and twigs, just like before, and he hears that shiver of laughter, again, and he is crying now, letting out incoherent words, please, God, help me, please, and he senses, even in his panic, the glow of light that means the edge of the copse and he hurls himself towards it, blindly, and then he sees something that makes him stop so suddenly he has to reach out and grab a tree trunk to stop himself falling over.

An airborne shadowy figure, arms wide, floating in the sky, beyond the black bronchial spread of a leafless tree. It's a vision—an angel—come to save him, to guide him! Or is it the Devil, appearing to him in celestial form, to trick him?

Liam's jaw falls open to let out a scream or a prayer, he doesn't know which.

"You'd better shut your mouth," says the angel, "or you'll be swallowing flies."

His fists tighten, his pulse leaps. It is no angel after all—how can he have thought it was? It is none other than his sister, Enda, there in the copse, in her nightgown, perched in the lower branches of a tree, filthy feet dangling. She must have followed him here to see what he was up to. She is grinning down at him, her fiddle at the ready, bow in hand.

"Enda?" he gasps, almost fearful of the answer—what if it's not her but some spirit who has taken on her form, the better to lead him into danger?

By way of reply, she smiles and brings down her bow on the strings: a cluster of notes leaps out into the damp air, and Liam realises, with both relief and fury, that was the sound he'd heard, the noise that had frightened him out of his wits.

"Enda," he hisses, and he's almost sure it's really her and not some malevolent vision, because there is the raw edge of her thumbnail where she's chewed it, and there is the smut on her cheek.

"So," she calls, over the sawing music of her fiddle, "you want to be a priest."

He flushes scarlet, the heat rising to his neck, his cheeks. He is invaded, colonised by instant fury. How dare she come here and listen in on him?

"I—never—you shouldn't be eavesdropping like that—spying on me."

"I'm not."

"You are so. You can't just—you can't be—" He kicks the ground, so incensed is he. "I'm going to tell Mammy and—"

She fits her fiddle under her chin, and steadying herself with just one foot hooked daringly around a branch, she plays a group of notes and sings in a loud voice: "There was a young boy called Liam and he didn't want to be a mapper . . . He wanted to train as a priest . . . to wear a long dress and look . . . dapper."

With a bellow, Liam launches himself into the tree, grabbing at branch after branch, hauling himself up at surprising speed, fuelled by ire and loathing. He will stop her song, he will stop her mocking, if it's the last thing he does.

"I'll kill you," he hears himself scream, "so I will."

Enda lets out a peal of mocking laughter and scrambles higher, fiddle and bow tucked under one arm, and Liam, climbing after her, fixes his murderous gaze on the gleaming wood of her instrument. He will seize it and dash it to the ground, and good riddance to it. She is three branches above him, now two, and he is gaining on her and he sees a spark of alarm in her eyes now because she hadn't known he was this agile, this fearless, she hadn't noticed until now how much he's grown, and she's running out of tree: he has her, she's trapped.

He sets his teeth, and gripping the trunk with one arm, he lunges at her.

"Get off," she spits, her teeth bared, like a cat. "I didn't mean it. I was only messing. Stop now. You'll break my—"

"I'm going to smash it up, you see if I don't!"

"Liam, stop," she says, and her pleading tone is so unfamiliar to him, so thrilling, "please. I'm sorry. I won't tell, of course I won't."

But a kind of savagery has descended upon Liam. Fuelled by her fear, blind to the consequences, he makes a grab for her foot, as if he means to unseat her entirely from the tree, and seizes her toe in his hand. He has it right there, in his palm. At this point, had Liam been in his right mind, he might have paused: he and Enda have reached brinks like this before, where rivalrous bickering turns serious, where harmless fights tip over into danger. Liam, however, is not in his right mind. He yanks at her foot as she sits there, clinging to the top of a tall tree. He shakes it, a dog with a rat, with every ounce of his strength.

"Li," he hears her cry, "Li, don't, I'll fall—I'll—I'm sorry—please stop." But the terror in her voice only spurs him on. For once, for perhaps the first time, he has her. It's as if he's wearing blinkers: all he can think is that he's suddenly stronger than her, bigger than her; he is top dog. He's about to destroy that fiddle, her most precious possession, and then he'll deal with her.

Enda, however, is not one to give in. She tightens her hold on the tree, she squeezes her eyes shut, and she kicks out with her other foot, trying to free herself from his clutches. One of her heels connects with a part of him—afterwards she'll wonder if it was his shoulder or his chest, something soft and cloth-covered—and his grip on her foot is gone, she is free, and her brother is still there with her in the tree, but then there is a long moment of silence as he is pulled away from her, down to the ground below, his face a pale mask of surprise, his body dropping through the branches, cracking against them as he falls, flipped like a puppet, down, down, until he hits the earth with a thud.

And then Enda is alone in the tree once more.

Phina is deep in sleep, dreaming about ladders, salt-saturated and tilting with the motion of waves, when she hears the noise.

Her body reacts before her mind. There is a certain type of cry that sets a mother in motion before she's even aware of what she's doing: it's something in the pitch or the timbre that alerts the animal part of her brain to some manner of disaster.

One moment Phina is sleeping, deep in a maritime nightmare, the next she is out of bed, out of the house, the baby tucked into her shawl, hurrying awkwardly towards the sound.

"What?" she finds herself yelling, at the air, at which child she doesn't know. "What is it? Where are you?"

Her eyes catch sight of a figure streaking out of the trees up the slope: a blaze of auburn hair, white nightshirt, legs working like pistons. Enda.

Phina sets her course straight for her, a stone catapulted towards a target, and child and mother meet in the middle of the meadow where the donkey is tethered to a stake. Phina seizes Enda around the arm and looks her over. The girl's face is stricken, her hands green and grazed, but there are no obvious injuries.

"Mammy—Mammy," she gasps, "I'm so—so—sorry—I—"

"Whatever's happened?"

Enda points towards the mountain and the copse at its base with a shaking finger and utters the terrible words: "It's Liam."

Phina hands the baby to Enda, and for the first time in years, she runs: away from her daughter, up the slope, between the hills, along the stream, towards the trees. Her body is still sore and soft from the birth, her chest engorged, her innards not yet settled back into place, but still she runs like a startled hare, into the trees, through the briars and the leaves.

"Liam!" she screams, to the dark trunks, to the mossy stones. "Liam!"

The branches catch at her hair, the streams mumble and gabble. Phina turns, her bare soles skidding on pebbles and leaf-fall, and turns again, peering into the greenish shade. She has never set foot in these trees: Tomás has told the children, and her, that it isn't a safe place to be, and she had obeyed him but, nevertheless, here she is.

"Li!" she calls again. "Where are you?"

Behind her, outside the copse, she can hear the voices of Enda and Rose, the latter asking questions, and the former telling her to hush.

Phina stands still. She reaches for the frond of fern and grips it in her hand, and as she does so, a drift of sound reaches her ear: it is lower than the noise of the water, softer than the susurrations of the leaves. It is something like a sigh or an exhalation.

Her head snaps around. There, through the greenery, she catches a glimpse of something white, then the trees move over it and it vanishes, but Phina is off, dodging one trunk, then the next, and she is thinking, Dear God, is the child dead? and she forms the word, *please*, under her breath: *please. Let him live and take my life instead.*

Suddenly there he is, her son, stretched out and on the ground, between some small tussocks, at the base of a tree, his chest moving up and down in soundless gasps. He is dazed but coming round, blinking up at the light. She kneels, eyes darting about, taking in his injuries. His shin is clearly broken, bent at an odd and unnatural angle, a snapped bone pushing at tautened skin, and his face is ashen, with a duck-egg lump on the forehead. She lets out the breath she didn't know she'd been holding. Nothing here that won't mend.

By the time the girls arrive, both snivelling, the baby held in Enda's arms, Phina has already formed a plan.

"Enda," Phina says, "give the baby to Rose."

"But, Mammy," Enda whispers, "you told us—"

"I know what I said. That Rosie's too little to lift him. But she's to take him now. I need you to help me get Liam into the house."

Rose holds out both arms and takes the bundle that is Eugene, full of the solemnity of the task.

Enda shuffles towards Liam, and Phina indicates that she should take hold of his shoulders.

"He's not dead?" Enda whispers, as they heft him between them, Liam moaning and wincing with each jolt.

"Course I'm not fecking dead," he mutters.

"You mind your tongue," Phina says. "He's just concussed. And has a broken shin into the bargain."

Between them, they carry Liam down the slope, past the donkey and the cow, through the haggard and into the cottage, where they lay him by the hearth and cover him with blankets.

"Run now," Phina tells Enda, "for the sisters at the end of the village. They know how to set bones."

The two elderly women arrive with a stook of willow sticks and a powder that the older sister mixes with water and heats on the fire as the younger touches the tips of her fingers to Liam's snapped leg, the purpled and bruised lump on his head. "Why do you do that?" Rose asks, squatting down next to them. "Will it hurt him, can you make him better?"

"We can," the older sister says, "but hope."

The younger sister says nothing but mumbles and hums to herself as she presses her gnarled, wrinkled hands on different parts of Liam. Phina watches from the chair as she feeds Eugene; Enda sits at the table, plucking distractedly at her fiddle strings.

Without warning, without so much as a pause in her humming, the younger sister grips Liam's mangled shin and there is a horrible crunching sound, followed by an outraged shriek from Liam, as she snaps it back into shape. Then she wordlessly reaches for the heated pan. She ties splints of willow to Liam's calf and covers them with the greenish clay powder. Taking torn strips of cloth, she binds it, round and round, until the broken leg resembles a chrysalis.

When they leave, Liam is quiet. He chews the herbs they left for him, then sleeps until dusk. When he wakes, he looks at Enda and says: "I'm so hungry."

With meticulous and considered movements, Phina breaks first one egg then another onto a griddle. The shells she lays to one side: she will grind them up later for use on the vegetable path, for they are the best way to keep the slugs off her scallions and lettuces.

Watching her from the hearth are her two eldest children, Liam sitting in a chair, his leg bound and raised on a stool, Enda crouched beside him. She seems not to want to leave his side, Phina has noticed. Rose is asleep up in the loft; the baby is snug in his swaddling clothes in the cradle, violet lids twitching as he dreams his unfathomable dreams.

Phina scrapes the eggs onto two plates, adds a slice of bread, and hands them both to Enda. She observes that her daughter feeds Liam first, before herself, spooning the food into her brother's mouth with care, bit by bit, without being asked.

Phina positions herself before them, hands on hips. "What happened at all?" she asks them.

Enda and Liam exchange a glance. Neither of them answers.

"Well?"

"It was my fault," Enda mutters, "I—"

"We were just messing," Liam interrupts. "That's all. It was nobody's fault."

Phina looks from Enda to Liam and back again. Liam flushes under his waxy countenance, then Phina sees him tap his sister's arm with a finger, and something like a pact passes between them. She will never get the truth from them. They are keeping a secret for the other and she isn't to be told.

She sighs. She paces to the door and looks out at the darkening sky. She leans over the cradle to check on the child. As she straightens the bonnet on the baby's head, she says, without looking at them both: "The question now, of course, is what we do about your father. And the redcoats."

Again, Liam and Enda glance at each other, then away, as if the secrets between them are too potent, too dangerous.

"You, Liam, are supposed to meet him, and the division, tomorrow morning, at the clock tower in town. But you'll not be going anywhere," Phina continues, "so either we get him to delay his trip—"

"The redcoats will never agree to that," Liam mutters. "We'll lose the pay."

"Or your father goes alone."

There is an uncomfortable silence. Liam picks unhappily at a loose end in the sleeve of his jersey. Eugene in his cradle gives a squawk like that of a songbird that has sighted a cat. And Phina is distracted, oddly, by the sight of Enda, who is chewing the crust of her bread, apparently listening, her legs folded under her, but Phina wonders if she is actually thinking about something else entirely. Her daughter seems abstracted, as if the conversation has nothing to do with her, a matter between her brother and her mother, and she is merely waiting to see what the outcome will be. Despite everything else that's going on, Enda's sense of exclusion pains Phina in a way she can't quite identify. Why shouldn't Enda feel part of this, just because she is a girl? Added to this is the fact that Enda, Phina realises, is the one whose opinion she would like to hear: her mind is quick; she is uncowed by life, ready to embrace and parry whatever it might throw at her. Enda—Phina's fierce, impulsive daughter, whose intelligence does not mark her out for an easy life—is the most likely to come up with a solution.

"He mustn't," Liam is saying hoarsely, his face turned to the fire. "He mustn't go alone. We don't know what might . . . We can't let that happen."

Phina unties and reties her apron with nervous fingers. The truth of what Liam is saying moves through her, like blood through organs, like water through a landscape. Liam is right, of course he is. Tomás cannot go alone. What if he gets the melancholy when he's out there on the island? What if he doesn't make it back this time?

She glances again at Enda and is struck anew by the injustice of her daughter's position, by what she has lost in coming here to the peninsula. Her education, her friends, the possibility of training to be a teacher. And now only this: a decimated village on a windswept tongue of land, no schooling, no companions other than her siblings, and no future other than being taken in marriage by a farmer or a fisherman. Phina cannot see Enda as a biddable country wife. It makes her want to stamp her foot, makes her want to grab Tomás by the lapels and say, Do you see what you've done to her?

Phina shuts her eyes, purses her mouth. For a moment, behind her lids, inked in light, she seems to see the patterns of trees, the deltas of boughs spreading into branches spreading into twigs spreading into foliage.

"There is another way," she hears herself say.

~

The journey to the island is, as Tomás expected, arduous and long. The division's ungainly charabanc of carts, horses, sappers marching in approximate unison, equipment and supplies lashed to their backs, charts rolled into leather holders, accompanies them from the town, as far as the coast, where Tomás, two sappers and Liam are set down. The division continues on its way while Tomás waits for a favourable tide on the curved stone harbour of a village he has never been to before. It's a cluttered place with cottages crouched low beneath a cliff, half-seen faces peeping out from behind doors left ajar, then ducking out of sight when they see the soldiers.

The sappers doze in the shelter of the harbour wall, caps over their eyes. Tomás goes over his notes, the details of his commission. Liam, he is distantly aware, climbs up and over the rocks and along the cliff-face.

When their boat finally appears, on an outgoing tide, the boy seems eager to get aboard: his is a black shape at the corner of Tomás's eye that leaps from the harbour to the currach before the boatmen have a chance to beckon them forward, shouldering perhaps more baggage than his thin frame can realistically handle. Tomás is heartened by this, but doesn't of course praise him—it wouldn't do for the boy to get a big head. All the same, it pleases Tomás that the child seems to have caught some enthusiasm for the trip. As the currach detaches itself slowly from the harbour wall, the boatmen pulling and sculling on their oars, the people from the cottages coming out to watch, now that the soldiers are safely onboard, Tomás feels an unaccustomed lightness in his chest: he and his son, at work together. He pictures them, for years to come, striking out like this, the pair of them.

As the mainland recedes, he reaches out a hand and pats his son, only a little too hard, on the back. Then, so as the boy doesn't get the idea that life in a surveying division will be easy, he orders him to sort out their packs. Stack them neatly there, child, against the side, where no one will trip on them.

The boy turns instantly and bends to lift and tidy their things. Tomás, mollified, oblivious now to everything but the task ahead, turns to look across the water, and at a column of rock emerging from the smudged line that divides sea from sky. A light tremor of apprehension reaches him, like distant thunder, and he gropes for his logbook.

The island appears at first, he writes, in an uneven hand but that is only due to the pitching of the boat, nothing more, *as inhospitable as may be, solid dark rock—in all probability basalt—with a deep channel of dangerous water running through it at the velocity of a river-current. A multitude of seabirds, gannets and black-headed gulls wheel around the island in a mostly clockwise motion, driven by a prevailing wind in a direction of north-north—*

Tomás looks up from his page, wondering where they might find a landing on such a place, pulling his compass from his pocket, squinting up at the sun, to establish whether they have yet altered their course from west-south-west to south-south-west, as he predicted they would, when he is aware, at the corner of his eye, of a sudden movement, like that of a bird, but it is instead the cap being torn from the head of his son by the stiff breeze, and hadn't Tomás told the child to remove it before they set sail, but he didn't listen, and now he will have a cold head for the length of their stay. When Tomás glances over, to give the child a stern told-you-so look, he thinks his eyes are deceiving him or his mind playing a trick on him because he sees, or seems to see, not his son, but his daughter.

Tomás starts, turns his head and then his whole body towards the child.

There! Sitting at the side of the boat, one arm dangling over the side so that she may skim the water with her fingers, the two long plaits of her hair whipping behind her, is his daughter! Enda! Right there, bold as anything.

Tomás's hands convulse on the page of his book, snatching at his pencil. He turns the other way, and sees their pack, the boxes of supplies, the instruments, the boatman, the two redcoat sappers, who are leaning weakly over the sides, puking like puppies. No Liam.

"By God," he cries, letting book and pencils fall, lurching across the wooden floor of the currach, causing it to rock and pitch, and the boatman to yell at him to sit down, for the love of God, seizing Enda by the arm, "what are you doing here? Where's your brother?"

Enda turns and looks up at him in that brazen and provoking way she has, face set. She shrugs and says something but the wind snatches away her words.

"What's that?" Tomás shouts, shaking her by the arm, ignoring the boatmen who are still bawling at Tomás to sit down.

She repeats herself: a garbled account of a tree and a broken shinbone and a plan of Mammy's and the copse and something about a bonesetter, but three things are clear to Tomás: that he's been tricked, that Liam will not be assisting him on the island, and that Enda will have to stay for the duration of the project because the boatmen will not risk the winter tides after this.

A hand of a boatman reaches out and yanks Tomás down, and he acquiesces, numbly, unthinkingly.

The seabirds shriek and keen above his head, gliding in huge and invisible circles, and the merciless rocks of the island where he will spend months of his life loom ever closer, and Tomás sees himself as if on a map of the entire country, a pinprick, a fleck, tiny and wholly insignificant.

The two sappers seated on the planked bench at the stern of the flimsy vessel, one of whom lost his breakfast only minutes before, are distracted from their seasickness by the sight of the native labourer, a taciturn and grumpy chap whom it's usually hard to get a single word out of, becoming animated. The man, for no reason at all that the sappers can see, suddenly flings down his work and leaps up, lurching across the boat to engage in an animated and heated argument with his daughter.

The sappers perk up, their nausea forgotten, nudging each other.

The sea is choppy and freezing, and the island ahead, where they have been billeted for months, looks to be as cold as a witch's tit, and this piss-poor boat seems ill-equipped for such a perilous trip. For now, however, the dumb show at the front of the boat is providing a modicum of entertainment.

The labourer seems furious about something, and other people's anger is always amusing. He is a funny-looking chap anyway, with bandy legs, very few teeth, and the furtive, squinty look of most of his type. The soldiers watch, grin, as he gesticulates to the bay behind them, then to the girl and back again, the pair of them gabbling away in their impenetrable patois.

With an impatient bark, the boatmen pull the labourer down to a seated position and continue to row, as if nothing at all is happening, their backs to the wind, their oars scooping into the water, lifting, scooping again.

When the division had picked up the labourer's child at the clock tower, the soldiers had been flabbergasted, the taller sapper saying to the other, Good Lord, it's a girl—the man's bringing along his daughter, can you believe it? They had been expecting the son, like last time, and a female on such an expedition was unheard of. But then the natives here are unfathomable, always doing what you least expect—there's no reasoning with them.

As she had clambered aboard the cart, her father barely glanced up or acknowledged her arrival, but the two soldiers had both looked her over, immediately and instinctively, the way they, as men, were obliged to do when a female came near. She had curled into herself, chin down, avoiding their eyes, gathering her bundles around her, pulling her hat down low. And they came to the conclusion that she was not worth their notice: a scrawny and stringy type, flat-chested, not of an age or build to excite any particular interest and, what was more, wearing an ancient and patched boy's jacket, belted at the waist, with her skirts hitched up to resemble britches.

Here on this hellish sea-voyage, her father cuffs her on the shoulder and, as if sensing their gaze upon her, seems to order her to unhitch her skirts, to make herself decent.

"Don't worry," one of the laughing sappers calls, "we won't be laying a finger on her, guv'nor."

"Nah," the other shouts, "we don't like squirrels."

His comrade bursts into peals of laughter. The labourer turns his back to them, trying to make out that he hasn't heard them, but the flush on his neck says otherwise.

"We was only joking, Tommy," the first soldier calls, "just having a laugh."

To her credit, the girl doesn't seem to take a telling from her father. She pulls her skirts straight, as she's been told, but she argues back and kicks at their luggage, and the sappers let out a supportive cheer. She may have the face of a squirrel but she's got spirit and she's giving her old man what-for.

The argument ends with the father scrabbling angrily to pick up his books, a thunderous look on his face, and the daughter surprising them all. She begins to tap out a rhythm with her knuckle on the side of the boat, and then she starts to sing, in a high, raw voice.

It's a sea shanty, one the sappers also know, so they take up the song with her, as do both boatmen, and although none of them seem to agree on the words of the verses, or indeed the language in which to sing, all five join together at the chorus, which is a rousing tribute to life on the waves, and the two soldiers feel their spirits lifting. They have taken a liking to this odd girl after all.

The labourer is the only one who doesn't sing but sits brooding in the footwell, not meeting anyone's eye, scribbling away in his books.

They are still singing as the boat pulls alongside a low, rocky landing place, and the girl is the first on dry land, taking the rope and leaping nimbly ashore.

A couple of hundred miles away, the dog, Bran, is not happy. He paces back and forth along the perimeter line—recognisable only to himself—between the flat ground of the farm and the wilder terrain of the hills. Inside the house there are raised voices, a crash that makes Bran's ears flick forward, the rising wail of the baby. Nothing, Bran knows, has been right since Enda and Tomás went away. He watches, alert, as the door crashes open. Liam shoulders his way out, limping and listing on two improvised crutches, and with only a glance in Bran's direction, he strikes out down the hill.

A moment later, the mother hurries after him, wiping her hands on her apron. She seems about to call his name but stops herself, hiding instead in the lee of the cottage and peering around it.

Puzzled by all this, Bran shifts his eyes to Liam. Both dog and mother watch as Liam staggers jerkily over the pebbles, towards the stream, his bandaged leg held up off the ground.

Bran fidgets, scratches at the sod with his front paws. What to do? Should he follow the boy, who is clearly in no state to go off down the boreen? Bark? Go to the mother? Into the house? He lets out a whine of indecision and distress: the house is a complicated place for him. If all is well, if the air feels right and good, if the wind is blowing in the right direction, if there is the smell of food, he can be persuaded into it, but if feelings are running high, if the atmosphere is stitched with tension and yelling, like today, he will not come further than this invisible line.

Bran drops to his belly, rests his muzzle on his paws. He might look to anyone like an animal at rest but far from it: he has his gaze trained with great concentration on the house, on the hiding mother, the limping boy, every muscle tensed to leap up, if required.

A noise reaches Bran's ears and he lifts his head. The boy has fallen, the books in his bag slipping, scattering about the ground. In a flash, the mother darts out and gathers everything into her apron; she has her arm around the boy and she's half walking, half supporting him back to the house. The child is sniffling, saying he must get to school, he has lessons to catch up with, and the mother is replying, Not yet, you're not strong enough. The two of them go back inside the house, the door shuts.

Bran observes it all, attentive. Not so long ago, the man had strode away, carrying a pack on his back, muttering, Out of the way, you foolish animal, go on home, but Bran hadn't taken it amiss because rough words and imperatives were the way this man showed love, and the man was given to walking out. But a few days later, the girl, Enda, went off too, wearing Liam's clothing. Bran had circled her three times, sniffing at her feet, the jacket, the jersey, cocking his head to look at her, asking, What is the meaning of this? Enda had stroked him with a fervour that gave Bran his second instance of misgiving—where was she going and how long would she be and what did it all mean? What Bran took amiss most of all was this leaving, the brazenness of it, as if it didn't matter at all, as if they didn't care that it was Bran's job, his purpose in life, to keep them all together, here, safe. They just opened the door and walked away and left, first the man and then the girl.

Unable to bear immobility a moment longer, Bran leaps up from the ground and races around the house in long, loping circles. He leaps up at the window and the half-door, paws on the wood to look inside, catching a glimpse of Liam being settled by the mother in a chair by the fire, and Rose, her head bent over some task at the table. Bran then comes to a stop by the wall of the little byre. The baby, Eugene, has been put out to nap in the fresh air, swaddled in blankets so that only his face shows. Bran paces twice around the cleeve but he doesn't rest his paws on it—he has too much sense for that—but he puts his narrow nose over the side and snuffs at the child.

Eugene is awake, eyes open to the sky, and he looks at Bran. Bran looks at him. Perhaps the youngling can help, can settle matters in the house, perhaps fetch back the missing members of the family. But he is too small, Bran knows, he can't even stand on his two spindly little legs yet, and how slow are the young of humans, how vulnerable and defenceless. Child and dog regard each other, and Bran is suddenly certain that this child is an extraordinary one, that he can see right into Bran, that he knows everything without being told. It is a sensation both comforting and unsettling. It makes him want to lie down right here, as close as he can possibly get to the cleeve. So he does. He stretches out his great paws, his long legs, lays his flank on the sod, and falls into sleep almost immediately, and so does the child, and the two share the same dream: a landscape weighed down from above with great billowing clouds that part and merge, letting in the light and obscuring it, over and over again.

Report of Progress
To the Ordnance Survey Office,
Phoenix Park, Dublin
October 1866

From Mapping Division XI___ii
Sapr. P. Carbury
Sapr. D. Bentford
(Also present: Labourer & Chainboy)

Week 1: Access to the largest island has been attained, and camp set up. For the initial two days the division commenced, as directed by the Office, a walking survey of the island's perimeter in daylight hours, terrain permitting. Notes taken of landmarks, topography, notable features, both physical and human: herewith enclosed, with relevant sketches, labelled here as —

(Tomás pauses in his writing of the Report of Progress to observe that, across the camp, a tussle has broken out between the two sappers, Carbury and Bentford, apparently playful in nature, but you never can tell. He deems it best to pretend not to notice. They are only young lads, so what can you expect? Tomás sighs and reads back over what he has written. The dispassionate tone, the scantness of detail, strike him as correct. He does not, for example, mention to the Office that he sleeps in one tent, the sappers in the other, and that his daughter, Enda, for the sake of decency, has been lodged with a fishing family down by the cove, an irritant and an expense that Tomás had not, of course, foreseen. Enda, on the first day, a short time after Tomás had begun his walking survey, ran up to his side, dressed and ready, even though it was not yet dawn, saying how excited she was and how maps always made her want to know what was beyond their edges, didn't he wonder that himself? He had ordered her back to her lodging house: she may have tricked her way into coming here but he was not going to play along with any of that nonsense. Tomás dips his pen in the inkpot and returns to his Report.)

—labelled here as (i) the small, natural harbour on the northside; (ii) a knife-edged arrete, (iii) a limestone pavement, (iv) a stronghold of possible Viking origin, much injured by time and the hand of man, (v) an early Christian structure.

(Tomás replaces the lid on the ink bottle, wipes his nib. In their horseplay, the sappers have knocked over the water butt and crushed the tents: the lads lie in the flattened remains, laughing and cursing, slapping at each other's heads. Tomás tidies his papers, then rises. He has to get one of them to sign this week's Report. And he will have to reassemble the tents, when they decide to once more get to their feet.)

Week 2: The Division has been engaged, as directed, in interviewing the islanders. The dwellings here are rudimentary cabins constructed of mud and straw, with the exception of the factor's house, which is stone. The landlord's factor is not resident but visits twice a year. The islanders now number fewer than 30; they gather feathers and moss in lieu of rent; there is little distinction made here between the labour of the men and the women as both take to the work of spinning and knitting—

(He would like, Tomás reflects, as he writes, crouched in the shelter of a tumble-down wall, for Phina to see the patterns that emerge from their knitting needles. The diamond vents, the textured bobbles, like blackberries made of wool, the ridges and ripples, the blended colours.)

There is a flock of sheep, hardy and thick-fleeced, said to be the property of the landlord, which are unfenced and have the run of what pasture they can find. The factor's visits have the purpose of collecting said rent, and removing the fleeces and lambs to the mainland. What stray wool that may be found snagged to bushes, etc., may be kept by the islanders: from this is their knitting made. Signed, Sapr Carbury

Week 3: trig-point set up, measurements begun.

(His pen nib rests on the page, the full stop pooling more ink than is needed: he is too exhausted to write more. If more is required, what would he say? That he cleaned and assembled the instruments of measurement. With only a light wind off the Atlantic, the sappers yawning and grumbling, they ascended the highest peak of the island, where Tomás made his trig point. The sappers had seabird-shooting competitions and discussed which island woman was the best-looking: the daughter of the blacksmith or the wife of the publican?)

Week 4: measurements and calculations.

(He is forced to seek out Enda and, if not apologise for treating her so brusquely, to make amends. He finds her at the shore, knee-deep in a rockpool, helping with the gathering of cockles. He cannot do this without a chainboy, he says to her, someone to help him with his calculations. The sappers will never— But she cuts him off, with a grin, and says, what about a chaingirl?)

Week 5: measurements and calculations.
Week 6: measurements and calculations.

(Enda is suddenly nowhere to be found. Tomás searches the shore, the row of cabins, the pasture, the place where the women sit together, under a hedge, to knit. When he asks the islanders, they pretend not to understand him.)

Week 7: measurements and calculations.
Week 8: measurements and calculations.
Week 9: commencement of draft maps.

(The landlord has given the Office permission for them to use the factor's house for this work, so Tomás has set himself up at the table here, and has begun the initial sketching. He leaves the door open, for the air, and Enda passes by, one afternoon; she carries her fiddle under her arm. Tomás hails her, waves her inside, and asks if she would clean his pens. She refuses. Tomás tells her to clean his pens. She shakes her head. Tomás informs Enda that she is to sit down on this here stool and do as he bids. She smiles then steps out of the door, slamming it behind her. Just like that. Tomás stares after her, open-mouthed. There seem to be several people outside in the lane who greet her by name, and was it his imagination or did she talk to them in the island language?)

Week 10: draft mapping.
Week 11: draft mapping.
Week 12: draft mapping.

(Tomás has been told to knock on the door of the shepherd after dark: he wants to check the spellings and origins of some of the names of the island—the hills, the coves, the Viking stronghold—and one of the fishermen said he should come to the shepherd's cabin, for the whole island gathered there of an evening. He knocks, then steps inside. The interior is thick with smoke, candles spreading an oily yellow disc around themselves. Islanders sit on the tables and chairs, on the floor, men and women, youngers held on knees or on shoulders. Several dogs lie on their sides by the fire. Someone puts a cup into Tomás's hand; he doesn't take a drink usually but feels to refuse would not be conducive to his purpose here. The liquid blasts his mouth and gullet with a fiery heat. Two young men shuffle up to give him a space on the bench, and he sits himself down, one hand on his knee. From a corner of the room there is the sound of musicians. There is a drum and a pipe or whistle. The tune is slow and lilting; an elderly woman near the fire is singing a chorus about flowers and a river. When this tune comes to its close, Tomás decides, he will stand, he will make for the shepherd, who is sitting in a chair at the table, his head turned towards the music, and Tomás will get out his papers, explain to him, to everyone, what he is about, and ask them all to confirm the names of the hill, the stronghold, the coves. Tomás clears his throat in readiness, takes a second sip of his drink, and as he does so the tune changes, all of a sudden, without pause, into one that is fast and wild; it is greeted with whooping and clapping, a few get up to dance, and Tomás sighs because now he'll have to wait until this is over. The musician this time is a woman with a heavy curtain of hair and she stands to play, stamping her feet, her body bent around her instrument, and everyone in the room stares at her, rapt, held in the net of her music. Everyone, that is, except Tomás. He is looking around, deciding who are the best people to speak with, the ones least intoxicated, when the young man next to him leans over and says something in his ear. What was that? Tomás asks, bending closer. I said, says the man, she's a rare one, is she not, your daughter? Tomás is about to say, What would you know of my daughter, when he realises, he sees, that the woman playing, the woman with the heavy hair, is indeed Enda. His daughter. The music in the room comes from her, her fiddle, her fingers, her bow. Tomás gapes, split down the middle between shock and admiration.

His daughter: she has loosened out her plaits, she shakes her head as the tune gains speed, as the notes flood from her hands, and her hair shimmers and snakes in the candlelight, and her foot under her skirt stamps out the rhythm, and the children dance and the islanders drum their hands and call out their approval. Tomás lurches to his feet, stumbles forward. He wants to say, Stop; he wants to say, Where did you learn to play like that?; he wants to say, What would your mother think, come with me now, come away from here. Hands are grasping at him, pulling him back, and the young men on the bench are laughing, saying to him, Leave her, leave her be. They push him to sit down between them, half gaolers, half companions, and they are saying to him that a couple on the island, a man and a woman, who are grand musicians, have taken Enda under their wing, have been teaching her every day, but he knew that, sure, didn't he? Tomás cannot speak, cannot take his eyes off Enda, the movement of her wild hair, the swan-like elegance of her bowing arm, the sweat that glows on her brow, and he thinks of what she said about wanting to travel beyond the edges of maps, to find out what was there, and he recognises in that moment that she has gone beyond the limits of his paternal reach, far beyond, that she will never again reside within it.)

Week 13: draft mapping, name checking.
Week 14: draft mapping, name checking.
Week 15: completion of draft mapping.
Week 16: completion of field books. Departure.

—Conclusion of Report of Progress
Signed, Sprs. Carbury & Bentford
February 1867

Hard to pinpoint exactly when they realise Eugene is not as other children.

When Enda and Tomás return from the island, Eugene is almost one and there is nothing particularly unusual about him at that point;

he stares at these two people, of whom he can have no recollection, taking in his father's huge beard, his sister's incessant fiddle-playing, with a composed and evaluating stare.

Phina has been relieved, in their absence, that he is such a quiet baby, so watchful there in his cradle, gazing intently up at the roof or the sky, or whatever happens to be above him, barely making a cry, even when he is hungry. He reaches to grasp things in his left hand, but there are many like that, she tells herself. Loud noises make him flinch, cause his face to pucker in shock: a door slamming in a breeze, a sudden bray from the donkey, a shriek of frustration from Enda, a bucket set down with a thud.

Nothing unusual in that, Phina says to Tomás, by the time Eugene turns two, and her husband nods, without a word, clapping his cap to his head. Phina catches the widow with a thoughtful look on her face, singing to Eugene as he sits by her spinning-wheel, then letting the wheel slow as she says, You sing now, Eugene, on you go. And Eugene looks at the turning of the spokes, the paddling of the treadle, but makes no sound. Phina snatches him up, presses him to her hip, kisses his soft hair. He is interested in what he can hear, she thinks, defensively, as she walks away, just doesn't want to make the noise himself.

More difficult, by the time he is three, then four, for Phina to explain away Eugene's continuing silence. There are many theories as to why he never learns to talk. Phina: He's taking his time. Rose: He has me to speak for him. The widow: There's something stopping his tongue. The sisters from across the estate: The faeries stole away the real child, and left this silent one in the cradle. Father Joseph: The boy is simple.

The most plausible one of all comes, surprisingly, from the younger fisherman who says, one day, when Eugene is five years old and is working hard, lifting sods from the creels on the donkey's back and taking them, one by one, to the drying store, "He doesn't speak because that would be letting things out, when he only likes to be taking things in."

Impossible for Tomás, who is nearby, helping with the turf, and Rose, who is also lifting sods into the store, to disagree with this assessment. As for Eugene, he gives no sign of having heard the man, laying his small hands on two cuts and pulling them to his chest, but he folds it into himself, to turn over and consider later.

Eugene has a sound for assent (a rising *ah-a*) and another for refusal (a growling *ur*). He has a gesture for hunger (a fist pressed to his stomach), for cold (arms wrapped around himself), for tired (his head lolling sideways), for affection (a hand laid on another's cheek). Eugene's approach to communication is, in Liam's view at least, one of admirable necessity and purity: the child has devised his own way of saying what he needs to say and no more. There is no ambiguity, no dissembling about his brother: just a person's straightforward requirements to exist.

To Eugene, the world is that which is in his immediate vicinity. The red yarn tied to the bedpost, as a talisman for protection, and how it is sometimes seen to hang on the mattress side and sometimes on the room side; the pads of the dog's paws, some pink and others black, their roughness, the fringe of fur that grows between them; the orange starbursts of lichen that adhere to the cottage's external walls; the twin dark holes of the donkey's nose, through which warm air is blown.

He likes to put the harness on the donkey, to fasten each buckle, one by one. He likes to stand near Rose when she is stirring something in the pot because she'll hand him a spoon to lick, and the burred grain of the carved wood is an interesting contrast to the fur of his tongue. He likes to collect bits of coral from the strand, perfectly smooth, angular, like tiny whitened trees. He likes to wrap himself in his mother's shawl, if she happens to discard it on a chair, until only the top of his hair pokes out.

Words, words. How obsessed, how concerned people are with them. Here, Eugene, eat this. Take this. Put this on. How are you today, little man? Let that alone and come with me, hurry now, fetch your jacket. Apple, ap-ple, can you say that for me, can you, can you try, ap-ple? What's the matter with him, deaf is he, simple is he, poor soul, does he not understand? What does he want, can he not hear?

Eugene hears. Eugene understands. He understands it all, every conversation, every silence, every arrangement of words and the gaps between them, every interchange, everything said and everything not said. He hears it all, sees it all but, like Bran, he has no need of or interest in speech.

He also hears things no one else does, the noises beneath: murmurs and mutterings and utterings, cries and expostulations, tales and mumblings, from the bushes and the streams and the turf and the air. He hears that the dry-stone wall of the haggard is opposed to moss growing on its humped back, so he sets about scraping it off with a scallop shell, which causes his father to yell and grumble at him about dislodged stones, but he doesn't care. He senses that the stream flowing out of the copse joins the bigger streams further down the hill, but with reluctance, and that the waters hold themselves apart from each other, and separate again as soon as they reach the sea. He feels that the bog is set against the faery fort, for reasons he cannot quite fathom, so he will never visit both in the same day.

Furthermore, he sees that his father and Liam are similarly set against each other and that the reason lies deep within them both, like a seam of glittering quartz through a rock: Eugene cannot work it out but knows that the same seam is present in both of them. He observes Liam growing taller and taller, until his head is above Tomás's, and he sees how Tomás doesn't like this, it doesn't sit easily with him. He sees that Liam is away from the house more and more, spending long hours at the schoolhouse and more at the chapel; Liam begins to talk of a place called a novitiate, or a House of First Formation, where he wishes to go, and things called vows, which he wishes to take. Eugene sees the prickle of blame and fury between his father and Father Joseph for this (and how Eugene dislikes the priest, with his soft yet wheedling voice, and his hands, which are always so eager to imprison Eugene's or ruffle his hair, the chapel, which smells disturbingly of burned reeds and mildewed whitewash).

He sees that, in spite or perhaps because of his father shouting about apprenticeships and the squandering of chances, Liam will leave. Eugene intuits that one day his brother will pack up his books and walk out the door and that he won't ever really return, that his exit will have a finality and a closing to it. He sees that their mother knows this and that it forces a crack through her chest, that her heart is already a little bit broken by it.

He sees that Rose will stay, willingly, and so will Enda, but unwillingly. There are moments when he senses something coming off Enda, something like the licking tongues of flame—he pictures them as writhing, black, airy things with the shape of eels—and he knows to keep clear of her then. He sees that when she thinks no one is looking, Enda takes Liam's books and reads them; if anyone comes upon her, she slides them into her apron pocket. Eugene can tell when Enda is beset by feelings so strong she cannot contain them, and he knows that, before long, she will take down her fiddle from where she keeps it above the door, so it is away from the heat of the fire and also the damp of the floor, and she will head out towards the shelter of the ring fort and she will play there, to the birds, to the tree, until she feels back in herself. He knows this because he often follows her, keeping out of sight: he likes to hear the torrent of her music, the notes that are isolated from each other and the ones that blur together to make a grouped sound.

And Rose? Rose is his magnetic north, the sun around which he orbits. He will go to bed only on the pallet next to hers; he will sleep only once she herself is asleep, and even then the rest he has is a quivering, shallow thing, from which he can be pulled by a passing breeze, the creak of a door hinge, the turning over of the dog, a dream in which a hooded stranger throws seedpods into the embers of a fire. Eugene's waking hours are measured by no clock but by Rose's activities and location. Where she goes, he goes. When she milks the cow, he will sit with his back to hers, leaning against her: she always gives him the task of dipping a finger in the froth and drawing a cross on the cow's hide, as their mother taught them. They have a ritual that when he has the froth on his finger—and it isn't a sensation Eugene likes, and Rose knows this, of course, because she knows everything—he will look at her, eyebrows raised, and she will answer the question she knows he is asking: We draw a cross on the cow, she will say, her lips curled in a smile, as a charm to keep her safe. The word "safe" is his cue to make the cross, so he does, every time, and he lets out a guttural chuckle, because he likes the idea of a charm, and he likes the smooth side of the cow, and the milk releasing into the bucket, and he knows that Rose will give him a spoonful of the cream, and that later they will take some along to the elderly neighbour who lives over the hill.

Some days, if his mother and Rose are busy with long and repetitive tasks, he gets a desperate restlessness in his legs, and the only way to relieve it is to pace from wall to wall, letting short moans out of his mouth. At these times, Enda might take him with her to the lough to collect the eggs, and they will spend some hours there: she will tie a length of rope to a branch of the hens' tree and fasten the other end to his waist so that he can splash in the shallows, learning to work his arms in time with his legs so the water supports him, so he can fly on the surface, the birds doing the same above him, and Enda will practise scales and melodies on her fiddle, every now and again breaking off to tell him he's doing well, he's almost afloat, he's doing three strokes, now four, now five.

His mother has sewn Enda a special blouse in a smooth fabric to wear when she goes out to play at weddings or a wake or sometimes a dance. The blouse is looser around the armpits and tighter at the wrists, she's told him, to allow for the action of the bow. When she goes out playing, she takes Bran with her, and he, Eugene, often accompanies them. He likes the walk there, along the road that he can see from their house. Enda doesn't like her hand to be held—she says she needs to keep it supple for the fiddle strings—so he keeps one hand on the fur of Bran's neck and in the other he holds a fistful of her skirt tight against his chest. This is not, as Enda believes, because Eugene worries about getting lost or left behind: he possesses, just behind his eyes, a natural sense of where he is and how one direction relates to another, how a road links up to a second, then a third. He keeps himself firmly between Enda and Bran on these walks because the walls and fields and trees away from the house whisper to him in unfamiliar voices, and he fears they might lure him to places unknown.

While Enda is playing, it is his job to mind Bran; Eugene will sit to the side, watching his sister, his back pressed to the wall, the dog stretched out over his feet. Enda will let him carry any pennies she has been given for her playing because he likes the slithery feel of coins as they clink together in his palms.

Time is not a concept of which Eugene has a grasp. His siblings grow. The voice that comes out of Liam's mouth is suddenly the growling and rumbling of a large man's, but they all get used to it, although Eugene finds he misses the light, fluting tones of his brother and sometimes goes to him and puts his fingers into his mouth to see if he can prise it out again (Liam puts up with this for a moment or two, then eases away Eugene's hand, saying, That's enough, Euge). His sisters acquire forms and stature that resemble their mother's. Strands of silver appear in their father's hair, and these spark intriguingly in the light, and soon his temples are completely white. Bran's muzzle does the same. Growing seems strange to Eugene: that he can step out of the door a slightly taller boy than the previous day is peculiar, unsettling. He doesn't like it.

The day he sees that his hand is no longer smaller than Rose's is when he runs through the bushes of the boreen and doesn't come back for a long time, even though they are all calling for him. He stumbles through the solace of the bog, its brownish ooze lapping over his bare feet, and when he reaches the higher ground, he kicks and thumps at the soil, hurls handfuls of it into the air, grips its dampness in his fists and squeezes and squeezes until he notices that it has turned to dry clods between the slits of his fingers. He sits down on a stone, distracted, his rage forgotten, examining these wedges of peat, the way they have taken on the lines and contours of his fingers and palms, the way they fit back so perfectly into his hands.

He feels something hard inside one, and for a moment he is loath to break the clod apart, so lovely is it, but he is curious to see what it might be—a pebble, perhaps a cowrie, and Rose would be pleased for him if he had found another shell to add to his collection—so he rubs away the crumbs and smears of turf and sees a gleam, a smooth curve, and then he has it in his blackened palm: a ring, made of gold, an interlocking pattern with curves and circles, two tiny scaled animals swallowing the legs of each other, caught in eternal and complicated twinship, the symmetry of it pleasing, the way his eye can follow one of the lines and meet it back where he started, the way one animal's mouth holds the feet of the other. Eugene stares at it for a long time, tilting his head one way, then the next, following each animal three times around with the beams of his eyes. Then his gaze drops to the marshy ground at his feet. He pushes his feet deeper into the wet, toes pointing downwards. What else might be in there? What other treasures could he find? He flexes his feet back and forth, the ground shifting, sucking, and he feels something—hard, unyielding—and Eugene is interested. He slips the ring onto his thumb for safekeeping and digs down with his hands, the bog water instantly invading the fabric of his trousers, claiming him, as if it wishes to draw him in, to make him part of itself. He digs, tossing handfuls behind him, and before long, he finds what looks to him like a human arm, crooked at the elbow. He feels no surprise, just a flicker of curiosity. What would a person be doing here, down in the earth? He clears more soil, working upwards, and here is the whorl of an ear, a cheek, a mouth, lips partly closed, a neck and, round it, a string of plaited leather woven with cowrie shells and a knotted rope. Eugene sits back on his heels, considering her. The person, a girl, he thinks, seems to be asleep, eyes shut tight against the world, as if she finds it too harsh, too jarring. He pulls away more of the soil and there is her shoulder, around which is wrapped the long swirl of her hair. He pats her with a solicitous palm. She ought to wake up. He sees, for the first time, that her arms are around something and, digging further, he finds the ear and muzzle of a dog. It is so like Bran that for a moment Eugene is thrown: why is Bran here with this girl and wouldn't he be terribly cold? But then he remembers that Bran has gone to market today with Rose.

It is indeed a puzzle. Eugene sits there, with the bog-girl, for a while. He sucks the peat off the circles of the ring, feeling its ridges and scales against his tongue. He puts a finger to her face. He thinks that she, too, doesn't like to speak. He likes her stillness, her silence, her closed-up face, her grip on her hound. He feels that she, like him, loves her dog. She seems more like him than anyone else he has ever met. He thinks that she needs him, Eugene, to take care of her, the way everyone takes care of him. He spends a while holding her hand, his fingers curled around hers, then realises he is hungry because he didn't eat his breakfast. So he uses his feet to push the wet earth back over the girl and her dog—gently, gently, ever so gently, because he doesn't want to wake them up—replacing their blanket of marsh and bog earth, and he slops his way back to the house.

His family ask him about the ring—how did he come to have it, where did he find it?—but the questions don't interest him, so he merely shrugs and makes a gesture towards the bog. Enda slides it from his thumb, which Eugene isn't entirely happy about, and they pass it among them, holding it up to the light, Tomás fetching his spectacles to examine it more closely. They talk about it for a while, saying it must be old, very old, and perhaps they should show it to the widow, or the sisters from down below, or the priest, but Eugene shakes his head, rapping the table with his curled knuckles. Rose is the last one to hold it: she slides it onto her finger and regards it there for a long moment thoughtfully, turning her hand one way, then the other. Then she says, I think we should give it back to Euge. He found it. He should keep it. And she takes it off and puts it into his hand, closing his fingers over it, one by one, making him its protector and custodian.

Eugene partly gauges the passage of years by observing his siblings and his parents; another part of him measures it in terms of storms. A gale blows in from the sea and it lifts part of the thatch; Liam and their father climb up together onto the slippery roof, with the wind snatching at their clothes, and they toss twine to each other, over the hump of the house, their voices trying to find the other, and Eugene doesn't like this, he doesn't like it at all: not the sky, which is angry and low, not the yellowish light, not the way the gale whips his hair around, and certainly not the way his brother is up there, standing on the gable end, gesticulating, coils of twine over his shoulder. Later, another storm comes and this one is wet and wild: the thatch stays on but the rain leaks through and his mother puts pots and buckets about the place to catch it. The streams and rivers burst their banks; their hillside becomes a flood. Eugene removes his boots and goes splashing through the currents and the puddles. Everything is new, everything is different: the field, the donkey's place, the haggard are flowing with water, swallowed by the river. The yellow irises are up to their necks, valiantly keeping their heads above water. Eugene worries about the bog-girl and how she'll be faring, so he wades up to the boreen, which is rushing and bubbling with noisy silver currents, but he finds that the bog is still a bog, the same as always.

It is after another storm, one from the south, with low and venting winds, the sea heaving up great banks of black weed and broken shells, that he and his mother walk out to check on the neighbours, and on the way back, his mother tells him she has a strange feeling, terrible strange it is, just here, and she puts the heel of her hand against her clavicle. Then she says, Oh, Eugene, and clutches at his arm, the front of his jacket, and he doesn't like this, she should know he wouldn't, so steps sideways, and when he looks again, his mother is lying on her side, her face turned to the ground. The basket is upturned and all the things in it are scattered around her: a cloth, the straw that held the eggs, some kale from the widow, a handkerchief. Eugene spends some time putting these things back. Then he sits on the hillside, waiting for his mother to wake up and walk to the house. She doesn't. She lies where she is and doesn't answer when he makes an enquiring noise, doesn't respond when he taps her hand. Eventually, Eugene wanders away. He goes to the place where there is a row of smooth rocks emerging from the sod, like the backs of whales coming up from the sea, and it's possible to walk along them, and he does this, back and forth, for a while, looking out beyond the cliffs, where sea-witches are whisking white froth off the top of the waves with their brooms. When he returns, he finds his mother is gone, as if she hadn't been lying there at all. The basket, which he has repacked, is still there, so he takes it in his hand, intuiting that this is what she would want him to do, and walks up to the house.

Inside, everything is different. Rose's face is streaming with tears, like the ground after the wet storm; Enda is sitting at the window, her fists rammed into her forehead, and those tongues of fury are writhing around her. His mother is lying on the bed, which is a more usual place for a sleep, her feet making a V, her face turned up to the rafters, and someone has placed coins on her eyelids. Most disturbingly, his father is bent over her, his face pressed to her middle, his hand gripping hers, and he is crying, not tearful crying, like Rose, but a kind of roaring, and out of the storm of it come words but they are not in any particular order and Eugene cannot make sense of them.

Eugene puts his hands over his ears, surveying the scene. Rose's leaking eyes; Enda's rage; his father making the horrible sound. He cannot parse this situation; he cannot fathom these various behaviours, what it all means, what might be expected of him. The only possible course of action is to make himself disappear, to occupy the smallest space imaginable. He climbs the ladder to the loft, lifts the lid to a chest and wedges himself in next to the blankets kept there. Here is a place to think, a place to preserve some of the necessary space and silence around himself. He props open the lid with a twig from his pocket, so he can watch what happens next.

It turns out to be this: Liam bangs in through the door, his face flushed and distraught, and the priest is with him. Eugene's father leaps up and shouts, Get out of here, don't you dare, and Liam says, Stand aside now, and Tomás says, He'll not have her, I'll bury her myself, here, on this land, and Liam says, No, you won't, she'll have a proper service, with a mass said, it's what she would have wanted. Eugene wonders why they are shouting about burying, why they wish to place Phina in the earth; he thinks his mother would not want this because doesn't she always brush at the clothes when they have mud on them; she tuts if he comes home with soil on him, dirt she calls it. Then he thinks of the bog-girl and he wonders if his father means to put his mother with her, down in the wet and mulch of the marsh. Why, though? Why are they so set on putting Phina into the land?

It is confusing indeed. Eugene presses himself lower into the chest and the blankets as the house fills with people, neighbours, who bring food, who embrace the girls, who shake Tomás and Liam by the hand, and say, Sorry for your troubles, and She was a good woman, and She was taken too soon.

The lid of the chest is lifted, after a time, he doesn't know how long, and Enda offers him her hand and helps him step out. Then he is taken with them down the hill, to the chapel, and there is a gash in the soil and into it goes a long wooden box. The priest is saying words and Rose and Enda and Liam are crying, and Tomás is trembling, his legs making the fabric of his trousers ripple, and this distracts Eugene because he is trying to copy his father, to make his own legs tremble like that, but then Rose whispers something to him. Mammy's in there, Euge. And she points at the box, which is now resting at the bottom of the pit. Eugene looks at it. Mammy's gone, Rose says, and Eugene waits to be told where she's gone, and when she's coming back. And he must look as if he doesn't understand, because Rose says again: Mammy's gone. Say goodbye now. Eugene doesn't like this idea, not one bit. There will be no goodbye; he will not say it, he will not think it, he refuses. So he shakes his head, to Rose, to the grave, to the priest, to the air, to the box they say his mother is in, he shakes it back and forth, emphatically, desperately, sealing up his mouth, like a mussel-shell.

PART THREE

SAIL THE WIDE OCEANS

It is nightfall in Calcutta, on the third evening of Liam's interrogation. Two candelabra are being placed by servants at either end of the table. Liam gazes at them and then at the faces of the committee members, which, above their dark robes, are rendered as unsteady, coruscating masks.

He rubs a hand over his face: his eyes ache inside the dry hollows of their sockets. Surely this can't go on much longer—they can't keep him here for ever, can they? One of the men is talking at length, his face furious, his chin trembling in outrage. Is it Portuguese the man is speaking or perhaps Latin? Liam cannot tell—the man's words reach him like the sound of birds—or maybe it is that he no longer cares. The man is asking him about his life just before he went into the priesthood.

"My mother had just passed away." Liam cuts across the man's words and the utterance hurts his parched mouth. "A matter of weeks before I left."

"And your father?"

Liam stares at the man, mute, wrong-footed. My father, he wants to say, why would you ask about my father? The committee wait for his answer, their pens poised above their papers. On the candelabra, Liam counts six candles in each, which means a total of twelve. The same number as the apostles. This coincidence strikes Liam as hugely significant, or perhaps it is of no consequence at all, perhaps—

"Your father," another man raps out, making Liam flinch, "was he encouraging about you taking orders?"

Liam goes to speak, then realises that his mouth has somehow twisted into a soundless line: he is unable to utter the word "father" or even "Tomás," and he does not know why this is. Sweat breaks out on his brow, his upper lip.

"He—I—I . . . my—my—" he hears himself stammer "—my fa— Well . . . he . . ."

Liam lets the breath leave his body, closes his eyes to the glare of the twelve candles, the four faces peering at him through the chamber's heavy miasma. His pulse is suddenly clicking painfully in his throat; his hands are slick with cold moisture.

He tries to calm himself, to think his way back to those weeks between his mother's death and his leaving for the novitiate: if he forms a reply to this question, maybe then they will let him go. The interrogator is asking about the time before he entered the House of First Formation, so he duly tries to picture their broken household, his mother's empty chair, how he longed to be gone—it couldn't come fast enough.

An extraordinary thing, however: his thoughts will keep returning, insistently, to the well, and the day he first walked into the copse. It is perverse, it is unfathomable. What has this to do with his taking orders? He buries his face in his hands, seeking a response to the question, trying to picture his mother, as she was, laid out on the table, the neighbours gathering in the room for her wake. But his mind, like a troublesome and headstrong steed, will not heed the command: it offers him instead the image of a person standing on a distant hillock, blurred by fog.

He presses the nails of one hand into the palm of the other, finding that he is on the verge of tears but wanting to keep them at bay, for he refuses to give this committee the satisfaction of breaking down in front of them. He considers telling them about the time on the hillside, the day their lives were set off-course, or maybe even on-course, because who is to say that the six of them were not destined to end up exactly where they did? Perhaps they might then understand. He would like, instead of answering their futile questions, to describe for them his abortive apprenticeship, and the process of mapping, the complex labour and responsibility of it, its peculiar mix of science and storytelling, mathematics and artistry. He would like to tell them about the exorcism, his father's melancholy, the terror and upheaval of it all. My father, he would say, by way of a beginning, was ever a man of few words. Even knowing that it is hardly likely to help his case, Liam feels the urge to relate the tale to them from its strange start. It might, he thinks, go some way to explain what has happened here, in India.

He looks out instead at the consoling shape of the dark banyan tree, its massive width of trunk, the peculiar crutch-like aerial roots. His vision seems beset with a bewildering palimpsest: parakeet feathers, the tree, lightning-bolt flashes of Calcutta dusk between its branches, his sisters and Eugene standing at their mother's grave with the priest, grey veils of drizzle, shallow turquoise inlets, his father bending over his loy with a sharpening stone. He realises three things; they apprehend him as triple truths. That he will, as soon as he is able, return to where he came from, to the peninsula and his family. That he will never speak of Tomás in this room, to these furious men. That his father is somehow antithetical to these men, to the Church. Like magnets held together, his father and the Church will always repel each other.

It comes to him that he is about to speak, so he stands up.

"It was the parish priest's fault," Liam hears himself announce, and the members of the committee frown. "Father Joseph was his name. It was him put me up to it. If you're looking for someone to blame, it should be him. This is his fault."

Consternation among the committee. Two of the men raise their voices to pepper Liam with furious refutations; one glares at him balefully, pen at the ready; the other his hands over his ears, as if to shield them from Liam's words.

Liam lowers himself back to a seated position. It all seems so clear to him suddenly, the petulant priest and the choice he laid out for Liam: he could have his father, who loved him, or he could have the Church, which did not. As he grips the edge of the hard wooden bench in the sweltering dim room, Liam cannot for the life of him fathom why he chose the latter.

"Tell us," the man with the pen urges, once more, "about the weeks leading up to your departure for the priesthood."

At the table, as they eat their porridge, Liam shifts in his seat and clears his throat, and Rose looks at him expectantly, her heart brimming with hope.

With every passing moment of every day she is waiting for him to say that he is putting off his entry into the priesthood, at least until the hay is in or the turf footed or until the winter. He's going to say it, she is certain, because he wouldn't be leaving them now, surely, not just after their mother's passing. He is about to say that he intends to write to the novitiate and tell them he won't be coming this year but perhaps the next. Rose smiles in readiness.

The five of them are eating in silence, Enda absently drumming out a rhythm on the table with her fingers, Eugene leaning up against her, Tomás sitting a little apart from them all, his scarf already wound around his neck.

Rose sits straighter, certain that Liam is about to speak, to tell them he is going to delay his departure; she is ready to spring up and embrace him, the minute he has the words out.

Liam does not meet her eye. He shuffles his feet beneath the table, opens his mouth and says it is twelve days until he will leave.

Enda pauses in her drumming, glancing first at Tomás, then Eugene. Rose gets unsteadily to her feet, leaving the dishes on the table. She doesn't know what to do; she cannot look at her brother. Blindly, she snatches up the creel of laundry and heads out the door, banging it shut behind her.

Outside, the day is fair and the rain has held off, despite the grey-bellied clouds that have slumped, exhausted, to the hilltops. Rose marches her burden to the washing stone, a large flat rock at a bend in the stream, and she wades in, trampling and soaping the clothes with a tearful, venomous exertion.

In truth, she could have left the laundry but the weather may turn—they may not get a dry day again for a while. It has nothing to do, she tells herself, with her sudden urge to get outside, to leave the confines of the cottage, to get away from Liam and his pronouncements, his certainties, his self-satisfied packing and preparing, his ostentatious scripture-reading at all hours.

From where she is, at the washing stone, she can look up at the house. She sees Eugene moving from the gable end to the donkey's enclosure, and back again. He seems to be conducting some kind of internal debate, counting off something on his fingers, and she wonders with a pang if it is Liam's remaining days. Bran has stretched himself out in Eugene's path so that the boy must step over the dog as he moves, and Rose thinks that after this, when she's finished the laundry, she'll take them down to the shore for a while: Eugene loves to run in circles with Bran on the strand. It will distract him from what Liam said at breakfast. She sees Enda come crashing out of the half-door, their father calling after her to mind the cow, to take it up to grazing; she sees Enda ignore this, hastily knot her shawl and, planting a quick kiss on Eugene's hair, hurry away.

Her sister, Rose thinks, might come and help her. Enda might wonder if Rose needs another pair of hands with the laundry. She watches Enda's bright head disappear, swallowed by the tangled branches of the boreen, and she grips the block of soap in the icy claw of her hand as if she might hurl it after her. Instead, she makes herself dip it in the water to lather it, and scrubs listlessly at a stubborn stain on a shirt of Tomás's. She doesn't know what might have made it: soil or ink or grease or goodness knows. She finds that she wants to say aloud: Whatever does he do to get himself so filthy? Then someone else might say: Here, use the salt. And she might reply: We've the back of the task broken now. She feels all these words there, in her throat, like a stuck fishbone.

Her mother's passing has left an ache in her, a wrongness, as if a hand has pulled out the loops and ribbons of her innards, then stuffed them haphazardly back in. Every moment of every day, she has to remind herself of the unbelievable fact that her mother is gone, that she won't see her again. She doesn't know how this can be. How is it possible that when she climbs down the ladder, Phina will not be there, not at the hearth, not in the haggard, not drawing water at the pump, not visiting neighbours?

Phina, it seems to Rose, was like the hinge on their door, or the pin at the centre of a wheel. Phina was crucial to their structure and function. Without her, they are lost.

Rose does her best. She gets up early, coaxes the fire into flame; she pours out the flour from the jar; she scatters in the soda so that the bread will be ready. She milks the cow, she collects the eggs, she looks after Eugene, she takes a needle and thread and she tries to mend their clothes, she really tries. Somehow, though, whatever she does isn't enough: her darning unravels, her stitches aren't strong enough, the tears and rents show through.

Enda will disappear for hours on end, returning damp, her skirts clotted with mud; in the evenings, she is out, more and more, with her fiddle, playing at crossroad dances or fairs; she rarely sits down to eat with them. She doesn't get paid for her work, or barely, but she says she is collecting tunes from all over the country, and this is better than any wages could ever be. Any pennies she is given, she saves in an old tobacco tin. For the first few weeks after Phina's passing, Eugene had brought their mother's apron to Rose over and over again, asking for her with an upwards sound, his face confused. Rose had had to shake her head, say, Mammy's gone, Euge, she'll not be back. Eventually, she took the apron from its hook and hid it; then Eugene crammed himself under the table, regressing to the habit of sucking his first two fingers.

Since the funeral, barely a civil word has passed between Liam and their father. Liam spends all his spare hours at his books or with Father Joseph—taking instruction, he calls it. He doesn't say much to any of them, beyond how long it is until he enters the novitiate: four weeks, three, now two, now only twelve days.

Rose slaps a petticoat to the washing stone, again and again. She has listened to Liam count down the days he has left but she cannot let herself hear it: to lose another person is unthinkable, that they were once six in this house, now five, soon four, is unbearable. Please, she said to Liam last week, clutching his shoulder, can you not put it off a little longer? He was polishing his boots, yet again, a fastidious cloth over his trousered lap, a brush in hand, and he looked up at her. The Lord, he said piously, waits for no man. He had sounded so like Father Joseph that Rose could have sworn the parish priest was there in the cottage with them. Behind Liam, across the room, Enda, fitting a new string to her fiddle, rolled her eyes.

You're asking me to put it off? Liam had murmured, under his breath, almost to himself, as he polished his boots. Her entreaties had congealed in Rose's mouth as she foresaw what would unfold: he would leave, and Enda would be off with her music, and she would be left to keep the house together, to look after Tomás, who had become as silent as Eugene. Liam was the only one to whom Tomás paid any attention, who caused Tomás to raise his eyes from the fire and speak. It was, admittedly, often rambling words of anger and accusation, but that was better, surely, than glowering silence. Liam would leave and be sent far away on a mission, and this was what their mother dreaded, that the Church would swallow him whole, like a whale, and there would be nothing left for them, that they would lose him altogether.

"Don't go," Rose had whispered, taking hold of his wrist. "Liam, please, don't go."

Liam held her in a long gaze, his hair aflame in the light of the fire. He glanced over her shoulder, at their father, at the other end of the table, perusing a map of his own devising. When Rose had asked him what it was, Tomás had said nothing for a long time, so long that Rose had thought he wasn't going to reply. Then he had murmured that it was something he'd started years ago, a map of the thin places, the points of confluence between our world and other worlds, and some further baffling things, and Rose had no idea what to say.

"I have to," Liam muttered, putting down one boot and taking up the next. "I can't stay here, Rosie. I'm sorry. I simply can't take another second of Da and his nonsense. And the novitiate is all arranged. Father Joseph says—"

At the mention of the priest, Eugene set up a loud wailing, and Rose had to stand and comfort him, to pat his shoulder in the way he finds soothing, to assure him that Father Joseph wasn't coming here, and to remind Liam not to talk about the priest in front of Eugene: can't he see that the boy is frightened of the priest? Liam had been puzzled, asking why would that be, and Tomás was muttering,

Sensible child, and Enda was whisking her shawl off the back of her chair, asking, What's all the noise, Euge, what's wrong?

And Tomás. Rose does not know what to do about Tomás.

Since the burial, he has been disturbingly quiet. He sits mostly in his chair. He doesn't seem to hear them or see them. If someone puts into his hand a cup of tea or a plate of stew, he will consume it, without pleasure or appetite. He sleeps late into the day, showing no interest in the crops outside or the beasts that need tending. At Rose's urging, Liam has had to leave aside his books, his boot-polishing, his study of the scriptures, take the hoe and the loy and dig out the weeds, has to repair the walls where the stones have fallen. Your father is grieving, the widow says, when she calls on them, let him be.

Rose is trying her best. She is worn to a husk ensuring the five of them are fed and worked and rested. She is trying, in the face of enormous odds, to keep them all together, but if she must now be the pin in their wheel it is one that has become rickety and uneven, the spokes pulling apart with every jolt and pothole along the way. She doesn't know how her mother did it, for all those years. If Mammy is looking down on them from Heaven, Rose hopes she is not disappointed in her. She doesn't know how much longer she can keep it all turning.

Enda has taken to sitting up on the thatch of an evening. It is the only way to avoid the stormy atmosphere between Liam and Tomás. She must climb onto a barrel to reach the byre roof, and from there she can crawl along the gable end to reach the highest peak. Below her, the packed straw and willow feel solid; she can straddle the ridge with one leg bent up under her. It's possible to hear the rumble of her family's voices coming up the chimney, to gauge whether or not Liam and Tomás are arguing or ignoring each other. She can see far out into the bay to the rear and the deep gulley of the sound ahead; to her left is the village, to the right the stone face of the mountain; at her back is the bog, which is filled at this time of year with a carpet of trembling flowers; and just behind that hillock is the ring fort, where on a day a long time ago she and Rose found Bran (or

Bran found them). And no one can see her up here, only the birds passing overhead—the gulls and the geese and sometimes a pair of long-necked swans. She is close but invisible.

It is a mild, late-summer evening and she has returned from playing at a wedding two villages over, where a young woman was marrying an older and widowed man, taking on his seven children. Enda saw nothing much to celebrate in that but she played anyway and the young woman danced with her sisters and her cousins, her face flushed with pleasure and abandon, and once with her new husband.

Enda is up in her place on the roof, watching Eugene down below. He checks over his shoulder once or twice before working the handle of the pump, then inserting the very tips of his fingers into the gush. The silver of the water meets the gold band of the ring he wears on his thumb and she sees him shiver with the shock and pleasure of it. She smiles to herself. She knows, and he knows, that if Tomás catches him doing this, he'll come over and remove Eugene's hand from the handle, telling him not to waste water, it's a precious element. But Eugene loves the pump, the cold flush of it, the draw and sucking motion of the handle, the first few dry gulps before the water appears. Enda sees no reason why he can't play with it: the child has little enough to make him happy.

She is just about to call down to him, Good on you, Eugene, you carry on there, when it occurs to her that her position up here, near the wisped and fragmenting clouds, might be like their mother's. Is Phina somewhere among or above them, watching, observing, unseen? Enda knows that if it were at all possible, it would be what her mother would want: she would refuse Heaven, turn down the everlasting, if she could remain close to them.

The thought that Phina could be nearby, unable to reach them or communicate, is so harrowing that Enda has to push the spiked ends of the thatch into her palms. She thinks she will swing her leg back over the ridge and make her perilous, sliding descent—she'll go to Eugene and see what way he is—when she hears voices coming up the boreen. Two of them, rising and dipping in what sounds like a dispute.

Eugene, below, drops the pump handle and scurries away, towards the donkey, and Enda realises that Eugene had recognised the voices before she did. It's Tomás and Liam, coming up the hillside, engaged in a row.

"All I'm saying is—"

"Listen to me, now—"

"You never, not even once, pay attention when—"

"Hear me out, for the love of—"

Enda shifts so that she is lower to the roof as they round the corner of the house. Tomás steps in front of Liam, forcing him to a halt.

"I—I beg of you not to do this. It's that damned padre who's put all this nonsense into your head. You mustn't shut yourself away in that place just because of what he's said, do you hear me, you could—"

"Da," Liam says, with quiet menace, "I am going to the novitiate. It is what I want, what I have always wanted. I will become a priest, with or without your blessing and—"

"I have no argument with the idea of faith, you know that. But can you not put your faith in what is beneath your feet? The rocks under the earth, the inexorable shift of soil down a mountainside, the pull of the moon on—"

"Da—"

"And when we die, we surrender our bodies to the earth and we become earth. It is the end of one story but the beginning of another."

Liam sighs and covers his face with his hands. Enda can see that he wants to push past Tomás but is holding himself back from doing so.

"You have your beliefs," he says, through his fingers, "and I have mine. We will both of us need to respect that—"

"Do you recall the day we found the well?" Tomás's voice is so soft that Enda has to strain to hear it. "What a day that was. And do you remember—"

"What I remember," Liam says, with sudden violence, pulling his hands away, "is being terrified. Of you. Of that place," he stabs a finger towards the copse, "of everything. I was a child. A child. And you left me there, on that hillside, in the rain, abandoned me, discarded me, like a—like a—" He gives an inarticulate noise, half sob, half scoff. “There's no point in discussing this,” he mutters, sidestepping his father and walking off. “No point at all.”

“I said that you'd sail the wide oceans,” Tomás calls after him. “Do you remember that?”

At the doorway to the house, Liam pauses, his head bowed. “I do and I still might. God's work can be done all over the world, to spread the word of—”

“I have something for you, son.” Tomás strides towards him, fumbling with something in the inner pocket of his jacket—Enda sees the white flash of paper in the gathering dusk. “Your mother and I talked of this, before she passed, and it was what she thought was best, the priesthood was the last thing she wanted for you. The idea of you emigrating would break my heart, as it would have broken hers, but if you must leave us, we would rather see you on a boat than walled off from the world with the Jesuits and—”

Liam has taken the papers and is turning them over in his hands. “*Permission to emigrate*,” he reads, in a wondering tone.

“And money for your passage, to Québec.” Tomás indicates, pointing. “It's all set up. I sent instalments in your name. We thought you might—”

Liam is shaking his head, refolding the pages, trying to hand them back. “Da, this is madness, sheer madness. You can't spare the money for this. I'll not be going, I'll—”

“No need to make up your mind now. Keep it all by you,” Tomás says, sliding the papers into Liam's jacket pocket. “Your mother . . . your mother always said that there was a thirst in you, a curiosity, and she thought . . . we thought this would . . . A vast country it is, thousands and thousands of square miles of good fertile soil. There are forests so high you can't see the tops of the trees, with huge rivers cutting through them, and mountain ranges like nothing we have here. And you know what else? There are no viscounts, no landlords sapping the lifeblood of the country. Imagine what a young man of your talents could make of it. Consider the idea, won't you? Think it over.”

A moment later, the haggard is empty, almost as if this conversation had never taken place, Liam vanished into the house, Tomás up the slope to walk the field. Eugene reappears from wherever he has been hiding and he stands at the pump, staring after his father. Enda rearranges her legs and slides down the thatch, coming to land with a thud near the door.

Eugene doesn't turn, just flaps a hand towards her in greeting, which makes Enda wonder if he'd known all along that she was up there. She comes over to stand beside him, following his gaze, to see what he's looking at. The hill, perhaps, or the fast-scudding clouds, or the V of curlews overhead.

"Will we work the pump?" Enda says, because it is the least she can offer him. "I'll keep watch for Da."

~

The days elapse both quickly and slowly. Twelve days until Liam goes, then ten, then six, then three, then the morning of his departure is upon them.

Liam wakes in his pallet under the thatch for what he knows will be the final time, Eugene curled into a ball next to him. He will leave today. It is very simple: he will rise, he will tie his bootlaces, he will open the door, he will step outside, and then the leaving will be done.

He turns his head towards Eugene and sees that his brother, too, is awake and following with his finger the path of a slater as it crawls up and down the inhospitable terrain of their rumpled blanket. Liam croaks out a good morning, and Eugene says nothing, watching the grey armour-plated back of the insect as it toils up a gulley of wool. Liam reaches out and flattens the incline with his fingers and the slater rushes forward but when Liam looks back at his brother, expecting Eugene to be pleased, he finds that the boy is regarding him with a penetrating, intent gaze.

Instantly, Liam is swamped by guilt, as if he ought to be begging his brother's forgiveness for what he is about to do. He tosses back the blanket, as if to free himself from this feeling, and rises, lifting his clothes from the stool, smoothing them down.

The leaving, now it is here, needs to happen quickly. He cannot delay. If he remains a moment longer with Eugene, his quizzical gaze and the wanderings of the insect, Liam thinks he is in danger of wavering—he might offer to stay.

He kneels, winding his rosary into his fingers, pressing his hands together, finding the stirring words of the matins prayer, at the forefront of his mind: *All the earth doth worship thee, the Father everlasting, to thee all angels cry aloud, the heavens and all the powers therein.*

Afterwards, he stands. He touches the rafters above his head. The girls and Eugene are down in the kitchen, getting out plates, stepping around each other. He watches for a moment: the smoke from the sullen morning fire, the oblong of light coming in from the half-door, Eugene kneeling to blow on the embers, Rose slicing bread at the table, Enda fetching butter from the press.

His instructions are to take nothing with him, for he is embarking on a new life, and what little he will require in the way of worldly things will be provided. He turns, surveys the low space of the loft where he has slept every night of his life since he was ten years old: the girls' bed, the blanket chest, the wicker chair. He folds his spare britches and jacket and lays them on the stool for Eugene; his woollen hat he places on Enda's pillow; on Rose's, he leaves his handkerchiefs, edged by the hand of their mother. His certificates, his papers, his schoolwork, all record of his life up to now, he tucks under the pallet: he has no need of them but cannot bring himself to commit them to the fire.

He tells himself quite clearly that this is the last time he will be here, that his life is now God's, that he is leaving, but at the same time he finds he cannot believe it. Surely he'll be back here tonight, laying himself down on this pallet next to his brother. That he might live anywhere else, with anyone else, that this chapter of his life is over, makes no sense.

He moves down the ladder and through the kitchen—he cannot risk eating breakfast with them all—and he stands on the threshold, the cottage behind him, its door still open, as if he could still change his mind and turn back. He takes a final look at what is before him: the mountain, the donkey, the haggard, the tops of the copse trees, just visible. He pulls in a lungful of the peninsula air, then lets it out.

He is joining the Jesuits, the Society of Jesus, a select religious order, a strict and closed one: the college he is going to takes only a handful of postulants each year. Father Joseph has told him that only the very best, the most studious and committed of men, the ones most suited to rigorous study and contemplation are admitted. He couldn't be more pleased or proud, he had said yesterday, when Liam had gone to take his leave, his hand on Liam's head for a final blessing. Liam wanted to clutch at his fingers, to say to him that he was frightened, he was afraid he wouldn't be good enough, clever enough, that the famed severity of the Order might be too much for him, but he held his tongue, swallowed his fears, submitted to the blessing.

In the doorway of the cottage, Liam drops his gaze from the mountain to his siblings, who are standing beside him here, outside the house, Rose leaning against Enda, arms tightly around her neck, and Eugene crouched next to Bran. Rose is looking at him imploringly, as if hoping he might even now decide to stay with them, but Enda's jaw is set, trembling. She will not cry, Liam sees, or at least not now. Eugene has one hand on Bran's scruff and with the other he holds the hem of Liam's britches between finger and thumb, as if this grip might keep his brother with him. Bran is hanging his head, peering up at Liam, and Liam finds he cannot look the dog in the eye, and what nonsense is this—what has he got to be sorry for? Why does he feel as if he is betraying the animal by leaving?

Tomás stands at the far end of the haggard, his back to them. He has the loy in his hands, its ash handle inverted, and he is sharpening the blade with a stone, the scraping sound, metallic and harsh, piercing the early-morning air.

Suddenly decisive, because it has to happen, he has to go, Liam steps forward. He grips his sisters by their shoulders, pressing a kiss to their cheeks, Rose's wet and saline, Enda's cold as marble. Rose hugs him with a fierce pressure, pushing a small wrapped loaf into his pocket; Enda circles his arm with her fingers for a fleeting moment, then steps back, away from him, her face shuttered up, turned aside. She must not weep, he sees, so that Rose can. Liam places a hand on Eugene's shoulder, feeling the tension in the boy's collarbone, and Eugene, still crouching on the ground, once again takes Liam's hem, but this time he grips it with his whole fist.

Liam cannot touch or look at the dog, cannot bear that disbelieving gaze, so he straightens, moving away, trying to free himself from Eugene's insistent grasp.

"Da," he calls. "Da?"

His father still stands at the haggard wall, loy shaft in one hand, sharpening stone in the other. He has paused in his movements but doesn't turn around.

"I'm away now, Da," Liam says, his voice carrying through the damp dawn.

At his feet, Eugene gives a growl of protest; Bran paces in interlocking circles, letting out high whines of distress.

"Will you not come and bid me goodbye?" Liam says, or tries to say, but he finds that, halfway through the sentence, his voice is wavering and that he might break down in tears.

"Da?" he tries, one last time, because he would like to feel that there exists between himself and his father a modicum of understanding.

He watches as Tomás lifts the stone, with slow deliberation, and resumes the downward strokes on the blade, as if nothing of any note is happening behind him, and Liam feels each rasping sweep as if it is applied to his skin, to his very ribs and chest.

Liam turns away—from his father, from the house and the fields and the mountain. He tells himself to ignore the stricken faces of his sisters, Bran's yelping, Eugene's high-pitched noises, his father's stubbornly turned back, his maddening silence. He ignores the fact that, to allow him to leave unmolested, Rose must catch Bran by the collar and Eugene by the arm and take them both into the house; he ignores the knowledge that Enda walks behind him, following him, to the corner of the house, where she calls to him, goodbye, goodbye, drawing out the two syllables into a kind of incantation.

He ignores all this not because he feels no love for these people but because he feels too much: he is strangled by it, choked by it. He wishes, as he forces himself to walk away, that there was some way of telling them all this: if I looked back at you, I would be paralysed, stuck, like a man up to his waist in quicksand.

He leaves. He walks away. Down the boreen, down the hill. At his back, he hears the dog barking and howling. He tells himself he will pray for them, he will see them again, though there is no certainty of this. To train as a Jesuit requires years of study and self-abnegation, then long missions in far-flung corners of the world.

Halfway down the boreen, he is pulled up short by a strain of music. Enda's fiddle. He cannot see the house from the green declivity where he stands but he can hear the notes, the melody, and he can picture her, in the lee of the cottage's end, giving him a tune to send him on his way, and is it his imagination or is she playing the same tune she played that time in the copse, when they had fought so bitterly in the tree and he fell, the moment that sealed his fate as not a mapping apprentice but a priest-to-be? He thinks she is, and it takes all his strength and faith not to double back to her, to say, You see it, don't you? You know, as I do, that was another day that changed everything.

Rubbing his hands over his face, he sends up a prayer to St. Ignatius, who established the blessed holy Order that Liam will shortly join, asking for strength and guidance on his journey.

As Liam makes it down the boreen, through the village, past the gates to the manor house, along the road, neighbours come towards him, with prayers and pleas, and some wish for grace, others murmur blessings upon him, and he draws strength from this, and he is sure he feels the presence of St. Ignatius beside him, like the flicker of a lamp.

Near the estate border, a phaeton comes around the corner, and there, sitting next to his groom, cigar in mouth, is the viscount himself, with his wife and two of his daughters in the seats behind him. The viscount gestures curtly for Liam to stand aside. But Liam does not. He continues to walk down the middle of the road. Because he is leaving. Because he is about to be accepted into the Society of Jesus. Because he is no longer a paying tenant of this man or his wife or his horse-faced daughters. Because he feels the protective shield of St. Ignatius, who was after all a soldier and a rebel before he received visions that led him to God.

The viscount's groom—a young man who lives inside the manor gates—is forced to slow his pair of horses to a walk. Liam steps past the phaeton and its occupants. He doesn't salute them, as he is supposed to, according to the rules of their tenancy; he doesn't even glance their way. He is aware of the viscount's short temper—the man could very well beat him for impudence—but Liam doesn't care. He is leaving. He will become a priest, a most exalted and learned one; he will make St. Ignatius proud.

As he passes between phaeton and hedgerow, he hears snatches of the cross-currents of conversation between the viscountess and her daughters, their words drifting around him like airborne seeds: *lilac bombazine with a pale fur trim*, and *a pretty yearling, untrained but showing promise.*

He walks away from the phaeton, without looking back, and is soon over the estate line, then the county border.

It is a day's walk to the House of First Formation, which is set at the end of a long and winding carriageway in green parkland, at the heart of a county to the east of the peninsula. Dusk is settling on the land when Liam moves through the stone gates. His elation is waning now, from exhaustion and also nerves, and he trudges along, following the curves of the carriageway. Glimpses of the house reveal themselves to him through the trees: a line of battlements, the point of a turret, candlelight trembling behind a windowpane, the bone-white length of an empty flagpole.

He feels weakness, tremulousness, in his knees, a trickling sensation in his gut. Blisters have formed on his heels, burst and then re-formed, and they sting and seep into the uneven darns of his socks. He would do anything to be able to lie down and shut his eyes, perhaps sleep for a night and a day, but he knows this will not happen. He is about to step over the threshold of the building where he will undertake the first stages of his priesthood. He is about to meet his spiritual adviser, who will guide and judge him, and also the other novices, men who have chosen, like him, to devote their lives to God. They will be expected to form a close bond, a brotherhood, to assist each other in their vocations, and serve the Jesuit community as a whole.

Liam puts his hands into his pockets, takes them out again. He tries to ignore the thunderous growls of hunger from his belly, tries to master this bodily need when so much else is at stake. He takes the final turning in the carriageway and there is the house: a crenellated grey stone castle, to which several asymmetric wings have been added. To the left is higher ground, an outcrop of smoothed rock—evidence of glacial activity, he finds himself reflecting, before he firmly crushes the thought—and to the right a fenced area containing rows of vegetables and, beyond them, a line of beehives. Off to the side, near an orchard, he sees a group of young men, several of whom hold a hurley, and they are jostling and running, tossing the *sliotar* between them. There is the noise of laughter, the distinct thwack of leather against wood, the thud of footfalls, the calls of the men to each other. Unease fills Liam. Will he be expected to join the game? Might these men be his fellow novices? The young men wear collared shirts and trousers held up by braces; several have smartly oiled hair. There is something forbiddingly moneyed about them: they have the patina of wealth, of expensive schooling. They are not, Liam is sure, from the country, like he is. Not one of them wears a pair of strong, mud-heavy boots.

The young men jostle and shout in the failing light, diving for the *sliotar*, their shirts pale as moths, as if unaffected by the solemnity of the life they have bound themselves to. Liam waits in the shadow of the building, watching, unsure if he should go over and greet them—but he hasn't the skill or the coordination for hurling, never has had—or whether he should knock on the imposing iron-studded door.

His dilemma is solved for him (and isn't this, he will point out to his questioners, as he sits before them in Calcutta, looking back along the years at himself as a gauche and uncertain would-be novice, partly why he joined the Jesuits in the first place, to have life's decisions taken from him, to be able to follow rules and forms instead of thinking for himself?). The front door swings open to reveal an older priest with wire spectacles and an almost entirely hairless head. He looks at Liam with an appraising gaze, asks what is his business here. Liam falters, clears his throat, gets out that he is here to begin his novitiate, and he says it with a questioning tone, as if asking permission. He speaks his name, his worldly name, for he knows he will be given a new one. And the priest nods and says they have been expecting him and that he has arrived in time for supper. He then asks Liam if he renounces the world, and everything in it, if Liam is prepared to enter a preparatory week of solitary silence, if he is willing to embrace the three eventual vows of poverty, chastity and obedience, and Liam says, Yes, Father. He says, Father, I will.

To ease the ache in his back and knees, Tomás has seated himself on a thick tree root that has ruptured the soil, as if coming up for air, before diving back down again into the moss. Open across his lap are the pages of a field book. He has hooked his spectacles around his ears and is perusing the day's measurements and notes, undisturbed by the arguments and curses coming from the motley group of people in front of him. At his feet is a pot of ink with a pen resting in it.

Tomás glances up at the sappers and the two chainboys who are trying to right a cart, which has become stuck in a watery ditch, the sappers bawling orders at the lads, who are thigh-deep in the filth, pushing from behind. The cart is loaded with wooden boxes of supplies, instruments, packs and folded tents; a taller sapper hauls at the harness of the donkey, which is panicked and braying; his two compatriots are disputing among themselves the best way to free the wheels from the ditch. A short distance away, the corporal stands with the lieutenant, smoking and gazing out over the townland.

The commission is to survey and revise a parish in Cavan: the letter Tomás received had said they were needing a civilian assistant for the duration of a month, no more, and that the work was expected to be light and reasonably straightforward. Tomás had not wanted to take it but had been persuaded, against his better judgement, by Rose. She had said it would be good for him to get out of the house and into work: they needed the money, as the rent had gone up again—the viscount's land steward was claiming that the value of their acreage had risen. No point in arguing that this was due to the work Tomás and his sons had put into the land, all that backbreaking drainage and planting and harvesting and fertilising he and Liam and Eugene had done over the years.

Rose had been insistent. They had to find some way to meet the new rent price, she had said, so Tomás was to write back this very minute to say he'd be reporting at the barracks as soon as possible. Tomás had grunted, displeased. He hadn't been out with a surveying team for a long time, not since Phina passed, and he had no wish ever to go again. He was too old for that life now, he told Rose, and hadn't he said often enough that he had his own work to be getting along with, his version of the maps?

But the matter of the raised rent remained and his daughters had the situation sewn up. Rose had packed his knapsack for him as Enda helped him grease his boots, the two of them talking brightly: wasn't it a piece of luck, the letter arriving just when they were in need of money? And the letter said the work would be light, and over in a few weeks. Wasn't Tomás happy to hear they still wished him to work? Too old for that life, indeed: here was the proof that he was still a man in demand.

Tomás regards the scene before him: the mud, the ditch, the stuck cart, the soaked and shivery chainboys, the yelling sappers. There is no such thing, he wishes to say to his daughters, as light work in this world. He sighs and looks back to the field book on his lap, running a thumb down the columns of calculations. He himself made all the measurements, wrestling the instruments into place with the help of the chainboys, neither of whom had ever done such tasks before, but the taller sapper had totted up the final figures.

Tomás can see that several of these are unsound and will need to be corrected. He taps his teeth with the end of the pen, glancing up furtively under his cap. How to fix the figures without incurring the anger and resentment of the sapper, or insulting the corporal, who has added his signature to the page?

The sappers aren't looking his way, but kicking the wheels of the errant cart, slapping the donkey on its rump, and telling the lads what to do; the corporal and the lieutenant still have their backs turned.

With a swift movement, Tomás reaches down and plucks the pen from the inkpot. He lifts his eyes once more, to check that he isn't being observed, and strikes a neat line through four—no, five—of the sapper's calculations, writing the correct figure next to them, in his slanting, exacting hand. He eyes the paragraphs under "Remarks," before adding a mention of the town's new grain store and a culvert, intended for the building of a railway, and then he swiftly blots the page with his sleeve.

He is just considering whether or not he should make a draft map of the townland tonight or wait for tomorrow's surveying calculations when he becomes aware that the sappers are shouting the same two words, with rising insistence.

"Oi, Paddy," the taller one is yelling, or perhaps it's the shorter one—Tomás doesn't know.

"Paddy—oi, you!"

Tomás regards them, distantly, as red shapes bobbing back and forth in the hinterland of his spectacles' focus, his mind still engaged with culverts, the azimuth and its reference meridian.

"He's talking to you, mister," one of the chainboys says quietly, deferentially, his shoulder still pressed to the backboard of the cart.

"Me?" Tomás says.

He stands, removing his spectacles, sliding them into his breast pocket, putting the pen back into the inkpot and shutting the cover of the field book—the marbled card, the cloth binding, so familiar to him—and folding his arms over it, protectively.

"You," one of the sappers is yelling, pointing at him, inexplicably angry, while the other is castigating the chainboy for talking in the wrong language, which they well know isn't allowed, boxing him on the ear. Tomás feels a stab of guilt: such a young lad, and it was his fault that the boy had spoken like that, without thinking. It crosses his mind, of course, as it does several times a day, that it might have been Liam here with him instead of this scrawny northern lad, had that damned priest not turned his head. For the first time Tomás feels relieved that it isn't. He wouldn't want his son to be forced to stand up over his knees in filthy ditchwater, uselessly heaving at a toppled cart, shouted at and struck around the head.

Still the noise of yelling rings in the air. The taller sapper has let go of the donkey's harness and has come towards him, still shouting, still gesturing. Tomás tries to listen to what he's saying but his accent is unfamiliar. The sapper is angry, clearly, and wishes Tomás to do something, but Tomás cannot tell what it is. He stares back, puzzled. Is it the mathematics? Did the man see Tomás correcting his work?

Without warning, the sapper lunges forward and seizes Tomás by the collar, yanking him down off the verge. Tomás withdraws into himself, an animal under attack: he cannot defend himself, he cannot strike a redcoat, so his only hope is to make himself as small as he can. He hears the seam of his jacket strain and tear, but his main concern is for the field book, for it not to fall, to keep all that carefully written ink out of the ditchwater.

"Do as I fucking say, Paddy," the sapper is bawling, as he drags him along, "and put your fucking back into it."

It comes to Tomás that the sapper is wanting him to help push the cart, and he hears one of the chainboys saying, "Ah, now, sir, you can't be asking a man of his age, it wouldn't be right," and he tries to gesture frantically to the lad to stay quiet, if he knows what's good for him.

Sure enough, the shorter sapper roars at the boy to shut his bloody mouth; he lunges forward and bangs both of the chainboys' heads together with a sickening knock, just as the taller sapper snatches the field book from Tomás's hands and tosses it aside, onto the verge, and shoves Tomás towards the cart, into the ditch, into the freezing muddy water.

For a moment, his boots resist the wet, as if taken by surprise, but then he feels it invade, via the eyelets, via the laces and the tongue, through the seams, up through the sole. He'll never get them dry, not for the whole rest of this job.

"Right, lads," he says, wading towards the two chainboys, who are sniffling and crying, swiping at their faces with their sleeves, and one has a bloody nose, his shirtfront scarlet with it, "we'll need to wedge the wheels with a plank of some kind. Can you see anything like that roundabout? Have a look, now."

The boys stumble, dripping, out of the ditch, casting about for various sticks, at which Tomás shakes his head, saying, Something flatter, something stronger, until they come up with two squat lengths of wood. The one with blood down his front is still crying.

Tomás takes the wood, giving them both an encouraging nod. He leans down, pushing his hand into the ditchwater, up to the armpit, feeling his way, and wedging a plank under the first submerged wheel of the cart. He then wades his way around to the other side.

"When this one is in," he says, seemingly talking to the chainboys, but actually addressing the sappers and their officers, who have come over to see what all the commotion is about, "we'll count to three—"

Tomás bends over again, groping in the freezing water for the curve of the wheel.

"—then we'll push from the back, and the donkey can pull from the front—"

He grasps at a spoke, then slides his hand towards the outer rim, following its orbit down towards where it rests in the mud.

"—and we'll be out in no time. All right?"

He fumbles with the wedge, trying to slide it between wheel-rim and ground but the mud repels it; he has to lean forward to push it into place, the front of his jacket and the brim of his cap drinking up the water, the cold taking hold of his torso. He tries twice, then three times. On the fourth go, he thinks he has it, almost, just another inch or two.

It would have been effective, Tomás's scheme to free the cart, for he was always skilled in the way of practical solutions, in the business of angles, pressures and forces. It might have worked; the cart might have rumbled, slowly at first, but then more easily, up out of the ditch and on its way; the division might have continued on to its destination and set up camp and kept at its work, assessing its distances, making its maps.

As it is, none of this happens, or at least not on this day. For just as Tomás is making the final adjustment to the angle of his wedge, in order to free the wheel from the mud, so that the cart may roll onwards, the taller sapper goes back to the donkey.

He reaches out to grasp at its bridle, and the gesture is impatient, it is rough, and the donkey, being a wise animal, senses this. It also knows that this person is the same one who was yelling near its sensitive ears and slapping its rump not so long ago, so the donkey does what any sensible being would do when faced with so obvious an enemy.

It lurches away to escape the grabbing hand.

The cart, buffered by one artfully placed wedge, creaks and shifts. It jerks forward, pushed by the weight of two chainboys at the back, and hauled by a dissatisfied donkey and a furious sapper, who has triumphed after all and got hold of the bridle.

Tomás's hand, however, is at that very moment between road and wheel. When the cart moves, he is trapped, by the fingers, by the palm, and then the cart rolls on, the momentum carrying it forward.

By the time everyone has realised that something is amiss with their civilian assistant, who is near face-down in the filthy water, cursing and screaming in his native language—no one thinks to rebuke him this time—it is too late.

Tomás's hand, the right, the one that can draw coastlines and marshes and castles and contours, the one that grasped Phina's to lead her off the ship, the one that can conjure a landscape in inks and pictograms and lines and calculations, can wield a loy and a spade, can dig and slice turf, is no more. Where once there was a hand is now a mere mess of pulp and bone, useless and crushed, a bloodied stump, dripping with ditchwater.

Tomás is taken, in the very cart that crushed his hand, to the nearest town, where the sappers are dispatched by their commanding officers to find a doctor to treat the poor blighter. They are gone for several hours. The corporal and his lieutenant disappear into an inn, leaving the cart with the chainboys, telling the unfortunate man to keep his chin up.

The cart stands in the middle of the town square, the donkey dozing in its harness. As the sky above Tomás turns, shade by shade, to purplish-black, the chainboys sit by him, damply, telling him it'll not be long now, and Tomás acquaints himself with the pain.

So large and unwieldy is it, like a creature lashed to his back, a hulking ghoul with harsh furnace breath that it blows on Tomás's forearm, up his sleeve, into his shoulder, down his neck. It has a bruising, tendonous grasp on his wrist. It shifts itself into many forms: it is throbbing, it is darting, it is aching, it is cold, it is scalding. He cannot shake it off, he cannot free himself. He tries to keep silent, to still the tongue in his head, but as night comes and a dour drizzle starts to fall, he's aware of a shameful and intermittent groaning that he's sure is coming from himself.

It is almost entirely dark by the time the sappers return. They smell of smoke and whiskey, are full of good cheer, and they have a doctor with them, a portly country man in a three-piece suit, whose speech is slurred and whose touch, when Tomás feels it on his sleeve, quivers with drink.

"You see his hand?" one of the sappers says. "What can be done for it?"

"Can I see it?" the doctor repeats, squinting, his soft and shaking fingers easing back the sleeve. "Can I me hole. How can I possibly see it when there's nothing left to see?"

He tells the sappers that Tomás must be taken to the hospital in the next town, and quickly, before infection sets in. He doses Tomás with laudanum, gives them the bottle, charges them several shillings, and goes on his way, into the night, whistling to himself, his pockets jingling.

Laudanum dreams, Tomás discovers, are both real and unreal, breeze-filled, their edges frilled with light. He floats just above fields of corn, of barley, his feet grazing the wavering tips. He stands on a strand, up to his ankles in pale foam, tiny waves dragging the sand out, grain by grain, from under his feet. He sees Phina coming towards him along a road, and he stops, holding out his arms towards her, filled with longing and happiness at the sight of her, and although she smiles at him, she keeps walking. I thought you were gone, he calls to her. I am, she says, over her shoulder, but you know where to find me, and as she walks away, he sees that she carries under her arm a small wooden boat with tall masts and tiny sails. But I don't know, he shouts after her, I don't know where to find you, where do I find you, where?

As he dreams, and sleeps, acts are performed on his body. At the hospital, doctors in gore-stained aprons saw through the bone and gristle of his arm, removing the mess of his crushed hand. They amputate just above the wrist, stitching the skin closed in a kind of envelope seal. After a day or so, as Tomás lies insensible in his hospital cot, red lines, like border-demarcations on a map, begin to appear from under the bandages, to crawl up his arm.

He is sent back to the operating room, and this time they amputate at the elbow. They re-stitch. They re-bandage. The two surgeons glance at each other. One of them shrugs. They are not very hopeful.

Tomás, however, begins to rally. He is nothing if not resilient. As he lies unconscious, his stump strapped up, his body starts to gather its resources, musters its troops.

The laudanum keeps him submerged, his vision filled with the drift and flash of finned fish. Or he finds himself on a high crag, the wind pressing at his back, and resting on a table in front of him is a bowl of clear yellow soup, at the bottom of which lie pebbles and pen nibs. Or he is watching a battering ram swinging back on its ropes, and back again. Or he is standing in a stream and ahead of him are the figures of two people and he thinks they are Liam and Enda, for one carries a Bible and the other a fiddle, but he finds he cannot tell which is which because they both seem to have the same face and wear the same clothes, and he feels in his marrow that one of them is in great danger but he cannot tell which. Or he is on the strand with his younger son, Eugene, and the boy is holding the heavy turf spade and beside him, on a slipe, is the dog, and Eugene is speaking about the sea, about tides and currents, and his voice is beautiful—low and melodious—and Tomás says to him joyfully, I didn't know you could talk, and Eugene turns to look at him, the turf spade over his shoulder, and says, There is so much you don't know, so much you don't see.

At that very moment, on the ward, the nurse administering to Tomás observes that the man flinches or twitches in his sleep, as if receiving a blow, but she assumes that he is merely registering the pain of his injury, so she goes on with the job of changing his dressing.

Unaware of the disaster that has befallen their father, or the narcotic dreams in which they feature, his four children continue with their daily lives: as far as they know, Tomás is off with the redcoats, working on their maps. As the nurse secures Tomás's bandage with a deft pin, Rose is tying a shawl over her head, preparing to wade through the lough to collect the eggs; Enda scurries along a road that cuts past a church, her fiddle gripped in her hand; Eugene is taking the cow up to pasture. Liam is at the top of a ladder, in the library of the House of First Formation.

He holds a cloth in his hand and he stands up near the curved ceiling: he has been instructed to wipe the dust from the top shelf of books. Each day, he must divide his time between the six principles of the Order, ensuring that no single one is neglected. Under his breath, in an attempt to quell his nausea at being so vertiginously high, Liam recites them, in what he hopes is the correct sequence: *cura personalis*, discernment, *magis*, service, *ad majorem Dei gloriam*, and—what? Liam pauses, his fingers resting on the gold-tipped pages of a large leather-bound volume that looks as if it hasn't been opened for millennia. What is the sixth principle? Liam looks at the rows of books, at the window, the top of which is currently level with his knee, and how he hates heights, hates to be up here at the top of this ladder, how it brings back to him that time when he fought with Enda and fell from the tree: the obscure rage that filled him, the sickening drop as he plummeted down, the useless flail of his limbs, the crunch of impact as he hit the ground. He has avoided climbing anything ever since but he has to perform this task of dusting the topmost books, he cannot refuse because service is one of the portions of life as a postulant. He doesn't, cannot, look down, at the library below him, the floorboards and the rugs and the desks and the discs of lamplight that each encompass a book or manuscript and the head of the particular scholastic which is bowed over it.

One of the heads below must sense his gaze because it swivels, looks up, and the face is blurred and indistinct and, not for the first time, as he hurriedly resumes his dusting, Liam wonders if his eyesight is all it should be, if he doesn't perhaps require spectacles. He can see what is up close, what is within range of touch and grasp, but beyond that, the world is increasingly fogged for him, inaccessible, and didn't his mother always say to him that all those books would ruin his eyesight and he should—

It comes to him then, like a beam of sunlight: finding God in all things. That is the sixth principle. Liam sighs and strains to reach the tops of the volumes on the shelf behind. He always forgets that one. It is, he thinks, secretly his least-favourite of all. Finding God in all things: the idea discomfits him. The concept that the Holy Spirit may reside in a jug, say, or a table, or a river, or a rock—and Liam sways, gripping the ladder, awash with sudden vertigo because he is startled by an awareness that this principle lies perilously close to his father's way of—

Liam squeezes his eyes shut and latches his fingers onto the highest rung. He finds himself to be not a grown man in a hallowed library but a child at a longhouse doorway, being held back by a priest in a black robe, and beyond the crack in a door is a barely human beast lashed to a table, and the person who has trapped him there, to torture and harass him is—

Liam presses his forehead into the leather spines of the books. He will not go down this route. Such thoughts must be banished. Father Joseph was his saviour, Liam must remember, the one who set him on the path to spiritual glory, and he must descend this ladder, as if nothing is wrong, as if he is the serene postulant he is meant to be, secure in his vocation, executing his tasks without hurdle or doubt. But Liam's hands are slippery and refuse to uncurl from the rungs; his feet have no wish to move. He has to press his lips together so as not to let out small whimpers of distress. Liam sends up a prayer for forgiveness, for assistance: *O God, come to my aid, O Lord, make haste to help me.*

Curiously, as Liam is steeling himself to descend the ladder, at the same time, a hundred miles or so to the west, Liam is also waiting in a queue on a harbour wall.

He is dressed in trousers that are held fast at the waist with a length of twine. He clutches his papers and his ticket in his hand.

The queue around him is restive, distraught: people shove and fidget; some weep; some shout angrily, accusing others of cutting in or stealing their goods. All around, people are in fierce embraces, bidding farewell, probably for ever, to relatives or friends they cannot bring themselves to let go of.

Liam, however, is dry-eyed, pale of face, entirely alone. No one has come to see him off. He sets his back against the country of his birth, and turns instead towards the great febrile sea between him and his destination. It is shifting, deep blue-green, speckled with foam, punctured here and there by the hungry beaks of diving birds. He will, as his father once predicted, sail the wide ocean. He will leave. He will not give way to sentiment, he will not cry. He will go to Québec and make a different life for himself.

This Liam shuffles forward, slowly, towards the gangway, inch by inch, his boots—he has stuffed them with straw for he has heard that it can be brutally cold out at sea—taking their last steps on his homeland. The harbour, he notices, is built from ancient rock, embedded with the tiny curving bodies of fossilised sea creatures—he quickly looks away for he has to keep his mind on the queue, the ticket in his hand, the knapsack of goods on his back, anything at all to fend off thoughts of his father and the siblings he is leaving behind. He tips back his head to look instead at the ship, its triple masts, the figurehead on the prow, its complex web of rigging, the powerful ropes looped and knotted to the quay.

Why are there two Liams? How can Liam be in the library in the House of First Formation, learning about the six principles of the Jesuit Order, and also on a harbourside, about to board a ship, to become a migrant, heading for a new land?

One Liam is making his hesitant way down the ladder, rung by rung, intending to sit at a desk and learn by heart a portion of the Jesuit rules or perhaps a psalm or ecclesiastical hymn. The other? His hair, newly shorn, is mostly tucked into his cap; it is, like that of the first Liam, still the colour of new coins, but perhaps slightly finer. His hands are narrower, the fingers longer. There is a tell-tale callus on the right-hand thumb. His face is eager but wary; there is a suppressed nervousness, an anxiety, about this one, as if he might burst into laughter or tears at any moment. Impossible, really, to tell the difference—for anyone who doesn't know Liam or his family. Anyone who does know them, however, might guess straight away, which may explain why the second Liam, every now and again, darts nervous looks over his shoulder. Will he, he is thinking, be found out? Can he get away with this? Can he pull it off?

As Liam in the House of First Formation opens the Book of Psalms at the allotted page, the second Liam reaches the front of the queue. He shows his ticket and his papers and his passage documents to the harbour official—and how his heart punches and kicks against his ribcage and the bindings wound around it, for if it is to go wrong, it will be now—but the official just glances at them and waves him past. And this Liam stoops to pick up something that has been resting on his feet and takes the gangway with hasty, disbelieving strides, shouldering as he does so a fiddle strapped into its case.

At the very same moment, Rose flings open the door of the cottage and yells her sister's name into the hills.

"Enda? Enda!"

She turns to Eugene.

"Where can she have got to?"

Oceans are not blue, Enda discovers. They are not the azure of the bays and inlets of the peninsula, where yellow-shelled creatures cling to rocks and frail scarlet seaweed waltzes in the clear, froth-fringed waves. Neither are they the mild cerulean of her father's maps. This ocean, the one she is crossing, yard by yard, day by day, week by week—and to call it a singular "ocean" rather than "oceans" seems an error because its vastness, its boundlessness, its terrifyingly endless expanse implies plurality, how can something this large be one ocean alone?—is shifting and various, impossible to pin down.

On dry and windless days, when the sails above them hang limp in the air, the waters are flat and dull as a sheet of metal. If the winds start to rise, the waves become puckered and troubled. And there have been times when gales scream and rip through the masts, and the seas boil up into great dark peaks striated with sinister white lace, and the ship is pitched down one incline then up another, a small vessel toiling across an aqueous mountain range, and the sailors lock down the hatches and no one is allowed out on deck, and the cramped quarters of steerage become a slithering purgatory of upturned waste buckets, belongings, water, wailing and terrified children, knots of people on their knees desperately reciting the Mysteries.

Enda has been assigned a bunk with five others: two men, their wives, and a boy of around six. She wedges herself between the child and the partition: she doesn't want to put herself, even dressed in Liam's clothing, next to either of the men, and she worries that if she were by the women one of them might discover her secret. She sleeps, fitfully, her arms locked around her fiddle, a scrap of blanket over her head; her money she has sewn into the lining of her jacket.

Liam's jacket.

And she dreams of nothing but water: streams, pumps, wells, gutters, springs. She is wading into the inlet at home, a creel for dulse and mussels on her back. She is dousing a barrel of washing in suds. She is swimming down a river, and the current is warm and cradling, and she knows Rose and Liam and Eugene are behind her, and then, without warning, there is a weir, the river rushing down its drop, and Enda is falling.

When she wakes, with a flinching start, she feels the keel and haul of the ship, hears the squealing of its boards and joists, and the slumberous sighs and snores of her bunkmates, the pukings and mewlings, the squabbles over space, and it comes back to her where she is, what she has done, that she cannot go back, she can only go forward, and even the familiar hollow lightness of the instrument in her arms cannot stop her sobbing into her sleeve.

What has she done? Why did she leave? Enda staggers around the dark and oppressive hold, pushing her way through the crowds, the press of unwashed bodies, cursing herself: impulsiveness has always been her downfall; she never thinks before she acts; will she ever learn? The people around her are in family groups of four or five or more. There are grandparents holding fast to the coats of small grandchildren; there are brothers and sisters and cousins, who all huddle together; there are couples with unwieldy broods of children. They will arrive in the New World insulated and consoled by each other, perhaps to be greeted by more family. Enda, however, will be alone, will need to find her own way, and she has no idea, no plan, as to how she will achieve this. She is, she thinks, the only passenger who has no one, and this is nobody's fault but her own.

Rose is expecting Tomás back soon; any day now he'll walk up the boreen with his mapping bag on his shoulder, come in through the door and hang his cap on the peg.

She has been planning in her head, all these long weeks, how she will give him dinner before she tells him about Enda. She'll get him sitting down, put some boxty or some salted fish in his stomach to ease the shock of it, the deception and lies of it, Enda's cruelty at not even saying goodbye. For Enda to scheme like that, to steal Liam's papers, and run away across the sea: it takes Rose's breath away. She has, she knows, been waiting for her father's return so she may vent her fury and hurt, and receive the balm of his.

Now, instead, as she lifts her head from milking the cow, she finds not Tomás but two soldiers coming around the gable wall, carrying between them what at first sight appears to be a heavy sack. Rose blinks. Why would soldiers be bringing her a sack, and one wrapped in cloth at that? She blinks again. The sack is the body of her father, Tomás.

Rose staggers upright, startling the cow and upsetting the milking pail, and cries, What is this?, rushing forward, and she is certain that Tomás is dead, the soldiers have killed him, and why would they do such a thing? Then she sees the rise and fall of his chest: he is alive but deeply asleep. Kneeling beside him, she demands: What happened? But the redcoat lads have to lean with their hands on their knees, catching their breath, gasping and complaining about the climb up the hill, the weight of the man. When they are able to answer, they talk over each other, rambling and confused, something about an accident, a cart, a spell in hospital, nearly died, lost his hand, medicine. The way they speak is so jerky and tight-mouthed that she has to ask them to say it all again, which they do, ending with the fact that they had orders to lash him to the back of a horse and deliver him home, so here he is. They are, by this time, taking off their hats, winking at her, offering her tobacco, saying they would have come sooner if they'd known she was such a looker; they'd have urged the horse up to a canter. Rose steps past them, taking the proffered medicine bottle, and calls for Eugene to come and help her. He won't, however, come out of the byre until the redcoats leave, so she waits beside the insensible Tomás until she hears their boots departing.

Eugene and Rose put their father to bed, then stand there, taking in the state of him, bit by dreadful bit: face gaunt, body wasted and thin, the ominous bandage, the sling that holds the half-arm to the chest. How can this have happened, and after everything else? It is too much: her mother, Liam, Enda, and now this. She finds it hard not to believe this family is under some kind of curse. With hands made slow by shock she takes from her apron pocket the brown-glass bottle given to her by the soldiers and administers the strange liquid with the dropper. She and Eugene wait, gazing down at their subdued and motionless father, slumbering like a giant in a folktale. Eugene hovers his fingers over the bandaged stump, over Tomás's flickering eyelids. He bends down, as if he might whisper something in his ear.

With the aid of the bottle, Tomás remains unconscious for three days. Rose and Eugene tiptoe around, unwilling to rouse him. Neighbours come, to tut and pray over him: the widow, the bonesetting sisters, the younger fisherman (who is in fact well over fifty by now). The liquid in the bottle runs low; Rose gives him the final drops late one night. She wonders what will happen next.

In the thin, milky half-light of dawn, Tomás wakes with a roar.

It is a hoarse, atavistic sound, ripped from deep inside him, full of sorrow and ire. It is the lament of an injured animal, the grief of a fallen warrior at the close of a battle. It wakes Rose and Eugene up in the loft. It sets Bran instantly barking and leaping at the door.

Before Rose can make it down the ladder, Tomás has thrashed his way out of bed, yelling, stumbling about, upturning fire-irons and pots. Eugene has his fists pressed over his ears, his face flushed and fearful. Rose scrambles down the ladder, seizes Bran by the collar, and tries to get a hold on her father, who is on his knees, plucking at the sling, trying to pull himself free.

"Da," she cries, as he slips from her grasp, crawling towards the window, where he pulls himself up to stare wildly out as if he, like Bran, believes that enemies are breaching their defences. "Da, you're at home, with us. Your arm—"

Tomás gasps. Rose sees that he is looking down, for the first time, at his loose and empty shirt sleeve. He lifts his left hand and touches the absence there, his fingers groping for what is no more.

"You were in hospital," Rose says, trying for a reassuring tone. "The soldiers brought you back. You nearly died of the infection. Do you remember—"

Tomás lets out a shaky, uneven breath, pulling himself up so that he is leaning against the wall. He fumbles at the buttons of his shirt with his left hand, trying to push them through the cloth. He manages one, but he can't seem to get a grip on the second, his fingers slipping, a muffled sob escaping his lips.

"Will I help you there, Da?" Rose says softly, biting her lip, because it is a sight past bearing, her father, a man of such coiled strength and strange talents, brought so low, his light so diminished. She steps forward but Eugene is already at Tomás's side. At nearly thirteen, he is catching up in height with his father, and he reaches out with hands that are gentle and capable, working his way down the buttons and easing the shirt off, taking great care not to touch the amputation. Rose watches, dazed: in the midst of all this panic and uproar, she is struck by the sense that she is seeing the adult in her brother for the first time, the grown man he will be. Eugene folds the shirt neatly and lays it on the table, then turns back to Tomás. He seems to understand what their father needs, which is for him to examine his body and what has been done to it.

Tomás stands unsteadily in his cottage, by the ladder, his breath coming in rasps, looking down at his bandages, his stump, his chest, the remaining arm.

"Gone," he whispers hoarsely, as if trying to make sense of the word.

"They'd to cut it off," Rose says, "to save your life. They thought you mightn't live, but here you are."

Tomás, in only his underclothes, lifts both arms, trembling, holding them out, as if comparing their lengths. The left hand curls and opens, fingers flexing. He turns it palm-up, then circles it at the wrist. He stares at it, then at the vacancy of its missing counterpart. The forefinger and thumb on his left hand come together, as if grasping something, then stretch apart, as if letting whatever it was fall.

Then he turns and looks about the room, and his face is frightened, like that of a scolded child. He sways dangerously on his feet and Eugene steps forward, grips his shoulder, helps him to a chair. Tomás is muttering something about punishment, at last, retribution, comeuppance, it all being his own fault.

"Don't be saying that now," Rose says soothingly, as she tucks a blanket around his legs. "Punishment indeed. You'll have done nothing wrong, sure, and—"

"A lifetime of working for the enemy," Tomás mutters, letting his head fall back to the wall, his face ghastly pale. "I told your mother, I told her, I told Liam, I told them all that I was finished with it, and now look where it's got me."

Rose goes off to fetch breakfast, a cup of water, a warm jersey. When she comes back, she finds Eugene sitting on a stool at Tomás's feet, holding his hand, as if he is still a young boy. Tomás is rambling, incoherently and disjointedly, with long hesitations and gaps, about a grave and not enough stones or stones that were too heavy and some hungry swine and a child at a window and a person long ago who lost an arm or was it a leg? Rose doesn't catch it all. She assumes it is something he heard in hospital or a type of delirium caused by the shock and perhaps the medicine. Eugene, however, listens intently, his gaze fixed on his father, and he nods gravely at intervals, still holding his father's hand in both of his, as if he understands the story Tomás is telling, or as if he'd known it all along.

The novices have fasted all day. They have taken only water while going about their duties and devotions. Liam's stomach has gone through cycles of growling and rumbling, then silence, then darts of pain. He has felt weak and enervated, almost as if he couldn't manage the allotted walk around the cultivated woodland, still less up to the compulsory task of conversing in Latin with the other novices.

Now, as he sits on the long bench in the refectory, he feels filled with nothing but an impatient fury. The novice master, Father Byrne, stands at the lectern, reading aloud to them from some tract or other—Liam screws up his eyes to see that the title is *Practice of Perfection*—while all the time wafts of their dinner come through the open door to the kitchen.

Liam folds his hands in his lap, one cupped inside the other. He tries to breathe in only through his mouth. The reading will be finished soon, he tells himself. Father Byrne's sonorous, measured voice can go on only so long. And then their collation will be brought, they will pick up their cutlery, they will be permitted to eat. Baked eggs, he has heard, are what is permitted after a day of fasting, the purpose of which is to teach them humility and obedience.

That he feels neither—only rage and hunger—Liam endeavours to ignore. He tries to set his face in an expression of humility, even obedience, but all the while such thoughts are rattling about inside him: what is the purpose of making us fast, and for so long? Why does Father Byrne speak so slowly? Why does he pronounce the word "Christ" as if it's tri-syllabic? How are we to stand it? That fella opposite me, Cox is his name, what a peculiar face he has, as long as a boot. Is it eggs I can smell or something else, and who was it told me we'd be getting eggs? How much longer, how much longer?

At the sight of Father Byrne removing his spectacles, carefully, and closing the cover of the book, Liam feels himself straighten up. It will be now, it has to be. A sign will be given to the kitchen and out of that door will come trays bearing food, any minute, any—

But what is this? One of the novices, an older man called McGrath, is getting to his feet and mumbling something. Liam leans forward to catch what is being said, what is holding up their meal now.

"Reverend Father and loving brothers," McGrath recites, "by order of holy obedience, I tell my fault—"

It is too much. Liam trembles with the effort of not burying his head in his hands, not laying his forehead on the table in despair. They are to speak their faults and receive their penances? Now? When the food is so near, yet so far?

McGrath admits to breaking two plates yesterday, and Father Byrne nods, saying that this is indeed a fault, albeit minor, against their religious poverty. McGrath is asked to kiss the feet of the reverend fathers at the nearest table. The novice next to McGrath stands. He says he did not clear the ashes from the fire grates as well as he might. He is duly told to eat his meal in the corner on bended knee. On it goes: someone folded down the corners of a book, someone else failed to clean all the wax from the chapel candlesticks.

When it comes to Liam's turn to stand, he gets through the part about order of holy obedience, but when he says, "I tell my fault," he cannot go on. His speech dries up. His mind is a grey blank, a desperate hollow, filled only with a crazed longing for food.

"I tell my fault," he says again, swaying slightly, "and . . . and . . ." what comes next? He must say something about a defect or a failing in himself, he must indicate that he wishes to learn obedience, that he wishes to grow in virtue, but all he can think about is eggs. Eggs from the little islet out in the lough, his mother wading through the waters to fetch them for their breakfast, boiled on the fire. Their thin carapace, then the white casing, which would yield to a spoon-tip, inside which was the molten yellow core, slightly crystallised at the edges, and—

"If I may," comes a voice from across the table, and Liam sees that Cox, the man at whose face he had been staring, is getting to his feet.

"Reverend Father," Cox is saying, his head bowed in humility, but under his brow his eyes are darting to Liam with a calculated beadiness, "forgive me for speaking out but I wish only to aid my brother here. I speak in the spirit of charity when I say that I have observed a fault in him, and my own holy obedience enjoins me to bring it to his notice."

"Go on," Father Byrne says, leaning with one elbow on the lectern. "What fault have you observed?"

"That of impatience. And inattention. And lack of humility."

Anger sweeps through Liam, like fire through field stubble. He may leap across the table and strike Cox about his lugubrious face. How dare this man say of him that he is—

"Twice during mass today, I saw him yawn. During meditations yesterday, I saw him gaze for a long time out of the window. When he was asked by a reverend father to polish his shoes, he was heard to sigh."

Father Byrne turns to Liam. He tells him that the word "obedience" comes from the Latin, *ob-audientia*, and they, as novices, must therefore take it to mean not only the following of a rule, but also the aspect of listening or, more specifically, the desire to hear the voice of God. To be obedient is to be listening to God. Father Byrne tells Liam that his penance is to go shoeless for the rest of the week.

They sit. Grace is said. Food is brought. It is not eggs but a thin soup the colour of pondwater. Liam is made to remove his shoes with all eyes upon him before he is permitted to eat his soup, hands shaking, head lowered.

What does it mean to lose a hand? A person can no longer button his own jacket or tie his bootlaces. He must school himself and his remaining hand to raise a spoon to his mouth. It takes him twice as long to milk a cow or dig a drill. He might try to write something with his left hand, but what comes out is the scratched scrawl of a child. He will spill water over his exquisitely inked cross-sections of a mountain range, the paper ruined, the geological symbols blurring to abstract cloud trails. He will discover that the lack of half an arm somehow sets his feet off course, unbalances him, and that when he stumbles he hasn't two hands to catch himself. He gains bruises down his thighs, along his flanks. He collides with doorways, shelves, table corners, rafters. When he is told that his eldest child, his daughter, the headstrong one, has taken herself and her fiddle across the water, never to return, that she deceived them all, that she didn't even say goodbye, he will discover that one hand isn't enough to wipe the tears from his face. He will wish to smash something in the wake of this discovery—a bowl, maybe, a cup—but he will find that his left arm hasn't the strength in it, even for this. He will rise in the morning with the phantasmagoric sensation of a hand—and how miraculous it had been, how nimble and wise, how had he not marvelled at this every minute of every day when he still had it?—resting at the end of his shirt sleeve, its fingers curled, its nails bedded into their half-moons, its palm ready to hold whatever he wishes it to.

But the hand is gone, it is no more. The incompetent redcoats took it from him, and he will never see it again.

Tomás has been back at home for almost a month when he raises his head at the table, like a man waking from sleep. He seems not to see his daughter, sitting opposite him, sawing a knife down through a loaf of bread; he doesn't look at his son, the youngest, who is spreading butter on each slice that drops from Rose's knife, one by one, making sure the butter reaches right to the edges, the way he likes it.

Both his children, however, jump when Tomás suddenly speaks, for the first time in days: "What are we to do?"

Rose pauses, midway through cutting. She looks at Eugene, she looks at Tomás. "About what, Da?"

Tomás pushes away his bowl of soup, wipes his mouth. He lifts the shoulder of his injured side. "The state of me," he says. "I'm good for nothing. I'll never work again. I can't hold a pencil, can't write a word. I can't even till my own land. You and Eugene can't work those fields on your own."

Rose clears her throat, sits straighter. She casts a glance towards Eugene before she speaks. "After mass last week," she says, and if the words have a rehearsed quality to them, it is because she has been speaking of nothing else, to the widow, and to Eugene, for days, whenever she's out of Tomás's earshot; she has been expecting this conversation and she is ready with her reply but she must tread carefully because, as the widow pointed out, her father is not an easy man, and for this to work she must make it seem like his idea, "I was talking to . . ." here she is horribly conscious that she must avoid mentioning Father Joseph, and the fact that this scheme is all his ". . . some people, and it was suggested that we might write to the mapping office in the city about . . . com-pen-sa-tion."

Rose has had to practise saying this word, taught to her by Father Joseph as she stood with the widow outside the chapel, its odd emphasis on the third syllable. She likes the word: it has a safe, reassuring ring to it. Father Joseph had, of course, heard of Tomás's accident—he was kept informed of most goings-on in the peninsula and people were always keen to talk of the troubles of others—and he had come up to Rose to find out more. You can't let those redcoats get away with it, he had said to her. It's not right.

"Compensation?" Tomás repeats slowly.

Rose nods and tries to remember what else Father Joseph had said, and she remembered being surprised by his vehemence, his insistence, because it was well known that no love was lost between him and Tomás. Father Joseph had said that Tomás had been injured in the line of work: the army or the mapping office surely owed him for that; they must pay for what they had done to him. Compensation. Hadn't Rose's family suffered enough?

"Father J—" She stops herself just in time. "It was said that because the accident happened while you were following orders, that you were injured in the line of—"

"Exactly!" Tomás shouts, banging the table with his fist, setting the spoons and bowls leaping and clattering. "It's exactly that! Those feckers did this to me. They took my hand."

Tomás, agitated, stands up, and begins to pace around the table, muttering about obeying orders, about blackguards and beatings and inebriated doctors, and the irony of him not being able to write the letter, and who on earth hereabouts can they find to write such a thing? The girl hasn't the learning, and neither does the widow or the fishermen.

Rose must keep her face still, her expression perplexed, throughout this rant. She must sit with her hands in her lap, apparently deep in thought. Who, she must appear to be wondering, should we ask to write the letter?

All of a sudden, Tomás subsides, falling silent. Rose waits, her mouth pursed, not daring to glance up at him. Has he arrived at the one and only solution to this problem? She thinks perhaps he has. He is staring at the table, his face twisted into a grimace, as if in pain. He seems about to speak, then stops himself, then changes his mind.

"That fella," Tomás gets out, in a gruff and strangled voice. "Whatshisname. That priest of yours. I wonder would he do it?"

Rose allows herself to gasp with surprise. "He might. He has the learning after all. Will I walk over there and ask him? Tomorrow. Or the day after."

She watches as Eugene goes to the pegs by the door and takes down his jacket, which he puts on, and her shawl. Tomás takes it from him and passes it in a bundle to Rose.

"Now?" Rose stands, reaching for it. "Will I go now?"

Tomás nods, once, furious yet relieved, then waves her off with a curt gesture.

Enda stands at the stern, looking out at the water as yet uncut by the boat. The sun beams down on the hold passengers having their time up on deck; a fresh but unthreatening wind fills the sails, and the boat is skimming along nicely over a tranquil sea. Around her, she hears accents from the north, from the east, from cities, from farms and fields. There are young men and women, awkward and shy in their newly tall bodies, tiny babies wrapped in blankets, ancient and toothless old ladies with bonnets tied firm, children who charge about in herds, from one side of the tilting deck to the other. No one else, not a single other person, is travelling alone.

She feels a sickening wave of something gathering behind her eyes, which sting and smart, and she turns to face the direction they came from. Their vessel leaves a smooth, filigree-edged road on the ocean that vanishes and erases itself so that they can never find their way back, even if they want to. Then she hears that a man next to her at the rail is speaking to her.

"What was that?" she says, forgetting momentarily to put on the low voice of a man.

He gestures at the fiddle case, as always strapped to her back. "Will you not give us a tune, son?"

Enda stares at him for a moment, the word for "son" resounding in her head, and for a moment she sees, with a lacerating clarity, her mother carrying baby Eugene on her shoulders, her father and

Liam standing facing each other on the hearthrug, the older man imploring the younger to stay, not to go into the Church, to be his apprentice. Liam is the son, the *mhac*, she wants to say, and Eugene: They are the sons. But I am the one who has gone.

The man is still regarding her, his snaggle-toothed mouth held in a hopeful grin. Enda makes herself nod. A tune. Of course.

She brings out the fiddle into the sea air, fits it under her chin, lifts the bow in her hand, tests the strings, adjusts the pegs. Both instrument and bow feel almost weightless in her hands, utterly familiar. Her fingertips rest on the strings, awaiting instruction, the horsehairs of the bow are poised above the bridge. Enda takes in a breath, glances around: the man at the rail is watching, and a couple of others are gazing at her, without curiosity. She doesn't know what to play, how to begin, she doesn't know how to start, and yet she does, or her fingers do, and they move themselves into position without her, and her other hand comes down, and the strings seem to leap eagerly towards the bow, and music surges out, notes following notes, and she somehow finds the rhythm of it, or it finds her, and she plays there, standing by the ship's rail, her foot in her straw-stuffed boots keeping time, people sitting up and taking notice, some moving closer, others clapping along, and at one point she hears a singer find the melody and the voice—a woman's—dips below and then above the fiddle, inserting words and phrases into the sound, twining around it like ivy, and Enda smiles in acknowledgement, slowing her fingers so that the singer can add her own embellishments, the voice turning on a note, like a child playing hopscotch, skipping over another. The singer's face is blank, her eyes shut, turned away from the blast of the wind, her back against the scuttlebutt; her child stares at her, open-mouthed; an older woman, next to her, listens intently, tears spreading through the creases of her cheeks. An obscure part of Enda wants to go to her and speak her secret, to say, I'm not a man, I'm a woman, like you, but she, too, shuts her eyes, and plays. She plays a song about rushes, an air about a battle; she plays a seafaring melody, which the sailors up in the rigging sing along to, a ballad about a man and his lass, a long song about fish in a river, and another about green hills. She plays until her fingertips are sore, until the instrument is warm under her chin, and the horizon is drinking down the red orb of the sun.

That night, she dreams not about water but about the old widow on the peninsula. She is standing in the doorway of her cottage, beckoning to Enda as she passes by. At her feet is the cedar chest and she opens its lid and says, Why don't you get in? and Enda says, I can't, I'll never fit. The widow shakes her head and says, You must get in or you'll be lost. Enda, wretched, says, But I am lost, I am. Then she wakes and the ship is as before: creaking its way across the blue-green-grey-stormy ocean, and she must go with it.

A week at sea, then another, then another. They are blown off-course, a sailor tells Enda, his lips cracked and split from the weather, by a north-easterly wind, which might add another week to their journey. Enda stops keeping count of the days. She surrenders herself to the crossing, her life at home becoming as unreal and insubstantial as the life she is heading towards. This vessel is her world now: she wakes, she douses her face, she accepts her water ration, her porridge, she eats the dry biscuits and hardtack, she plays the fiddle, she walks up and down the deck, she goes to her bunk, she sleeps for as long as she can, trying to ignore the sharp elbows and knees of the restless child next to her.

Water rations are reduced. A storm keeps them all below for three days, and Enda tries to move about the aisles in the darkness so that her joints don't seize with stiffness, while people all around her have lowered themselves to pray. A woman takes sick, then another, then some children. A baby dies, and the hatches are opened, and they are all ordered on deck, to empty their buckets, to air themselves, to sluice out the hold, to shake the lice and filth from bedding. The wrapped parcel of the baby's small body is committed to the waves; a priest holds mass on deck. Enda regards him with dull curiosity: his worn soutane, the rise and fall of his Adam's apple, the pallid scalp visible as the wind parts his thinning hair. She wants to ask him what made him want to be a priest; what was it that drove him to it? The baby's mother, a young woman with a blue-black plait reaching down to her waist, wails inconsolably, and continues to do so for days. No one tells her to hush, even at night. Her husband pats her hand, in a numb and helpless daze. An elderly man who, it has been noticed by some, possesses a good and thick coat, also passes, and the priest once again prays as the sailors, their caps stuffed into their pockets, slide the body into the water. Nothing is said when, a few days later, one of his sons is seen wearing the coat: the crossing is cold, colder than any had imagined. A boy falls ill with a fever and a rash, but recovers. Another child succumbs, then a third. The sailors, Enda notices, wear their scarves up and over their noses and mouths, so she does the same. Three children die, and then two women, and five men. Several groups of people elect to remain on deck at all times, even throughout the night. Enda decides to do the same, bedding down on her bundle, still with her fiddle clasped in her arms. Whenever she wakes, she presses her fingertips to her forehead to check for fever, just as her mother used to do. She doesn't want to die here, for her body to be dropped from a plank and swallowed by the restless, shifting waves, to be devoured by sea creatures, and her family never to hear of her again. The boards are unyielding, pressing up into the joints of her hips and the bones of her shoulders, but above her are the scatterings of stars, and Enda thinks about how she once had to explain to Liam that they were not holes in the dark fabric of the sky, through which the light of God was showing, but distant forms, and he had refused to believe it. They have to be something more than that, he'd said. As she lies there, under constellations brighter and more perfect than any she has ever seen, Enda wishes she could say to him that she sees what he means: they cannot be mundane matter—they must be celestial illuminations beaming down.

The next day, in a grey and damp dawn, the cry goes up that land has been sighted, and everyone comes up on deck to jostle at the rails and watch the promontory of Nova Scotia, at first no more than a wavering graphite line on the horizon, but then gathering itself together from the veils of mist, acquiring form and dimension.

Rose stands beneath the clock tower, hands wedged in her apron pocket, her gaze directed upwards, beyond the rooftops of the town, towards the sky. This is always her place on market day, just as it was the widow's, before Rose took on the task of selling their goods. The clock tower is placed where the road splits in two, and several lanes converge. It is, Rose knows, the best position for a stall: many others have tried to take it, but the widow has always been fierce in seeing them off.

The eggs are arranged in two baskets on the ground in front of Rose, with the widow's dried dulse in a creel beside her. The market is busy today, the streets thronged with people, chickens, pigs, carts, horses. There are farmers from up-country, some of the gentry from a big house, with their tweed shooting suits and silk cravats and their loud voices; there are children running between stalls, and women bartering for goods. On the other side of the clock tower a man is selling heads of cabbage; Rose is able, through the heavy mire that clouds her mind, to form the thought that she should use the egg-money to buy one before she takes the road home. She could fry it in butter with slices of potato. It would make Eugene happy, for he loves fried cabbage. Maybe their father would agree to take a plateful or—

Rose sighs, the vague thought of cabbages detaching itself and trailing off into the air, like a piece of cut thread.

Her head is like that, these days. It cannot hold an idea or a notion for long. She has become a leaky vessel, a frayed garment, a bucket with a hole, a sack eaten away by mice, and everything trickles out of her, gone for ever. During the crisis of Tomás's accident, she was too preoccupied to think or dwell, but lately she has felt herself to be weighed down by cares, or stranded in a mist.

What it comes down to is plain: if anyone else leaves her, she feels she may dissolve, like soft rock in water. Her mother, taken too soon, too suddenly. Her father, who walked out one day to do some work, and was returned to them insensible, his hand gone. Liam, who warned and warned them that he would leave, and then, appallingly, did so. And Enda? Rose finds herself more and more angry with her sister as the days go by; she cannot think about Enda's treachery, her deceit, without working herself into a pure and righteous fury. Tomás's accident kept these thoughts in abeyance for a while, or perhaps Rose wondered if Enda might come back to them somehow, might change her mind and return from the dockside, saying, I thought I would go but in the end I couldn't do it.

To take the papers, to leave, to sail away, without so much as a word to any of them. To have planned it all but said nothing to Rose, her only sister, no farewell, no explanation. Rose had initially refused to believe it possible: Enda would never betray her like that; she would never take the emigration papers and her tobacco tin of saved pennies and her fiddle and lie to Rose's face about where she was going that day.

A day or so after Enda disappeared, Rose had gone out beyond the haggard to feed the donkey, and near the copse and the streams, she came upon strange scatterings of bright strips. For a moment, she couldn't understand them, couldn't tell what they were. They looked like tethers or bindings, and they possessed an odd familiarity, and then she saw what they were: Enda's hair. She must have come up here, with a pair of scissors, and cut it off, severed the length of it from her head, all the better to pass as the man named on the papers she had taken from beneath Liam's pallet. Only then, as Rose scrabbled about on the ground, snatching up the strands of hair, rage and grief tearing through her like a gale, did she fully comprehend what Enda had done. Enda had gone, had left her, had hatched this plan and not told her, had abandoned her here, to look after their father and their wordless brother, in this lonely place. She would never come back. As Rose knelt on the grass and moss, she was aware of a horrible cawing noise coming out of her, like that of a furious gull. Enda had gone and Liam had gone, within weeks of each other, and neither of them knew of Tomás's accident, and how was she to manage, because here she was, left out, just like when they were children, unheeded, the last to know.

As she stands by her eggs, she thinks she will never again utter her sister's name, that it will be relegated to silence for evermore. She thinks that if Enda were to appear to her now, before her, in this marketplace, Rose would not forgive her. She might very well strike her; she could not be held back.

She has barely sold anything today. The beautiful domed shapes of the hens' eggs remain where she put them this morning. She knows it is because she is standing with her back to the clock tower, not catching anyone's eye. This is no way to sell, she can hear the widow—or is it perhaps the voice of her mother?—telling her. You'll be heading home with empty pockets. You need to call out, catch people's attention. Fresh eggs, best eggs, laid this morning, dulse for you, go on, shout it loud, with a smile on your face.

So Rose breathes in, and calls: "Fr—" She has to stop and clear her throat, and it occurs to her, in that moment, that she hasn't spoken at all, today, not once, since she woke, she and Eugene sharing a silent breakfast then making their way down to the lough, their father out God knew where, on one of his secretive wanderings. She might lose her ability to speak altogether if she goes on like this, with no one to talk to.

"Eggs," she croaks, the sound not even reaching the people passing right in front of her—a woman holding two children by the hands, a frozen-looking boy with no shoes, and the eldest son of the viscount, who is raising his arm to greet the knot of gentry across the street, calling to those of his kind over the heads of the townspeople as if they are simply not there.

Something about this young man riles Rose, fans a flame of anger in her. Him with his silver-buttoned waistcoat, his smouldering cigar, his yellow-patterned cravat folded just so about his fleshy neck. Suddenly, her fury has a direction in which to travel: it has a target. How dare he? she's thinking. How dare he strut through this town, looking like he's never lost anything or anyone in his life, decked out like that, when his father—

"Eggs," she bawls, just as he's passing her by, causing him to jerk his head sideways and bring up a protective hand to cup around his ear, "fresh this morning! Get your eggs here! Fresh eggs, fresh this morning."

People wander over. The woman with the two children buys a dozen, and Rose slides the money into her pocket. The jangle and slide of coin over coin is a comfort: it gives her a feeling of purpose. Eugene will like to look at them, one by one, when she gets back tonight—he will run his thumb over the markings, noting to himself the numbers inscribed there. He will stack them in piles, then rearrange them according to whatever private rules he has made for himself.

A family of five stops at her stall, and fills their basket; a woman with barely any teeth in her head wants a half-dozen eggs to feed her sons. Then one of the gentry comes over, a lady in slender-toed button-boots, drawing leather gloves off her white hands, and Rose tries not to stare at her but it's not often she sees someone like this up close, and everything about her is fascinating to Rose: the delicate pin-tuck pleats of her starched collar, and the way it brushes against her jaw, and Rose would like to know if it itches at all, and the tiny blue stones that hang by golden hooks from her earlobes, the way they shimmer and pull the daylight into their centres, the pale softness of the skin on the cheeks and across her nose, as if she's never been out in the sun. When she speaks, her lips part over straight shining teeth, and Rose has to shake herself to listen.

"I say," the lady says, "how much for a handful of the moss?"

Rose doesn't correct her, doesn't say, It's not moss, it's dulse, it's from the sea, not the land.

Before Rose can answer, the lady twists her neck to speak to someone behind her, and Rose sees it is the viscount's son again, still with the stinking stub of a cigar in his mouth, the man who will one day inherit the estate and take their rent and direct their labour. It is the first time she has ever seen him at close quarters but she has heard much about him: that he once horsewhipped his groom at a point-to-point, that there is trouble between him and his father, the viscount, because of all the debts he runs up, and that as a boy he used to tie burning sticks to the tails of sleeping dogs. Rose examines him and observes that his sleek good looks are somewhat marred by a pair of slack, moist lips. He stands there, feet apart, glancing at his watch, wholly unaware of this imperfection, and Rose finds herself tempted to point it out to him, just to see what he would do.

"Simply marvellous for keeping chills away," the lady is saying to him. "I swear by it."

The man laughs, a short bark, thrusting his watch back into his waistcoat pocket. "If you say so."

"Do you doubt me?" She taps him on the arm playfully. "You stir it into hot water and then, hey presto, you knock it back."

"Rather you than me," he drawls, removing the cigar from his mouth and flicking the ash to the ground. As he does so, he shifts his attention from the woman to Rose, and his eyes skate over her, from her face all the way down the front of her apron and back. His gaze is belligerent, interrogative, as if saying he will look at whatever he likes, for as long as he likes, as if daring her to object.

The lady is addressing Rose again, asking how much for the dulse, and Rose is relieved to be able to turn towards her. And because of her discomfort, and because of the horsewhipped groomsman, who bears a scar on his face to this day, Rose names a price so excessive that she's sure the lady and the viscount's son will draw back and walk away. There is a strong urge in Rose not to sell the dulse, collected so carefully by the widow at low tide, to these people, to let them walk away without it, to condemn them to a winter of endless chills and bad chests. *Hey presto,* she thinks, what a way to talk. But, astonishingly, the lady gives a nod with her angular chin. She reaches up her coat sleeve for a small velvet bag adorned all over with glistening beads arranged in triangles. Rose watches, mesmerised, as the elegant fingers draw apart the strings, as they count out the correct coins—a shocking amount, Rose is ashamed to watch—and then hold them out in a neat stack.

Rose takes them, releases them into her apron pocket, telling herself that it will please the widow, it will see her through the winter, and hasn't the widow paid enough in tithes and rent in her lifetime to more than line the pockets of the gentry, didn't the woman lose her whole family to the Great Hunger and these people and their ilk did nothing? All the same, Rose gives the lady not one but two handfuls of the dulse, and says, God bless you, at which the lady bestows upon her a gracious smile, saying, Thank you, dear, before turning away and taking the proffered arm of the viscount's son, and together they rejoin their friends.

Rose has no idea that she is being observed from across the street. Tomás stands with one shoulder pressed into a wall, most of him hidden from sight, his right sleeve, sewn shut, tucked into his jacket.

Several minutes ago, as he was making his way along the street, he realised that the girl selling eggs over by the clock tower was his daughter. Ever since the amputation, he finds he loses track of the day of the week, the times of the day, the rhythms of his house, if in fact he ever knew them.

He hadn't noticed that it was market day, hadn't been aware of Rose preparing to come. In truth, he has never had much of a sense of how women decide which days they will do the washing and peg it out to dry, which days the cleaning and the sweeping, how or when the clothes are mended or the socks knitted. Such conversations have always woven like smoke through the air about his head, and he has never paid them any mind: leave the household to the women and he will get on with his work.

Except—Tomás has to shift to the other foot, pass his left hand across his brow at the thought—there are no women now. There is only Rose.

Ever since they received a reply from the mapping office, Tomás has taken to what he thinks of as walking out. What else can a man like him, without a right hand, do? He cannot work but he has now the ease of knowing he has money in his pocket, sent to him each month: at least he knows that the rent will be paid, the children provided for. Whenever the mood takes him, he packs himself a small inventory of essentials—a rolled-up blanket, a pair of dry socks, a spare shirt, a cup, a compass—and off he goes, on foot, in whichever direction feels right. He might be gone for two or three nights, perhaps a week. He will not be deterred from this; he refuses to let the redcoats take this as well as his arm.

There are men around here who disappear, like him, for nights on end, who lose whole chunks of days to the drink. They take up with a friend in a shebeen or an inn, and sink beneath the surface of alcohol—they might wake up in a town two counties over, with no idea how they got there, dishevelled, their pockets empty.

This is not Tomás's way. He has never been one for the drink, never flushed away his wages or land like that; he has always been careful with money. He has taken the precaution to hide enough to keep his children for several years, in the event that anything happens to him, and he's shown Rose where to dig to find it. And now, since they wrote asking about compensation—he will not think of it as Father Joseph's letter, no, he will not—he receives a regular payment: the mapping office sent a reply, on headed and watermarked notepaper, signed by a commissioner, and it concurred that Tomás had been injured-and-disabled "while carrying out orders" and would be sent a surprisingly large amount each month for the rest of his life. A "stipend" is the word they use. This letter Tomás had also given to Rose, for safe-keeping. Never let it be said that he doesn't know how to take care of his family.

Work, the making of maps, the measuring of land, the moving along with a division, is at an end for him. He will never again follow the survey carts, never handle a theodolite, never point out to a chainboy where he must stand, never help to unravel the links of the measuring chain along undulating ground, never fill the columns of field books, never calculate triangulation or altitude; he will never again write that most beautiful of words, "azimuth." He will not take up a pen and draw the meandering mark for a coastline, or a miniature tree for woodland, or the dotted lines of parish boundaries. Most devastating of all, he will never finish the project he has been working on ever since they moved to the peninsula—his own map and record of the country—and the loss of this purpose feels to him like the forfeiture of another limb.

Old age seems to have caught up with him in a sudden swoop. His joints ache and twinge in the morning, his heart performs a peculiar fluttering at times, and even with his spectacles, his eyes don't see words on the page or symbols on the maps so well.

He will attend to his land and his beasts; he will attend to his remaining children. He has, however, been robbed of that most important task, the one he believes he was born for, or perhaps survived for, the one to which he had always intended to devote his twilight years: his version of the map, a true cartographic representation of his country, which would have erased and disregarded its conquerors. Such a map will only ever now live inside his head, for his left hand has never had the agility for inscription and detail, and the only other person who might have done it, his first-born son, is gone.

Tomás has decided, in the wake of this loss, that he will walk out as much as he can: if he cannot draw this country, he will stride through it; they may have taken his hand but he will damn well trace it with his feet. He finds himself ever conscious of his dwindling years, the narrowing down of his stretch of time here on earth, always aware that disaster can befall a man at any time, and he wishes very much, still, to find the valley with the road. He craves this now, more than ever, more than anything. If he cannot have his map of the land, he would like at least this map of himself. It burns within him, the desire to find where he is from, to walk the soil where he began.

It cannot, he is certain, elude him for ever: he is following a simple process of elimination. If anyone can find it, surely he can. He has a copy of the map of the entire country—a smudged one that was being discarded, where the engraver or the printer used too much ink—and he will walk along every lough and every path in the land, if he has to, but he will find it, he will.

A noisy clatter of women with shawls over their heads come down the lane behind him, carrying baskets in outstretched arms, chattering and laughing, and Tomás has to step aside to let them past.

In the days after he'd been told about Enda's disappearance, when he'd risen from his bed and was staggering about the place, he had discovered, laid out on the little table in the back bedroom, the faulty map, as well as a selection of his old draft maps of the neighbouring townlands. For a moment, he had been perplexed as to what they were doing there: who would have had the temerity to touch his work and leave precious papers like these in the open, vulnerable to dust and daylight? He had been nursing his maimed arm against his chest, working himself up to confronting Rose and Eugene, and then it came to him why the maps were there, arranged like this. Enda must have consulted them before she fled. She had gone through his papers and found his sketches—the ones he had made for the redcoats, and kept, because he was fond of the look of them—and he cursed himself then, cursed his vanity, cursed the redcoats for their relentless acquisitiveness, their clamouring for ownership. But, curse or no curse, the fact remained that his daughter had used his very own work to find her way.

Perhaps he should have known, should have seen it coming. That time when, as a child, she had got herself onto that boat out to the island so remote that once she was there, once they'd arrived, and the trick she and Liam had played on him became apparent, it was too late to rectify it, to send her back. That, Tomás thinks, as he stands against the wall in town, his eye trained on Rose and her egg stall, was the seed of these current troubles.

If Tomás had seen through the ruse before they left, if he'd thought to look at the child, maybe Liam could in time have been persuaded to become his apprentice, might never have fallen under the influence of that charlatan priest. If Enda hadn't spent those months out on the island, with the people there, with the musicians who took her under their wings and taught her every day on the fiddle, the lot of them playing together until her eyes were dreamy and distant, maybe she would never have got such notions in her head.

Hadn't Tomás said to Phina, again and again, that the girl spent too much time altogether playing that instrument? Didn't Phina think it was making the girl a little odd? Always off to find a session where she might play. Always asking people to give her a tune, to sing something to her—she collected music, she used to say. No man might be tempted to court her if it was known roundabout that the girl was given not to cooking and mending but scraping out tunes all day and all night, sitting on a rock in the rath; no man would come near her, and then where would she be? He had no idea, he'd railed, why the girl was so headstrong, so intransigent, so unswerving in her ideas, so bent on traipsing about the countryside when she should be at home.

It comes to him now, as he leans against the wall, pack on his back, that Phina had looked at him, eyebrows raised, and said: I wonder where she'd be getting that from?

Tomás brushes away this recollection. It is easier for him to keep himself filled with fury at Enda, at his maiming, than to dwell on Phina. At the thought of his wife, loss engulfs him, as if he's fallen into seawater, his head swallowed by the bitter waves. He has to clench his remaining hand into a fist so as not to let out a sob that might attract the attention of passers-by. It is unthinkable, senseless, that she is gone. How can it have happened that he is the parent left and not her, when her daughters and her mostly silent son had such need of her? Instead, Liam is away, Enda has vanished, and he is still here, bafflingly, with a broken Rose and a confused Eugene, and Tomás hasn't the knack of helping them.

Over at the clock tower, Rose is handing something to a family with numerous children, and they are giving her money, and Tomás is pleased to see this. Poor Rose, with so little to give her happiness, her sister gone, and only that brother for company. It occurs to Tomás that he could go over there, stay beside her as she sells the last of her eggs and dulse, help her carry back the wares she will buy.

He pushes himself away from the wall, however, with his eye on the empty road before him, giving Rose a final glance over his shoulder. She now has a young gentleman loitering near her stall, looking more at her than at her baskets. Tomás pauses, frowning. There is something vaguely familiar about the young man and it comes to Tomás that it is the viscount's son, back among them for the summer. He considers again going over there: Rose is a beauty, always was, and he doesn't want the likes of the future viscount paying her notice. It won't be long, Tomás thinks, until some gurrier will climb the hill to ask him for her hand, and what will he say? Phina would have known what to do, would have been able to size up the suitor with a glance. Tomás adjusts the straps across his shoulders. The young gentleman has moved away, Tomás is relieved to observe; Rose has given him no welcome, then.

He pulls the compass from his pocket. As he looks down into its familiar, expressionless face, its quivering needle, a strange thought occurs to him: Enda, his daughter, had been a far better assistant than Liam. Out on the island, when he had permitted her to help and when she wasn't off with those musicians, she had set herself to her tasks with great enthusiasm and concentration. What's this for, Da? Why do you do that? Is this granite or limestone? How do you know? How do you measure the distance between here and there? He hears these questions so clearly, in her high and piping voice, that it is as if he might turn around and find the young Enda beside him, her face tilted up to his, awaiting the wisdom of his answer. Tomás is struck by the notion, as he turns his head to see that there is, indeed, no one with him, no small Enda, no one at all, that she would have made the perfect apprentice. She would have carried on in his footsteps, had things been different, had the cards fallen another way. Instead, she is gone, and he will never see her again.

Tomás lifts his shoulders, shrugging, as if trying to shift a weight from his back. He pockets the compass and turns his face towards the road heading north-north-east. He brings himself back to facts: the here and the now and the why. He believes he has spotted two possible valleys on the badly printed map. He will go now, this minute, a journey of a day, perhaps more, on foot, but he can always find a place to sleep overnight—a dry overhang of rock, under the canopy of a sheltering tree, he is used to such hardship—and he will decide if either of them is the right place. He is determined to find the valley. He must have this knowledge. He will locate it if it is the last thing he does.

PART FOUR

OFF THE EDGE OF THE CHARTED WORLD

ENDA'S SHIP GLIDES UP A NARROW CHANNEL WITH HIGH AND thickly forested banks rising to port and starboard. She elbows her way to the side, where she stands, stunned, unable to bend her mind to the idea that the journey is over and they have arrived. That she would one day land in this place called Québec and have to face her new life had until this moment seemed abstract and unlikely: she has only got as far in her planning as disguising herself, managing to pass as her brother, and surviving the passage without being discovered. For the last two months, her life has shrunk to the confined dim hell of the ship's hold and its narrow set of concerns: when she would wake, what she might eat, if she would be allowed on deck, how she might wash and dress in privacy. Now, here she is, about to be released into a strange city, alone, and her tasks are rapidly multiplying, chief among them such terrifying necessities as finding a place to stay and some way to earn a living.

Other boats, larger than hers, with taller masts, some with steam engines expressing clouds, like silent thoughts, from their funnels, are travelling alongside. These passengers are waving handkerchiefs and calling out across the water; others are singing, a hymn of some sort in a foreign tongue; people on her own ship are on their knees, offering up prayers. Enda sees a painted sign saying that the ship nearest to them has sailed from Germany, another from Hungary, or Italy or Lithuania or Norway. All these ships are converging down the ever-narrowing channel, on one destination: an island, their point of entry, beyond which lie the jumble and smokestacks of the city of Québec. The captains of each vessel are vying with each other, Enda sees, racing to make it to the harbour first. It frightens her, in a deep and profound way, that so many hundreds of immigrants are about to disembark, all at once, for surely this will make her task harder. How can one city, one land, have enough work, enough places for all these people?

When she steps off the gangway, Enda discovers a new kind of sickness: her skull is still filled with the unquiet tipping of waves, and her legs seem not to work, to fulfil their purpose of keeping her upright. The dockside, the stacks of luggage, the sailors looping ropes as thick as a man's leg, the weak grey sky above her, the ranks of uniformed harbourmasters, the shoving hordes of disembarking passengers, all seem to shimmer and fragment before her. She is forced to pause, one hand on a wall for balance. Holding on to it, she tries to keep upright. She is pushed one way, by a phalanx of men with blue neckerchiefs, shouting happily to each other in a harsh and yammering tongue; she is pushed the other by a severe-faced family in beaded headdresses and square-toed boots. Enda sees that she has to join a queue to get inside the immigration building, and she takes a few tentative steps away from the wall, but it is hard to find the end of the queue when so many people are swarming and yelling, and even harder when you're alone and there is no one to shove back when you get jostled out of the way.

Enda cannot make an inroad into these crowds; she finds herself squeezed out to the edges, nowhere near the queue. She needs to dive in and force her way through the cross-currents of immigrants on the quay but it's near impossible. She cannot seem to adjust to the stability of land, its stolid immovability. It is as if her legs are stuffed with rags, and petals of glaring brightness are blooming, disturbingly, at the edges of her vision; she staggers, her pack and fiddle sliding sideways off her shoulders, and she falls into a person to the left of her.

She is apologising as she sinks down, knees meeting stone, and she is snatching blindly for her instrument, a cold fear clutching her that it might strike the ground and break into pieces—and what a desperate omen that would be—when the person turns and catches her by the arm. It is a woman, newly arrived, Enda supposes. Except that she is like no one Enda has ever seen before: she is tall and strong-looking, with emphatic jet eyebrows. Weighty black plaits are piled on top of her head like a dark coronet, affixed there with what look like tiny silver spears. Enda, unable to stop herself staring, takes in the thick, layered skirts that pad the woman's lower half, the floral stitching on her bodice.

Next to her, Enda feels like a very different animal: scrawny and dowdy. The woman says something, quickly, over her shoulder, in a language that is jerking and consonant-heavy, to a man behind them. He is bearded, with a wide-brimmed hat and a dark coat over a striped shirt, and he is also, Enda can see, from her crouched position on the dock, powerfully built, with the same angular set to his face. He is taking in the scene around him, frowning, strong white teeth biting down on his lip, while carrying an array of bundles and boxes, as if they weigh nothing at all. He takes a firm grip of Enda's other arm and lifts her to her feet.

Enda might have found him and his wife forbidding, perhaps even alarming—she might have extricated herself and moved away from them—were it not for one of their items of luggage. Slung across the man's chest is an accordion. It is foolish, she knows, to trust these people just because one of them is a musician, but she cannot help feeling that they will see her right, somehow, that they will take care of her.

Between them, the strangely attired couple, apparently untroubled by the shift from ocean to land, link an arm each between hers and haul her along. Unlike her, they seem excited to have arrived, gazing around, pointing and exclaiming to each other. Enda is trying to say thank you, and the dark-haired couple merely nod, continuing their conversation above her head. As they shove their way into the queue, the man reaches out to tap his knuckle on Enda's fiddle case, and Enda, recalling stories of the thieves and pickpockets who lurk on docksides, smiles nervously back. He says a word to her, then another, still rapping on the case, as if trying out different languages on her. He has a gaze that is both stern and also probing, as if he is able to see right into people, their nooks and crannies and all they might hide there. It unsettles Enda, makes her shift her eyes away from his, in case he manages to glean some secret from her.

Suddenly, a recognisable word comes through the strings of syllables, like a distant signal. "Violin?" he is saying, in a heavy accent.

Yes, Enda nods vigorously, violin.

"You are a violinist?" he says, looking her over in his unblinking, assessing way. "I am a teacher of music." He touches his palm to the accordion. "Also languages. You play in an orchestra?"

"I . . ." Enda hesitates, wondering how to explain the lack of orchestras on the peninsula ". . . no. How many languages do you speak?"

"Three. Almost four. I don't know how many of them will be useful here."

They are inside the immigration building now, under a kind of glass canopy, being ushered between low wooden railings, so narrow that they have to stand sideways. Up ahead is a large, tiled atrium with a domed ceiling, at the end of which is a row of desks, at which stand stern-looking officials with pens and large ledgers. It seems to Enda that the dome is collecting the din of what is below: the chatter of hundreds and hundreds of different tongues. She asks the man where they have come from, and he utters a name, a complex one, possibly beginning with *k* or perhaps *z*, with multiple syllables and harsh collisions of sounds. Seeing Enda's incomprehension, he smiles for the first time.

"You have heard of the Baltic Sea?" he asks.

Into her mind flash the world-maps her father would occasionally draw for Liam, to test him, pointing out certain countries or rivers or seas and asking him to identify them; Enda would watch, over Liam's shoulder, repeating the answers silently to herself. She nods, not trusting herself to speak.

"Our town is on its shore."

"But what is your country called?"

The man grimaces, rolling his eyes; his wife, who has been regarding them keenly, raises her brows, and he seems to translate Enda's question for her, which causes the woman to emit a scoffing, mirthless laugh.

"It is not so simple to answer," he says. "When I was a child, the soldiers in our town square tell us we are part of Russia. Then some other soldiers in a different uniform come and they tell us we are Lithuanians. And then a third set say we are Austro-Hungarian, and—"

The man with the accordion suddenly breaks off and points, indicating that they are next in the queue. With a deep breath and a grin, he says something to his wife, who, in an awed whisper, repeats the word to Enda but Enda shakes her head, mimes incomprehension.

"*Grozzle*," the man says, or seems to say, delving into a leather satchel around his neck.

The woman nods: "*Grozzle*."

They look at each other, tears standing in their eyes, then the woman leans her head into his chest and gives a tremulous sigh.

Enda is still mystified until she sees a signpost reading "Grosse Île."

Grosse Île, she repeats under her breath, *Grozzle*, which is, the sailors told her, the name of the island but also the entry point into the country, through which all immigrants must pass. It is the place where everyone who has survived the journey must produce their documents and submit themselves to be approved and recorded. *Grozzle*—Grosse Île. As she reaches into her pack for her papers, she seems to see her father, bending over one of his meticulous field books, with columns for names in different languages and dialects. An urge to share this misunderstanding arrows through her, and she is already arranging it into a story for him, arriving here, her landsickness, the two kindly strangers from the shores of the Baltic Sea, their tale of slippery nationalities, their pronunciation of "Grosse Île," or Big Island, but then she remembers that she will never be able to tell him, that he will never hear these words.

This is where her impulsive decision has taken her, that rummaging she did among Liam's papers, the ones he left under his mattress, in search of something to read, and how fed up she'd felt that day, she forgets why now. And then she came upon the emigration documents, the money for the passage, and how hastily she'd snatched them up and stowed them in her tobacco tin, with her savings, thinking how might she pull it off, would she dare, what a lark it would be. She never really thought she'd get away with it, certain that she'd be turned back at the harbour, sent home, but instead she'd been waved onboard and before she knew it, there she was, shut in the hold, sailing across the Atlantic.

Never to see them again.

The woman with the plaits has to take Enda's documents from her trembling hand and place them on the immigration desk; the man's arm is still tucked through Enda's. His forearm is pressed to her side, to her ribcage, and too late, she realises, to the side-swell of her breast beneath its bindings, and as Enda leans forward to answer the official's questions, she is aware of a flicker of surprise passing through him. When she leans back again, he is withdrawing his arm from hers, looking at her shrewdly, as if he'd known from the start that there was something not quite right about her. As the three of them wait in front of the admissions desk, Enda looks back at him mutely, imploring him to say nothing, to do nothing, and after a moment, the accordion player lowers his eyes, and she understands that he won't speak out, won't reveal her secret.

Enda glances back at the official and sees that he is writing in a large ledger on creamy paper, consulting the documents in front of him, lowering an ink-stamp and slamming it down, sealing a document that says a man called Liam emigrated to this country in this year of Our Lord, and is free to reside within it as a citizen.

She takes a sharp breath in, surveying the piece of paper, held in a hand that quivers in time with the hasty and unsteady rhythm of her heart. She is here. She has done it. There is no going back. She pictures her journey as a tiny sewn line that has picked its way from the beleaguered dog-shaped country of her birth, to this one—an eastern shore of an unimaginably vast continent, a place where land is plentiful and fortunes are there for the taking.

Or perhaps not quite. Beyond the immigration desks, before they are ushered to the next checkpoints, Enda disentangles herself from the couple, thanking them profusely: she will go on alone, she tries to tell them. The man is shaking his head, gesturing with urgent movements, checking around himself for officials, pointing towards the next set of desks.

"Medical," he is muttering in her ear, "medical. There will be a medical check. Do you understand? Your papers don't match your . . . person."

Aghast, Enda sees, with a collapsing sensation in her chest, another long queue, at the end of which doctors and nurses are ushering people behind curtains and asking them to remove their clothes. She had had no idea this would happen. She is speechless. She is appalled. She clutches her piece of stamped paper that permits a man by the name of Liam to enter the country: no one will take it from her, no one can.

Her new friends are shrugging, discussing the issue in their language. The wife is laughing incredulously, bending over, removing one of her numerous skirts and indicating that Enda should step into it; she is tying it around her waist and pulling her towards the queue for women. Enda has to lift the hem to walk. She enters the country in trousers and a skirt, one on top of the other; she enters as both herself and her brother, a spliced Enda-and-Liam.

She doesn't, however, enter it yet. Because behind the medical curtain, stripped down to her underclothes, she is examined by people who don't glance at her papers for long enough to register the ticked box on the form that states "male" because it is quickly discovered that she has a rash on her abdomen and a burning temperature. *Fièvre des navires*, the doctor declares to the nurse behind him. Both doctor and nurse step back quickly and don masks. Enda is ordered to stand away from them, away from the queue of other immigrants. Before she has cottoned on to what is happening, she is being hustled down a different corridor towards the quarantine hospital. She tries to say to the staff that she has to go back, to return the skirt to the kind woman, but it is not allowed. She is to be taken to the quarantine hospital and there she will stay until further notice.

A bird, perhaps a skylark, is in flight above the peninsula, wings unfurled, gliding south on a volatile thermal current, looking down to what lies below. She has been nesting on a particular estuarial incline here for three summers now, building a place to lay her eggs in a rushy declivity not far from the inlet.

What might she see as she flies towards her nest? The long and crooked length of the place, rolled out into the water, with the yellow stretch of sand at its lower tip. The smaller bays on its northerly and south-westerly shores, one where periwinkles collect during storms, in perilous banks up near the dunes, the other filled with whitened coral nubs, held there by the protective arm of the headland. Boats bob here, tethered to stones in the natural harbour, or pulled up onto the coral, high above the waves' reach. The low-lying machair where, on this breezy spring morning, a host of flowers trembles, clinging by their shallow roots to the sandy, shell-peppered soil.

The bird, heading to the brackish, estuarial shallows where the river spreads itself into the sea, might also see an intricate network of roads, paths, boreens, lanes, all linked together, cutting passages through the terrain; she would see the dry bog, like a brown-green pincushion pierced with white blooms, and the wet bog, a darker spread. The larger lough, the surface of which is today pleated and ruffled by a gusting wind, and the five smaller ones, pooled in the landscape's hollows.

The skylark dips and soars over fields enclosed by their stone walls, the clusters of trees, the cottages and houses—those with roofs and chimneys, and those without. The grassed-over ruined cabins, if the bird happens to look down at them as she flies, would appear as pale ghost-shapes on the land, like watermarks on a document.

The sea would be evident to her, as it always is to any creature—mammalian or avian—that lives on the peninsula: its colossal expanse and strength, its cold, turquoise depths, its saline scent, its restless presence at the fringes of the land, its power for ever eroding some parts of it and building up others.

Hard to miss, too, the manor house, built on an elevated plane, with its peaked roofs, chimney stacks, stable-block and yard, the walled kitchen garden, the tract of cultivated lawn and espaliered orchard and ornamental lake. The long, snaking gravel driveway, its stone gates topped with carved birds of prey. The ice-house. The glass-house and pineapple pit. The Regency conservatory. The curving verges of grassland.

And there, on the terrace, taking his morning tea, is the viscount.

He doesn't sit at the table, which has been carried out here for the purpose of his breakfast, laid with cloth and cutlery, where his wife is currently seated, along with three or four daughters. No, the viscount stands at the balustrade, brooding, looking out over his parkland, one hand holding his teacup, the other balled into a fist in his pocket.

The skylark passes unseen, directly over his head, and to her, his thoughts are a tangible line rising from his cranium, like steam: she flies right through them, she pierces the nimbus of his ruminations as a needle passes through cloth.

Scraps of it cling to her brown and cream feathers: stray filaments of his mind. This Darjeeling is too steeped. Too long in the pot. Must call in on the solicitor today. These bills, however am I to pay them? Son in with a bad lot. Better keep him here to learn the ropes. Need to tell him I'm unable to clear his debts for him any more. Don't let on to his mother. This country is changing, not what it used to be. Difficult times ahead, perhaps. Now, where has the groom put that stallion? See if the beast will be ready for the races. Call into the stables, then whistle up the dogs. Soon as I've finished this tea.

The skylark flaps her wings, as if to shake herself free of the viscount's troubles, and continues in a southerly direction, towards the estuary, and if she were looking closely at what was below it, she might spot a tiny manikin, moving from field and beyond, upwards, to the highest point on the whole peninsula: Eugene.

He is traversing the bog, where he comes most days, after he has finished his morning tasks, and before he starts those of the afternoon, hopping from stone to stone in his bare feet with practised ease. He has rested near where the bog-girl lies for a moment or two, catching his breath, communing with her in silence, before going on his way.

He likes to climb the highest hill every day, at noon or thereabouts. He likes to push himself through this ritual, feeling the hammering of his heart, the racing of blood through his veins as it tries to keep pace with his exertions.

At a piercing noise above him, Eugene looks up, shading his eyes. A lark, female, wheels through the sky, setting her course between land and cloud. Eugene guesses she will be heading back to her nest, with food for her young. He watches her, one foot raised above the other, for he, too, for a moment is thinking like a lark or an estuarial bird, but then she is gone. He lowers his foot and climbs the remainder of the way.

At the top of the crag, a frisky and insistent wind harries him, tugging at his lapels, trying to tunnel up his jersey. Eugene turns his back on it, ignoring its rude parries. He crosses his arms, to keep in the heat of the climb, and surveys all below him.

His look-out hill, he thinks of this place. He can see along the length of the peninsula, and most of the road into town. He can see over the north inlet and the south, as far as the next headland, where on clear days he can make out the crumbling remains of an old castle. There is the fishermen's cabin, down by the harbour bay, and their currach, tethered to its usual stone. There the house of the sisters, with its line of turf-smoke, blurred by wind today, and the fence enclosing their goat. He can make out the widow's longhouse, despite a crosshatching of sea-mist between him and the shoreline, and it's just possible to spot the woman herself, bent over something beside the byre. Behind him, he knows without looking, is his own dwelling, the cottage, the haggard, the field. Rose might be outside, pegging out the washing or lugging the churn in through the open door.

But Eugene isn't thinking of Rose today. He is looking down at the manor house, at the conservatory, which, he sees, is collapsed at one end, its wooden spars and elegant panes shattered into a heap of broken glass and splinters. He is noting, too, unlike the lark, the overgrown garden, the laurel walk almost closed over, the algae-clogged lake, the amount of greenery and moss adorning the roof, the potholes on the driveway.

Hard, Eugene has heard, for a man like the viscount to be getting labourers or servants, these days, to be finding people to rake his gravel and mow his lawns. When Eugene accompanies Rose to market, he listens in to the swirl of conversation and from it he gleans all kinds of information. An earl was bludgeoned in his sleep, not far from here, only last month; a lord in County Sligo had his grain stores burned. Other landowners have beaten a retreat back across the water and stayed there, leaving their estates to run themselves and the fine houses to fall into disrepair. Their viscount, however, has dug in his heels. He is staying, he has told his tenants. He is not running scared from the new mood taking hold of this country; it will take more than a few peasant rebels with pitchforks to frighten him off his land.

And yet, Eugene sees, far below him, the same thing he saw only a few days ago: the viscount's land steward leaning down from his horse to tear from a gatepost a notice that has been nailed there in the night. The piece of paper flutters in the man's gloved hand before he crumples it up and shoves it into his pocket.

Eugene knows what the notice says because it has been the talk of the parish for weeks now: who might have written it, who nailed it up, who would dare write such rousing lines or take such a rebellious tone. In a fine and even copperplate hand, it addresses itself to "Those who pay rent by work and labour to the viscount." It exhorts them to "stand antagonistic and defiant in the face of this unmerciful exploitation, to resist, resist, resist."

With a kick of his heels, the steward urges his horse on to the next gatepost, where he rips off another three of the notices. Eugene watches closely. The notices, he knows, will reappear in the night, and the steward will have to remove them all over again.

Unseen, the skylark passes over Eugene's head, and she drifts down towards the estuary on a high cross-breeze. His thoughts, to her, are opaque: they don't cling in shreds, like the viscount's, but slip past her, unreadable. She is, anyway, thinking only of her nest, the four green and speckled eggs hidden there, and how she will sit upon them now and warm them with the soft feathers of her belly.

Enda is once more afloat, crouching in the prow of a ferry shuttling her across the muscled currents of the St. Lawrence river.

It is 1880: a leap year. Elsewhere in the world, an inventor is patenting his incandescent electric light-bulb. A mathematician is introducing his new pictorial concept for demonstrating the logical relations between sets. After a bout of heavy rain, there is a landslide in Nainital, and a hundred and fifty people drown after being buried in mud. There is a prolonged gun-fight in Australia, at the end of which a notorious bushranger outlaw is captured; months later, he will be hanged by the neck until he is dead. The First Boer War is beginning. Two circus impresarios join forces. A vaudeville star makes her debut on Broadway. There is an earthquake in Zagreb, which reduces the Gothic cathedral to rubble.

Enda has been in the quarantine hospital for more than six weeks. She has eaten at least a hundred meals. From other inmates, she has learned tunes from more than nineteen countries. She has slept in three different wards, the first of which had windows that looked out, a doctor informed her, on the graves of thousands upon thousands of people from her country buried on Grosse Île. They'd made it across the sea during the terrible famine, in a weakened and starved state, the doctor said, as he examined her, only to die as they arrived, sometimes as they crawled up the beach. Enda spent all her time in that particular ward at the window, staring out; sometimes, if the nurses weren't around to stop her, she would play airs on her fiddle, sending the music out towards the graves.

She is at last leaving Grosse Île, the small ferry cutting a path towards the city of Québec, through those of the huge ships passing back and forth. Their proximity makes Enda flinch—she grips the rail but not because of seasickness; she does not suffer from it. With her other hand, she guards her jacket seam, sewn with coins and notes. The wharfside buildings pull closer and closer still.

Enda chews at her lip until she tastes blood on her tongue. She tries not to look at a group of brothers and their sister in the prow of the ferry, the girl's arm through the older brother's, the excitement evident in their faces. You will be all right, Enda chides herself fiercely. You will not give in to weak thoughts. You will do this alone, if you have to. And you have to. No good giving up now.

Instead, she fixes her eyes on the city ahead. Québec, from the river, looks to Enda like a flight of stairs or a pile of books, buildings stacked behind other buildings, edging backwards up the cliff. There is the sprawl of the long dockside buildings—warehouses, wharfs—and then behind them a layer of tall brick edifices, with flags on their turrets and white window frames. There seems to be a patch of greenery, perhaps a park, and Enda can see tiny figures, grouped together, walking along paths. Vehicles cut past each other, along streets, through gaps. At the top of the cliff there are large houses or mansions, their gables turned to the water.

Excitement and fear vie within her. Here it is; she is here. She is about to enter the city. Any moment now, she will be one of those people moving through the tree-lined park, along the streets.

She has, in her pocket, the address of an apartment, given to her by an Ulsterwoman from the hospital. It is a curious stream of numbers, separated by slashes, followed by words in a foreign language that the woman said was the street's name. Enda could stay there for a while, the woman said, the rent would be cheap, and at least she'd have the company of her own people.

There had been something not wholly trustworthy about the woman, Enda is thinking, as the ferry pulls up alongside the dock, something in the way her eyes travelled over Enda's face and clothing, the way she laughed and clutched her arm when Enda said she had come over on the boat alone.

Enda would prefer not to have to use this address, not to go to these people from Ulster, but what choice does she have? She will stay for a night, perhaps two, certainly no more than three, until she finds a better option.

On the dock, she has to fight her way through crowds who have come to meet the Grosse Île ferry, through those who are waving and calling to the new arrivals, lurching forward to embrace them. Enda keeps her eyes ahead; she shoulders her fiddle; she asks an elderly man how she might find the street on the address but the man looks at her blankly. Enda tries another person, then another. She is able to communicate what she wants but the problem is that she cannot understand their answer. Trying to quell her rising panic, she shows the piece of paper to a woman carrying a bag on her shoulder; she squints at it, then nods, waving her hand in a direction away from the river. That way, she says, with a guttural lilt, that way. *Zat way.*

The city unfolds to Enda, like a map, as she walks, toiling up the slope. Streetcars, drawn by pairs of blinkered horses, rattle past, and carriages, driven by uniformed men wielding whips. She passes beneath awnings and signposts advertising medicinal powders, household wares, haberdashery, millinery, fresh produce, good clean meats of all varieties. On the corner of a steep flight of stone stairs, a gang of squealing children overtakes her, almost sending her flying, pursued by an angry man in an apron, shouting at them in furious French.

Enda trudges along a dusty street, up a staircase, then another, stopping to check the directions with anyone who can understand her or who can read the words written on her paper. Québec is so full, so busy, the streets swarming with dust and grit, the brick buildings solid and unapproachable, and the people so various, all speaking different languages, wearing outlandish clothes. The ladies in waisted jackets with fur collars, the men in high-domed hats.

Enda rests on the edge of a marble fountain, around which children push their dolls in tiny perambulators or bowl wooden hoops as they run beside. Nursemaids in starched caps sit on wrought-iron benches, surveying their charges. Dipping her hands into the water, Enda dabs the dust and sweat from her face with her wet sleeve; she carefully unfolds the red embroidered skirt from her pack and steps into it. Several nursemaids glare at her but she doesn't care. She ties the skirt around her waist, on top of the trousers, but never mind—she can remove them later. She takes off her cap and runs her wet hands through her growing-out hair. She smiles to herself: she is transformed. She is Enda again, not Liam. She has shed him and is back to herself—her new self.

She presses on, enjoying the flip and swish of the elaborate skirt's movement, leaving behind the shops and fountains, through some squares where the houses are imposing and smart, into a neighbourhood of low-lying ramshackle buildings. The people here don't move as fast as they do in the places with streetcars and fountains: they loiter, they stare. She pauses to ask a man sitting in a doorway if she's going in the right direction; he is eating what looks like some kind of vegetable smeared in a scarlet sauce and the smell of it is at once enticing and alarming. The inside of his mouth, and all his teeth, are stained the same bright red as he tells her that, yes, she must walk along this street, then another.

Dusk is beginning to fall when Enda reaches the place. She is greeted by a man wearing a grimy collar and tie; he pinches Enda's cheek in an overly familiar way—and Enda is momentarily shocked because during her weeks at sea she has forgotten what it is to be female. The man grins, stepping aside to let her in, and Enda discovers that, yes, these are people from her country, but an incredible number of them.

Beyond the door, in the room, which is on the ground floor of a makeshift slatted building, there are perhaps twelve or fifteen men and women, some sleeping on the boards, some on a bare bunk, others standing by the small stove, and more people by the window, looking out into the street. It is as bad as the hold of the ship, perhaps worse. Enda is told she can bed down by the door in exchange for a few coins. She is offered a plate of cabbage, for more coins, which she accepts, and tobacco, which she refuses.

The night is long, disturbed by people coming and going, by others snoring, by a man who arrives back the worse for drink, stumbling over Enda's feet. She keeps her eyes shut, hoping that if she doesn't look at him he will leave her be. The next moment, however, she is conscious of the blanket being lifted, then an inquisitive hand landing on her wrist and another being shoved unceremoniously between her legs, and then the person is at her, slobbering on her neck, breathing beery fumes into her face, scraping her skin with stubble. Enda twists sideways, hissing, revolted, bringing up her leg to knee him; the drink has made his reactions slow and she is able to land a hefty blow on the underside of his chin. He swears, grappling with her clothing, the conundrum of both skirt and trousers, muttering curses and obloquies, grinding the bones of her wrist together, but she can feel that his heart has gone out of it. She shoves at his shoulder, again and again, kicking him hard on the shins, and after a moment, he rolls off her with an offended air, as if she has been impolite not to go through with it, and he falls almost instantly into a noisome, snorting sleep.

The fear that he might make another assault keeps her awake until the sun comes up. She leaves, shouldering her pack and her fiddle, certain she will never return, and spends some hours searching for a boarding house for women. The first she finds is too expensive; the second is so grimy she can see the bedbugs crawling along the creases of the mattress. In the third, she is offered a bed, which she would have to share with four others and a large, filthy dog; Enda says she'll think it over. It is the end of the day by the time she climbs the steps to the fourth boarding house, where a woman, whose accent reminds Enda of the soldiers her father worked for, shows her a room to be shared with one other, a nice clean girl from Belgium, the woman promises, and Enda nods. She is overcome with relief and exhaustion and wants nothing more than to hurl herself down on the bed and pull the sheets over her head.

The woman names a weekly price, to be paid in advance, every Friday; Enda agrees, and reaches into her pocket for her purse. But her fingers encounter nothing but the calico lining, sewn by her mother. Enda checks her other pocket. Nothing. A cold panic rinses over her and she feels along the lining, where she sewed her savings into the seam.

The stitches have been ripped apart, the seam opened. Her money has gone. The drunk man from last night was perhaps not as drunk as he seemed.

The woman is waiting, her hand out, one eyebrow raised.

"I had money . . ." Enda falters. "I did. I've . . . I've been robbed. There was a man and he . . . I'll have money by tomorrow, I promise, I just need . . ."

She trails away. Perhaps this woman will take pity on her, perhaps she will help her.

Within seconds, Enda finds herself pushed unceremoniously outside onto the steps, the front door slamming shut behind her.

Darkness has fallen. The streets are emptying. A few stray carts are toiling slowly along, the horses tired out, the candles low and guttering inside their glass lanterns. Enda walks quickly, wishing to give the impression that she has a place to go, a destination in mind. She moves away from the boarding house, holding tight to her fiddle, turns a corner, then another. She passes a grocery shop where a woman in a white cap is sweeping the floor, a child at her feet. She passes a house where a man with a pipe in his mouth is drawing the curtains, and a tavern where the windows are smeared with steam, behind which indistinct human shapes move, cleave and separate.

Who will help her? What should she do? It is important not to panic. She tells herself this.

She goes over the facts in her head. She is in a strange city, where she knows no one. She has had all her money stolen. It is night-time. She has nowhere to sleep. She could go back to the place she stayed last night and have it out with them. You took my money, she might say to the man. Give it back. But she fears worse might happen if she does.

Her feet lead her to the square with the fountain, the place where she shed Liam's identity and resumed her own. The gates have been locked; the place is dark and deserted, its gravel paths empty, but the fountain is still running, throwing its plume of silver drops up into the air. She stands for a moment, holding on to the railings. She checks over both shoulders, then grips a branch and the top of the spiked railings. In half a minute, she is on the other side.

She moves quickly, keeping to the grass, which absorbs the sound of her footsteps. At the bench where the nursemaids had sat in judgemental rows, she crouches. She pushes her fiddle and her pack underneath, then crawls in after them, pulling herself as far back as she can. She curls onto her side and tucks her hands into her sleeves for warmth. She is too frightened to cry.

Liam is also close to the ground, on his hands and knees, in the attitude of prayer, but he is in fact wielding a scrubbing brush and the hem of his robe is soaked in soapy water. He is on retreat in Rome, and has been instructed to clean the orange-brown terracotta tiles of the covered quadrangle, so he is working backwards. Scrubbing, sluicing, scrubbing, sluicing.

Three other brothers—scholastics, like him, in the *secundi* stage of their training—are similarly engaged on the quadrangle's adjoining sides.

For the first thirty days of his stay at the college in Rome, Liam has been instructed to remain silent. He must speak to no one save his assigned spiritual master, and then only in Latin. He must spend his days exclusively in prayer, meditation, study and also menial offices, such as the cleaning of the college. Later today, he will be required to memorise a portion of papal *bullae*.

Breathing hard, Liam sits back on his heels to rinse his brush in the bucket, and to wipe the perspiration from his hairline. He is aware that he is smiling. Despite the tedium of this most menial of tasks, his heart is ticking away inside him, like a well-wound watch. Ever since he arrived in Rome, staggering off the boat after a journey of four days, during which he was levelled by seasickness, he has felt suffused with excitement, with bliss. It must be, he knows, for he has been told so by his *secundi* master, his vocation at work; the delight he feels is the deliverance inherent in serving God. How he welcomes this sign.

He moves his brush back and forth among the bucket's bubbles, gazing out at the branches of the four trees in the quadrangle. Planted at a decorous distance from each other, each to a corner, they have leaves thick and lustrous, with blossoms opening themselves to the sun. The scent that comes from these blooms at nightfall is intoxicatingly sweet. In a few weeks' time, when the petals have fallen, oranges will start to grow in their place.

Liam can hardly wait. They will be green at first, he has heard, and that colour will gradually give way to a bright sunshine hue that signals ripeness, readiness to harvest. By that time, he knows, his retreat will be at an end. He will then be spending his mornings at lectures in philosophy, logic, mathematics, theology, and his afternoons doing "works."

It is the "works" that intrigue Liam the most. In pairs or threes, he and other *secundi* will be sent out into the city to visit the poor, or to teach in schools, to help in hospitals, to assist in the churches or cathedrals, in whatever capacity is required.

Behind him, he hears approaching feet—another brother, the reverend father, a spiritual master?—and Liam startles out of his reverie, leaning forward to resume his scrubbing. The tiles are worn and cracked, hoarding centuries of dirt in the gaps between them. However hard Liam scrubs, there is always more grime.

The footsteps come closer, then pass him by. Liam doesn't lift his head to greet the man—this is forbidden during these early weeks—but he glances up to see the gown of the philosophy master disappearing around the corner, to see that there is now a trail of dusty footprints for him to clean away.

Liam sighs but refuses to let this dent his mood. How could he, when the square of sky he can see above the orange trees is the purest lapis, when he will be finished with this task in less than an hour, when he can smell the scent of rosemary and baking bread coming from the kitchens, when the city of Rome is waiting for him, just outside the college walls?

He can feel it there, pulsing in the heat, its streets and houses lying in wait for him.

In only twenty more days—no, twenty-one—he will be walking through the college's large wooden doors. He will be permitted to draw back the iron bolts and step out. He and his fellow scholastics will then be free to move along the streets of which he caught only the briefest glimpse the night they arrived.

He has read that Rome has ruins of ancient temples and courthouses and villas and amphitheatres. That there is a cathedral with a hole in the centre of its dome, through which you can look up to Heaven. The Tiber river runs through the city's heart, how Liam is longing to see it, and crossing it is a bridge with stone angels standing like God's earthly soldiers along its sides. And a chapel with a painted ceiling, and a piazza filled with flower-sellers, and a church around every corner, each with its own bell-tower, all of which chime more or less together on the hour. Liam listens for their song at night, as he lies in his bunk.

For now, however, he must clean this floor.

Liam dips his brush and returns to the scrubbing with a new vigour. Only twenty-one more days.

Every night, Enda sleeps in the leaf-filled hollow under the bench. She crawls out before daylight, washes herself as best she can in the fountain, then takes herself off, before the park-keeper sees her.

She looks for work tirelessly, asking in the cafés and restaurants, presenting herself at the back doors of smart houses, knocking on the gate of a factory, then a paper mill. The problem, as it becomes clear to her, is that she has no letters of reference and she doesn't know a single person who can vouch for her. Also, she looks odd, she knows, with her man's jacket, her cropped hair, and her incongruous embroidered skirt. As the weeks go by, she becomes more and more shabby and unkempt, more pinched and cold and desperate.

She plays her fiddle on street corners, her cap placed on the pavement, into which people drop pennies, if she's lucky, so she can buy a roll at the bakery, even a cup of tea. But the nights are cold and her fingers are stiff and split, and she is often too scared by noises to sleep; her increasingly dejected air puts people off.

On an unseasonably frosty evening, Enda cannot face another night in the park. She hasn't the spirit for it, for climbing over the rails and lying in a bed of soil like an animal.

Enda wanders the streets, her mind dulled, her body aching, her feet frozen to numbness inside their boots. She turns down a narrow lane, then comes out onto one of the city's step-streets, where people are sitting behind their windows, beside their hearths or at the tables of restaurants. There must be a place for me, she is thinking, there must be.

There is a noise to her left, a whooping and a gust of merriment, and she sees a group of men coming down the steps, two or three at a time. They are shoving at each other, jostling, and when they see her, they stop. One says something to her, not in French but in some other language, and the others laugh, and Enda sees that she might be in trouble. Without thinking about it, she steps through the door of a restaurant, into its lit and warm fug, where people are eating and drinking and talking, as if nothing difficult has ever happened to them.

A waiter comes towards her, scowling, looking her up and down, taking in her filthy skirt, her wild hair.

"You must leave," he tells her, through tight lips.

"I had to come in," she says, breathless, "there was . . . I was . . ."

"Leave."

He opens the door and motions for her to step outside.

"Would you have any work, mister?"

"For you? No."

"Please?"

He pushes his spread fingers into her back and gives her a shove, propelling her back to the steps, the door shutting behind her.

The men seem to have gone but Enda cannot risk running into them again. She climbs up, away from the direction in which they were moving, and turns into a narrower street, on one side of which is a viewpoint, where people congregate in the daytime to enjoy the vista across the river. She doesn't know what to do, there is nowhere for her to go: her mind repeats these words, what to do, where to go, over and over again, uselessly and persistently.

She walks across the viewpoint, trailing her hand on its low wall, then past a school, around a further corner, and she sees, before her, through the darkness, a crucifix and the arched doorway of a church. She looks around, checking over both shoulders, then she pushes the chill metal of the handle, and to her surprise, it gives.

Serried pews of wood, an altar with a white cloth, a single candle burning beside an effigy, a statue painted gold.

Enda tiptoes across the stone floor, glancing around. There's no one here. She stands for a moment outside the confessional, listening, in case anyone is inside. But there is nothing, just the barely perceptible hiss of wax sizzling in its candle flame.

She lifts the confessional curtain and ducks inside. The relief of simply sitting down, of being off her feet, is immense. She stares glassily at the wooden walls, tucks her legs up under her, and lets her head rest on the slats behind her. Despite her exhaustion, sleep refuses her, and her eyes keep darting from one side of the confessional to the other, as if it might contain crucial written instructions for what she might do next.

When sleep does finally come for her, it is like a heavy woollen hood falling over her head. It is profound, deep, soundless and dreamless.

She is woken, much later, or possibly after no time at all, by a hand shaking her awake. She finds herself in a lightless, enclosed place, like a press or a prison, her legs numb, a smell of polish and candles filling her nostrils, and in front of her is a black silhouette in a long priestly robe.

Her mind forms the hopeful word: Liam?

It isn't him, of course. The hair is longish, wispy, grey, the hunched stature that of an elderly man. Letting out a yelp, Enda tries to leap upright but her legs fail to unbend, stiff as they are with pins and needles, and she falls back to the seat, pushing away the hand.

A voice says something in French, something intended to be soothing, followed by a question. When she doesn't respond, the man tries again: "Do not be afraid, my child."

It is the priest of the church, of course, looming over her in his soutane. The light behind him is ashy and bleached by dawn. Enda snatches up her pack, her fiddle, and makes as if to dart around him but the priest holds up his palms, like a man trying to calm a frightened horse.

"Please do not run," he says. "Let us sit." He indicates a pew. "Tell me why you are here, in my church."

Enda doesn't speak for a while. She sits, however, in the pew, with an eye on the door, and one hand on her bundle. The priest, beside her, hands laced together, waits with the forbearance of the elderly. She tells him, haltingly at first, of coming alone to Québec, her savings sewn into a seam (she doesn't divulge that the papers belonged to her brother). And she tells him about having ship fever, and about the man who stole her money, and sleeping in the park with the fountain, and the priest listens, his head on one side.

"And now," he says, "you have nothing and no one."

Enda flinches at this devastating analysis.

"I have my fiddle," she mutters, kicking her boot into the pew in front of her.

"Tell me your name, child."

"Enda."

"I would like to help you, Enda of the violin, if you will permit it," the priest says. "Because here it is not easy for a woman alone. Or safe. I would not like to see . . ." He trails into silence, as if reluctant to divulge what he is imagining.

"There are many in your position who fall into bad ways here," he says eventually. "I hope you understand me."

She nods, knowing yet not knowing.

"I would not like to see this happen to you. So, tell me, are you willing to work?"

"Of course."

"I think, for now, we must also find you a place to sleep. Do you agree?"

"I do."

"There is a household looking for a hired girl. They have asked me if I know of a God-fearing girl of fine character. It is a good situation, with a respectable family, who come to my church every week. The gentleman is a fur-trader. You will have to work hard but they will treat you fairly, giving you a bed and also a small wage. How would you like to be a hired girl? Can you do this work?"

"What kind of work does a hired girl do?"

"Cleaning, cooking, laundry, taking care of the house."

Enda closes her eyes briefly. She sees her mother, she sees Rose, sweeping the floors with their brooms, pounding salt into oatmeal, dipping linens in and out of suds, scrubbing at the table, the floor, the hearth.

"I can," she says.

Enda leaves the church with a letter from the French priest. She steps out into the dawn. She squares her shoulders and sets her course for the house of the fur-trader.

The woman who answers her knock at the back door—Enda mistakenly assumes she is the fur-trader's wife but later learns she is the cook—looks her up and down with a tsk-ing sound. Enda has attempted to tidy herself, to smooth down her hair. She is wearing Liam's old jacket over the red-embroidered skirt; she has hidden her bundle of possessions and her fiddle behind a bush.

The woman leans against the screen door and crosses her arms. She asks Enda, does she know how to clean and mop, can she do laundry, is she afraid of hard work? Enda answers, yes, yes and no. She finds she is telling herself to keep Rose at the forefront of her mind, how Rose would comport herself in this situation, how she always charms people on first sight. Enda breathes evenly, in and out, she tilts her head to the angle of Rose's, she produces a smile of such radiance and earnestness and trustworthiness—Rose's smile—that the woman's misgivings evaporate.

The woman shifts from one leg to the other; she adjusts her apron's tie, saying that a lot of people won't let Enda's people past the door but she herself isn't like that because her own mother came from County Down. She is willing to give her a chance. A week's trial. There may be an old dress somewhere in the house that could be altered for Enda, for she cannot go about the place like that. She eyes Enda's cropped hair but passes no comment, assuming that the girl's head was cut for sanitation reasons at the quarantine station.

Enda steps in over the threshold. She sheds her jacket, dons an apron and listens as the woman tells her where to find the mop, the polish, the cleaning rags, where the laundry is done, where the vegetables are scrubbed. She is shown a narrow bed in a room up in the eaves of the house, which is hers and hers alone. Enda places beneath it her bundle and her fiddle, and rests a hand on the patchwork coverlet, breathing out a long, unsteady breath.

She is a hard worker, of course, but not perhaps in the way the cook and the fur-trader family would like. Enda is expected to rise at five, rake out the grates, lay the fires, mop the floors, dust the mantels, with their porcelain figures, taxidermied stoats, chiming clocks, inlaid boxes, enamelled vases. She is later meant to serve the lunch, in a way that is helpful but unobtrusive, then clear the plates, and wash everything up, replacing the china in the cupboards and the pans in the kitchen press. In the afternoons, while the cook puts up her feet, Enda will do the laundry, clean the upper floors, sweeping the bedrooms, tidying away the family's clothes; she must make scones and bread for the children's tea at four o'clock. Then comes the serving of dinner.

The cook takes a shine to Enda, despite her shortcomings as a maid. The girl is good company; she'll say that for her. At the end of the day, when dinner has been served and cleared away, and it's just the two of them in the kitchen, washing up and tidying for the next morning, most hired girls will be sullen and exhausted. Not Enda.

The girl is always full of chat, will sing made-up songs to make the cook laugh, and often does impressions of the master or his wife or their guests. I have so many rings on my fingers, Enda will say, in an exaggerated French drawl, draping a dishcloth over her head to imitate the fur-trader's elderly mother, that it's simply too much to ask of me to raise my cutlery to my lips. Could you perhaps feed me, *mon coeur?*

Enda is not constitutionally suited to being a hired girl, the cook privately thinks. "Unobtrusive" is not an adjective anyone might apply to her. She doesn't have a servile bone in her body. She whistles while she sweeps, which the lady of the house is forced to speak to the cook about, who in turn tells Enda. She thumps the plates down on the table with a grin, as if they are made of tin, not fine china. She is sometimes to be found gazing out of the window; once the fur-trader himself is certain he witnesses the girl taking down a book from his library shelves. She asks far too many questions. Furthermore, she teaches the children songs in some Hibernian dialect, which their parents do not know the meaning of, and do not wish to. She is found, once, exhorting them to jump over a rope she has tied to a garden fence, which she is swinging in a circle, her sleeves rolled up. She plays her fiddle, albeit softly, late into the night, up there in the attic where she sleeps, and it may be heard, on windless evenings, in the bedrooms below, giving rise to clamouring from the children, who wish to be allowed to watch. It comes to the attention of the parents that she has given names to their famed collection of taxidermied animals, which the fur-trader finds disrespectful. All in all, while they recognise that the girl is a good sort, they find her presence in the house disruptive, oddly distracting. It is hard to put a finger on why but she makes everyone feel prickling and unsatisfied, as if her spiritedness is somehow contagious.

When summer comes, and the family leave the city for their country house, a large property on an island facing out into the ocean, Enda tells the cook that she thinks she won't come with them. She'll stay in the city; the boy who delivers the coal has told her of an inn that needs a maid. The cook nods gruffly, flicks her apron. Well, she blusters, at least I'll finally get some peace around here.

Always remember, Enda whispers to the cook, as she hugs her goodbye, that the squirrel on the stairs is called Cyril. The cook swats her on the arm and turns quickly away.

Enda works at the inn on the outskirts of Québec for several months, until the summer season is over, then finds a position in the kitchen of a hotel over the winter. The cold in this country takes her by surprise, she tells the cook, when she visits her on a Sunday afternoon—the fur-trader's family have returned from their fair-weather house. She had thought she knew about weather, had considered herself to be brave in the face of it, but the winter here is like nothing she has ever experienced. True enough, the cook says, her feet resting on the range. You need a proper coat, my girl, gloves too—you can't be going about in that thin jacket.

The freeze lasts for months; the chill seems to hang in the air, like a solid entity, like something you could kick a hole through. The snow is so thick it covers the windows, casting the rooms in a strange half-light. Enda washes up the pots in the hotel scullery, she lays the tables, she pulls the sheets off the beds, plunges them into the laundry tub, hangs them out on a line where they freeze into stiff, agonised ghosts. The strings on her fiddle shrink into themselves: she has to tune them and make sure she plays every day to keep them supple.

In the spring, which marks a whole year she has spent in the country, she decides on a whim to leave Québec, to go exploring. She visits her friend the cook, who shakes her head and says that Enda must have ants in her drawers to be so fidgety. Come back and see me soon, the cook demands, wiping her eyes. Promise?

Enda shoulders her bundle and her fiddle, waves goodbye and takes a ferry further down the river, to Trois Rivières, where she has heard from one of the guests at the hotel that a landlady is looking for hired help. She negotiates a bed in the basement of the landlady's rooming house, in exchange for the daily cleaning of the stairways, windows, kitchen and floors.

One afternoon, after she has finished her chores, she sits on the edge of her bed—no more than a bunk in a windowless cupboard—with a sealed letter on her knee. She has written to Rose, at last. I'm sorry, she has written, I'm sorry. I miss you. Please forgive me. Here is my address, if you would like to write back: I intend to be here for a while, perhaps even a year. I live in a town in the far north where three rivers converge; there are many paper mills here and they use the currents of the river to turn trees into paper, can you imagine? How are you? How is Eugene? Is Da doing well?

Suddenly decisive, she leaps from the bunk, seizes her fiddle and slings it on her back. She goes out and posts the letter, dropping it into the mailbox outside the main post office in the central square of the town.

After this, she walks along one of the three rivers, which cuts deep through a gulley, iron bridges arching over it. At a corner, where the endoskeleton of a building is being constructed, joists forming promises of floors and stairs and rooms to come, she pauses, looking up. A foreman with a book or ledger stands on what will be the first floor, a group of labourers around him. Someone else walks along a beam in mid-air, a breathless feat of balance. Two men are driving rivets through the ironwork, one hammer falling as the other is raised, a perfect synchronicity, an irresistible rhythm. When she hears the language they are all speaking, she reaches for the fiddle on her back.

The tune she plays mimics exactly the strikes of the twinned hammers: it uses the marching, two-four time as a base for the melody, which begins as simple, four notes circling each other, but then builds and rebels, one note pulling away from the other, turns and twists appearing, until the tune is flying, soaring, at double-time, going one way, then the other, up and down, around and around. It's a tune she knows well but somehow there, on the corner by the river, next to a would-be building, constructed by her countrymen, it becomes strange to her. It takes off in directions she hadn't known before, it pulls her into its vortex, and when it ends, she is cast out of it, alone, and she is breathless, feeling as if her skin has been lifted from her, and she is surprised to find herself back on the pavement.

Above her, there is a noise of cheering and clapping. The men have all come to stand at the front of the half-built frame, calling down to her, Play another, go on, so she does, a song this time, which they begin to sing, their voices colliding together, some more tuneful than others, but they all know the words, and even the foreman, an older man with a large belly, is singing. At the end, they clap again, and she bows, there in the street, and she is surprised to find that something is raining down to hit the paving slabs beside her: they are throwing something, and for a moment, she can't tell what it is. And then she sees that it is coins. They are reaching into their pockets and tossing money down to her, saying, Good woman, there, come back tomorrow.

Astonished, she collects it: never before has she had such a reaction to her playing. She fills the pocket of her cotton print dress, given to her by the fur-trader's cook. She takes the coins back to the rooming house, and puts them into a jar under her bunk.

The next day, she finishes her cleaning work in good time and she goes back, and plays for them again. Afterwards, when she has collected the coins thrown down, the foreman asks her if she will play at his apartment the next week—they are having a party for his daughter's engagement—and he will pay her for her trouble, of course. The day after that, Enda goes up the river, to a paper mill, where she plays polkas to the Polish workers as they leave their shift, the tunes she picked up while in the quarantine hospital. She positions herself in the logging district and plays drinking songs, or at the wharf to play sea shanties, and learns that it is perhaps best to dress herself as a boy if she is to make money in this way. So she tucks up her hair, most days, exiting the door of the basement in a cap and trousers, tightly belted around her thin frame. The landlady, watching from an upper window, her aged and malodorous cat tucked under her arm, takes a puff on her cigarette, narrows her eyes, then shrugs: she's seen all types come and go in her line of business. As long as the girl does her work and doesn't bring back men, she can dress as whatever she likes.

Liam kneels at the prie-dieu in the frescoed study, his fingertips resting on its warm wooden grain, his shins pressed to its kneeling pad.

"*Praeterea*," he is saying, "*patres doctissimi, quid haec doctrina nos docet . . .*"

Facing him are two fathers of the Society of Jesus, seated in armchairs. He is being examined in theological disputation, for the duration of one hour, and he must speak only in Latin.

"*. . . fortis et . . .*" Liam continues, and how his legs ache, how painful it is to keep up this kneeling position for the entire time, his legs may never straighten again, but he must give the impression of willingness and humility, he must "*. . . interrogans responsum est et—*"

"*Interrogans?*" the older priest repeats, "*Quare interrogans?*"

Liam is startled at the interruption. Questioning, the man has said, why questioning? Did he, Liam, say that, "questioning"? He doesn't remember.

The heat in the room is thick and languorous—if it were an animal it would be a cat, stretched out in sleep. Dust motes circle like fireflies in the ochre beams of light stealing in through the gaps in the curtains. Beyond the windows of the study, Liam can hear the clatter of feet, moving up and down the college's paths, the subdued chatter of other brothers, bursts of laughter, purposeful calls. There is a general air of excitement as the Jesuits are preparing for the Corpus Christi procession, carrying back and forth candles, flowers, vases, wine, copes, dalmatics, tinderboxes, ticking each item off a list, exclaiming about the June heat, helping each other, dropping things and having to turn and pick them up.

How he wishes to be out there, offering to shoulder boxes of candles or to brush down the brocaded garments.

Instead, he is undergoing his examination. He has, his spiritual director told him, excelled in his scholastic studies, and has completed them in a startlingly short time. If he passes this examination today, he is to be sent away from Rome, far away, to India, where his Order is said to be making great strides and progress.

He has not told them that the journey fills him with dread—over a month at sea!—and he fears he may not survive it. He has taken a vow of obedience and must go wherever they bid him. Liam will soon earn the title "Father," followed by the fuller, more expansive version of his name: Father Gulielmus. People will then address him thus, and how strange it will feel to him, the moniker hitting him at an angle. He will be a father and yet have no children, and never shall. Everyone he looks upon will be his child—man, woman, young, old.

Still kneeling, with beads of moisture gathering on his lip, Liam tries to pull himself straighter. His examiners are looking at him quizzically, one with a frown on his face. There had been a question; one of them had asked him something. What was it? Liam racks his brains, his gaze darting from one to the other.

Interrogans: that was it. They asked him why his response to this particular religious doctrine had been questioning.

Very well. Liam squares his shoulders, shifts his knees.

"*Quia*," he declares, evincing a confidence he doesn't entirely feel, "*mens et spiritus . . .*"

Outside, a candelabrum is being carried through sunlight, and the cast image of its outline ripples over the folds in the thin curtains, complex and stately, like the ghost of a tree.

Enda waits and watches for a letter from home: it comes close to an obsession. It is the first thing she does when she comes into the house: she asks her landlady every day, Has anything come for me? The answer is always no, and the landlady gives her a long look, from the feet up, as if wondering what might be wrong with her, if her family will not write. Enda develops a crushed feeling about her ribs, a curious ache in her sternum. Rose has not written; Rose has not replied; Rose may never reply. Enda knows that Rose cannot write, never having really attended school, but there are others around who can write for her, can inscribe her spoken words: the priest, for one.

That her sister has not forgiven her can be the only reason. From all the way across the ocean, on the other side of the world, Enda begins to feel the burning beam of Rose's anger. She remembers a tinker coming to the Lanes one day and showing their mother his basket of wares. The one that had struck Enda had been a circle of thickened glass, the tinker showing them how it concentrated the rays of the sun and, if you held it over a piece of wood, you could create fire, bring forth smoke, could make burned striations and marks in it. And it feels like that to Enda, as if she is being scorched by the focused, inescapable beam of Rose's fury, all the way from the peninsula.

Some shift or change takes place in Enda now, almost two years since she left. As well as the ache in her sternum, she loses the knack of sleep: she cannot receive its mercy. She can drop off, after she's been out, playing perhaps for a dance or at a wedding, but something in her clamours for attention at the darkest hours of the morning, rapping her on the skull, hauling her to wakefulness, so peremptorily that she sometimes comes to and finds herself tangled in the sheets, her mind thronged with home. She might lie there, thinking about the house, the way the door hinges squeal in hot weather, the smoke trapped in the rafters, the smell of hay off the mattresses. Lying awake in her bunkroom, the heavy heat of summer spread over her like twenty blankets she can't throw off, she thinks about the lough, and how your feet appear through its peaty waters, the slippery coating on some of the stones so you need to tread carefully so as not to lose your balance. She tries not to think of Eugene and Rose, tries to bat away or smother thoughts about how they must have searched for her, how it must have come to them, perhaps slowly, what had happened. The confusion Eugene must have felt, how it has always been hard for him to comprehend where people are when they're not in front of him, where people go, what absence is. The vulnerable nape of his neck when he is bent over some task—peeling potatoes for Rose, arranging his bits of coral in stacks—and how fine his hair is, how he will only ever permit Enda to cut it, and when she does he has to shut tight his eyes because he loathes the noise of the scissors, metal against hair shaft, so she does it as quickly as she can, the ends of it falling like dark feathers about him.

It is a nightly torment, the jolting awake and the skeins of thought that bind themselves around her. All day, she is here, in her new life, cleaning the rooming house, making the beds of the lodgers or scrubbing the front step, but it's as if her mind wakes her in the dark hours to say: Here, you haven't thought about home enough, what about the donkey, the way its long ears swivel when it hears you coming, or what about the noise of the streams after the spring thaw, can you recall that particular timbre of gurgling and rushing, can you?

The worst of it is not that she can't sleep, that she is coshed by exhaustion, her face mealy pale, her limbs leaden, but that it is starting to affect her playing.

On a day when she has slept for perhaps two or three hours, she has set herself up in the early evening outside a tavern where men drink after a working day. Dressed in her brother's clothes, a cap pulled down over her narrow face, she has the fiddle in position, its case open at her feet to receive whatever coins people might drop into it, and she is halfway through an air about an enchanted tree. A small crowd has gathered in the doorway of the tavern; several men are singing and whistling along with her, with varying degrees of skill. Her breathing is in time with the meditative rhythm of the tune; everything, she is telling herself, is fine. She is holding herself together, in this cold northern corner of the New World, all alone, keeping a roof over her head.

She is managing. She tells herself this. Not many could do what she has pulled off. Not many would have the stomach or the ingenuity for it. She knows this. She should be proud of herself.

And yet she isn't. As the months go by, as the years stretch between the here and now and home, she feels less and less at ease in herself. And this tune! Its mournful, lilting strains, its minor chords that climb and fall, the drone of the next string that must lie underneath it. Enda feels the notes vibrate through her, down her veins, through her bones, and in her head blossoms a vision of the peninsula—field-boundary walls that undulate over every bluff and hollow, the water lilies that crowd into wet ditches in early summer, the surface of the lough that quilts itself in a breeze, the cows that turn their large eyes upon you, the darkness that rises up from the hills at dusk. The music she plays is the land: it summons it; it conjures it here, to this street corner. It is enough to drive her mad. How can she be here and there, all at the same time? She is a person divided, split in two, a tree sundered by lightning.

Her fingers on the strings feel suddenly enervated and trembling. She can barely move them towards the next note. Her breathing is either too fast or too slow for the melody—she cannot tell. She notices that two or three men have emerged from the kitchen door of an inn opposite; one leans on a wall, smoking a cigarette, watching her.

She slides the bow up, then down, in an abrupt flourish, ending the tune in the middle of a verse, and keeping one eye on the group over the road—there is something unsettling in the way the one with the cigarette is staring at her so intently, and she feels her leg muscles tense, as if readying themselves to run—she attempts to launch into a French march, a fleet and rousing song about a hero triumphing in battle, but somehow she cannot do it, the music deserts her. Instead of feeling the tune, its verses and chorus, laid out before her like a path she has trodden many times before, each turning and curve familiar, she feels herself to be on a cliff, with nothing before her but a foggy void.

She feels the fiddle slide from her chin and she grips its neck with slippery fingers, her bowing arm falling to her side. Across the street, she is aware that the man with the cigarette is approaching. She sees the orange tip of it coming towards her, closer and closer through the dark. The man is tall and muscled, an apron tied around him, his sleeves rolled up.

Enda takes a step back. If she cried out, would her countrymen in the tavern doorway come to her aid, would they fight this stranger? They are not as tall or as smartly dressed as him, but they are wiry and fierce, they would help her, surely. But they might discover she is a woman and then—

The stranger with the spattered apron has arrived before her and now he is bending over, and for a wild moment, Enda thinks he might be bowing to her. Then she hears a chink and he straightens up and she sees that he was, in fact, only putting some money into her case.

"Thank you—*merci*," she says, or tries to say, but because no air seems to be reaching her windpipe, her voice comes out as a hoarse gasp.

The man remains before her, leaning with his hand on one knee, looking at her. No light from the tavern window falls on his face so that he appears to her as a silhouette in the darkness, like one of the cut-out figures from the shadow-theatre booths she has seen at carnivals. He says something to her, twice, both times a question, but it's a word she doesn't recognise.

"What was that?" she says.

He repeats it, twice. "Grozz," he says, slowly and clearly, "Île." He points at himself, his finger turned into his chest, and then at her. "Grozzle."

Then it hits Enda. Grozzle. Grosse Île. He is the very man she met in the immigration queue, the one who helped her at the medical station, who somehow saw through her disguise. He is the same yet different—his hair is shorter, his beard gone, his large overcoat replaced by a shirt and an apron. She lets out a laugh—a poor, forced version of one—and feels the panic drain from her.

"I remember you!" she says. "You had an accordion."

The man nods vigorously. "Indeed, yes." The word comes out of his mouth as *yis* or *yish*, or halfway between the two. "I still have it but not with me at this moment, otherwise I might have played with you. But I am working this evening, as you can see."

"At the inn?"

He nods. "In the kitchen. Which is, of course, too hot for an accordion. And my companions might throw it into the stove by accident. Or perhaps on purpose. No, I would not bring it here."

"You're a cook?"

"For the winter," he says, with a rueful shrug. "At home, I was a teacher. Here, I am a cook." He tosses his cigarette end to the ground. "It is not so bad. At least I am fed."

"That is always good," Enda says, tucking the fiddle under her arm.

"I liked your playing very much."

"Thank you."

"You switched, though," he says, looking at her sideways, "from a very beautiful, sad tune to something different. Why was that? Why did you cut short the first tune?"

"I . . ." Speech deserts Enda: she cannot think how to explain what happened.

"The first was so perfectly suited to your playing, and you delivered it so skilfully. It brought us out of the kitchen to listen. And then," he brings up a hand and mimes something disappearing, his fingers opening, like someone releasing a moth, "it was gone."

Enda shrugs, unable to speak. He regards her, arms crossed, his eyes searching her face. It comes back to her now, his way of looking, his unsettling ability to see through people's dissembling and disguises.

"Forgive me," he murmurs, after a moment, "I am told that I ask too many questions. And here I am, again, asking too many questions."

She taps her knee with the end of her bow, shakes the hair out of her eyes.

"How is your wife?" she asks. "I still have her skirt. Perhaps she would like it back."

"Wife?" he says. "Not wife. Sister."

"Sister?" Enda absorbs this, twirling a button on her jacket around and around on its stem. He glances at her and they look away.

"You may keep the skirt—I'm certain my sister hasn't thought about it since. She lives up the river, in Québec, with some cousins of ours. She preferred not to accompany me here, to Trois Rivières, but to stay in the city. We talked many times about the girl-boy from Grosse Île: one minute, you were there, and then you were gone. We wondered what happened to you."

He looks up and down the street, at the men lurching out of the saloons, at the sputtering gas lamps.

"Tell me," he says suddenly, with a frown, as if it has just occurred to him, "are you here alone? In this part of town? No one is with you?"

Enda shakes her head. "It's fine. Dressed like this."

He makes a sceptical huffing noise, and when she raises her eyes, she sees that he is looking over her head, gesturing to his companions, who are standing at the kitchen door. He says something to them in their language and they reply.

When he speaks to her again, it is in a low voice, almost a whisper: "I think perhaps you are tired, yes?" he says. "And also hungry."

He leans forward and takes the fiddle from her hand with a gesture of surprising gentleness. To her surprise, she lets him. She watches, as if from above, as he expertly loosens the bow, as he packs the fiddle into its box, as he collects up the coins and hands them to her, asking her name. When he stands up, he loops the case around his own shoulders. He tells her that his name is Anatole and that they can step inside the inn and eat together—he has finished his shift for the night and it is time for his supper. This part of town is not a good place for her to be, he says, even if she is dressed like this. He gestures up and down her outfit. He would not like his sister to be here at this hour, not at all. Enda stands on the muddy street, uncertain, dithering, then remembers how he and his sister helped her before, how kind they were. There can be no danger in this for her, she thinks, surely. As if he has intuited her thoughts, he tells her that she need not worry, he is her friend. So they turn and go into the inn, Anatole holding open the door for her. He points her towards a table, then disappears through a doorway hung with sacking, returning with two steaming bowls. Enda discovers that it is thick broth, purple in colour, and there are five dumplings bobbing on its surface, interspersed with discs of oil. Her stomach stirs uneasily and seems to turn over, and she thinks she will not eat it, but she takes a small sip from the spoon, so as not to appear rude. Then she takes a mouthful, and another, and suddenly her bowl is empty, and her body feels hot at its core, like a volcano, and Anatole laughs and nods, saying, It's good, yes, it's what you need, his teeth ripping at a crust of bread.

He tells her that in the evenings after work in the kitchen, he plays his accordion, mostly in his quarters, a room above the inn that he shares with five other men. He has not thought of playing in the street or outside bars for money, as she does. When the spring comes, he says, he will stop working at the inn and go upriver with a crew to a logging camp, where they will fell trees. He has done this for the two previous summers: it is hard work but it pays better than the kitchen, and he must save money to pay for passages for his parents and remaining siblings.

From a chair in the corner of the inn, a musician begins to play. Enda and Anatole fall instantly silent. The musician is an old man with a set of pipes, his boots planted either side of the stool; he works the bellows with his elbow and alternately hums along or turns his head to converse with someone to his right as his fingers move over the dark holes of the chanter. Anatole leans towards her to ask if the man is from her homeland and she nods. They listen to the melody, which is at first playful, then mournful, then back again, and at the end they clap. Anatole drums his spoon on the table, which makes Enda smile, and the old piper tips his hat at them, his eyes lingering on Enda with a fleeting piercing look, before he begins another tune, the name of which, Enda knows, is "The Girl with Red Hair."

She rips the bread on her plate into small pieces and pushes them into her mouth, listening. She cannot know that the elderly man with the pipes in the corner of the inn is, in fact, of great significance to her. There is no way for either of them to discover that they are linked. The old man tells no one these days about the family he left behind, his wife and all their pretty children, whom he intended to fetch and bring here when he was settled, and how even now he is twisted and bent inside with a bitter regret that he ever emigrated alone, that he didn't have the money for them all to sail together, that he got on that boat with only his pipes on his back, leaving them there. He tells no one that he went back to find them, but the cottage where they had lived was a ruin, inhabited only by stupid-faced cattle, and a neighbour told him they had all gone, died in the Great Hunger, but there had been one child, a daughter, who survived and was taken to the workhouse. He never speaks of how he had rushed there to seek her out, to reclaim her, only to find no trace: she, too, had gone. The old pipe-player keeps these things hidden deep inside him. There is no way for him to know that this daughter, lost to inaccurate records of the workhouse, gave birth to the child he now plays a song for. Perhaps there is something familiar to him about the oddly attired copper-haired girl who sits with a fiddle at her feet, next to an intense-looking man with rolled-up sleeves, in the corner, both of whom pay such close attention to his playing. Perhaps the girl—or is it a boy?—reminds him of someone he knew long ago, a cousin or a sibling, or one of his own long-dead children.

Enda and Anatole stay for two more tunes, and then they leave, Enda passing, unaware, within arm's length of her grandfather, and the old man will think of this red-haired girl, and how he would have liked to hear her play, until he dies, a year or so later, quickly and without warning, in his bed. Enda, however, will walk out of the inn and never think of him again.

Anatole insists on accompanying her back to her rooming house: you shouldn't walk about so late, he says. He tries to carry the fiddle for her but she does not let him. I don't like to let it out of my sight, she says, and he says he understands. He asks what her plans are, if she will stay in Trois Rivières, and she says she doesn't know. She doesn't say that she cannot cast her mind forward, she cannot envisage the years ahead, here, in this town, in this country, and in that moment she discovers that there is an intention, nestled within her, like a fossil in a rock, to go home. She could get on a boat and sail back. She could return to the peninsula, beg their forgiveness, tell them she will stay this time, she won't ever leave again. It's not impossible. She could do this, if she saved enough, if she worked for several more years and didn't spend anything.

When he asks her what she's thinking about, she doesn't tell him, but she finds herself instead speaking of how she wakes not long after she falls asleep, that she has horrendous dreams, that she feels so weighted down that she sometimes feels she cannot put one foot in front of the other.

"It sounds," he says, as they round the corner to her street, "as if you are homesick."

"Homesick?" she asks, in wonder.

"Yes." He shrugs. "Why not? It happens to us all. This whole country," he swings his arm around in a semicircle, "is full of homesick people. The homesick and the lonely."

As she reaches the door of the rooming house, she hears his voice out of the darkness.

"Perhaps," he says, "we can play one night. Fiddle and accordion. Together. What do you think?"

Enda considers this. She considers him, standing there in the blackness of the night, his arms folded against the cool air. She considers the faint anxiety in his voice as he asks her this question.

Yish, Enda thinks, and nods. "It's a nice idea."

When she goes into the house, her landlady is still awake, waiting for her to come back, she says, with only faint disapproval, because a letter has arrived for her. Finally, the landlady thinks but doesn't say.

Enda snatches it from her: a letter from home, with news of them all, with tidings, perhaps even love. She carries it off to her room and pulls out the folded paper, opens it, hands trembling, and if she could drink this ink with her fingertips, draw it into her body, she would; if she could breathe in the peninsula air sealed into the envelope, she would, but in her agitation she can do no more than scan the lines, eyes darting from word to word, from top to bottom.

In her hands is a single, short paragraph, written by Father Joseph. There are no expressions of love or anger or, indeed, anything coming close to an emotion at all. It is dated four months ago, and it says that he seeks to inform her that her father, Tomás, has passed away.

When Rose and Eugene finish bringing in their hay, they take only a moment's pause, shaking the stiffness from their arms and shoulders, wiping their brows, and drinking from the pump, before Rose turns and says to her brother: "I wonder will we go down and make a start on the widow's field?"

Eugene, replacing the ladle carefully, makes no sound.

"The sky is clear," Rose murmurs, looking up, "but rain might come in quickly. We'll go now, will we? We will. I'm not too tired, are you? I don't think you are."

She has developed the habit of holding both sides of a conversation, Eugene has noticed. For a while, he wasn't sure if he liked it, but now he thinks he does. Her words possess the motion of a saw moving back and forth through wood, or the swing of a pendulum: soothing and restful. It requires nothing of him. He can listen, and nod, or not, and she will carry on regardless.

Rose reaches out her hand to take Eugene's, and he lets her, and she toys, as she always does, with the gold ring around his finger, her fingertip following its circular patterns. When they get as far as the end of their boreen, he extracts his hand from hers, and folds his arms around himself. At fifteen, Eugene is tall, the tallest of them all, Rose often thinks, and has the strength of two or three men. Which is fortunate, the widow remarked the other day, because all the other men have fecked off. Eugene will apply himself to whatever task needs doing: feeding or milking, digging or scything, fencing or walling, fishing, trapping. There's a part of Rose that, when she watches her silent and mysterious brother bringing down an axe through wood or driving a plough through a field, wants to drag to his side all the people who called him "simple" or "useless" and say: Look. Do you see? I dare you to tease him now, go on, I dare you. She wants to yank them up the hillside by their collars and show them the loft full of tied stooks of hay, the walls and fences without a hole, their lean-to stacked with turf, their beasts placid and plump, and say: Guess who did all that? Not so useless after all.

The whole peninsula came to their house for Tomás's wake and passed the night with her and Eugene, bringing bread and bottles, which people handed round, and the talk turned to that way Tomás had of ending conversations by simply walking away or cutting a person off. He didn't mean any rudeness by it, the widow said. He was never one for goodbyes, the fisherman observed, never would he ever say that word. He would just stop speaking and be on his way. And then they began to talk of the time they had first met Tomás, when he appeared among them, and how suspicious they had been of this map-man and his boy, with their instruments, their questions, their inquisitive way of walking about the land.

Rose had turned her face to the embers in the grate. It seemed to her that their life in this house had been a slow process of subtraction: they had been six, and now it was just her and Eugene. Only two.

In the peculiar way she'd always had, the widow appeared at her elbow, sitting herself down in the seat next to Rose. She had her knitting in her hands, needles working against each other, winding up the wool—the colour of wet moss—into something that was possibly a sleeve.

"You'll come and live down with me," the widow said, out of the corner of her mouth. "You and the boy."

Rose had shaken her head. "We can't be—"

"Just for a while. Until you get back on your feet."

"We'll be grand here," Rose had said, gesturing around the kitchen, where her father's body was laid out on the table, pennies over his eyes.

The widow gave her a sharp look. "You can come back up during the days. You'll need to mind the fields, the animals and the hens. But you'll sleep down with me."

"It's good of you, but—"

"If you stay here," the widow urged, in a whisper, "the loneliness will kill you."

Rose had been struck dumb by this. She had glanced at Eugene, standing by the door, then back at the widow.

"Besides, I could do with the company," the widow said, in her normal voice, her needles clicking, and then she played her trump card: "It's what your mother would have wanted. God strike me dead if I left you and the boy up here to fend for yourselves."

So Eugene and Rose brought their blankets and their clothes down the hill. He slept in the widow's loft and Rose by the fire, Bran stretched out next to her, the widow in her back room. In the mornings, Rose and Eugene would help the widow see to her cow and crops, and then they would take to the lane, Bran trotting before them, nose to the ground, doubling back on himself if he found an interesting scent, and climb the hill up to their old home, returning to the widow's at sunset.

Today, however, sunset is still far off, and they have work to do and hay to bring in. Bran has gone ahead of them—he doesn't like mowing days, as his people must spend hours in one field, and it makes him restless—and he is waiting for them when they reach the village, chewing on a stick he's found somewhere. Eugene lifts the scythe from his shoulder and begins on the widow's furthest field. Rose follows behind, mindful to keep her distance from the swinging of her brother's arm, gathering up the hay in armfuls and tying it into stooks.

It is seven months now since Tomás passed, which feels to Rose like no time at all and yet an endless stretch of days. Death baffles her, every time she brushes against it: the finality of it, how there is no bargaining to be done, no way of saying to it, If I give you this or do that you must give my mother or father back to me, release them from your clutches. It is the inarguable force of their absence, and the conundrum of what to do with what they leave behind: the boots, the combs full of strands, the spoon worn smooth by their fingers, the shawl draped on a chair, the bonnet on the peg.

She would like to go to Eugene and ask him, How does it feel for you, what do you think of our father's passing, tell me, how does it strike you? She could have done this with Enda, or Liam. Either of them—if they were ahead of her with the scythe, cutting away, felling the stalks—would have stopped the mowing, would have turned around, perhaps even hugged her hard, and told her how they felt, what their thoughts were on the matter. They might have helped her tidy away the things, found a new use for them. As it is, Rose has no one to talk to about it.

Tomás was found, Father Joseph told her when he'd climbed the path up to their house, a couple of days' walk from here. Lying on the ground, beneath the shelter of a tree, his blanket roll under his head, looking for all the world as if he was asleep. Several people had walked by him, the priest had said, before it had dawned on one of them that the old man lying by the roadside wasn't resting but had passed away. All the signs, he said, suggested it was a peaceful death. Tomás had lain down to sleep and not risen again. May we all meet our end thus. And Father Joseph had looked as if he had concluded his duty in telling her, and that he might be off. But Rose had been curious, unsatisfied by this story. Where was he found? she wanted to know. Father Joseph was vague: a valley, he said, some distance away, a neighbouring county.

A valley? Rose had repeated. Yes, my child, the priest said, a valley surrounded by high hills, I'm told, with a lough running through it. A beautiful place, by all accounts. But whatever was he doing there? Rose had asked. And the priest had said: We may never know. He was given to mysterious wanderings, was he not? Your father was a man of strong character and there were unplumbed depths to his mind. We must consider him now at peace, his worldly struggles at an end. He is in the arms of God.

Rose sneezes violently three times, and sets down her bundle to wipe her nose on her apron. Eugene, over in the far corner now, for she cannot keep up with the speed of his mowing, doesn't look round.

At peace, my arse, she thinks, as she bends to gather the next armful. Tomás was never and will never be at peace: he was the most unknowable, dissatisfied, edgy, turbulent person she'd ever met. Never was he still, never was he content, but always fidgeting, always up out of his chair, saying he was away to mend something or straighten something, or bolting out of the door to see to a task or walk off somewhere. When she was little, she used to run after him sometimes, try to hang on to him, saying, Da, will I come too? His was a hand impossible to hold, always stiff and unyielding, the fingers refusing to curl around hers, so that she couldn't keep her grip on it. He would stride along, her hand sliding off his, and if he noticed she was there, which was never a given, might look down at her in surprise and say, Is it you, away back to the house, off to your mother now.

It bothers her, she realises, as she upends the stook so that it leans against the other; it nags at her, in a visceral and prickling way, that he should have died in the open air, at the side of a road, so far away from them. He should have been in his bed, with his family around him. It strikes Rose as a lonely, miserable way to die: alone, outdoors, with people walking past you, not knowing you, not seeing that you'd gone. It is like the passing of a wild animal, or—

At this half-formed thought, Rose's mind pulls aside, like someone veering away from a cliff-edge. She knows that people—thousands of them—died at roadsides, in ditches, in the rubble of their homes, outside churches, wherever they fell, not long before she had been born. Neither of her parents had ever spoken of those times, but she, Liam and Enda were aware that they had no grandparents, no cousins, nobody, and Phina had once told them that Tomás had rescued her from a terrible fate, that he'd come for her and taken her away with him, but she wouldn't elaborate. Rose has always been aware of a darkness, a roiling cloud, in her parents, a sense of rupture, a lack of rootedness. She has for ever carried, like a heavy bag strapped to her back, the sense that she wasn't able to assuage their losses: she was too small, too ignorant, to aid them, to make up for what they lacked. She didn't know how to ask them about it, how to form those questions, where to begin, what to say. And now it was too late. They were both gone.

Rose straightens, pressing a fist to her back. She is filled with sudden and baseless fear, a chill water welling inside her. She is lacking too much; she is unprotected; there aren't enough of them to be safe. She wants people, her people, around her; she wants walls, high ones, to keep out the ravening night, the baying enemies. She wants—what? Her sister, her older brother. She wants her mother. She wants her father not to be dead; she wants him to have said to her, as a child, Yes, you can come along with me, let me show you where I'm going and let me tell you where I've been, and for him to have gripped her hand, firmly, as if he would never let it go, would never leave her, would never just walk out the door and not come back.

She and Eugene are not enough, but there is nothing to be done. She puts that same hand, dusty and filthy, into her mouth, and she whistles for her dog, and instantly, he leaps from slumber to action, and over the half-mown field he comes, bounding towards her, ears flying back, mouth open in a canine grin.

Placing his sandals with care, Liam edges along the cultivated rows of neatly spaced sprouting leaves—they are some kind of layered vegetable resembling a scallion but with a sourer tang. The local people have a word for it that sounds like "ulli" and they fry it in hot, spiced oil, with nuts and lentils, sometimes with freshly caught fish: Liam often cannot resist buying food from market stalls as he walks between the school and the mission-house, because the brother who cooks here on the edge of town tends to boil everything to a colourless and flavourless pulp. Liam didn't know it was possible to make meals taste so awful. The market-stall food, however, has begun to tempt him almost every day, because of the way it makes his mouth and tongue tingle with turmeric, cardamom, tamarind, cinnamon and galangal—the very words themselves are delicious.

Liam straightens to stretch the muscles in his back. Even though it is not long since dawn, the people of Cochin are already up and about: the track that winds past the mission-house and along the canal is filled with those clattering out to the fields or making their way into the markets or fishing nets of town. The canal itself is thick with *kettuvallam* piled high with sacks and goods, and long, slender boats, paddled from the rear.

As Liam makes his way along the rows of vegetables, bending to remove weeds, he greets these passers-by with a nod or a word: some reply and others ignore him. The day is already hot, the humidity so intense it's as if he's wading through water, as if the wide, slow-moving canal has lifted itself up and permeated the air. It mists his spectacles; it turns his robe to sopped lianas that cling to his back and legs. Scratching in the earth to winkle out a particularly sinuous root, he cannot help but reflect that his father would be amused to see him thus.

Liam can almost picture Tomás here in south India, leaning on the wall behind him, his black cap pushed back on his head, watching as Liam pulls the weeds. How he would laugh, the wheezing cackle that always makes him pound his chest with a fist. All that learning, he would say, and they have you scratching about in the dirt, tending scallions. This is where all that Latin and scripture got you? You'd have been better following in my footsteps after all.

Swiping at his brow with the back of his hand, Liam glares at the wall. My days are very varied—he is addressing the imagined Tomás now—some mornings, I might be teaching mathematics to schoolboys, or working on a translation of an ancient astrological text, and on other days, yes, I may be working in the Order's garden, but it doesn't mean that—

A flicker of movement to his left alerts him to the presence of a face, perhaps two, of his brethren, behind a window in the mission-house, looking down on him, standing and arguing with his invisible father. He bends quickly to a weed. When he straightens again, the window is as before: an impenetrable surface reflecting the cluttered buildings at the edge of town, the canal that moves itself through the dropped green handkerchiefs of rice fields.

In the distance, along the flat valley, through the shimmer of heat-haze, Liam can see people bent, like him, over their crops. There are two figures pulling a plough through a shallow stretch of water, its reflection of clouds and sky rippling and splintering, re-forming as the people move on.

Liam crouches beside his basket, as if he is looking inside it but he is in fact taking a moment's pause. The heat is vicious today and how he wishes for a hat like the people here wear, large and woven into a bowl shape, giving merciful shade. When he spoke of this to the spiritual adviser of the mission-house, the man had frowned at him and said they were required to keep themselves apart, differentiated, so that they may be looked up to as the leaders and saviours they are.

Leaders and saviours, Liam is muttering, as he stands and lifts the basket of weeds to his shoulder, leaders and saviours, and then he realises he is being irreverent, ungodly, and he stills the tongue in the burning cage of his mouth. He may yet be being watched, he thinks, as he walks, suddenly self-conscious, too aware of how his legs move, to the place outside the high perimeter wall to tip unwanted greenery.

Shaking the basket only a little too vigorously, and watching the weeds tumble out, Liam's train of thought is interrupted by a slight but distant sound, like a shout, or a call. Perhaps a bird, perhaps a child? Liam glances up but sees only the splintering light on the waterway's surface, the bobbing shapes of boats. He is turning back to the mission-house gate when he hears the noise again.

This time, Liam shades his eyes, straining to see. There, on the track, shoving his way through the crowds, is a figure, dressed in a yellow *mundu*. The man moves with urgency and purpose; people step aside to let him pass; something about the way he holds his arms bent at the elbows, with the hands cupped together, strikes Liam as odd. What does he carry?

Without knowing why, Liam lets the basket slip from his fingers. He moves towards the man, away from the mission-house, which is not permitted for him at this hour—he will only be able to leave later, to teach his mathematics classes—but he cannot ignore this person. The man is shouting something: he is heading for the mission-house,

Liam is certain, he has seen him. He has been sent by the Lord, and he, Liam, will aid him, will assist him with whatever trouble has beset him.

Liam hurries towards him, along the canal path, his heart hammering. The man is closer now, still yelling—inarticulate, grief-stricken syllables, perhaps not words in any language. Although Liam knows he could still improve, he is just about able to converse in Malayalam, more fluently than his other brethren, though it would be committing the sin of pride to acknowledge it. So Liam raises his voice and calls to him: "What is it? How may I help you?"

He likes these words: they are authoritative yet kind, they strike the right fatherly note. He is helping this man; he is doing what he came here for.

Several feet away, the man falls to his knees, like a tree struck by an axe. People gather and mass around him, murmuring.

"I need . . ." the man gasps, still with his hands cupped together ". . . your magic."

"My magic?" Liam repeats uneasily, as he comes to a stop in front of the man. I have no magic, he wants to say, none at all, I am merely a servant of the Lord and magic could not be further from—

"Please," the man says, and Liam realises it is not only sweat running down the man's face, that tears are coursing from his eyes. "Help me."

He lifts his hands, curving them open in supplication, and Liam glimpses, before he averts his eyes, a human child, small enough to fit within the nest of the man's palms. Liam has to steel himself not to rear back in shock. The child is perfect, a masterpiece in miniature: tiny curled hands, minute lips, eyes shut tight, a lick of dark hair on its head. Liam swallows, his throat clicking with dryness. "I am sorry," he says, "I cannot—"

"Please," says the man, in terror, "you must do your magic. Make him live. My wife . . . The child came too early."

"Ah," Liam says, and sees with horror that the man is thrusting the tiny being towards him, intending for Liam to take it. Instinctively, he steps back, withdrawing his hands into his sleeves. "Forgive me but—"

"You. You can make him live. Everybody tells me, take the baby to the big stone house. The men there have magic."

"No," Liam says, "you . . . misunderstand. We have no magic, exactly, just—"

The man struggles to his feet, gulping, as if unwilling to swallow the fact that Liam cannot or will not help him, that his child will not be brought back to life. A sizeable crowd has gathered around them now, people peering to see, shoving at each other, talking among themselves, in words so fast and slippery that Liam cannot grasp them. The man begins to wail and ululate, holding the stillborn child in his hands, and Liam is reminded, in a flash, of Eugene, years ago, picking up a fledgling, found on the boreen, fallen from its nest: he had held it thus, lovingly in his palms, and taken it back to the house, where he fed it on mashed worms and milk, with unutterable patience, and it had survived. How astonishing is his brother. Liam closes his eyes at the memory. What a person, one in a thousand. He had the magic, Liam thinks, in a somewhat crazed way—the heat, the miniature and silent child, the man's grief-filled howls are all perhaps conspiring to unhinge his mind. For he is certain, as he stands there, uselessly, in his sandals and robe, that if Eugene were here, he would know what to do, how to console this poor man.

Liam recalls himself to the task before him. There is, of course, only one way to comfort this man, to assuage and alleviate his distress.

Liam clears his throat and, pressing his palms together, says: "Let us pray."

The man's head jerks up. He glares at Liam, or Father Gulielmus, clutching the body of his stillborn child to his chest, and he spits out a string of words that Liam recognises, with a cold spiral of dismay, as a hex, a particularly unpleasant one, involving the loss of loved ones. Lunging at Liam, he shoves him, hard, with his free hand. His face as he does so Liam will remember for the rest of his life: its expression of disgust, of betrayal, will rise to Liam's mind, when he faces the committee's interrogation, and again when he is an old man, far away from this place and this life, and it will never fail to fill him with shame.

Liam stumbles backwards, partly due to amazement and partly to the blow. He feels the earth tilt, feels the rough and stony surface of the path come up to meet him, first his elbow and then the base of his spine. Then he is sprawled in the dust and the grit, his back aching, spectacles knocked to the dirt. He watches, mutely, as the man hurries away from him, back the way he came, as the muttering crowd disperses, until Liam is alone, the boats on the waterway sliding past him, like embarrassed and indifferent strangers.

Anatole waits for Enda each evening outside her rooming house. Sometimes, he is smoking a cigarette and she can see the glowing tip moving like a firefly as he lifts it to and from his mouth, and she knows then where he is in the dark, where she must aim for. When she gets closer, she can often smell the inn kitchen off him, a throat-catching scent of onions and oil, the odour of a hundred dinners. He is usually already mid-sentence by the time she reaches his side: he talks about the other cooks in the inn, who has a cough, who always cuts his hands when chopping carrots; he talks about the logging work he will soon be doing upriver, how high the trees, how dense the forest. He talks about the different names for the lumber they will cut: Douglas fir, western hemlock, red cedar, spruce pine fir, yellow cedar, ironwood, hop hornbeam, white larch. He describes for her the bunkhouse where they will all live, the snoring and the fights, those who hoard food under their bunks, inviting rats, which the loggers like to take turns to kill, with the blunt end of their axes. And he asks her questions: what has she learned on her fiddle, who is staying at the rooming house, where has she lived before this in Canada, will she stay in Trois Rivières?

Each night they walk to the part of town where people gather to drink whatever wages they have scraped together. The two of them might be invited to play inside one of these places, or if the weather is fair, they will play outside on the street. Enda might pick the tune, and it could be from her country or his or someone else's; if Anatole doesn't know it, he will press his fingers to the buttons of his accordion, his ear bent towards her, his face watching hers, intently, carefully, and he will fill the pleated leather with air, pulling a low hum from the instrument, and then his other hand will start to inscribe the melody from the black and white keys. Sometimes, he will launch a tune and she will listen for the chord sequences, and will join, lurking underneath the melody until, like a dancer, she knows she can bring her fiddle forward to assume the lead.

The box at their feet fills with coins, sometimes only a few and other times enough to feed them afterwards. Anatole is scrupulous in counting it out, dividing it equally, and handing her half. He tips the coins into her cupped palms with a nod.

One night, he reaches out and inserts two fingers into the pocket of her jacket. They are standing at the mouth of an alleyway. Not a good idea, he says, to handle money out in the street; and Enda watches his hand, as it latches itself into the fabric, as it tugs slightly, causing her to take a step towards him, and she has no idea why or what will happen next. When she looks up at him, to find the meaning of this strange act, she finds that he is looking down at her, his gaze unflinching, his face suddenly serious and still. Why, she wants to say, why do you pull me by the jacket towards you? How dare you?, and she has no idea what might happen next and the breath is motionless in her chest, nothing passing in or out. Then he simply lifts his other hand, still without taking his eyes from hers, and he slides her share of the coins into her pocket.

Later, she lies in her narrow bunk in the windowless cupboard where she sleeps, tucked in behind the kitchen range, and she gives herself what her mother would have called a good talking-to. What a fool she is to have discovered within her even this faint flicker of hope. She isn't pretty, like Rose, she isn't the sort of woman men go for: she is too unusual, too irritable, she spends half her life scrubbing floors in a filthy apron, the other half dressed like a lad and playing a fiddle, and she carries within her, like a thorn under her skin, the memory of once being laughed at for looking like a squirrel. Anatole has a pleasing stance, a fine and open smile: she has seen women's eyes linger on him.

She turns to the wall, furious with herself for her sudden tears, scrubbing at her face, disgusted by her self-pity. She throws herself back down to the thin mattress, resolutely shutting her eyes. This will pass, she tells herself, teeth gritted, whatever it is, this fancy, this weakness, it will disappear as abruptly as it came.

The next night, he does it again: the hooking of his hand into her pocket, and she wants to say, What are you doing, you'll tear it and it was stitched by my mother for my brother and it's all I have of them, but his touch is gentle, his musician's fingers well used to the fine gradations and shifts in pressure, and he empties the coins into her coat, and then he does a strange thing. He lifts his hand and slides his thumb along one of her eyebrows, and then the other. Enda stands there, dumbfounded. His face is rapt and solemn: he applies himself to this task with seriousness. She doesn't think anyone else has ever paid any attention to her eyebrows, has ever touched them, these swoops of colour on her forehead, and she doesn't know how to respond, but he lets his hand drop and he turns away, saying something about his visit to a flour mill that day, and about the foreman, a man no one likes, who tripped over a sack and fell into a heap of flour and how happy it made them all, how comical the man looked. Like a ghost, he says, then laughs.

That's funny, Enda says faintly, a man covered in flour.

Without discussing it, the following night, everything changes. It begins in the same way, with him reaching for her pocket, but Enda, to her consternation, sees her own hand darting out to intercept his, and how enormous his hand feels, when entwined with hers, what breadth there is to his palm, how smooth the skin of his fingers, how ragged the nails, but also how warm it is, and there is an answering grip coming from it: her own, much smaller hand, raw from the floor soap, from the scrubbing brush, from the mop and duster, with calluses on the fingertips, is being enfolded by his. Then, suddenly, he has her, all of her; he has taken possession of her whole self, and he is lifting her off her feet, carrying her deeper into the shadows of the alleyway that runs alongside the inn where he works, and he is pressing her up against the clapboard wall, as if he would affix her there, and Enda somehow knows that she will always remember what is happening to her.

Without discussing it, they pause; they lean sideways and place their respective instruments carefully on the ground, and then he lifts her again, with both hands spanning her waist, and she thinks, fleetingly, of the moment he and his sister tied the skirt around her at Grosse Île, but then she doesn't think of that any more because he is talking, saying her name over and over again, and he has his face pressed into that part of her where her neck meets her shoulder—what can be the name for that part of the body, why does it not have one?—and then he is quiet, for once, and he kisses her on the skin of her jaw, then cheek, temple, mouth, his movements deliberate and unhurried, and he is muttering something to himself, or her, a brief phrase in his own language, and how beautiful it seems to her, the sound waves make when the sea rakes through pebbles on a shore, and then she stops thinking altogether. She becomes solely sensation: the shocking whiteness of his chest under his loosened shirt, the soft scrape of his stubble against her clavicle, the bewildering things her body wants to do or wants from his, and knows how to do, the plush press of his mouth on hers, the silk-firm slide of his hands over her ribs and stomach and more, the fathomless lock of his gaze on hers. She would remember it all; it will return to her, at unbidden moments, for the rest of her life.

The day has felt wrong to Eugene since the beginning. When he woke, he could feel that the wind was coming from the south-east, which was an unusual direction altogether, and it was skimming up and over the widow's roof in irregular gusts, some strong and prolonged, others skittishly brief. In the byre, the widow's cow was bellowing, calling out to someone to come and milk her, even though the dawn had barely broken and she was never normally seen to at this hour. When Eugene swung his feet out of bed, he found his boots, as always, beside the pallet, but they had been switched over, left to right, the laces knotted and pulled out of their eyelets.

He didn't like the look of all this. Outside, the air was warm—unseasonably so for early autumn—and sudden cross-breezes tugged at Eugene's hair in a way he found unpleasant. The sea, when he came around the side of the house, was grey and swollen, resembling a pot about to boil, with white-crested waves gliding in from beyond the breakers. As he walked to look at the grass in the lower field, he was startled by two ravens lifting out of the undergrowth, and Eugene was uneasy, for everyone knows that a raven leaving the ground on which you walk means a death before nightfall.

He didn't like it, he didn't like it at all, so later, when Rose said the bread wasn't rising and mentioned that she was intending to walk over to the far side of the town to deliver some spun wool to a family there, Eugene had put down his spoon with a bang and shaken his head.

"What is it, Euge?" Rose said. "You don't want me to go? Is that it?"

Eugene had nodded, once, very firmly.

"Whyever not?"

And when he had directed his gaze, pointedly, to the bread, she had laughed.

"Because the bread didn't rise I shouldn't go over with the wool? Eugene, that's—"

He had let out a growl and tapped her on the wrist, his signal to her that he meant what he said, that he needed her to listen to him. Rose had stopped laughing and covered his fingers with her own. "Very well, Euge. I'll stay in today, then, will I?"

He laid a hand to her shoulder briefly.

"Have it your way," she'd said, and got up to stir the fire.

Eugene has walked up here, to the old house, to cast his eye over their land, to see that the hay is drying, to check on their hens and collect the eggs. The wind is even more noticeable up here: the hens, when he wades towards them through the lough, are all roosting in the tree. None of them have laid this morning. He stands for a while, fists on his hips, in the lee of the ring fort, or rath, as their father referred to it, deciding what best to do with a day such as this, and he comes to the conclusion that to dig would do no harm, to turn the sod in the widow's upper field before the cold of winter sets in.

He is glad, as he fetches the heftiest of his father's spades, to think of Rose and the widow safe in the house, where nothing can reach them, except perhaps a twist of the peculiar wind reaching down the chimney.

Rose, however, does venture out later in the day. It's only as far as the shore, she reasons to herself, which is in calling distance of the house. She tells the widow that she's away to the strand to collect mussels at low tide. She will bake them later on a hot stone, for their supper, and Eugene won't know she has broken her promise because she'll say she fetched them yesterday, and he may not even ask because he loves a baked mussel, after all, and he'll be distracted by the eating of them.

So she whistles for Bran, and the two of them take the lane out of the village and then the path that drops down to the shore. The strand, she is saying to Bran, we're off to the strand, because the stretch of yellow sand is his favourite place, where he, despite his advancing years, will sprint in crazed circles, yapping and letting his tongue fly out in the wind, round and round her, his long legs kicking up sprays in his wake.

But Rose never makes it to the strand that day, for when she reaches the place where the path splits in two, one fork leading down to the sea and the other climbing up to the cliffs, she sees the figures of two men. They are not men from the village—she knows this straight away—because even through the half-light of dusk she can see that their physiques are thickened and well-fed, and that they are wearing the layered and buttoned clothes of the gentry, their throats muffled with white cloth, their hats high and brushed to a sheen.

She also sees that they are dangling something between them and she would have thought that it was perhaps an animal they had slaughtered, because she knows they do this for sport, a rabbit or a fox, except that the creature is wriggling and making a noise, and such a desperate, unholy sound it is, a squealing and a yipping, and Rose knows instantly that the creature is a young pup, they have it strung up by its neck, paws flailing helplessly in the air, while they take turns to land blows with their whips on its soft grey hide and belly.

Without thinking, Rose moves towards them. The pup is so like Bran, it is him in miniature, it has to be one of his, for he has fathered many around here: the same sleek, pale underside, and the feathery back, the long, curved tail.

The taller man—and Rose recognises him as the viscount's eldest son—lifts the arm holding the whip, and she hears him say that the pup is a cur, a scoundrel, that he will teach it a lesson it won't forget.

"Ah, please," Rose calls out, for she cannot help herself, "don't be hurting it. It's just a baby."

The men turn towards her and their faces are incredulous. The landowner's son still has his arm raised, his mouth open, but Rose doesn't care. She steps forward and puts her arms around the young dog, lifting it so that the collar no longer strangles, feeling the tremble and the terror racking its slender body, and it whimpers, recognising at once a sympathetic touch, burrowing its narrow nose under her hair and into her neck. There now, she murmurs to it, over and over again, you're safe, you're safe, and in answer it darts out a tongue to lick her ear.

The viscount's son is still holding the leash, so that he and Rose are connected, the puppy between them. She hears him murmur something to the other gentleman, who gives a short snickering laugh, and for the first time Rose wonders if what she's saying to the puppy is true: are they safe?

She lifts her face from the animal, and its fur is so familiar, so warm she cannot believe herself to be in any real danger.

"You can't be beating it like that," she says imploringly. "You can't—"

"Is that so?"

The landowner's son seems amused, his head on one side, his riding crop tapping the side of his boot, but Rose is not fooled: she can see the glitter and shift of his anger, like the current beneath a frozen sea.

"And who are you to tell us what to do?"

The manner of his speech strikes Rose as peculiar. The words are clipped and separate yet he hardly moves his lips as he utters them.

"I'm—" She is about to tell them her name, but she veers away from it, for these gentlemen will not care. "I . . . I've a dog just like this one," she says instead, because it seems important to establish this. "I'm certain he must be the father, they are the spit of each other anyway, and perhaps—"

"Are we to listen to this?" the other gentleman cuts across her, addressing the viscount's son, and his voice is different, more drawling, the words blending into each other, the way cream turns to butter, "or is there some other use we might put her to?"

Now the landowner's son lets out a laugh but there's no mirth in it. He reaches out, still with the crop in his hand, and takes hold of Rose's wrist, his fingers closing around it. It is a leisured movement: he is in no hurry, it says, there is no urgency here. He will take his time. The other gentleman who, she now sees, carries a gun in the crook of his arm, is not so gentle. His hand seizes the lobe of her ear.

"I had no idea," he murmurs, "that you had such pretty tenants. Why did you never say? You might have—"

The sentence is never finished. Rose kicks out, her boot meeting his shin, and she tears herself from the grasp of the other. Then she is running, as fast as she can, still with the puppy in her arms, she is heading back to the brae, at the end of which will be the widow's fields, and the village, if she can only make it that far, and surely she has an advantage for she knows this path and they never come this way, she could walk it in the dead of night, she only needs to get clear of the dunes, up the bluff and then—

They catch her effortlessly, of course. This time there is no hint of gentleness. One of them seizes her by the hair; the other kicks out the legs from under her so that she lands with a sickening thud that drives the breath from her. For a moment, all she can think is that she might have injured the pup in her fall but she hears it skitter away, yelping. Her mouth is filled with grit and sand; one of the gentlemen has his full weight on her shoulders so that she can barely breathe, barely scream; the other is at her skirts, yanking them up, forcing apart her legs.

She hears them laugh and say something about how she, too, needs to be taught a lesson.

Then Rose hears something else. A barking, a snarling, and she knows that Bran has come. He would have gone down to the strand ahead of her and then wondered where she'd got to and returned to find her. She hears one of the men curse, then let out an effeminate shriek, and she knows that Bran will have lunged at him, going for the throat, aiming to sink his teeth into his windpipe. She feels the men's hands and legs and bodies vanish from her so that she is free to stagger upright, stumbling on the soft sand, grabbing at the marram grass for balance, and behind her is a terrible growling sound and the panicked cries of the men, and she wants to say, Run, Bran, run away, but before she can turn around, a single shot rings out, followed by an awful silence, and she knows that they have killed her dog, they have put a bullet through his fierce and loyal heart, that he will never again run circles on the strand, that he tried his best, that he would have done anything for her, that he cannot save her now. She stumbles away, as fast as she can, up the dune, blindly, her hands snatching at the darkness, but of course they catch her again, and this time they are furious and determined. They don't speak a word: they strike her so hard across the head that she thinks her ears will burst, and she is felled there, among the spiked grass. One of them kneels on her wrists and the other tears the fabric of her skirts from hem to waist, and he raises himself up to unfasten his britches, and Rose thinks it is the viscount's son and she finds herself wondering if that is how it works with these people, that he gets to go first because it is his land, his tenant, whether this is an unspoken agreement between gentlemen like this, and how strange that is, and she tells herself that when it happens, and it will happen very soon, any moment now, as soon as the landowner's son has unfastened all those buttons, she will close her eyes, she will shut them tight, because she will not give them that, she will not let them take that as well, she will not look at them while they do this, she will not allow them inside her head.

But Rose never does close her eyes, and the viscount's son never gets to the final button on his britches, never gets to take what he believes is rightfully his. Because, as Rose steals a last look at the sky, where clouds race across an expanse of indigo and the brittle piercings of stars are showing themselves, the outline of her brother, Eugene, appears above her, above them all, between land and sky, and he has a spade over his shoulder and he brings it down, first on the head of the viscount's son and then on the upturned face of the other.

The widow has used the day to card and spin her wool, feeding its delicate fronds into the machinery of the wheel, and watching with satisfaction as it resolves into smooth yarn. She is just considering what colour she may dye it, when both halves of the door burst open and Eugene steps in.

She looks at him, from behind her wheel. She holds herself as still as the plaster icon of a saint, taking in every detail. Eugene is breathing hard, as if he's run a long way. There is mud on his boots and his hands. Across his face and in the V of his shirt are fine sprays of what looks like blood. Under his arm, he cradles a small dog that resembles Bran; the animal looks back at her with a sorrowful expression.

Stiffly, because her joints don't give as easily as they used to, she stands, she goes to Eugene, she takes one of his filthy hands.

"What is it?" she says, with more calm than she feels.

Eugene tugs at her, indicating that she should come with him.

So she does. She takes her shawl from the hook, the lantern from the hearth; she pulls on her clogs, and off they go. Darkness hasn't yet fallen fully and it is possible to see the shapes of things, to find a difference between shadow and night. Around the byre, through the field, along the path, over the dune, where Eugene takes the lantern from her and holds it up high.

Three shapes lie before her in the marram grass. Two gentlemen in tweed suits, with horsewhips and a gun, both their heads staved in; one is the landowner's son and his forehead is slashed in an ugly, jagged line, black wings of blood around his temples. The third shape is harder to make out. She takes the lantern from Eugene, moves towards it, and it resolves into the body of Bran, stretched out at an awkward angle, lips drawn back over his teeth, a dark hole in his chest, and curled around him, her face next to his, is Rose. For a moment, the widow believes that the girl is dead too, that Eugene and the puppy are the sole survivors of this grisly scene, but then she sees the shuddering rise of Rose's ribcage, her hand moving to smooth the fur between Bran's ears.

The widow looks from Bran to Rose to the bodies of the gentlemen. She crosses herself; she utters a quick and automatic prayer. What happened? she says. What— She stops herself. Get up now,

Rose. Up you get. Come on, we've our work cut out for us and we only have until dawn. Get up off the ground, I tell you, Rose. Do you want to live or die?

She instructs Eugene to run back to the byre and bring the slipe. Quick as you can. She takes Rose's hand and together they wait on the dunes above the strand. By the light of the lantern—a glowing circle of yellow—she examines Rose's face: the lip split and bleeding, the left eye swollen closed. She sees the ripped skirt, the petals of bruising around her wrists. It'll heal, she whispers, it'll all heal. Then she thinks about how to put it, how to ask, what words to use, and she does not know if she can bear the answer, before saying, in a low voice: Did they get their way, those devils, did they? Rose seems to consider this, then shakes her head. Good girl, the widow says, passing an arm about her shoulders, good girl. And they watch as Eugene comes towards them, hauling the slipe behind him.

The widow tells them both that they must load the two gentlemen onto the back of it. Rose turns aside. I cannot, she whispers.

You must, says the widow. You need to push them off the cliff, make it look as if they lost their way and fell to their deaths. It's the only way, the only hope we have, and a slender one at that.

Eugene slides his hands under the shoulders of the viscount's son and heaves. The head—what is left of it—lolls back on its stem of a neck, pieces of bone and gristle falling to the sand, onto Eugene's boots. He sets his teeth together, straining, face reddening with effort, trying to shift the body, which is rigid now, stony, and Rose sees that she must, indeed, help, so she bends and takes the legs, clad in woollen stockings, and together they heave him onto the slipe, then return for the other.

When the slipe is loaded with both dead men, their whips, their gun, whatever clods of sand have soaked up their blood and brains, Eugene and Rose drag it along the path and up the track to the cliffs. The way is rutted and steep, and this is no weather to be out. A turbulent wind lashes their backs, snatches at their clothing; rain hurls itself into their faces. The accusing eye of the moon appears at intervals between the clouds. At the top, where the land falls steeply away, where half a mile below foams an angry sea, a gale blows so loudly they cannot hear each other. They have to rely on gestures and glances. The gentleman friend goes over first, swung between them and released into the air, then his gun and his hat; the viscount's son is next. Eugene loses his grip just as they are about to fling him seaward, and Rose falls forward, onto the body, her elbow landing on the soft part of his belly, making her retch, then Eugene yanks her upright, and together, exhausted, they roll the dead man to the lip of the cliff and push him off. Rose inches forward to see the shape of him fall through the thin light of the moon, as if into the mouth of Hell, coat flapping, legs flailing, jaw stretching wide as if wanting to give an account of himself but finding nothing whatsoever to say.

Eugene is given the task of burying Bran. He carries him up the hillside and digs a grave just outside the haggard wall, in the sheltered spot where the dog liked to lie in the sun. Rose and the widow build up the fire and feed into it the bloodstained clothes, her torn skirt. When Eugene returns, the storm he sensed at the start of this longest of days has begun: the wind is hurling itself at the walls, rattling the doors for entry, rain is scalping the roof, and the widow nods grimly. Luck is on our side, she says, for now. It will wash away the footprints up to the cliffs, she says, and the tracks made by the slipe. She serves them both a cup of tea and a slice of bread. Rose says she cannot eat; the widow says she must. Rose rises from the table and says she will go to bed.

The widow shakes her head. She gestures to Rose to sit down. From out of her apron, she brings a small pouch of worn leather, tied twice around with twine, and a folded letter in an envelope that looks half familiar to Rose.

"The two of you," she begins, her voice trembling only slightly, "must take yourselves off. Tonight. Now."

"But where? And how can we—"

The widow holds up her hand. "You know this is the only way. Those gentlemen will be missed. The alarm will be raised. There'll be people out searching for them by morning. The bodies might be washed up in a day or two and it might look as if they took a fall from the cliff in the dark, or it might not. Either way, the pair of you need to be gone. Before daylight."

Rose begins to cry. Eugene shifts in his seat.

"None of that now," the widow says. "Unless you want them to string you both up on a gibbet—and they will, you know that—you've to keep your wits about you and get yourselves gone. You'll walk south to the port. It's the journey of a day or so. Take this money and buy yourselves passages across the sea. You'll go to Enda, of course. Here is her letter, with the address on it."

"We can't take your money," Rose says, tears coursing down her face. "It's yours. We can't—"

"You can and you will."

"Then . . . you must come with us," Rose exclaims, turning to Eugene, as if seeking his approval, and he stares back at them both, his face blank, as if he's having trouble comprehending their change in fortune. "We could all go, all three of us. What's left for us here? We must—"

"I'm too old for all that. And who would mind the cow? I'll not be going anywhere."

"But it's your money, you need it and—"

The widow takes a breath so deep and long that it strains at the seams of her bodice. "You must know that what little I have was to have been yours. Since your mother went, and then your father, it was always my intention. Who else would I have given it to? This way, you're only getting it before time."

She reaches across the table and, in an unaccustomed demonstration of affection, she cups a hand around each of their faces.

"You're to get away from here, the pair of you, to find Enda, to live long lives. Do you hear me?"

She removes her shawl with shaking hands and wraps it around Rose, tucking the ends into her belt. She tells them she will take care of everything, she will go up the hillside and close up their house, will bring the livestock back down with her: they are not to give it all a second thought. She packs dried fish and dulse and hard bread into their bags. Eugene stows the puppy in his shirt, and the widow gives its head an awkward pat.

Go now, she says to them, and be quick. Don't stop on the road. I won't say goodbye.

They go through the door, the widow, Rose and Eugene, and Rose is crying again, her chest heaving, high-pitched sobs coming out of her, and the widow shoos them away, like errant geese, and she cannot watch them leave, will not see the road swallow them. She gives them a single nod, then turns and blunders into the byre, latching the door behind her; she crouches down, her hands groping for the milking stool, the bucket, anything. She should fill the churn; she could make a start on the butter. She might. She could.

But instead, she lets herself sink into the straw. First her own children and now these ones, who were delivered to her by God and His goodness, to fill one of the empty houses. Her life has seen too many endings, too many leavings, more than can be borne by one woman, and that's the truth of it.

The widow kneels on the straw in the byre, clinging to the lime-washed wall. She leans her face into the warmth of the cow and, despite herself, strains her ears above the sound of the wind to hear the footsteps of Rose and Eugene as they walk away.

Liam stands in his schoolroom in Cochin, hands clasped behind his back. It is, he is telling himself carefully, a day like any other. It is a Tuesday—no, a Wednesday, an ordinary morning. He has risen, he has prayed, he has breakfasted, and now he is here, teaching these boys. He is not in the vegetable garden today but the school. It is just another day, with nothing remarkable about it.

He has placed himself at the front of the class, the better to keep an eye on the rows and rows of boys seated at desks. His hair is combed down with oil; from his sash hangs a cane switch for the punishment of bad behaviour. He has a frown on his face and looks for all the world like a mathematics master, listening as his pupils recite an algebraic theorem, a studious Jesuit who will brook no inattention, no breach of discipline.

Look more closely, however. Today his face is turned not towards his pupils but to the street outside. His lids are half lowered against the diamond-cut dazzle of the sun. His left foot twitches up and down, up and down, hinting perhaps at restlessness within. The switch at his waist is supple with lack of use—the boys in their desks know that they are unlikely to receive a beating from this particular master and they like him for it. They are not to know that Liam has been chided for this by his superiors.

If a person was standing close enough to Liam, or Father Gulielmus, as he is known here, they might catch a hint of clove, even hibiscus, and that person might ask themselves is it normal, is it permissible for a Jesuit to wear scented oil in his hair, would that not be considered a somewhat worldly indulgence for such a man?

Liam shifts his weight from his right foot to his unquiet left, and lets out a just-audible sigh as his eyes follow the progress of a *tonga* across the street and then up the slope, the horse straining between its shafts, the ding of its harness bell leaving a bright shivering circle of sound in the warm, saline air.

Cochin has long, straight streets lined with awnings, beneath which open-fronted shops sell spices and silks and bales of printed cotton and towering triangles of coconuts and jasmine blossoms threaded on strings. There are clusters of palm trees, the leaves of which rattle like swords in the wind, and a seafront where rows of elaborate fishing nets stand with elegant, outstretched arms that can be lowered, like genuflecting pilgrims, into the water. The wealthy colonialist families live in pink-tinted houses with ironwork balconies; they travel about town in huge-wheeled rickshaws, high above the dust of the street. Liam sees their gloved fingers drawing up the pleated canopies so that they may shield themselves from the sun.

The poor—among whom Liam spends a great deal of his time, when not in the classroom, perhaps a little too much, his superiors have observed—live near the swamp, a hollow depression in the landscape, hidden from view, filled with huts put together from whatever materials can be found. "Scalpeens" is what these dwellings would be called at home, Liam has reflected, but here the Order refers to them as "shacks." The trodden-dirt pathways of the swamp-village are familiar to Liam: he alone knows his way through the straw-and-clay cabins, for he has taken it upon himself to draw a map of the place.

He took great pleasure in the work, thinking it would be useful for the brethren who work alongside him in tending the sick and the poor. He worked on it in his cell, late at night, composing it in ink of blue-black, marking in the swamp, crosshatching the dampest areas, using the symbol for marshy ground, taking care to include each individual dwelling, even the names the inhabitants had given to the pathways. When he handed it, with no small expectation of praise, to their spiritual leader, the Provincial, the man had put on his spectacles, held it for a long moment at arm's length, brows raised, then turned a searching look on Liam.

Was it then that Liam felt his faith loosening in its foundation, like an unsound tooth? He doesn't know.

Early this morning, as he was consuming his breakfast of maize porridge, a ragged and stained letter was handed to him. On it was a postage stamp of his home country, and Liam saw by the franking marks that it had taken nearly a year to reach him: the Order had initially sent it, in error, to Rome, and since then it seemed to have lingered for an entire winter and spring in Bombay, before making its way to him, here in Cochin.

Liam had set aside his bowl and opened it. The letter was composed of several paragraphs, signed "your old friend, Father Joseph," and it told him that Liam's father, Tomás, had departed this life, not long after suffering a disfiguring accident, and was now with God. He was buried next to Liam's mother, may they both rest in eternal peace.

Puzzling, Liam thinks, as he stands before his pupils, that he should have had no notion of something so visceral, so significant. In some obscure way he feels cheated or hoodwinked. Would it be an unfair expectation that he might have received some sign or intimation of this, being a man of the cloth who has devoted his very life to the Lord? Could God in His wisdom not have taken the trouble to let Liam know in a dream or a vision or in one of His mysterious ways that his father had been injured and had died?

If the boys at their desks were to look up at this point and observe their master, they might notice a quivering in the hand that reaches up to dab at his face with a handkerchief.

No such trouble was taken. No such vision or dream was sent to him. His father died—there were no details as to how and why—and has been buried for more than a year, and Liam has been going about Cochin, teaching, hearing confessions, weeding the vegetables, helping the poor and dispossessed, blithely trusting that all at home was as it should be, not the wreckage described by Father Joseph.

What was it the letter had said? Liam has to strain to remember. That Rose and Eugene were gone to live with the widow, the cottage shut up. No reference at all to Enda, and Liam would like to know why she is also not living with the widow. Where has she got herself to? Could she have married and be living elsewhere? Why would Father Joseph not mention her?

This incomplete account of his family's dissolution, the unknown accident suffered by his father, his death, had caused Liam to stand up from the refectory table with a start, his bowl and spoon clattering to the floor, the letter crushed in his fist. He was aware of the other priests murmuring and exclaiming among themselves. The Provincial had laid his hand on Liam's shoulder and steered him from the room. After a few discreet questions, he had suggested that Liam forgo his duties for the week, even perhaps go into retreat, but Liam had shaken his head. No need, he had said. Work is the best medicine for me.

There is much, in this town, for Liam to be doing, besides teaching these boys, besides overseeing the construction work, which are the main duties assigned to him. A church is being built not far from here, funded by generous donations from ship-merchants and spice traders and tea-plantation owners: an edifice of stone and marble, in alternating stripes of lemon-white and malachite-green. It will be a towering monument to God, the Provincial tells them. It will bring people from miles around to the word of the Lord; its splendour will persuade doubters, will beckon many into their fold. It will include a college, in a side-wing, where young men may train as priests.

The other Jesuits here are from all over the globe: between them all, Liam knows, they speak sixteen languages. They spend their days at prayer, at work, instructing the faithful, in silent contemplation, talking with tact to the people from the pink and balconied villas: they might be prevailed upon to offer funds to the cause, perhaps a topaz frieze for the interior of the church's vestry or a gold-winged eagle-lectern for the pulpit. Liam tries to avoid this particular duty, preferring to go out in the evenings or the early mornings to distribute maize, milk, clothing, whatever medicines can be spared, to the inhabitants of the swamp-village.

Liam cannot suppress his unease at the sight of the church raising itself from the ground, its walls creeping upwards. It is his allotted task to check and recheck the engineer's calculations, and he does so, unfailingly, every day, unrolling the charts and plans with a leaden heart. He has prayed for guidance, implored God to help him appreciate the beauty of the building, and recognise the purpose of the Order's presence here in this country. Increasingly, however, it sickens him to see the men from the swamp labouring in the midday heat on the malachite façade, on the marble buttresses, their children crouched in miserable groups on the ground, wielding rudimentary hammers, breaking apart stones.

His hands, clasped behind his back, tighten around each other as the schoolboys intone their algebraic principles. It is not just the construction of the church that is eroding the conviction that has sustained Liam for most of his life. It is not only the filth and the poverty, the clay shacks, from whose walls protrude twigs and rushes and matted hair and old fabric. It is not merely the ordure that runs down their pathways, the carcasses of dogs and goats that lie, bloated and discoloured, in full view. It is not the biting insects that mass in storm clouds over the swamp. It is not just the children at whose bedsides Liam must pray before he supervises their burials, their tiny bodies shrouded in rough sacking. It is all of this yet none of this.

In the end, what erodes the effigy within him into rubble is something so prosaic, so imperceptible, Liam cannot explain it to anyone—not his brethren, not the Provincial. He cannot explain it to the committee of stern and angry senior priests who summon him to Calcutta to interrogate him, or even people he will meet later in life, those to whom he will have to say that he was once a priest, that he spent years in the Church, that he was not only a priest but a Jesuit—until one day he wasn't. He will, of course, realise over time that it is best not to disclose this; he will learn it is not something to throw into conversation but instead something to steer around, as a ship navigates past a submerged rock. Best not to divulge, unless he wants to elicit either judgemental silence or a slew of unanswerable questions.

On this day, which is like any other—apart from the letter, of course, apart from that—Liam moves up and down the lines of desks, the shining heads of the boys. The usual brisk trade wind is eddying through the town, finding its way around corners, up alleys, through window frames, down gutters. Through the windows, as he paces, he glimpses men sifting through a sackful of gnarled ginger roots, a boy pulling a horse by its bridle, two government officials sitting at a table outside a *chai* house, holding clay cups in gloved fingers. At an ornamental fountain is a group of young girls in frilled dresses the colours of hyacinths, their pale hair swinging down to their waists, watched from wooden benches by their mammas, their bird-like voices reaching Liam in the schoolhouse. An elephant topped with an ornate, carved howdah lumbers past at a stately pace, and Liam observes the bobbing heads and the profiles within, a young man with a blue turban leaning out from the silk cushions, laughing, to throw a green-skinned papaya to a passer-by.

Around Liam are the sons of wealthy traders, in starched white collars and ironed blue smocks, their leather-clad feet swinging above the parquet, their little elbows propping up their heads. It is the theorem of Pythagoras that they are reciting.

The square of the hypotenuse of the right-angled triangle, the boys intone, with varying enthusiasm, *is equal to . . .*

Liam glances out once again at the people drinking *chai*, the beady-eyed mothers under the trees, the elephant as it rounds a corner, half listening: *of the right triangle*, his mind echoes, *square of the hypotenuse.* Only yesterday, one of the older and more unruly of the boys had grumbled about having to learn Pythagoras's theorem, saying what possible use could it be to any of them? Liam had expounded to them the exquisite simplicity of it, and how it was the exact formula that enabled surveyors to calculate distances, to create maps. Imagine, he had said to them, the whole vast extent of this country, divided up into triangles: that is how they were able to do it.

That had been yesterday, only twenty-four hours ago, but it feels like the distant past, and now it is a different day, the one in which he received the letter, the one in which his father is gone. He slaps at a mosquito investigating his ear, coming to a stop between desk and window like a wound-down toy, his back to the boys. Misgiving is moving through him like something hard to digest. Strange that Father Joseph would be the one to tell him of his father's passing. And how can his father be dead? A world without Tomás in it feels like an impossibility. It doesn't make sense to Liam. That he will never again be able to return, to walk into the village and up the hill, to find Tomás mending a wall or divining the direction of the wind or drawing maps at the table, is so peculiar that it makes Liam feel dismantled, unbalanced, as if he might fall if he took a step to the side.

The Provincial, this morning, had knelt by Liam and prayed with him, concluding that Tomás was now "in the Kingdom of Heaven, in company with Christ." It was a sentiment that had caused Liam to let out a bark of laughter, which the Provincial had tactfully chosen to ignore. Liam, pacing now between window and door, is struck anew by the ridiculousness of these words: Tomás was a man who believed only what was in front of him, what he could touch or see, the soil and the rock and so forth; he believed in pools imbued with ancient spirits, and where does the soul of such a person go? Will it be wandering for ever? Will he—

The thought that this is exactly what Tomás would have wanted stops him in his tracks. Liam finds, as he stands in his classroom, that he is not harbouring the slightest concern about the state of his father's soul, as a priest ought, and this is stupefying to him. It is the same feeling of exposure he gets when he wakes from a nightmare of finding himself naked while conducting mass or hearing confession. According to the doctrine of the Church, his unbeliever father will be wandering in Purgatory, perhaps even condemned to hellfire, but Liam cannot locate the smallest flicker of anxiety about this.

Because, and Liam must pick his way, tread carefully, has to query himself here—why? How can he not feel concerned for his father's eternal rest? Because Tomás didn't believe any of it. Because Tomás put his faith only in what was before him or under his feet. Because none of it is real. Because Liam finds within himself only the absolute certainty that Purgatory, Hell, Heaven, none of it exists.

sum of the squares, the boys are saying, *of the two adjacent sides*—

None of it exists.

He recalls, suddenly, Father Joseph, in his schoolroom, saying to Liam that it was time for them to make a start on trigonometry. The priest had been all excitement, laying out on Liam's desk two wooden rulers at an angle to each other, but Liam had said, Oh, I have that learned already, my da taught me when I was his chainboy because we use it for the maps. He had thought the priest would be impressed with his scholarship, but Father Joseph's face had darkened with something akin to jealousy. He had withdrawn the rulers. I see, he had said, in a cold voice. Very well.

None of it exists. Are those his words, his thoughts, or are they Tomás's, projected into Liam's brain from afar, along the beam of some powerful supernatural theodolite perhaps, from the graveyard where his mother and father lie alongside each other?

He sees, for the first time, in a dismaying rush of insight, that Father Joseph had only ever wanted one thing: to separate Liam from Tomás, to come between them, to replace one father with another. And Liam had allowed himself to be turned away from Tomás, from all his family.

How like his father's his handwriting is becoming, as he gets older. Liam can write a word on a page and he will think, in surprise, There is my father's *p* and here is his *f* and how odd that it comes to a man one day that he cannot uproot his father from him, like an unwanted plant from the soil. There are no boundary walls between them; the two are one and the same.

There goes another elephant, with a purple howdah this time. And an open carriage. Across the street, a servant wipes a table with a red cloth, and when he flaps it in the air, the stunted branches of a pruned almond tree release a nimbus of scolding green parakeets.

Liam is wondering if perhaps he is going mad. Are these the ravings of a person who has taken leave of his senses? A priest offended that his pupil already knew what he wanted to teach him; a priest who sought to sever the bond between father and son by steering the child towards taking holy orders. Can Liam really have been so blind as to allow this to happen? The enormity of what he has lost, what was taken from him, surges through him like floodwater.

The parakeets are veering around the tiled roofs of the street, looking to Liam like the tail of a green comet. And Liam is suffused with a longing to talk to his sister, Enda. How he craves to see her again, just for a moment, even an hour. She would know, she could tell him—she was there, she witnessed it all. Where is she, exactly? He wishes fervently that she were here, that she might burst into this room, swinging the door open and covering the space between them with her quick stride to tap him on the shoulder so that he might turn and face her. She would dismiss all these boys with a decisive wave of her arm. Away and get yourselves into trouble, she would say, shooing them out into the streets, these small, scrubbed children. And he, Liam, would take her to the *chai* house, where he would order the hot, thick, milky beverage for her, and a plate of the sticky, syrup-drenched sweets. He would like to watch her devouring those in that way she has, which is pure pleasure, pure appetite, with not a thought given to how she looks.

He wishes they were all here, Enda and Rose and Eugene. With him, at the *chai* house, eating sweets and watching the birds and the elephants and the young girls, as the sun sinks down below the red-tiled roofs.

Liam is not meant to think these things, or feel them. The Jesuit Order is his family. He has cut all ties with the world. But as Liam looks down into the street, as the boys behind him go to the beginning of their recitation again, he wonders: Has he? Has he cut all ties? Does his life and his heart belong only to God? Or is he, in fact, losing his mind, overwhelmed by insights, like his father before him? Is it not only his father's handwriting he has within him but his propensity for madness as well?

Another *tonga* appears, going down the hill now, wheels squeaking, its bell sounding a jangling, insistent note. Sunlight glances in a series of lancing splinters off the polished brass on the horse's harness, making Liam wince and cover his eyes.

When he opens them again, the scene below him is unchanged:

the mammas on the benches in the shade, lorgnettes raised to their faces, men sorting their ginger root, the palm trees rattling their desiccated leaves, the young girls with their arms linked together. The parakeets have settled in the branches of a different tree. But, for Liam, it is as if he has never seen any of this before, as if he is a different person.

The sensation is akin to a sudden immersion in cold water on a hot day—a bodily shift, a sense of complete alteration or release, the passing from one element into another. The word "relief" passes across his mind, like the shadow of a cloud on a landscape. More than anything, he is aware of a curious sense of cessation somewhere within him, as if a rumbling battle in which he has long been engaged has come to its weary end, and he and his opponent are at last laying down their arms and calling off their troops.

For a moment or two, Liam cannot tell what has taken place, what has occurred within him: he is like a man who has misplaced something precious but cannot yet tell what it is. Liam experiences an urge to pat down his pockets, searching for what might be missing, what has been stolen from him, watch or wallet, penknife or comb, until he remembers he has no pockets, that he no longer carries such items or, rather, is not permitted to possess them.

He turns one way, then the other, as if expecting to find a robber or a pickpocket behind him, dimly aware of a faltering in the boys' recitations—the more alert of them have perceived that all is not well with their mathematics teacher—but there is nothing there, just a sea of parquet floor and an array of confused faces.

It occurs to him that it has gone, like a tide pulling off a strand: his faith, his trust, his belief, his conviction. It has simply vanished, drained out of him. He does not have a sense of why or how. All he knows is that it is no longer there, that his life as a Jesuit is over.

Weeks later, in Calcutta, Liam says precisely these words to the committee, over and over again. It is hard to know exactly how long he has been held here because he has lost track of the passage of time; he was forced to travel for days and has been permitted to sleep only fitfully and given very little food. The Jesuit fathers and spiritual advisers have come and gone, and others have taken their place at the long table with the candelabra, but he, Liam, has been obliged to remain on this bench. The Jesuits do not like to let go of a man, once they have him; if Liam is to free himself, it will not be without a struggle.

"You say your faith has gone," one of his questioners is saying to him now—Liam thinks it is the priest closest to the table's end. "Define 'gone.' "

Liam sighs and dabs with his sleeve at the moisture on his neck. Ever since he set in motion this chain of events, by saying to his Provincial, as they stood together beside the half-built church, that he felt he had irrevocably lost his faith, his existence has been precisely this: angry men putting questions to him. First the Provincial, who kept Liam in his private study for hours, making him go over and over the moment in the schoolroom, praying with him, exhorting him, telling him he was being tested, he was overtired, grieving for his father, it was only understandable, and would Liam give it more time? Liam had refused. He had, against the Provincial's wishes, spoken to his brethren, told them of his intention to leave the Order. The Provincial became angry; he dispatched Liam on a long, overland journey to his superiors here in Calcutta.

Liam pushes his hair out of his eyes. If they want definitions, he will give them definitions.

" 'Gone,' " Liam says, in the manner of the eager-to-please schoolboy he once was, "the past participle of the verb 'go,' meaning lost, departed, passed beyond reach."

The men lean towards each other, muttering. Liam catches the phrases "put trust in" and "test of patience." Without warning, the door to his right flies open and someone sweeps assertively into the room; beyond the door frame, Liam catches sight of two young novices, who are straining on tiptoe to lay eyes on this heretic, this apostate, before the door is swung shut.

The new man, Liam can tell, is the Superior Provincial, the man in charge of their mission in the whole of the Indian sub-continent: he will have received a directive from Rome and come here for the sole purpose of seeing Liam. They have summoned this most imposing of presences as a final attempt at keeping Liam within the Order.

The man does not take the proffered seat but stands there, drawn up to his full impressive height, regarding Liam, hands clasped before him. His voice, when it comes, isn't booming or domineering, as Liam might have expected, but stealthy and assured. He asks if it is true, the rumour that has reached his ears, that Father Gulielmus wishes to leave.

Liam tells him it is. He sees this man for what he is: the final hurdle he must clear before he is released, before he is allowed to leave. And he tells him that his joining the Jesuits had been a mistake, a misplaced youthful urge to set himself against his father. He was, he says, inveigled into it by a priest, a man who took against his father's atheism; he believes now that the priest was just out for revenge. His father's passing has made him see this, as well as recognise how flimsy his faith had been. It had been mere topsoil, not bedrock, he says to the man, with a smile. Do you understand me? My faith was nothing but a stratum of sand or grit, destined to be swept away by a storm.

The Superior Provincial stares at Liam for a long time, well after Liam has finished speaking. Then he steps forward. He reaches down and removes from around Liam's neck the tasselled ebony crucifix and its length of knotted leather. He utters not a single word but points towards the door with an urgent finger, in the manner of a man who fears contagion, indicating that Liam should stand, leave, walk away from them all and never come back.

Anyone observing the passengers packed into the ship's dim hold might have taken the young man and woman with the little dog for a husband and wife: she has her arm linked through his the whole time, leaning towards him to whisper words in his ear. He doesn't say much, doesn't meet anyone's eye or respond to any remark made to him, fixing all his attention on the animal he keeps stowed inside his shirt. The girl is a rare beauty, too, with hair sleek and shining as a raven's wing, but the young man seems not to notice or care. Some of the more observant travellers may have noticed the similarity of their brows, the set of their mouths, and decided they are brother and sister, or cousins perhaps. Others have taken note of the girl's bruised eye, her split lip, and their eyes have wandered questioningly to the knuckles of the young man, and resolved to steer clear of him, not to rile him in any way. Nobody wants trouble, especially so early in their voyage.

All, however, are taken aback when, a day into their journey, a rumour goes around the darkened hold where they must spend most of their time, that they have in fact been sailing east, not west, and before they set sail for Québec, they will first put in at Liverpool.

People stand up at this news; they rap the ceiling above them, they rattle the locked hatch, demanding an explanation. No one told them this when they bought their passages—they were told they would be heading straight across the ocean. Glancing about her, Rose squeezes Eugene's arm, murmuring to him in the darkness, telling him not to worry, that the sailors have told someone, who told someone else, who told her, that some passengers will leave the ship here, and the sailors will take on barrels of water and food for the journey.

"All's well," she says to Eugene, who trembles beneath the fabric of his jacket, who gives all his attention to the puppy, slipping her bits of dry biscuit, allowing her to lick his fingers with her narrow, pink tongue. Rose knows that Eugene hates the ship, the dark and damp, the proximity of so many strange people. She takes his hand and reminds him what is happening, creates a version of it that can settle in his mind, like a snowdrift: they bought two passages for Québec, they will be at sea for many days, they can walk on deck, in the fresh air, once a day, but otherwise they will be down here, Eugene must look after the puppy, has he thought what they'll call her, and after a good long while they will land in a new country, far across the sea, where they will find Enda, and won't Enda be surprised to see them, and the three of them—no, four, if they count the dog—will live happily ever after. It is a story she crafts just for him, the narrative of their new life. She says it to him whenever she senses his panic rising, his heart pounding, in the hope that the words will form a framework for him, a sense of direction.

She does not mention the spade, the cliff, the slipe, the broken heads of the gentlemen, the stormy night that snipped their life in two. Will Eugene be thinking of this? Are his dreams, like hers, peopled by bleeding, faceless monsters, by dogs running over hills, by the sound of tearing fabric, by gunshots, by whips and marram grass, with serrated sides that cut the thin skin of palms? Impossible to know.

The ship idles at anchor for a day, then another. The steerage passengers are allowed on deck, and Rose looks down on the grey stone buildings of Liverpool, the oily harbour water, the ragged children running along the dockside, and she is surprised because she thought everyone in this country wore fine clothes and had shoes on their feet. She looks up at the rigging, the masts and sails, and wonders at how fragile it all seems and how this craft will ever reach the other side of the world. She peers at the bolted door beyond which, someone tells her, the gentry travel, with damask chairs, china plates, silver knives and forks, and beds with sheets.

When the ship sets sail again, the hold is fuller than ever. The wind is fair and strong and it carries them down the channel of water between the two countries, and when they round the headland, Rose feels the change immediately: the waves are fuller, with a deep rolling motion; they have intent and purpose.

On the afternoon of that same day, a sailor opens the hatch above them, and tells them they are past Cork, that they will soon be at the last *terra firma* before the Atlantic; it will be the final sighting of their homeland and they may come up on deck to see, if they wish, to bid it farewell.

The hold is silent for a moment, then there are some startled murmurs. Some people translate what the sailor has said; others get to their feet.

Eugene elbows his way through the crowd and is first up the ladder. Rose has to wait until others have climbed up and out into the wind and spray, and she is worried that she will have missed it, this last glimpse. When, finally, she is able to climb on deck she cannot find Eugene, and she pushes her way through people who are crying and praying, holding out handkerchiefs to flutter in the breeze. The land looks so close, so green, to Rose, as the ship slides along beside it: she can make out fields, the meander of walls, grazing cattle, a line of trees, a bay of white sand, the thatch of houses. Someone is singing now, and others joining in; a woman is keening, collapsed into the man beside her.

Rose turns away from this, catches sight of a familiar cap and eases her way towards it. Eugene is standing at the rail, both hands gripping the side of the ship. His face is unreadable, his gaze fixed on the low-lying headland, a town visible in the distance: the southernmost tip of their country.

"Do you see?" Rose asks, tapping his finger, where he wears a swirled gold ring he acquired from goodness-knows-where, he would never tell or show her. She leans in to see his face because she doesn't know if he's understood, because she wants him to be able to say goodbye, to know what's before him, because why shouldn't he have this right, like everyone else? "This is our last sight of home, Euge. After this, it's—"

He cuts her off by pressing his forehead into hers, with an intensity that startles her, and she winces because her temples are still bruised and aching but she doesn't pull away: signs of affection from him are like butterflies—they flit by unexpectedly and you might not see another for months. Then Eugene does a strange thing. He reaches into his jacket, lifts out the puppy, and places it in her arms, with deliberation and tenderness. She takes it, of course she does, feeling the soft wisps of its pelt, its unquiet, restive warmth, drawn from her brother's body. For that moment, as they stand together at the rail, watching the coastline slide by, Rose believes Eugene has given her the puppy because he wants to wave at the land, their land, but almost in one movement, as she is settling the animal, tucking it under her arm, he turns and grips the rail of the ship—she hears the click as the back of his ring hits the wood—and, unbelievably, he vaults over it. It takes a fraction of a heartbeat: he is there, beside her, and then he is gone, off the ship, beyond reach, arms outstretched, legs pedalling in vacant, salty air, a bird flinging itself from a rock.

Those present will later say that the girl—sister, cousin, whatever she was to him—screamed, that she howled his name, she put her boot on the side of the ship as if she, too, would throw herself over, that she had to be restrained, that it took four men to stop her following the boy into the sea, that the quartermaster had to come and tie her to the rail. Some of the women sat down with her, wiped her face with their skirts, put their arms about her shoulders, rocked her to and fro, pulled out their beads to send up a prayer for the boy. They brought water and hardtack, for her and for the puppy she had clutched to her bosom, and tried to console her, tried to say that he was in a better place now, he was with God, his earthly suffering was at an end, that the sailors had been heard to mutter afterwards that it took some like that, queerly, it had happened before, some simply cannot bear to leave, but the girl just wept, burying her face in the animal's fur.

Others remarked, that evening, hadn't he seemed a peculiar one, from the start? Never gave anyone the time of day. It had happened so fast you didn't see the poor lad hit the water—he'd just been snatched, behind the ship and away, by the wind. As if he was a gull, or an angel. Those who had been by the stern at the time claim that they saw him fall into the waves, pulled into the road-like wake of the boat, the merciless green waters closing over his head as he was dragged down to the deep.

None of them said the truth: that in the moment they saw him jump the rail, they had all been feeling the same impulse, that their muscles were taut with the exact desire to leap from the ship, cold sea and certain death be damned, that they wanted only to get back, by hook or by crook, to their home, to undo what they had chosen, to die rather than to leave—anything but that.

As Rose's ship sets a westward course, sails strained by a stiff wind—it's a small but doughty vessel with many such crossings to its name, as well as a dark history in the capture and transportation of enslaved people in its rotting recesses—a clipper carrying a cargo of tea and spices is weighing anchor just outside Dublin.

Two seamen and the purser row in and report to the officials, who have come out to greet them, that there are no contagions onboard. They wish, they shout across the choppy stretch of water that separates them, to put in here to offload a lone passenger and twenty chests of tea, to take on fresh water and whatever vegetables and live poultry can be had, and then be on their way—they come from the tropics and are bound for the frozen north.

Their papers and ledgers are taken into the customs office for examination. The seamen and the purser scull and bob in the choppy waters of the port; just within view, the passenger onboard waits under the slackened rigging, pack and bag at his feet. Then the signal comes that they may dock.

The clipper is seen to turn, three men working their strength at the wheelhouse, and half an hour later, she is alongside the wharf, the gangplank lowered.

First to disembark and set foot on soil (or, in this instance, a silty and malodorous puddle of rainwater collected in the dip between stones) is the passenger, a gaunt man, sickly of visage, with rain-sopped hair and a sunburned forehead. He is dressed in an unusual and old-fashioned velveteen jacket, too large on the shoulders, with brocaded lapels; the waistcoat beneath is in a matching fabric. His britches are worn but have gold buckles at the knees. If the people on the docks knew the word "dandy," they might have used it for him (it shall not be recorded here what word they did use for him).

Liam—for it is he, in an outfit obtained from a saffron merchant in Calcutta, traded for a signet ring, a leather-bound Bible and the Order's robe, may God or whatever is the good in the world forgive him—leans to pick up his luggage. Dusk is infiltrating the sky and streets before him, and he finds, after weeks of seasickness, that he is ravenously hungry. All he can think about is securing a place to sleep and some dinner for his empty belly, and then, in the morning, he will decide what he's about.

Several lodging houses turn him away—he cuts, he knows, a peculiar figure, dressed as he is—but he finds an inn on the south side of the river willing to take him. He consumes a plate of tepid stew, then crawls into the lumpy bed and drops, as if from a tall tower, into a profound sleep, which seems to consist of narrow lanes and alleyways down which he must run, pursued by animals he believes are dogs until he turns to find, disturbingly, that they are malevolent-faced swine, with enormous tusks.

He is jolted awake, either by hearing a loud shout or making one—he does not know—and he lies there, heart hammering, unable to remember where he is. Where is the creak and groan of the ship's timbers, where the nocturnal pulsing insects of the mission-house? Can he be sure the ferocious pigs weren't real, and what on earth is that unconscionable sound?

Liam lifts his head from the chilly mattress. From the room below comes a hooting and a carousing, a drumming of feet, strains of music, a deafening roar and then the chime of laughter. He sits up crossly, slides out a leg to drum his heel on the floor. It is ineffectual: the noise intensifies, the music reaching a pitch. There is the whoop and clatter of dancing, a shattering of glass.

He lies back, fuming, the insufficient blanket wrapped around him. Hours pass, or seem to, and the disorder below shows no sign of abating. Eventually, Liam stamps out of bed, pulls on his clothes and descends the stairs.

In the doorway of the bar, he comes to a stop. Before him is a scene of inebriation, of wrongdoing, the like of which he has never seen in the course of his sequestered existence. A man in the corner, who appears half asleep, his head resting on his chest, beats time on a *bodhrán*; next to him a piper plays a hectic, circling tune, and a woman stands with a hand on his shoulder, eyes closed, her dress hanging low on her bosom, singing. Bottles and bottles of stout line the tables and the sawdust-covered floor. Furniture has been pushed back to accommodate a wild and tumultuous jig, an arm-wrestling match by the door between two shirtless men, and Liam is certain gambling debts are being laid down. Most shocking of all, there are—he flails for the correct term—*clinches* occurring. He cannot think of another way to express it. Clinches. Between men and women, in the shadowed recesses of the smoke-hazed room.

He puts a hand half over his eyes. Please, he says, ladies, gentlemen, please. There are people trying to sleep.

His voice is overridden by the din. Not a single face turns in his direction. A woman stumbles past him, laughing, shoving him aside, her face flushed, her skirts hitched up. Liam catches a flash of stocking-tops, white flesh spilling over, before he looks away.

I beg you to desist, he shouts. I for one have paid for a night's rest.

Again, no one takes notice of him. Incensed, he seizes two bottles and chinks them together, and the music at last falters to a halt. Everyone turns.

This is no way to conduct yourselves, he thunders, as if standing at an altar with the heavenly host in his hands instead of two empty stout bottles. You must reflect. On your souls. On the eternal reckoning they must one day face. Drinking, he says, but at a slightly diminishing volume for he senses, strangely, that his command of the crowd is slipping away. I said, drinking, he repeats, his voice wavering, disporting, keeping others from their rest. Need I remind you all, this very night—

Liam is astounded to find that, instead of a receptive and cowed silence, the whole room is erupting with a sudden noise. For a moment, he cannot identify what it is. The people are pointing his way, doubling over or leaning for support on each other. He looks from face to face, puzzled, the stout bottles cold in his fingers. It is as if he is an explorer in an unfamiliar land, watching unknown beings behave in a way he cannot parse.

Then it comes to him what the sound is. Hilarity, giggling, shrieking. These people are laughing at him. They are jeering and pointing, slapping their legs, throwing up their hands in mirth. They do not respect him. They will not heed him, now or ever.

He is filled to his very marrow with a creeping horror. The crowd guffaws and hee-haws, all at his expense. They exclaim, they hoot, they hawk derisively onto the sawdust, they wipe their eyes. Someone offers him a smoke; someone else yells that he's to take a fecking jar or feck off. He hears himself referred to, variously, as a "*gom*" and an "*amadán*." The man with the *bodhrán* wonders aloud what kind of get-up that could be, just look at the fancy knickerbockers on him. The music resumes. The people drift away, return to their drinking, their dancing and their clinches.

Liam backs out. He makes his way slowly up the stairs, step by exhausting step. As he shuts the door of his room behind him, he finds he is still holding the empty bottles. He places them on the windowsill with scrupulous care, as if they are indeed communion vessels. It comes to him as incontrovertible fact, as he stands there, looking out into an overcast dawn, that he has for ever forfeited the status, the camouflage, of a priest. He is like a snail with its shell ripped away. All the prestige that was automatically conferred upon him as a Jesuit has gone. He has given it up, stripped himself of it. If he had come down those stairs dressed in his robe, the people would have listened. They would have immediately and respectfully dispersed, muttering abject apologies. Yes, Father, of course, Father, we're very sorry, please forgive us, Father.

He is nothing now, Liam realises, as he moves across the room and pulls the blankets back over himself. He is no one.

Sleep eludes him for the rest of the night. By morning, he is sitting on the edge of the bed, hands on his knees, head bowed. He had planned to leave for the peninsula as soon as he woke but now he is beset by doubts, by misgivings. He cannot present himself to his family, to the peninsula, in his current state, jobless, homeless, dressed in these eejit clothes, barely a penny in his pocket, requiring them—who have little enough as it is—to give him shelter, to feed and clothe him. How could he ever have thought of facing them as he is now? A failed priest, a renegade, a nobody. The shock they will feel when they learn that he abandoned them, just after their mother's passing, to undergo all those years of training, to become a man of God, only to leave and return to them, cap in hand, with nothing to show for himself. He is filled with shame for what he has become. What an insufferable prig he was to them.

Everyone on the peninsula and in town will assume he was defrocked, forced out of the Order, guilty of some terrible deviant crime that has banished him for ever: no one will believe he chose to leave. On market days, as soon as he returns, foul gossip about him will spread, fuelled probably by those who were jealous of him at school. How will he shield his siblings from the opprobrium of it all? How will he ever face Father Joseph again? How will he explain to the widow, to the fishermen what happened? This is not a country that looks kindly on those who leave the Church. How could Liam have forgotten this?

More than anything, he cannot wipe from his mind the expressions of the people last night as he stood there in his velveteen suit, shrilly exhorting them all to behave: the scorn, the ridicule on their faces. It scorches him, it cuts him.

When he steps out onto the street, later, with no clear sense of where he is headed, his feet lead him to the river. He looks east, out to sea; he looks north, towards the hills. He gazes at the bridge, at the twisting current beneath it; he turns and looks west, towards the city and the countryside beyond, the way obscured by dropped scarves of fog. He closes his eyes and grips a coin in his pocket; which way should he go, what should he do? According to the grooves of habit, his mind begins to recite: *In the Name of the Father, and of the Son, and of the H—* Liam's eyes spring open. What is he doing? He looks down at the disc of copper in his palm. A cloud is drawn off the sun and a yellow light beams down on him, standing there, and a sudden shadow greets him, stretched out on the ground, attaching itself to his feet. Some corner of his mind is persevering with the prayer he swore to himself he would never resort to again—*as it was in the beginning is now and ever shall be, world without end.* To blot it out, he flips the coin. Tails, he tells himself, for going home; heads, to stay here awhile.

The penny spins and oscillates in the air, flinging itself up against the milky sky, and Liam goes to catch it, and he almost has it but feels it slip, inevitably, through his fingers, glancing off his palm. He never was good at such things. It lands on the ground, bounces off a stone, rolls sideways, and Liam chases it, trying to stamp down on it to stop its wayward course. It veers over the cobbles and down, down into the river, where it disappears with a singular plop.

Liam stands, looking at where it fell. He imagines it spinning and falling through the murky water, coming at last to rest on the silty bottom. He will never know what answer it gave, and this seems to compound everything, to confirm all his worst fears. He is useless, he is a failure. He can't even toss a coin.

He has no idea what to do or where to go. He lowers himself to a wall because he is aware that the old injury in his shin is aching, as it sometimes does, even now. He thinks about how his leg looks normal, entirely healthy, but he knows, and it knows, better. He thinks about the day it happened: him dropping into the well his saint's medallion and how it fell, turning and turning, much as the coin just did into the river.

He raises his head. He looks at the river, flowing inexorably towards the sea. That day, in the copse, he'd had two choices before him—the priesthood or the mapping—and it was decided for him, in a way, by the breaking of his leg, by Enda taking his place as chain-boy. He had been pulled along by events, like a boat on a current.

Liam considers his leg. He considers the penny, now at the bottom of the river. He hoists himself to his feet. A decision, all the time he has been sitting on this wall, has been coalescing in him, and it is his to make this time, no one else's. He will not go to the peninsula today, not yet: he cannot put his family through any more; he will not load them with the shame of what he's done in abandoning the Church. He will establish himself here, in the city, first. He will write to them and tell them he's back and will visit them soon. Imagine this, he will say. I'm no longer a priest, and here is my address. Please write back.

Before anything else, however, he will find gainful employment. He will establish himself so that no one can ever look on him again with scorn. He will go back to them when he can hold his head high, not as a failed priest but as a citizen, a working man.

With her scarf tied over her mouth and nose, her knees pressed against the brass rim of the hearth, Enda scrapes at the ash and cinders in the kitchen range, gathering them into a small hill, then tipping them into a bucket at her side.

Some are still warm, with red-orange centres: these she leaves, poking them to one side. She places dry kindling around the embers, thinking, as she always does at this moment, of her mother's instructions—*in the shape of a little house*—for it was Phina who taught her how to relight a fire, how to revive it in minutes to a good blaze, and it is a skill that has never left her. She pokes twigs and scraps of newspaper and wood shavings around the house-shaped kindling, and is soon rewarded with a curl of smoke, then a flicker of flame, uncertain at first, but gaining appetite.

She brings a tendril of wood shaving up to her nose and inhales, sitting back on her heels.

Anatole has gone upriver for the summer, into the distant woodlands, with a large crew, to a logging camp, where they will work in teams to bring down the towering, sky-high trees. Larch, hornbeam, Douglas fir, red cedar, yellow cedar. He has promised Enda that he will stay away from the falling trunks and those in the camp who like to start fights to alleviate the boredom. He has to be careful with his fingers because how would he play his accordion if the axe or an angry logger took off a finger or two? And Enda had reached for his hand, pressed it to her mouth.

He has left the instrument with her, for safekeeping. He couldn't take it to the logging camp, he said: it was a rough place, the men crushed in together, the air too wet, the risk of fights and brawls too high. Seeing her face, he smiled and said: Do not worry. I know how to stay away from trouble. They had been in their alleyway, away from the streetlamp's circle of light, and he had been fastening her blouse, button by painstaking button, and she had been watching his fingers working from hem to neck, recalling how, not so long ago, they had gone in the other direction. She had been leaning up against a windowsill, one foot resting on the alleyway's opposite wall, and his imminent departure had seemed abstract, far-off, but now he has gone, the accordion is silent, its pleats folded, stored away under her bed, and he will not be back until leaf-fall, when the men have done all the cutting and felling they can, before the biting winds of winter drive them back to town, and then he will be paid.

Enda feeds a log into the range, surrendering it to the fire. The flames resist it at first, sniffing it like a suspicious cat, then curl themselves around it, satisfied. She places another against the first—her mother coming, again, to mind—and then another, and soon she can swing the iron door shut, raise herself to her knees, and haul the bucket of cinders off to the back step, where she flings its contents onto the ash heap and slams the door.

Enda must sweep the stairs and the parlour. She must mop the hallway and the kitchen, then polish the mantels. When this is finished, she is free.

She would write him a letter but he had told her that no mail will come in and out of the logging camp all summer—the river is not navigable by boat, he had said, only canoe. If she needed to reach him in an emergency, she could call at the timber merchants' offices in town and they might be able to get a message to him. He had held her head in his hands then and said, with his mouth pressed to her temple, that he would be back, at the end of the summer, he promised her this, and would she wait for him, please, would she make him that promise, would she wait and not go anywhere, because when he came back he would come to find her and he thought that then they should perhaps get married. Enda had listened, wonderingly, and they looked at each other for a long moment, and the thought crossed her mind that their children would have either her very blue eyes or his very dark eyes, and which might it be? And then she realised that his "perhaps" denoted a question, he was asking her and he was waiting for the response she had yet to give, so she nodded. Yes, she said, of course, yes.

So now she waits. She finds herself to be the woman in all stories, in all ballads and myths, waiting for her man to return—from battle, from sea, from mountain and, in her case, from forest. Against all her instincts, she has to stay put at the rooming house, so he knows where to find her; she must remain here, a limpet on a rock, until he gets back. In these new and makeshift towns, people vanish all the time, move on, never to be heard of again: she can't be one of them. She made her promise and she is determined to keep it.

It is a long summer—hot and dry, the trees in the town unmoving, the flags in the square limp on their poles, the boarders in the rooming house fractious and thirsty. Enda does her chores listlessly: she reasons that she can be done with the mantels quickly, with the merest flick of her duster, and that she can get away with just moistening the middle of the floors—the landlady's eyesight is not what it should be. She tries, as she goes about with her mop bucket, not to picture the axe-men and their swinging blades, the crash of immense trunks to the forest floor, the wild people said to inhabit the dense woodlands who release arrows and spears from the leaf canopies, who hide themselves in the branches and undergrowth to observe these tree-felling interlopers.

Her feet feel every day as if they are made of lead; her limbs seem to be silted up. In the evening, she sits on the back step, her chin in her hand; at night, she can't find a comfortable position in her bunk. The days tick by with agonising slowness. She is waiting, she is waiting, and she has no aptitude for it. Her shoes slap and drag as she moves. The landlady, noticing at last that the house is steadily gathering dust and smut, reprimands her and tells her she could fill her position in a minute, so pull those socks up, girl.

Socks. The very idea makes Enda want to boak—their woollen clutches, their hot and sweaty interiors—but she lowers her eyes in a pretence of contrition and says, Sorry, madam, I'll mend my ways.

And she does try. She clatters pail and brush about with apparent zeal. She unhooks all the curtains, without being asked, and beats the dust out of them in the yard. She takes a wire brush and cleans out the range. She polishes the brass door-knocker until it gives back a reflection of her face.

She imagines what she wishes might be happening: the loggers packing up the camp, clearing their bunks, cleaning their axes for the last time, throwing away their empty hooch bottles, then lashing it all to canoes. She pictures Anatole carefully wiping his axe and rolling up his bedding. She wills herself to see him hiking back through the forest, along the hidden trails, the other axe-men behind him, the whole gang of them returning, coming back to their wives and children and womenfolk, back to the sawmills and the paper mills and the inns and the taverns for the winter.

The weeks pass, day follows night follows day, the season turns; the leaves on the trees in the square, when Enda goes to stand beneath them for the relief of the shade, have a definite crisping to their edges. She pulls one off, just to be sure, and carries it home, joyfully, where she pins it to the wall by her bed.

It won't be long. Anatole will be back any day now. He will be coming through the forest, making his way through the cedars and the larches and the firs and the hopwoods, towards her.

On his third day in Dublin, the city of his birth, Liam takes himself to a particular street, the name of which he has seen all his life at the bottom of papers and on notebooks: Phoenix Park, which strikes him, when he sees it on a street-sign, as preposterously symbolic of his current state. He walks the pavement one way, on the opposite side, he walks it the other. He stands for a moment at the bottom on the steps, then grips the railing—much as his brother, Eugene, did, on the deck of the ship, but this is, of course, unknown to Liam—and he climbs the stairs.

In the vestibule of the offices of the Ordnance Survey, Liam removes his hat, he straightens the unfamiliar-feeling tie around his neck, and he tells the secretary at the desk he has been an apprentice to his father, he is a skilled mathematician, an experienced surveyor and is looking for employment.

He has thought carefully about this, lying awake at night in his inn; he has circled round and round the idea, in his mind, and also during his days wandering the city, the concentric shapes getting smaller and smaller until he sees he has no choice. What other work would he possibly find? What opportunities would be open to a former priest? He could teach, he supposed, which would involve enquiries about where he has taught before, and then it would come out that he had been in the Order, and he left, and the whys and the wherefores of that. It would open him to judgement and questions he does not wish to answer; people would look at him with disgust and accusation. There is no other way forward for him.

He has swapped, at a market stall, his outlandish velveteen outfit for a jacket and trousers, discreetly patched, that more or less fit him. He has wandered for miles, along the pavements, through the squares, around the edges of the parks, out to the docks, to the Lanes, where he stood for a long time, watching children playing with improvised swings tied to streetlamps, taking turns to fly through the air. He has seen new houses half built, their roofs open to the sky; he has seen shop fronts and dray horses and carriages and trams and dogs barking at bicycles and men stumbling out of bars and young girls holding babies in their arms.

Women: he has watched them covertly and, for the first time, from under his brow: fair ones, young ones, older, slim, curved, smart, shabby, with curled hair, with straight, thin and careworn, young and smiling. Would he ever? Could he? That it is a possibility for him now turns his mind to the sheer whiteness of unmarked paper. What manner of woman does he like? He has watched a courting couple on a tram, the woman with her hand tucked through the man's. Her narrow wrists, her hair smoothed and tied back with a sky-blue ribbon, the way she held her drawstring bag hooked over a single finger, moved Liam almost to tears. He has seen a barefoot woman—a lovely creature with large brown eyes and chapped lips, absently biting the seam of her glove—selling bound posies of flowers at the gateway to a park, and he had to hold himself back from proposing to her on the spot.

At the desk of the Ordnance Survey office, he gives his father's name, the map sheets they worked on, the years of his father's employment, his job title. He is asked to sit on a bench, where he waits for several hours. Eventually, towards the end of the afternoon, a harried man with wire spectacles comes to speak to him. Liam tells him again about his father, Tomás, about the surveying they did together out in the west, in the north, in the far-flung island (he crosses his fingers behind his back, not mentioning that it was his sister who assisted there) and the man goes away to check.

A second man, dressed in a suit, appears and asks him to spell his family name, in both languages, please. Liam is asked if he can read and write, and he demonstrates his skill in several tongues; he is given calculations to complete and he works them out in his head in a flash, before inscribing the answer with a neat flourish. He is then ushered up the stairs into a room where, on a desk, lie a number of surveying instruments, including a theodolite and, yes, a surveying pole.

Liam picks them up with sure and steady hands; he demonstrates his knowledge, his experience, his ability to calculate and measure, then to translate this into first text and then cartographic runes. The men nod, looking at him carefully, catching each other's eye with an unspoken meaning. Someone else comes in with a stack of ledgers and there, Liam sees, is his father's handwriting, slanted and meticulous, filling the columns of field books, and how happy, Liam thinks, it would have made Tomás to know that his work has been kept like this, with such care, filed away so systematically. Here are his listings of landforms, villages, lakes, boundaries, their names, explanations and histories. Here are the courses of streams, the amount of water flowing from which escarpment, which side of a mountain, the size and depths of lakes, their geological formation.

The signature at the bottom of each page is not his father's, of course, but that of the army officer in charge of the division, so Liam has to swallow a surge of fury and injustice to say: That's him, that's my father, we wrote these together, he and I.

~

Enda holds Anatole's promise at the forefront of her mind, as a person entering a dark room will bear aloft a candle. He will come back for her. They will be married. When she feels downhearted, she tells herself to think about the house they will have together: a table, two chairs, a bed—what a thing!—and a shelf where an accordion and a fiddle will sit.

Another week passes, then another. Enda clears the grate; she swishes her mop about the floor. She goes to the square and sees that all the leaves lie on the ground, desiccated and curled. They rattle against each other in the cold wind and collect against her boots.

Other thoughts are beginning to crowd her mind, seeking entry, but she will not permit them. She finds it harder and harder to rise in the morning: she is so tired. How relentless this life is, how repetitive; she is almost ill with it, a peculiar sour taste in her mouth, her nails splitting and cracked.

She blunders through her chores one day, then walks out to the timber merchants' office, trying to ignore the fact that the air rings with cold, that she should have worn a shawl and mittens. She knows where it is, a large, double-fronted building off the main street, with blue-painted gables and a cupola above the door. Anatole pointed it out to her once, saying that his logging crew was part of this company, that all the trees they felled belonged to these merchants.

Inside, the place is hushed. Dark-wood panelling and opaque glass segment the large room into separate offices. Men in ties and jackets move between the partitions, their shoes clicking on the flooring.

Enda hesitates by the door, then sidles up to the nearest desk, where a clerk with a pince-nez stands, holding a piece of paper close to his face and simultaneously writing something in a ledger. She places the tips of her fingers on the edge of the desk and clears her throat. She has put on her best dress and clean cuffs. The clerk makes her wait for a long moment before he glances up at her, eyebrows raised, apparently shocked to find her there.

Folding her hands together in an attitude of meekness, she says she is enquiring about an employee of the company. She gives Anatole's full name, and she begins to tell the clerk what she knows of the logging camp, its position in the deep forest, where the tallest trees grow, up a narrow and un-navigable tributary of the river, but the man shuts his eyes behind his spectacles, and tells her he knows nothing of this matter, and to please leave because she is taking up his valuable time. He lifts his pen from its holder and continues with his work, as if she isn't there.

When it is clear that the man isn't going to address her again, Enda turns away.

She hurries along the river, with no clear idea of where she is going, her hair flicked into her eyes by an icy breeze, her stomach roiling, her arms half raised, as if to fend off an enemy. Something must have happened: this is the only thought she will allow herself. Something might have happened: the grammar of this is more comforting. Something has happened: this conjugation frightens her very badly because she finds she knows it to be true.

Enda tilts her face to the sky, as if to calm herself, as if to find a different answer to the puzzle of what is occurring, both inside and outside herself. Anatole hasn't come back. He promised he would return, and his accordion is here, and he would never abandon her, abandon that, so something must have occurred—might have occurred—to delay him. Some other work perhaps, some other opportunity; he will be back soon, she feels, very soon, and if he isn't, if he never returns, she doesn't know what she will do, because, because—

Here, she pauses, as if reluctant to take a further step, pressing the side of her fist to the smooth trunk of a tree growing beside the river; she doesn't know its name but it has dark berries hanging in clusters, a few smooth shiny leaves still clinging to its branches.

What she has been refusing to think about, to admit to herself, all these long weeks, must now be faced. She must name it. She must turn her attention to it. She doesn't know, cannot see, how she has got herself into this—she gropes for the right word, one that doesn't alarm her too much, alighting eventually on "situation." She doesn't know how she got into this situation, but she cannot ignore it any longer.

He had said he was being careful. That was the word he used. I will be careful, he said. Always careful with you. I don't want to give you trouble: he had also said this. Don't worry: this, too, was something he had said—no, breathed—to her, in the alleyway, before, well, before. And she had trusted him. Like a fool, like an eejit, like so many before her. She had said, she actually remembers herself saying—and she would like to strike herself about the face at the memory—I trust you. She had said this. She had said: Don't stop.

So she finds herself perplexed because she is sure he was careful—he is a man of his word, she is still so certain of this. But how, then, has this happened? How is it she both sickens and hungers for food? How is it she hasn't had her monthly visitor since just before he left? Whatever in God's name is she to do now?

Blindly, Enda leans over, grapples for a stone and hurls it towards the water. It falls with a meek plop into the shallows. Furious now, she snatches up several more, throwing them in arcs, watching them fall with separate coronets of spray into the river. Then, breathing hard, she turns and marches back the way she came, rounding the corner to the main street so quickly that the wind nearly lifts the hat from her head.

At the desk in the loggers' office stands a different clerk. This one is younger, with a fine smattering of acne over his cheeks, and long pale fingers. Enda leans over and taps the top of the ledger to get his attention. She repeats her enquiry. She spells the name "Anatole" again. She says she isn't leaving until they send a message to him.

The clerk stares at her in faint surprise. Then he opens the very ledger in front of him. He runs one of his ink-scarred thumbs down a list, turns a page. He examines another column, turns another page, glances up at her again. He shuts the ledger with force and places both of his hands upon its cover, as if hiding something from sight, and he swallows, his Adam's apple bobbing up and down in his throat.

"Hmm," he says. "Wait here."

He walks across the room and behind a partition. Through the blurred glass, she sees him leaning over the desk of another clerk. They confer. The seated man peers around the partition at Enda, retreats, and the men confer again. Then the second man reappears, rising from his chair and coming towards her, across the office, fastening the buttons on his jacket. He says that he gathers she is enquiring about one of their employees, an axe-man, who was recently working for them upriver in an encampment, is that correct?

Enda says: "Yes."

"May I ask," the clerk says, spreading out his fingers across his lapel, "what is your connection to him?"

"You may not."

"Well," says the clerk, flushing, "I regret to—ah—inform you that there was an accident at that logging site, some weeks hence. The man in question was killed."

Enda examines the two clerks in front of her. The fraying necktie of one. The livid and angry-looking pustules on the jaw of the other. Their fingernails ingrained with black rims of ink.

"An accident?" she parries, as if this is an argument she can win. "But he's an experienced axe-man. He—he—he told me he knew how to stay out of trouble. He can't have been—"

She will not say "killed," she will not, because to say it would make it true, it would mean she accepts their explanation, when it cannot have happened, it cannot have taken place, there must be some mistake.

The two men exchange a glance. The young clerk fiddles with his cuffs, running a finger around them, as if they are too tight.

"It was in the river," the other clerk says, "I believe. The timber was being sent downstream but the trunks became jammed and this man entered the water to release them—which, by the way, is not a practice recommended by the company—and he became trapped beneath them. His body was recovered further downstream. That is all I can tell you."

Enda stares at the clerks. Their words are so perfunctory, but her mind is filled with the rushing of currents, the crash and power of the river, the jumble of wet tree trunks, their awful roll and weight, how they might overpower a man as if he were no more than a beetle, his head disappearing beneath them, his shirt filled to heavy saturation with water, his hands stiff with cold, unable to find a grip on the merciless wet bark, and what in God's name was he doing entering the river, why was he asked to do such a dangerous thing?

"But . . ." she hears herself say, and she has no idea what will come out of her mouth next ". . . I have his accordion. I was . . . to keep it for him, he left it with me for . . . safekeeping and—"

"In that case," the younger clerk exclaims, as if pleased to be able to be of use, "you could send it to his wife."

"Wife?"

Enda finds that speaking this word aloud has done something strange to her: her throat prickles with a horrible dryness and her lips feel too frozen to move. She isn't sure she will be able to say anything further.

"You mean—" she rasps out an approximation of speech "—his sister? The one living in Québec?"

The clerks regard her, the younger one with pity in his gaze. No, they say, wife. He had a wife and children, up in the city, a boy and a girl, they believe, and the company intends to take care of them, in accordance with their policies. They can let Enda have the address, if she just waits a moment, do you hear, wait here, wait, where are you going, it won't take a moment, just wait.

Enda finds herself outside again, and it has begun to hail, and the pavements are covered with perfect miniature spheres of ice, and it is still falling, striking her on the head, and the sensation is like the sting of sewing needles dropped from the sky. She turns a corner and another, her feet carrying her somewhere, anywhere. She passes houses and street stalls, a group of children throwing a ball, a dairy where the rectangles of cobbles are outlined with thin opalised lines of milk. It hurts, she finds, to move her eyeballs inside her skull, and her hands feel at once freezing cold and burning hot. After a time, she discovers she is moving down the street where she lives, and she doesn't know how this day will end, how she will get through it, and the next, and the one after that, what she will do, how she will live now. The answer is about to appear, although she doesn't know it yet, for when she reaches the rooming house she takes to her bed, she pulls the covers over her head and she closes her eyes, tight, and even when the landlady comes to find her the next morning, to ask why the stove isn't lit, she will not open them, she will not move, she will not speak a word. When asked if she has a fever, Enda nods, tucking her chin into her chest.

The landlady, spooked by the rigid white face of her maid-of-all-work, retreats. There are rumours of typhoid in the town, and diphtheria. She backs out of Enda's cupboard-room, her handkerchief over her face; she leaves a pitcher of water for the unfortunate creature because no one could ever say she was an unchristian woman, and then she shuffles back upstairs, closing the kitchen door firmly.

Enda stays in bed for two days, then three. She watches the light filtering in from the kitchen rise, then fade, rise, then fade. She doesn't think she will ever be able to get up again, that she may just expire here.

On the fourth day, or perhaps the fifth, she hears a knocking at the front door, followed by the low rumble of conversation. After a short gap, there comes a knocking at the back door.

Enda rolls into herself, closing her eyes.

The knocking turns to a pounding. Then someone, unmistakably, calls her name. It is a woman's voice, low and insistent.

"Enda," it says. "Enda. Open the door."

Enda struggles to an upright position, dazed, afraid. The pounding comes again and, when she looks over, the door is juddering on its hinges.

She puts her legs out of the blankets and stands, unsteadily, pulling herself upright. She tiptoes across the kitchen flags, her bare soles cold against the stone.

"Enda!" the voice yells again.

Fearfully, Enda pulls back the bolt. She swings open the door.

There, on the back step, is a hallucination from Enda's past, a figure dressed up as a woman from the peninsula, a thin and shabby apparition with bare legs under a faded skirt, a heavy shawl folded across the chest. This person stands there, in the lee of the doorway, a bundle on its back, a length of twine clutched in one hand, at the end of which is a dog.

It is the dog that recalls Enda to herself. Bran, her mind tells her incredulously, it's Bran. The same starburst of white on the chest, the exact grey pelt. Then she sees that it can't be—this animal is too young, too lithe—and she is chiding herself for such a foolish thought, telling herself she is turning simple-minded, along with everything else. Perhaps she does have a fever after all.

When the shawled person with the dog says her name, it comes to Enda who this is, and the shock of it is like the lash of the hailstones. She cannot believe what her eyes are telling her; she must be going soft in the head, losing her reason. It seems to be her sister, but it can't be because she will be at home, in the cottage, and yet here she is, and pinned to her bodice is that blue tassel so beloved of their mother, but Enda must be hallucinating.

"Rose?" she whispers, because her voice is still gone, stolen away by the word "wife," said in the offices of the timber company. "Is that you?"

Rose, because it does indeed seem to be her, here, on the back step of the rooming house, where Enda lives, alone, is inexplicably furious and looking as if she might belt her, is saying, You jade, you turncoat, you left me, how could you do that?

Enda doesn't care about the fury, about all the hateful things Rose is calling her. She crosses the ground between them in two strides, she goes to seize her sister by the shoulders, she tries to touch the blue tassel with her fingertips, but Rose sidesteps her, and Enda is saying, over and over, I'm sorry, I'm so sorry. She offers Rose her hand, which Rose knocks aside. Enda asks her, Will you come inside, what dog is this, where's Eugene? and at this her sister falls silent, her anger punctured. She shuts her eyes. Her hands reach for the dog, her fingers plucking gently at the silk of its ears. Rose shakes her head, back and forth, back and forth, tears slipping down her cheeks.

Enda looks on, appalled, afraid. Eugene without Rose is unthinkable. Where can he be? Who is looking after him?

"Dead," Rose says, her voice flat. "Drowned. Off the side of the ship coming over. I couldn't save him."

Enda, swaying, puts a hand to her mouth. She murmurs their brother's name. She tells her sister, over and over, that she is sorry, she is so sorry, she should never have left, it was a terrible mistake, she has regretted it ever since.

She reaches out to Rose again but the dog takes the gesture as directed to itself, and it makes a delighted lunge for Enda, paws landing on her nightgown, tail whipping back and forth, ears folded, eager to make the acquaintance of this new person, to sniff out what manner of human this is. Enda, unable to resist, crouches, letting the dog lick her face and hands, running her hands through its tufts of fur.

"I should never have left you," she says, as if to the dog. Without looking her way, Rose—so much older, her face sallow and pinched—lowers herself down to the step, rests her head in her hands, muttering that Enda looks like death warmed up, what can be wrong with her?

"Come here to me," Enda says, still squatting next to the dog, her heart brimming with pity, with love, holding out her arms to Rose, and suddenly she is sure that she can tackle whatever is ahead of her, of them, that things will turn out, because her sister has come, Rose is here, and she won't be alone, ever again. "Come here to me now," she says, and the dog looks from one to the other, and back again, its eyes anxious and alert, waiting to see what will happen.

Liam has a pair of shoes in oxblood leather. He has a tiepin and a wristwatch. He has a suit in grey flannel. He has two pairs of horn-rimmed spectacles: one for every day and a spare. He sports a handkerchief, folded in three, in his breast pocket; he presses them himself, once a week, in his lodgings; he is used to attending to his own needs—his time in the Order taught him that, if nothing else. He has a choice of two ties. He is contemplating the purchase of a straw boater with a green-and-white grosgrain band. On his day off, he takes the tram out to the seafront and walks along the strand.

He writes a letter to the peninsula. Dear Enda, Rose and Eugene: the words move him unutterably. He tells them he has left the priesthood. He tells them he has missed them. He tells them he has a job and that they will laugh when they find out what it is. He pins two banknotes to the page. I will come out to see you, he writes. Then he amends this to: I long to see you all again, to see home.

There is no reply.

Monday to Saturday, he works at the offices. He is a diligent employee, skilled in mathematical calculation and in cartography. Like his father before him, he can render, freehand and flawless, a drumlin, a lake, the contours of a valley, the geometric boundaries of an estate, the wild irregularity of bogland, woodland both evergreen and deciduous. He can glance at an outdated map and at new lists and calculations and immediately divine what amendments need to be made. Times have changed, and with them the mapping-office rules: he is permitted to sign his own work, to spell his name however he desires, in whichever language he chooses. He and his kind are no longer automatically given the rank of "labourer": Liam's job title is "surveyor," and he is paid a living wage.

He is mostly in the city, where he lives a life of routine and regular structure, but for several months of the year, he is out in the field, making revisions to the ever-changing maps of the ever-changing country, checking measurements and calculations, noting down any alterations to the geographies, both human and physical.

He writes again to his siblings. I am doing well in the city. I am making maps and sometimes I have to refer to ledgers and books written in our father's hand—what do you think of that? I will call in when I am sent out west. It can only be a matter of time. I wish you well, I send my love and best wishes to you all.

Again, there is no reply, and this injures him. Enda can write, of course, and even if she has moved to a different house, married perhaps, his letters will find them because that is the way of places like the peninsula—no one just vanishes.

He is a willing, if quiet colleague, uncomplaining about long hours, not given to spending lunchtimes at the bar but quick enough to put his hand into his pocket when it's his round. He listens to the conversations around him but doesn't often contribute. If volunteers are needed to go out into the field, he is always the first to put forward his name. When it is discovered that he is sending postcards to the daughter of an innkeeper with whom he stayed for several weeks up in the north, he is good-natured about all the teasing he comes in for. The postcards, most of which are hand-drawn, increase in frequency, and when he comes back from his next assignment, it is several days before he lets slip that he and the innkeeper's daughter are married.

She is ten years his junior; when he tells her he was once a priest, because he wants no secrets between them, she laughs, assuming it's a joke. He assures her that it's the truth, that he trained for years in Rome, then lived in India, and she looks at him with wide, disbelieving eyes, then says best not tell her father. She cries when she has to leave the inn, and her parents, but recovers quickly, sitting beside him on the journey to Dublin, her gloved hand tucked into his.

He purchases the lease on a house not far from the Lanes. It is in a woeful state of disrepair but it has a door with a glass fan above it, a row of rusting railings outside. He installs tenants on the upper floors; he and his new young wife live in the basement.

I am married now, he writes to them, and we have a child on the way. I would love to hear a word, if you have the time. Please forgive me for whatever it is I did to offend you all. You are my flesh and blood. Your loving brother, Liam.

Several weeks later, the letter is returned to him, falling to the tiles in the hallway of his house. He picks it up on his way out to work, hat on his head, a maroon tie pinned to his collar, walking cane in his hand, and turns it over. Scrawled on the back, in blotted and uneven ink, are two words: "GON AWAY."

The misspelling and the brevity are devastating to him. GON AWAY. How could they go, all three of them? And where? He cannot picture them anywhere other than the cottage on the hillside, or down at the shore with the widow. That they might be living elsewhere is inconceivable.

He writes that very day to the widow herself, c/o Father Joseph at his chapel. Can you tell me where they are? Do you have an address? He signs it, Your Liam.

It, too, is returned to him only days later. A different hand this time, in looping pencil script: "BOTH DECEASED."

The creased, returned letters are propped on a shelf in the kitchen, along with bills, a hairpin or two, one of his library books. His wife, when she catches him looking at them, slides an arm around him. Maybe you should go out there, she says, when you get the chance, and you can find out what happened to them all. It would give you ease, I think. You might find someone who knows where they are, how to find them.

She's right, of course, Liam sees. But her time is near, and then the baby comes, a son, and his days are busy at his desk, and his evenings at home, and somehow months pass. He has two sons when it becomes known in the office that a man is needed to go out west, to the coast. The name of the place is familiar to Liam; it is perhaps fifteen miles from the peninsula. He puts himself forward, says he would be glad to take on the task.

He kisses his wife goodbye, he ruffles the hair of his elder son, he strokes the curved and milky cheek of the younger, and he sets out.

The mapping itself is straightforward. A new stretch of road here, the draining of a bog, the felling of a wood there, a few houses reduced to rubble, a field sold to a neighbour, a small inaccuracy to a place name, a number of redrawn lines to the townland boundaries. Many of the books and drafts he must refer to are in his father's hand: he finds Tomás all over the landscape, written into it, wherever he goes. That familiar, slanting script never fails to give him a jolt, and sometimes, if no one is looking, he will pass his palm over the pages, as if from the loops and crosses of the words he might glean some insight into that most enigmatic and taciturn of men.

On the final day, he takes the road leading south-west, a twisting, uneven track that skirts multiple inlets and sounds, leads him into woodland and out the other side. It is several miles before certain things begin to seem recognisable: that bare rock pushing up from the middle of a field, the slope of that roof, the line of white surf in the distance, the humped back of an island out to sea, the trees sculpted to italics by an unrelenting wind. He passes a line of cottages, then the chimneys of the manor house appear over the next hill; he traverses the crossroads where the lane leads to the town, and then he sees the peninsula laid out before him, the hill that is shaped like the spine of a sleeping dragon, the loughs pooled in the hollows, the dividing lines of stone walls, the sheer face of the outcrop, at the base of which is the cottage where he lived a great portion of his life.

As he walks closer and closer, things look at once familiar and strange. The estate wall seems lower than he remembers, its stones thick with leaf-rot. Were there always pink-gold lilies on the surface of the pond? Have swans and moorhens always nested like that in the reeds? Was the moss always a vivid yellow-green? Liam is simultaneously disoriented and certain of where he is: he is adrift, he is home; this place is both in him and out of him. And the question that keeps tolling through his mind is: who is he here, if none of his people are left?

When he reaches the village, the first shock is that the house of the fishermen is nothing more than its foundations, pulled down, Liam fears, by the eviction men. He stands for a moment at what would have been the threshold: he sees a shard of a bowl, the rusted blade of a knife. The next cottage he reaches, which used to house the two elderly sisters, has at its doorway a pair of leggy, sharp-nosed dogs, between which sits a small, besmirched child, who is solemnly eating an apple. The dogs keep their eyes trained on Liam as he passes, alert to his status as a stranger.

The widow's house looks much as before: the half-door open at the top to let in the air, feathers of smoke lifting from the chimney, a brown cow tethered to a stake, a hen roosting on the windowsill, a creel of seaweed propped up against the lime-washed wall.

Liam knocks, calls out a greeting. After a moment, a man comes around the side of the house. He is dressed in the canvas britches and smock of men in these parts, and he takes in Liam's suit, his polished boots, with something like alarm.

"What is your business here?" he demands, and Liam can see that every muscle in his body is tensed, ready to defend his home, his family.

"Good day to you," Liam says, and he uses his soothing priest-voice. "I'm sorry to be taking you from your work."

The man shifts on his feet. "Are you coming from the big house?" he says. "I've paid my rent, I've—"

"It's nothing like that," Liam says. "My family used to live up the way," he sweeps an arm towards the crag, the rath, "and I've lost sight of them. I'm here to see if any know of their whereabouts. We knew the widow who lived here before you. I wonder did she leave anything behind? Any letters or—"

"They went away, I heard."

"Who?"

The man nods towards the hillside. "The young ones from up the hill. A brother and sister. Across the sea."

Liam hears the clicking of a sudden pulse in his ear. He is too late, they have gone. He is a fool, an ingrate: why ever did he not come before? "There . . . there were two sisters. Do you know what happened to the other one?"

The man shakes his head. "I'm sorry for your troubles."

He goes inside the house to see if his wife knows any more; as the door swings open then shut, Liam catches a glimpse of the interior, the ladder up to the loft, the long table laid with spoons and cups. The woman is friendlier than her husband: she invites Liam to come inside, to take a bite or a drink of tea, but he refuses. She tells him that nobody lives up the hill now: the new viscount, a distant cousin of the old man who passed not long after he lost his son, God rest him, doesn't bother too much with his tenants—he spends most of his time away, abroad—but his land steward is the very devil of a man, always after them, always wanting to raise their rents or call in his thugs. Will you step inside? she asks again, and Liam, again, refuses.

He turns from the house, his eyes sweeping over the door and the byre, the strand behind it, knowing it is the last time he will ever see it. Darkness will fall in approximately four hours, Liam thinks, so he doesn't have long. He stands there, hesitating. He could leave, walk back along the track to the main road. He has, in a way, got what he came for: they have all gone, his brother and his sisters, and nobody knows where. Across the sea. There is nothing for him up the hill.

Hard to picture Eugene and Rose—for it must have been them who went together, no doubt Enda split away and is off somewhere marching to her own beat, her and her fiddle—in the New World. Impossible to envisage them anywhere but here. He feels himself to be small of heart, deluded, a person so short-sighted that he could not recognise that what he needed—his brother, his sisters—was here all along. He'd assumed, like a fool, that they would always be here, waiting for his grand return, and now he is the one left alone.

Liam eyes the mountain, the twin drumlins; he turns his head to look back the way he came.

His feet, his body make the decision for him. He is contemplating the distance to the nearest inn when he sees that he is, in fact, moving up the hillside, climbing the slope, and how potent, how arresting is this overwhelming familiarity. Each stone, each swag of moss, each patch of mud seems precisely the same, the fecund damp smell: he is at once a grown man with two children and a wife, and he is also a young lad, desperate to go into the priesthood, making his way home after a long day of instruction at school. And he is the small boy who came up here with his father, carrying a surveying pole, on a wet and breezy day, long ago.

At a bend in the path, he is startled to see a group of children bending over a stream, and for a moment he thinks that time has twisted back on itself and it is Rose and Eugene and Enda and himself, building a dam, sending leaf boats downstream, but no, of course it isn't, because isn't he standing here, a surveyor and cartographer, in a suit?

The children are scooping mud from the bottom and piling it up in thick, oozing slabs on the bank. One of them sees Liam and exclaims in surprise and they all scramble to their feet.

"Who're you?" says the oldest girl, a bold one with two fair plaits and the hazel-green eyes of the woman from down below.

"I'm Liam," he says.

"Where're you headed?"

"Up this way. I used to live there, when I was your age."

"In the old cabin on the hill?"

"That's the one."

The children eye and nudge each other; there is some conferring between them. The youngest pushes her hand into that of the eldest.

"Mammy says we're not to go up past the boreen's end," blurts out one of the boys.

"Is that right?"

"A *gruagach* lives there."

Liam raises his eyebrows and smiles. He hasn't heard this word for a good long while—his city children don't concern themselves with such things—and he is happy to be reminded of it. *Gruagach*: a goblin-creature, hard-working and secretive.

"Does it now?"

"It does," says the small boy, face flushed with glee, "and it comes out at night and might steal you away. Mammy says you can hear it on windless nights."

Liam shrugs. "I don't believe in *gruagacha*."

"Well, you'd better watch yourself, then, mister," says the girl, turning back to their game, and Liam feels himself dismissed.

He steps around them, careful to avoid their mud-towers, and as he walks away he hears them talking about the *gruagach*, the older girl claiming to have seen it, and how it looks like a man but is covered in hair and has yellow teeth.

The drumlins get closer and closer, the mountain looms over him, and he can make out the rings of the rath against the cirrus-streaked sky. He finds that the boreen is thick with branches and growth—it is clear that nobody has come this way for a very long time—but he battles on, twigs snapping and breaking as he pushes through them, the long spined limbs of brambles snatching at his clothes. When he emerges at the top of the boreen, he realises that the woman down below is mistaken. People are living here. There are rows of beans growing in well-turned soil; the haggard is swept and neat; turf has been stacked against the house; onions have been picked and left on a stool; there is grain and chaff on the quern stone by the back door; the air carries the scent of a fire.

Liam moves forward cautiously, calling out a greeting. The idea that a *gruagach* might burst out of the half-door, brandishing perhaps a cudgel, furious at this human trespass flits through his mind, and he scolds himself for such childish fears. Whoever it is inhabiting this place are people of habit and organisation—that much is clear.

Liam straightens his tie, brushes the leaves and twigs from his jacket. He lifts his hand and knocks gently on the door because it seems like the right thing to do. He knocks twice more, but there is no answer. He could, he supposes, lift the latch and step inside—he knows precisely how to work that door handle, how much pressure to apply, how you must turn it slightly to the left before giving it a sharp twist to the right—but it doesn't feel right to disturb these orderly people, who arrange their seedlings in such precise and straight rows. Let his memory of the cottage's interior be preserved; let it not be overwritten by whatever these new people have done to it.

Liam turns 360 degrees, taking it all in. The haggard wall, the white flowers coming out on the bean plants, the axe that he's certain was once wielded by the hand of his father, lying on top of a chopping block, the stacked ends of the thatch above his head. He wishes he could feel that time has collapsed, that at any moment the door might open and his mother step out, that if he tilted his head, he'd see Enda sitting high on the roof, staring moodily out to sea. He wishes he could close his eyes and believe he'd find Rose or Eugene, perhaps even Tomás, when he opened them. But there can be no going back. They were here for a while, the six of them, and before them, others lived here, and before them, someone else, and now they are all gone, and whoever cut that turf is here now. After these people will come someone else, and then someone else, and on and on it will go until the end of the world.

Because Liam feels this insight coursing through him, he heads, almost without thinking about it, towards the copse. Why not? is what he is thinking. Isn't it where his father told him to return, if he ever became lost? And isn't it where all this began, his father's garrulousness, the sudden move out here to the peninsula? Wouldn't his going there be the closing of a circle? Always, Liam carries within him the idea of what life might have been had his family stayed in the Lanes, who he might have been if he had never come west, never seen his father strapped to a table, never fallen under the spell of a resentful, score-settling priest. It is a lost self, a ghost twin, that Liam. He would like to ask his sisters if they feel it too: who might they have been if they had stayed? Now, he thinks, with a fearful wrench, he will never be able to put this question to them and it is all his own fault. He is the one who left them, he is the one who didn't write, even, to Liam's eternal shame, when he received news that their father had died. It was him who severed the ties that bound them, and look where it has got him: alone, on a hillside, his former home taken over by strangers.

So, why not go into the copse and visit the sacred well? He is an educated man, a wage-earner, a husband, a father. There isn't a shred of superstition or religion left in him. Let him stand before it for the last time: the well cannot touch him now.

Liam steps into the trees, smoothing the front of his waistcoat, surrendering to the green-lit glow. For a moment, he wants to laugh at himself, at the boy he was. How could he ever have been frightened by this place? It is a cluster of trees, nothing more, really quite unremarkable—stones, a network of streams. Some oak, some ash, a blackthorn there at the edge. Evidence of higher water, perhaps even minor flooding, in wetter seasons, low-lying layer of fern, small insects, a butterfly, birds overhead. A branch catches him on the cheek, and as he twists away from it, it rakes through his hair, disturbing it from the neat lines into which he combs it every morning. Really quite a pleasant place, after all, Liam is thinking, not anything to be—

The pool appears sooner than he had remembered. Natural bowl of granite, his mind is telling him, worn by the action of the spring over thousands and thousands of years. Water extremely clear. Remarkably deep, actually.

At the sound of a crack behind him, Liam's mind empties of thought. There is a shrivelling sensation at the back of his neck, a prickling, as if something has passed across it—a trailing cobweb, a tiny hand. He feels his heart falter and hesitate, the blood in his body stilling, then restarting at a galloping pace. He has, he cannot deny it, the distinct sense that he is being watched, or that he has somehow stepped outside linear time, that he might very possibly turn to find himself as a frightened child, standing there, regarding him.

Liam does not shift his gaze—he will not. He keeps himself motionless, just as he was, head bowed, not in any religious or superstitious sense, just because he was examining the well. He is annoyed to realise that he is clutching his hat in his hand, as if about to pray. A muscle just below his eye starts up an abrupt twitching, distorting the edges of his sight; it is tempting to reach up and rub at it but he doesn't want to move, doesn't want to attract attention. He will stay still, until this sensation, this suspicion, has passed, because he is not going to give in to any foolish illusions or tricks his mind might play on him. There is nobody here. Just him. Nobody at all.

A flash, a movement across the surface of the pool, as if something within it has writhed or moved, or someone has dropped a pebble into it, is all it takes. Liam flinches, turns, drops his hat, all in one movement, and then he is fleeing, hurrying and stumbling through the trees, and for the second time in his life, he is sprinting through the copse and out, away from this place, as fast as he can, and this time, he is swearing to himself, will absolutely be the last, for he is never coming back here again.

After this sudden flight, the man crashing and flailing through the branches, slipping on the moss and ferns, letting out noises of panic and fear, there is silence in the copse. The trees lift their arms to the wind and clack their fingers together. A bird hop-stitches its way up a trunk, from root to twig, before becoming distracted by a woodlouse hiding in a crevice of bark. The four silver streams flowing from the pool continue to weave towards each other and apart. The pool sits, implacable, inside its necklace of stone.

After a long interval, a shape might be seen moving through the trees, if indeed anyone were there to witness it. It picks its way soundlessly, with a certain grace, through the moss and the stones, placing its feet with care so that no footprints are left.

It looks one way, then the other, before bending to pick up the hat, which it examines for a moment, before reaching out to hang it off the outstretched limb of a tree.

Eugene—for it is he—has no idea that this hat belongs to Liam. He hasn't an inkling that the man he had been watching from his private perch in the canopy of an oak tree was in fact his brother. He had been weeding his vegetable patch, laying dung around the plants to make them grow strong, when he had heard a commotion in the boreen. He had canted his head to one side, listening to the unaccustomed sound of someone struggling up the old path, swearing and cursing the bushes and trees, fighting with the branches that he, Eugene, had eased together, woven one into another in order for them to grow into a mesh, a net, so that none would come this way. But, thought Eugene, leaning on his loy, whoever this was must be a determined, headstrong sort. When he heard the person's footfalls getting nearer, despite the thicket of briars he had cultivated, Eugene had laid down the loy and run to conceal himself in the copse, as had always been his habit on the rare occasion anyone made it up here.

He had watched the smartly dressed gentleman walk up to the cottage door—and Eugene doesn't like the gentry, the fine fabric of their clothing, the marks of combs in their oiled hair, but he isn't going to think about any of that—and rap upon it with his knuckles. Eugene had peered out from behind his tree as he examined the vegetable garden, the haggard wall, the stack of turf. When the man had made his way towards the copse, Eugene wasn't worried: he has myriad ways to make himself invisible. He had merely stepped further into the trees and up off the ground, rendering himself as still as a branch, as a rook, and watched.

It did not occur to Eugene to wonder who the man was. It did not cross his mind that this person might have any connection with him, beyond disturbing his day's work. That the man had hair the colour of copper did not register with Eugene: this is not the way his mind works. The concepts of familiarity or resemblance are not ones he comprehends. To him, his brother, Liam, is a lanky boy who wished to train for the priesthood. That years have passed and that Liam might have grown up and now look different does not occur to him. Liam was his brother who caused arguments and went away; this is a bespectacled man in a fine suit of clothes who is alarmingly curious about Eugene's home.

When the man leaves, finally, beating his way back down the boreen, Eugene waits until the cottage's shadow is almost tucked away under it before he ventures out.

If asked, Eugene wouldn't be able to say how long it is he has been here alone, how many years ago it was that he plunged into the sea, off the side of the ship, handing over the puppy and leaping into the waves. He is not one to examine motives. He doesn't think about the past, as such, because he sees no delineation between past and present, between the now and the future. He lives much as his ancient forebears did: on and by the land, watching the weather, feeling one season blur into the next. He knows that when the frost retreats back up the mountain it is time to dig and turn the soil; he knows that a wet spring will mean fewer apples on the tree by the lough; if a summer is dry, he should lift the crop early; if the bog-cotton is plentiful, there will be a good yield; when the mornings become cooler and mistier, he knows it is time to start footing the turf.

In the early days, he cried a great deal. He remembers this. He plunged off the boat, without forethought, without pause. When he saw the rocky shoreline sliding by, the patchwork of fields, when people around him cried out that it was the last glimpse of their land, it was clear to him: he would not be leaving, he would go back. And so he flung himself off and the sea claimed him greedily, the waves cold and choppy, reaching their huge arms over his head and forcing him down. He could feel beneath his wildly trampling feet the vast depths, filled with fish and monsters and currents, and he was sorry then: he longed for Rose, up there on the ship, and he longed for the pup, its sleek head, its wise gold eyes, but he could not leave.

When his head broke the surface, he hawked and coughed, spitting up all the bitter water, he gulped at the air, and he knew not to stay still, to kick his legs, to sweep his arms, pushing one handful of water behind him at a time, keeping his eyes on the shoreline in front of him. There were times when the land seemed to get no closer, despite his efforts, despite the ache in his limbs and lungs, and he thought he wouldn't make it, or not alive, and every hundred strokes he had to turn onto his back and float there, like a starfish, to gather his strength. And there were times when the waves were unkind to him, angry with him, when they dumped themselves over his face or pushed him off course. But he felt after a while that the tide was with him, the water racing towards the strand, hauling him with it, so when he became so exhausted that he thought he couldn't move any more, all he had to do was keep afloat and the rollers would carry him to shore.

When he came out of the sea, it was onto jagged rocks; they cut his palms and the knees of his britches. He was cold to his bones, his fingers white and withered, his hair streaming, and he was clawed by regret. He yelled, mouth wide, for all he had lost. He kicked at the brine, the seawrack that flipped itself back and forth in the shallows. After a while, sore and bleeding, he crawled towards the sand, pulled himself upright, shook the water from his ears and hair, and he made himself put one foot in front of the other.

He walked. He kept to smaller paths, woodlands, bogs, skirting villages, avoiding the straight walls of estates. He ducked into ditches if he heard the cloppetting sound of large horses. He headed north, then north-west, then west, adjusting his course according to the Pole Star. He slept under trees, in the shelter of walls, in the ruins of abandoned cottages. If his feet sprouted blisters, he lined his boots with moss; if he was hungry, he searched for bilberries on low-growing bushes; he cracked open mussel-shells on the rocks he pulled them from; he leaned over the wall of a pigpen and stole fistfuls from the bucket of swill; he crawled into a henhouse late at night and broke the eggs, raw, into his mouth, swallowing down the slippery mess.

When he finally reached the peninsula, he kept to the higher ground, coming up and round behind the cottage, so that he descended towards it from the mountain. He lifted the latch, he stepped inside, he sat down at the table. The air was cool and still, dust motes circling in the shafts of light, a soft and forgiving darkness lying over the stacked bowls on the shelf, the fire grate, the balls of wool in a basket.

Eugene looked around: he took his time over this. He cast his eye over every spoon, every cupboard, each chair, the rungs on the ladder to the loft, the flags on the floor. Then he bent over to remove first one boot, then the other. He laid his head down on the warm wood of the table, and he breathed and he breathed.

Several days later—long enough for Eugene to have cleared the grate and got the fire going, to have filled the buckets with water, to have washed and dried his clothes—the widow made an appearance. Eugene came upon her, standing with her fists on her hips, as he rounded the haggard wall, a bundle of kindling in his arms.

"Mother of God," she said slowly, when she saw him. "What in the name of . . . ?"

She came towards him, and seized him by the arm, which was something he did not like. "What are you doing back? Where's Rose? Is she inside?"

Eugene extracted his arm from her grip. He shook his head.

The widow moved towards the cottage, distraught, one hand pressed to her back, her stick gripped in her gnarled fingers, and pushed open the door. "Rose?" she called. "Rose!"

When Eugene came in behind her, dropping the kindling into the basket, she turned on him. "Where is she?" she demanded, raking his face with her eyes.

Again, Eugene shook his head.

"Are you alone?"

Eugene shrugged.

The widow frowned, her eyes boring into him. "Did she . . . sail on the ship?"

He nodded.

"And you?"

Eugene was still for a long time. Then he inclined his head, once, and he lifted a hand, forming his fingers into a curve, which he brought down in a swooping dive. He looked up at the widow, to see if she understood. He mimed swimming, and more swimming, then walked his fingers along through the air, for a long time.

The widow put a hand over her mouth. She lowered herself into a chair, his mother's, which normally would have bothered Eugene, but he found he didn't mind the widow sitting in it.

"Dear God," she said, then: "Poor Rosie."

She stared at Eugene for a long time, so long in fact that he decided to get on with laying the fire.

"Whatever will we do with you?" she murmured, then rose to her feet and disappeared down the hill.

The following day, she was back, a hen under each arm. They were for him, she said, handing them over. They belonged to him by rights. Take them out to the islet on the lough—he was going to need the eggs to feed himself. Then she told him to listen, and proceeded to say many things, some of which Eugene understood, most of which passed him by: the people at the big house did not seem to be looking for him, or for Rose, she said, but still he had to be careful. He was to stay up here, not to come down the hill, not to walk into the manor land, not to go to the village or the town or the chapel or anywhere. If he lit a fire, he should make it a small one. If he went anywhere, he was to make sure it was only after dark. And he should fill in the boreen, make it impassable, cover it over with old branches for now, and no one would come bothering him. Did he hear her? Would he heed her?

Eugene nodded. He turned these orders over in his mind. And he followed them to the letter, as was his way, for the rest of his life. He did as the widow told him. He collected fallen branches, he kept his fires small, he ate eggs for his dinner, he went down the hill only after dark.

If the people below knew he was back, living in the old cottage, nothing was said. On occasion, during one of his night excursions, he found a warm loaf there, at the base of the path. Outside the widow's house, near the threshold, there might be a scarf, knitted in blue wool. People—he didn't know who—left mealcakes, a round of goat cheese, a head of cabbage, a pair of stockings when it got cold.

Even when the widow passed on and other people moved into her house—Eugene could smell their strangeness, their newness, when he stood beside their windows at night—he kept to her rules, faithfully, doggedly, keeping himself apart, hiding away. He took only what he needed, and always left something in return. A pair of britches might vanish from a drying line, but the next day their owner would find a pail of cockles left at their door, gathered at dawn's low tide. The sharpening stone in a man's byre disappeared for a week or so, but was then returned, and attached to it was a donkey's harness, perfectly crafted from flax, interwoven with cowrie shells. Further along the shore, a currach might be borrowed overnight: the fisherman arrived in the morning to find it weed-streaked and briny, but pulled up carefully beyond the tide line, the oars neatly tucked beneath. A hammer was taken from a house on the other side of the estate, and in its place was a door-knocker, carved from birch.

In this way, Eugene lived his life, undisturbed, as he wished.

He stands, now, at the edge of the copse, under its canopy, watching the boreen, making sure that the man with the straw boater hat (or indeed without it) has left and isn't about to reappear. When he sees the interloper emerge down below, onto the village road, he steps out of the copse, putting one cautious foot before the other, scanning his land, his empire, for marks or transgressions. He looks over the vegetable patch and sees that the man's shoe has crushed only two seedlings; these he straightens with careful fingertips. He walks to the door and wipes with his sleeve the place where the man rapped his knuckles; he checks the stack of turf, he touches each stone of the haggard gate, he stands at Bran's grave.

When he is assured that all is as it should be, he returns to his work. The day is still warm, the sun high but slipping behind the rath now; the wind is low. He chip-chips at the earth, up one row, down the next, loosening the straggling weeds and stowing them in his basket. After the fertilising is done, he will wade out to the hens and collect the eggs, which he will eat for his dinner. Then he will repair the boreen—he will work all evening, if need be.

At set of sun, he goes back to the copse. He needs branches and foliage for the boreen, and it has occurred to him that the hat might make a fine gift for someone in the village—he could leave it in exchange for something grand, a kid goat, perhaps, for he has a liking for the company of goats, their peculiar oblong-centred eyes, their inscrutable obstinacy, and he could keep a couple here, for the milk and the cheese.

Eugene moves sideway into the trees, turning his body first one way, then another, gliding between trunks, bending below branches, placing his feet only in those places he's stepped before. He carries in his head the detailed and precise cartography of this place: he could find his way in the pitch dark, if called on.

The air is dank and peculiarly still. Eugene cocks his head, sniffing, he swivels his eyes up to the sky, down to the ground. There is something charged about the copse tonight, some alteration or shift, as if the man who came here has brought with him a breeze from a new place, or opened up some channel running through the trees. He places a hand to a trunk, as if to read the passage of water through it, as if to communicate his presence. All is well, he wishes to tell it, the intruder has gone.

He bends to lift a fallen bough from the moss, then another, both broken by the man in his haste to be gone. The branches feel slippery against his palm, not unpleasantly so. He moves further in, the light dimming: the leaves above him sigh and shift; a bird somewhere whirs its wings against the heavy air.

When he comes to the pool, it is translucent, the sky above it dark enough for the water to be holding its own with the dusk, giving its own light, finding its own boundaries. Eugene crouches. He reaches out and lays a palm on the water, perfectly flat, watching the ripples circle out from it. And because he has been hiding most of the afternoon and hasn't drunk from the pump, as is his habit, he does something he's never done before: he turns his hand, dips it, and brings the water to his mouth. It tastes, to Eugene, of peat, of leaf, of earth, of sky, both bitter and sweet. It cuts its cool path through him and Eugene feels it entering him, merging with him.

And then a fish makes itself visible, stirring the depths, drifting up in half curves from wherever it has been hiding. Eugene watches without surprise the unhurried flick-flack of its tail, the calligraphy of its body.

The fish speaks. Its voice, to Eugene, is thrilling, unprecedented, at once tiny and loud. It seems to rise up from the water; it wreathes itself through the gaps between trees; it shivers inside the leaf canopy; it vibrates along the water vessels in the roots and trunks; it locates the pool's water in Eugene's body where it has made itself into deltas and branches, and it causes them to quiver.

Give me the ring, it says.

Because it isn't in Eugene to disregard an instruction given, because he takes whatever is said to him, examines it and acts upon it, if he wishes, he moves his hands towards each other. He sees the answering reflection of their clasp in the surface of the pool. The fingers on his right hand find the ring on his left. They tug at it, drawing it from where it has resided for many years now, the flesh grooved around it. Then he holds it out, away from him, and he drops the ring into the water. It turns and turns, the gold of its interlocking creatures revealing then hiding themselves, over and over again. It flickers and spirals, down and down, and then it is gone.

Eugene watches the fish circle the pool, swimming lower and lower, until it, too, disappears.

Without the ring, his hand feels queer, at once naked and burning. Eugene shakes it to make it come right; he dips it into the water and swishes it there, disturbing the ripples, creating bubbles and splashes. As he raises himself, shaking off the droplets, he catches sight—he is sure, he will ponder it later, it definitely seemed so—from the corner of his eye, in the half-light, the outline of a person. It cannot be the gentleman from earlier, for it is not anyone he recognises or has seen before, and as it turns out, Eugene never sees him again. This man is large, his outline tall and broad, and he appears to leap or coalesce from the water itself, bounding on strong, muscular legs. He doesn't pause to address Eugene, or even acknowledge him, or to look around himself. Instead, he darts up and bounds away, through the trees, out of the copse and up the hill, as if he has enemies at his back, as if he has left something precious in that direction and he must get himself back there, as quickly as he can, to reclaim it.

Eugene stands watching the figure as it recedes up into the hills, over the crag, towards the rath, waiting to see what else might happen, if it will come back.

He will mull over the incident for the next few days. Eugene tends not to dwell on the reasons or explanations for things; his way of thinking is one of curiosity paired with acceptance. It happened; he had no understanding of what it was or why, and this does not bother him. A fish spoke to him, he threw in the ring, as bidden, and then a man rose from the water, forming or freeing himself from it, and ran quickly away. It is enough for Eugene to have seen this, to have been its witness, and he will fold it into his mind as one of the sights he has seen, one of the inexplicable events he has lived through. He will think of it again, every once in a while, over the coming years.

There will be many years for Eugene, as it turns out: he will live beyond a hundred. He will find, as he continues with his unusual existence on the mountainside, that he possesses knowledge both great and useful, that he contains everything he needs, has all he requires and no more. He knows, for example, that his parents' bones lie alongside each other in the churchyard, not far from a yew tree, the roots of which in time weave in and out of their whitened ribs. He knows that Enda and Rose are together, that Enda is still restless and still plays her fiddle, still collecting tunes, a dog at her side. That Rose earns money by making flowers out of wadded felt and that the blooms which come to life under her fingertips adorn the hats of fine ladies. He knows, too, that there is a child with them, a boy with blue eyes and copper-coloured hair who bears his own name, and he knows when a husband comes for Rose, and that he is a good man, who on warm evenings will take the boy, Gene, out into the street where the two of them will throw a leather ball between them, and that more children will come to their household, many more. He knows that Enda plays her fiddle until the end of her life, and that people come from all over to hear her. He knows, too, that Liam is alive and not so far away from him: Eugene feels him sometimes, when the wind blows from the east, can sense him on the air.

He obtains two goats, churlish but charming creatures that are tethered on long ropes to a tree and come into the house on cold nights. He acquires a dog, a mongrel pup with Bran's long legs and fleetness of foot, but a smooth and striped coat. It has an instinctive mistrust of the house and won't come further than the haggard wall, and Eugene respects this and builds a shelter for it by Bran's grave, and the dog is content enough, although it never takes to the goats.

Eugene lives long enough for the manor estate to be dissolved and redistributed, its house burned down, the landowning viscount (second cousin to the gentleman whose head Eugene once staved in) to face financial ruin. A fraught and bloody war will rage throughout the country, in waves, like a fever. He lives long enough for the children who live in the widow's house to grow up and have children of their own, and those children will tell their children about the *gruagach* who is said to reside on the hill, beyond the tangle of trees and brambles, and how the children must be sure to be good, always, because he comes down at night and peers through their windows and sees all, and they must put offerings for him on their doorsteps or windowsills, and the *gruagach* will always leave something in return. He will live long enough for some of the cottages on the peninsula to be bought up by city dwellers, who use them during the summer or to rent out to others.

And if these holidaymakers should find that shoes they leave outside have vanished overnight, or if they discover that some of their laundry is missing from the line, the peninsula people will give the same response, every time. There's one among us who needs such things and we must let him have them, for he is so old and wise that he could tell you all about the history of the land, should he wish to do so.

ACKNOWLEDGEMENTS

Thank you, Mary-Anne Harrington, Victoria Hobbs, Jordan Pavlin, Christy Fletcher, Conrad Williams and Emma Knight.

Thank you, Mari Evans, Jennifer Doyle, Hazel Orme, Ellie Freedman, Elaine Egan, Rebecca Bader, Jim Binchy, Lucy Howkins, Patrick Insole, Tina Paul, Joanna Smyth, Ellie Wheeldon, Eleanor Wood and Isabel Martin.

Thank you, Jessica Lee, Alexandra McNicoll, Lucy Joyce, Jack Sargeant, Steve Williams and Gosia Jezierska.

I'm immensely grateful to the archivists at An Chartlann Náisiúnta/The National Archives in Dublin, and those at The National Records of Scotland in Edinburgh. Also to various members of the extended O'Farrell family, especially my parents, my sister Bridget, and my cousin Sarah Kinsella.

Thank you, Ruth Metzstein, for reading my final draft; Fiona Miller, for expertise on the fiddle; Alistair Pugh, for explaining theodolites and the principle of triangulation; Charlotte Mendelson, for sending books and encouragement; Chris Peyton, for geography lessons in the 1980s; Seren Nolan, for help with classical references; Eilís Ní Dhuibhne, Sinéad Gleeson and Micheál Ó Conghaile, for their knowledge of *Gaeilge* and their generosity in sharing it. Any errors will be my own.

The Latin passage given to Liam on page 159 is taken from Pliny the Elder's *Natural History* (Book ii, Part V, Chapter 88).

Thank you, MS, who was here for the start of this book but not for the end: much missed.

Thank you, JA, IZ and SS, for accompanying me on visits to wells, for the loan of a silver fish, for dedicated donkey research, and many things besides.

Thank you, as always, Will.

And thank you to my great-great-grandfather: *go raibh suaimhneas síoraí air.*

A NOTE ABOUT THE AUTHOR

MAGGIE O'FARRELL was born in Derry, Northern Ireland, in 1972. Her novels include *Hamnet* (winner of the National Book Critics Circle Award), *After You'd Gone*, *The Vanishing Act of Esme Lennox*, *The Hand That First Held Mine* (winner of the Costa Novel Award), and *Instructions for a Heatwave*. She has also written a memoir, *I Am, I Am, I Am: Seventeen Brushes with Death*. She lives in Edinburgh.

A NOTE ON THE TYPE

This book was set in Adobe Garamond. Designed for the Adobe Corporation by Robert Slimbach, the fonts are based on types first cut by Claude Garamond (ca. 1480–1561). Garamond was a pupil of Geoffroy Tory and is believed to have followed the Venetian models, although he introduced a number of important differences, and it is to him that we owe the letter we now know as "old style."

Typeset by Scribe, Philadelphia, Pennsylvania

Book design by Betty Lew

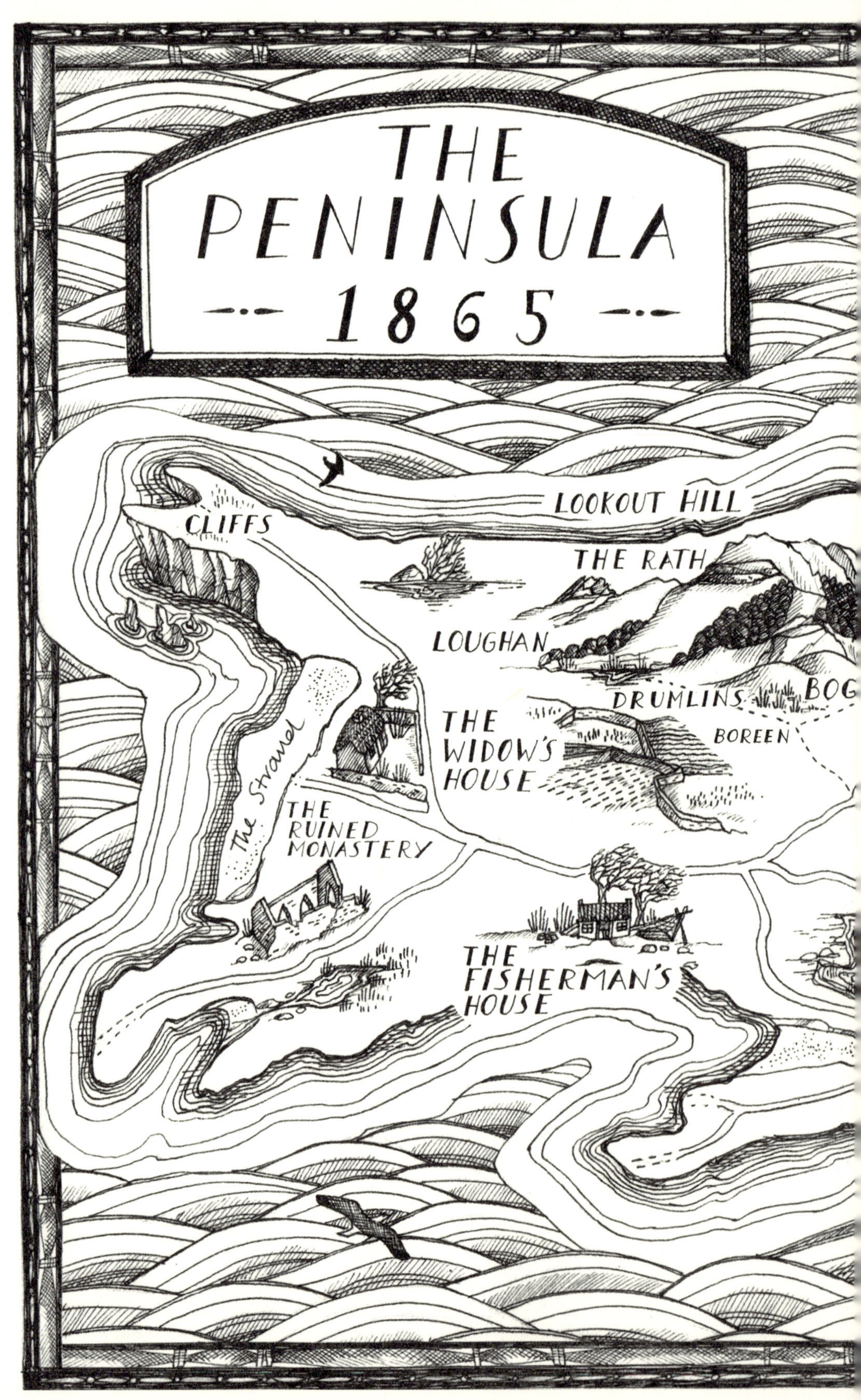
THE PENINSULA 1865
LOOKOUT HILL
CLIFFS
THE RATH
LOUGHAN
DRUMLINS
BOG
THE WIDOW'S HOUSE
BOREEN
The Strand
THE RUINED MONASTERY
THE FISHERMAN'S HOUSE